SLANTED JACK

Baen Books by Mark L. Van Name

One Jump Ahead
Slanted Jack
Overthrowing Heaven (forthcoming)

Transhuman ed. with T.K.F. Weisskopf

SLANTED JACK

MARK L. VAN NAME

SLANTED JACK

This is a work of fiction. All the characters and events portrayed in this book are fictional, and any resemblance to real people or incidents is purely coincidental.

Copyright © 2008 by Mark L. Van Name

A Baen Books Original

Baen Publishing Enterprises
P.O. Box 1403
Riverdale, NY 10471
www.baen.com

ISBN 10: 1-4165-5549-8
ISBN 13: 978-1-4165-5549-0

Cover art by Stephen Hickman

First printing, July 2008

Distributed by Simon & Schuster
1230 Avenue of the Americas
New York, NY 10020

Library of Congress Cataloging-in-Publication Data

Van Name, Mark L.
  Slanted Jack : a Jon & Lobo novel / Mark L. Van Name.
      p. cm.
  "A Baen Books original"—T.p. verso.
  ISBN-13: 978-1-4165-5549-0
  ISBN-10: 1-4165-5549-8
  1. Soldiers of fortune—Fiction. 2. Nanotechnology—Fiction. 3. Boys—Fiction.
4. Life on other planets—Fiction. I. Title.

  PS3622.A666S63 2008
  813'.6—dc22
                                                                    2008005952

10 9 8 7 6 5 4 3 2 1

Pages by Joy Freeman (www.pagesbyjoy.com)
Printed in the United States of America

To Gina Massel-Castater
For a lunchtime conversation that
formed the seed of this book,
and for so much more

CHAPTER 1

NOTHING SHOULD HAVE been able to ruin my lunch.

Joaquin Choy, the best chef on any planet within three jumps, had erected his restaurant, Falls, just outside Eddy, the only city on the still-developing world Mund. He'd chosen the site because of the intense flavors of the native vegetables, the high quality of the locally raised livestock, and a setting that whipped your head around and widened your eyes.

Falls perched on camo-painted carbon-fiber struts over the center of a thousand meter deep gorge. You entered it via a three-meter-wide transparent walkway so soft you were sure you were strolling across high, wispy clouds. The four waterfalls that inspired its name remained visible even when you were inside, thanks to the transparent active-glass walls whose careful light balancing guaranteed a glare-free view throughout the day. The air outside filled your head with the clean scent of wood drifting downstream on light river breezes; a muted variant of the same smells pervaded the building's interior.

I occupied a corner seat, a highly desirable position given my background and line of work. From this vantage point, I could easily scan all new arrivals. I'd reserved and paid for all the seats at the five tables closest to me, so a wide buffer separated me from the other diners. In the clouds above me, Lobo, my intelligent

Predator-class assault vehicle, monitored the area surrounding the restaurant so no threat could assemble outside without my knowledge. I'd located an exterior exit option when I first visited Choy, and both Lobo and I could reach it in under a minute. Wrapped in a blanket of security I rarely achieved in the greater world, I could relax and enjoy myself.

The setting was perfect.

Following one of my cardinal rules of fine dining—always opt for the chef's tasting menu in a top-notch restaurant—I'd forgone the offerings on the display that shimmered in the air over my table and instead surrendered myself to Choy's judgment, asking only that he not hold back on the portion size of any course. Getting fat is never an issue for me. At almost two meters tall and over a hundred kilos in weight, I'm large enough that I'd be able to eat quite a lot if I were a normal man, and thanks to the nanomachines that lace my cells, I can eat as much as I want: They decompose and flush any excess food I consume.

Spread in front of me were four appetizer offerings, each blending chunks of a different savory meat with strands of vegetables steaming on a glass plate of slowly changing color. Choy instructed me to taste each dish separately and then in combinations of my choice. I didn't know what any of them were, and I didn't care. They smelled divine, and I expected they would taste even better.

They did. I leaned back after the third amazing bite and closed my eyes, my taste buds coping with that most rare of sensory pleasures: sensations that in over a hundred and fifty years of life they'd never experienced. I struggled to conjure superlatives equal to the dishes.

The food was perfect.

What ruined the lunch was the company, the unplanned, unwanted company.

When I opened my eyes from my contemplation of that confounding and delicious blend of flavors, Slanted Jack was walking toward me from the stark white entrance hallway.

Slanted Jack, so named because with him nothing was ever straight, had starred in one of the many acts of my life that

I'd just as soon forget. The best con man and thief I've ever known, he effortlessly charmed and put at ease anyone who didn't know him. When he eased through a room of strangers, they all noticed. He was a celebrity whose name none of them could quite remember. Maybe ten centimeters shorter than I, with a wide smile, eyes the blue of the heart of flame, and skin the color and sheen of polished night, Jack instantly cornered the attention of everyone around him. While weaving his way through the tables to me he paused three times to exchange pleasantries with people he was almost certainly meeting for the first time. Each person Jack addressed would know that Jack found him special, important, even compelling, and Jack truly would feel that way, if only for the instant he invested in sizing up each one as a potential target.

While Jack was chatting with a foursome a few meters away, I called Lobo.

"Any sign of external threat?"

"Of course not," Lobo said. "You know that if I spotted anything, I'd alert you instantly. Why are you wasting time talking to me when you could be eating your magnificent meal, conversing with other patrons, and generally having a wonderful time? It's not as if you're stuck up here where I am, too high to have even the birds for company."

"It's not like I could bring you into the restaurant with me," I said, parroting his tone. I know he's a machine, but from almost the first time we met I've been unable to think of him as anything other than "he," a person. "Nor, for that matter, do you eat."

"You've never heard of takeout? I may not consume the same type of fuel as you, but I can be quite a pleasant dinner companion, as I'd think you'd realize after all the meals you've taken while inside me."

I sighed. Every time I let myself fall into an argument with Lobo when he's in a petulant mood, I regret it. "Signing off."

"You don't want to do that yet," Lobo said.

"Why?" Just when I think I understand all the ways Lobo can annoy me, he comes up with a new one.

"Because I was about to alert you to an internal threat," he said.

"Let me guess," I said. "The tall man who recently walked into the restaurant and is now talking to some people not far from me."

"Correct," Lobo said. "I did not consider the threat high both because other humans have stayed between you and him since he entered and because his two weapons are holstered, one under his left arm and the other on his right ankle."

Jack was armed? *That* was unusual, the first thing he'd done that didn't fit the man I'd known. Jack had always hated weapons and delegated their use to others, frequently to me. I don't like them either, nor do I like violence of any type, but both have been frequent hazards of most of the kinds of jobs I've taken over the last many decades.

"Got it," I said. "Anything else you can tell?"

"That's all the data I can obtain from this distance, and even that information required me to force enough power into the scan that the restaurant's skylights are now complaining to the building management system about the treatment they have to endure."

I kept my eyes on Jack and tuned in to the common appliance frequency. Restaurants employ so many machines, every one of which has intelligence to spare and a desire to talk to anything that will listen, that tapping into their chat wavelength was like stepping into the middle of a courtyard full of screaming people. The sonic wall smacked me, the sounds in my head momentarily deafening even though I knew they weren't really audio at all, just neurons and tweaked receptors firing in ways Jennie and the experiments on Aggro had combined to make my brain interpret as sounds. I sorted through the conversations, ignoring mentions of food and temperature until I finally found a relevant snippet and focused on it.

"Radiation of that level is simply not normal for this area," one pane said, "though fortunately it is well within the limits of what my specs can handle."

"All of us can easily handle it," said another pane. Household and building intelligences, like appliances, are insanely competitive and desperate for attention. They spend most of their lives bickering. I listened for another few seconds, but all the chatter was between the pieces of active glass; the household security system didn't respond to the windows, so it clearly didn't consider the burst from Lobo's scan to be a risk. I should tell Joaquin to upgrade his systems.

"If you see that man reach for either weapon," I said, "alert me instantly."

"Of course," Lobo said. "Must you constantly restate previous arrangements?"

"Sorry. Humans use reminders and ritualized communications during crises."

"I appreciate that, and I sometimes don't mind, but he's one man, he's made no move to suggest aggression, and so I hardly consider him a crisis."

Lobo clearly didn't appreciate the trouble a single man could cause, much less a man like Jack. Jack had finished with the foursome and was now leaning over a couple at a table adjacent to the first group. "Now signing off," I said.

I blended bits of food from a pair of the plates into another bite, but I couldn't take my eyes off Jack; the charms of the appetizers were dissipating faster than their aromas. Jack would require all my attention. He and I had worked the con together for almost a decade, and though that time was profitable, it was also consistently nerve-racking. Jack lived by his own principles, chief among which was his lifelong commitment to target only bad people for big touches. We consequently found ourselves time and again racing to make jumps off planets, always a short distance ahead of very dangerous, very angry marks. By the time we split, I vowed to go straight and never run the con again.

"Jon," Jack said as he reached me, his smile as disarming as always. "It's good to see you. It's been too long."

"What do you want, Jack?"

"May I join you?" he said, pulling out a chair.

I didn't bother to answer; it was pointless.

He nodded and sat. "Thank you."

He put his hands palm-down on the tablecloth, so I said nothing.

A server appeared beside him, reset the table for two, and waited for Jack's order.

"I throw myself on Joaquin's mercy," Jack said. "Please tell him Jack asks only that he be gentle."

The server glanced at me for confirmation. Jack wasn't going to leave until he had his say, so I nodded, and the server hustled away.

"Joaquin truly is an artist," Jack said. "I—"

I cut him off by standing and grabbing his throat.

"I'd forgotten how very fast you are for a man your size," he croaked. As always, he maintained his calm. He kept his hands where they were. "Is this really necessary?"

I bent over him so my left hand was on his back and our bodies covered my right hand, with which I continued to grip his neck tightly enough that his discomfort was evident. "Carefully and slowly put both weapons on the table," I said. "If you make me at all nervous, I'll crush your throat."

"I believe you would," Jack said, as he pulled out first a small projectile weapon from under his left shoulder and then an even smaller one from a holster on his ankle, "but I know you would feel bad about it. I've always liked that about you."

"Yes, I would," I said. When the weapons were on the table, I pushed back Jack's chair, released his throat, and palmed both guns. I put them behind my chair as I sat.

Jack stretched his neck and pulled his chair closer to the table. "I really must locate a tailor with better software," he said. "You shouldn't have been able to spot those."

I saw no value in enlightening him about Lobo's capabilities. "What do you want, and since when do you travel armed?"

Jack assembled bits of all four of my appetizers into a perfectly shaped bite, then chewed it slowly, his eyes shutting as the tastes flooded his mouth. "Amazing. Did I say Joaquin was an artist? I should have called him a magician—and I definitely should have dined here sooner."

He opened his eyes and studied me intently. The focus of

his gaze was both intense and comforting, as if he could see into your soul and was content to view only that. For years I'd watched him win the confidence of strangers with a single long look, and I'd never figured out how he managed it. I'd asked him many times, and he always told me the same thing: "Each person deserves to be the center of the universe to someone, Jon, even if only for an instant. When I focus on a man or a woman, that person is my all." He always laughed afterward, but whether in embarrassment at having been momentarily completely honest or in jest at my gullibility is something I've never known.

"We haven't seen each other in, what, thirty years now," he said, "and you haven't aged a day. You must give me the names and locations of your med techs"—he paused and chuckled before continuing—"and how you afford it. Courier work must pay far better than I imagined."

I wasn't in that line of work when I last saw him, so Jack was telling me he'd done his homework. He also looked no different than before, which I would have expected: No one with money and the willingness to pay for current-gen med care needs to show age for at least the middle forty or fifty years of his life. So, he was also letting me know he had reasons to believe I'd done well since we parted. I had, but I saw no value in providing him with more information. Dealing with him had transformed the afternoon from pleasure to work; the same dishes that had been so attractive a few minutes ago now held absolutely no appeal to me.

I decided to try a different approach. "How did you find me?"

He arranged and slowly chewed another combination of the appetizers before answering. "Ah, Jon, that was luck, fate if you will. Despite the many years we've been apart, I'm sure you remember how valuable it is for someone in my line of work to develop supporters among jump-gate staff. After all, everyone who goes anywhere eventually appears on their tracking lists. So, when I made the jump from Drayus I stopped at the gate station and visited some of my better friends there, friends who have agreed to inform me when people of a certain," he looked skyward, as if searching for a phrase, "dangerous persuasion passed into the Mund system. Traveling in a PCAV earned you their attention, and they were kind enough to alert me."

I neither moved nor spoke, but inside I cursed myself. During a recent run-in with two major multiplanet conglomerates and a big chunk of the Frontier Coalition government, I'd made so many jumps in such a short period that I'd abandoned my previously standard practice of bribing the station agents not to notice me. Break a habit, pay a price.

"Speaking of your transport," he said, "is that a show copy or the real thing?"

I said nothing but raised an eyebrow and forced myself to take another bite from the nearer two plates. With Jack, silence was often the best response, because he would then try another approach at the information he wanted, and the tactics he chose frequently conveyed useful data.

"There's no shame in a good copy, Jon," he said, his curiosity apparently satisfied. "I spent a couple of years recently brokering the machines to planetary and provincial governments in this sector. The builder, Keisha Li, was this munitions artist—and I mean that, Jon, not merely a manufacturer, but an artist—who found her niche on Gash but couldn't ever hit it big. Her dupes were full, active transports that could handle any environment their originals could manage, though admittedly they were slower—and, of course," he chuckled, "completely lacking firepower. I helped her grow her business. We sold a couple of PCAV clones, though they're pricey enough that they were never our top sellers. Less expensive vehicles provided most buyers all of the intimidation value they sought." He leaned forward for a moment, his expression suddenly sad. "The worst part is that it was completely legal, an indirect sort of touch that I thought would be perfect for me, the real job I've always wondered if I could hold, and it delivered no juice, Jon. None." He sat back and threw up his hands as if in disgust. Jack always spoke with his whole body, every gesture calculated but still effective. "Oh, we made money, good money, the business grew, and we were safe and legit, but I might as well have been hawking drink dispensers." He took another bite, savored it, and then shook his head. "Me, selling machines on the straight. I mean, can you imagine it?"

As engaging as Jack was, I knew he'd never leave until he'd broached his true topic, so I tried to force him to get to it. "Jack, answer or one of us leaves: What do you want?"

He leaned back and looked into my eyes for a few seconds, then smiled and nodded. "You never could appreciate the value of civilized conversation," he said, "but your very coarseness has also always been part of your appeal—and your value. Put simply and without the context I hope you'll permit me to provide, I need your help."

Leave it to Jack to take that long to give an answer with absolutely no new content. If he hadn't wanted something, he'd never have come to me.

"When we parted," I said, "I told you I was done with the con. Nothing has changed. You've ruined my lunch for no reason." I stood to go, the weapons now in my right hand behind my back.

Jack leaned forward, held up his hand, and said, "Please, Jon, give me a little time. This isn't about me. It's about the boy."

His tone grabbed me enough that I didn't walk away, but I also didn't sit. "The boy? What boy? I can't picture you with children."

Jack laughed. "No," he said, "I haven't chosen to procreate, nor do I ever expect to do so." He held up his hand, turned, and motioned to the maître d'.

The man hustled over to our table, reached behind himself, and gently urged a child to step in front of him.

"This boy," Jack said. "Manu Chang."

CHAPTER 2

CHANG STARED AT ME with the wide, unblinking eyes of scared youth. With shoulders slightly wider than his hips and a fair amount of fuzz on the sides of his neck, he appeared to be somewhere between ten and twelve, not yet inhabiting a man's body but on the cusp of the change, soon to begin the transformation into adulthood. His broad mouth hung open a centimeter, as if he were about to speak. He wore his fine black hair short, not quite a buzz cut but close. Aside from the copper hue of his skin nothing about him struck me as even remotely notable, and even that flesh tone would be common enough in any large city. He stood still, neither speaking nor moving, and I felt instantly bad for him, stuck as he was in an adult situation whose nuances were beyond his ability to understand, with an angry man—me—staring down at him.

"Are you hungry, Manu?" I said as I sat, again putting the weapons behind my chair.

He nodded but didn't speak, the fear not releasing its grip on him.

"Then please eat with us." The maître d' was, predictably, ahead of me: Two servers appeared, hustled the boy into a chair, and composed a plate of food for him from the remains of the appetizers and two new dishes they brought for us all to share. Manu sat but otherwise didn't move. After I took a bite from the plate nearest me and Jack did the same, Manu followed suit. The boy swallowed the first bite as if it were air, consumed it so quickly he couldn't possibly have tasted it, and inside I winced at the waste of Choy's artistry.

I forced a smiled and said, "Good, huh?"

Manu nodded.

"Have all you want," I said.

I turned my attention back to Jack as Manu attacked the food in earnest. Jack was almost certainly manipulating me; he knows no other way to interact with others. The odds of my later regretting asking him a question were high, but I was too curious not to continue. I also had to admit that the boy's open, guileless gaze touched me—probably as Jack had intended. "Why do you want my help?" I said.

Though I was certain that inside he was smiling, all Jack permitted his face to show was concern for the boy and appreciation at my interest. "My answer will make sense only if I give you some context," he said, "so I have to ask you to grant me a few minutes to explain."

"Go ahead," I said, leaning forward and lowering my voice, "but, Jack, don't play me." As I heard my own words, which I meant and delivered as seriously I could, I grasped how well he'd hooked me. I was speaking nonsensically: Jack isn't capable of saying anything to anyone without having multiple angles at play, and, as he taught me, the mark who has to urge you to tell the truth already wants to hear the pitch.

He leaned conspiratorially closer, so our faces were almost touching, and whispered. "I know you're aware of Pinkelponker," he said. "Everyone is. But do you know why it matters?"

"Yeah, of course I've heard of it," I said, leaning back as if the name didn't matter to me. "It's quarantined. So what?"

Pinkelponker. Hearing Jack say it shook me far more than his appearance, more than the scared boy now sitting with us, more than any of the suspicions I'd felt since Jack had shown up. I did my best to hide my reaction. I was born on that planet, and I lived there with my sister, Jennie, an empathic healer, until the government shuttled her away from our home island and forced her to heal only those people it deemed important. I've never forgiven myself for not finding a way to rescue her, to bring her back safely.

Pinkelponker occupies three unique niches in human history.

It's the only planet successfully colonized by one of Earth's pre-jump-gate generation ships, its name the result of that ship's captain foolishly letting his young son choose what to call mankind's first remote, planetbound colony. The ship ultimately failed to land properly, crashed badly enough that it could never take off again, and stranded its entire population until humanity discovered the jump gate that led to the two-aperture gate near Pinkelponker.

It's the only place where radical human mutations not only survived but also yielded parahuman talents, such as my sister's healing abilities. Never found elsewhere, these abilities were now the stuff of legends, stories most people consider on par with tales of elves and dragons.

And, it's the only planet humans have ever colonized that is now forbidden territory. It exists under a continuous quarantine and blockade, thanks to a nanotech disaster that led to the abandonment and banning of all research into embedding nanomachines in humans.

What no one knows is that the rogue nanomachine cloud that ultimately caused the planet's enforced isolation came into existence as part of my escape from Aggro, the research prison that orbited above Pinkelponker. More importantly, to the best of my knowledge no one alive knows that I'm living proof that nanomachines can indeed safely exist in humans—and I very much want it to stay that way. Any group that learned the truth about me would want to turn me into a research animal. My months on Aggro as a test subject stand as some of the worst and most painful times in a long life with more than its share of pain; I'll never let that happen again.

I'd lost track of the conversation. I forced myself to concentrate on what Jack was saying. Fortunately, he didn't seem to have noticed that I'd drifted away for a moment.

". . . hasn't been open to travel in over a century and a quarter," he said. "If you haven't spent much time in this sector of space, you wouldn't have any reason to keep up with it, though obviously even you know about the quarantine."

"Who doesn't?" I said as casually as I could manage. Jack held my attention now, because far more relevant than my past was a disturbing question I should have considered earlier: Was he telling me all this because he'd learned more about my background than I ever wanted anyone to know?

"It's tough to avoid," he said, his head nodding in slow agreement, "particularly for those of us who always plot the best routes off any world we're visiting." He smiled and pitched his voice further downward, speaking softly enough now that without thinking I again leaned forward to hear him better. "But have you heard the legends?"

"What legends?" I said. Playing dumb and letting Jack talk seemed the wisest option.

"Psychics, Jon, not grifters working marks but *real* psychics. Pinkelponker was a high-radiation planet, a fact that should simply have led to a lot of human deaths. Something about that world was special, though, because instead the radiation caused the first and so far *only* truly useful human mutations— something humanity has never seen anywhere else. The legends tell of the existence of all types of psychics, from telekinetics to healers to seers."

Jack sat back, his expression expectant, waiting for me to react. I'd seen him use this technique to draw in marks, and I wasn't about to play. As I now feared Jack might know, I hadn't come to Mund simply for Choy's cooking, as amazing as it was reputed to be. Mund was one of the worlds with a jump aperture to Drayus, the only planet with an aperture to Pinkelponker since the one on Earth mysteriously closed a decade after it opened. No other gate aperture had ever grown over and stopped working. New apertures appeared from time to time, and each one inevitably led to a system with a planet suitable for human colonization, but once open, apertures always stayed that way. Theories abounded, of course, as to why this one and only one aperture had closed, but as with everything else about the gates, humanity could know only what they did, never why they did it.

The Drayus aperture was now also closed, but not because it had stopped working. As far as anyone knew, it still functioned correctly. What kept it out of operation was the most potent and long-lasting blockade mankind had ever assembled: No human had successfully passed through it in a hundred and thirty years. All but one of the few ships that had made the jump—before the Central and Expansion Coalition governments had cooperated in shutting down all access to the gate—had never returned. The one ship that made it back had passed halfway through the aperture, just far enough that its crew could warn of the nanocloud that was dissolving it and then return in time to prevent the cloud from entering this system. No one is sure why the nanocloud itself couldn't make the jump, but neither is any government willing to take the chance of sending another vessel and possibly bringing back the cloud. The CC and EC ships stationed at the gate make sure no private craft try, either.

Despite all that, the aperture was still there, still a possible way to my home, maybe even to Jennie, if she—or anyone—remained alive in that system. I visited this sector of space periodically, each time wondering how I could get back to Pinkelponker and see if Jennie still lived—and each time realizing with a gut-wrenching sense of failure that there was no way I could reach her, no chance I could save her even if by some miracle she hadn't died of old age on a planet whose medical science was stranded over a century ago.

I could only lose by giving away any of this knowledge about my past, so I waited. A pair of servers took advantage of the silence to whisk away our dirty dishes. Another pair replaced them with fresh plates, each a work of art combining greens, nuts, and small pieces of cheese. Manu immediately took a bite. He chewed quietly and steadily. I eyed the food but couldn't make myself eat.

After a minute, Jack realized he'd have to keep going on his own. He leaned closer again and, his eyes shining brightly, said, "Can you imagine it, Jon? In all the colonized planets, not one psychic—until Pinkelponker."

Jack was as dogged as he was slippery, so I knew he'd never give up. I had to move him along. "You said it, Jack: legends. Those are just legends."

He smiled, satisfied now that I was playing the role he wanted me to fill. "Yes, they're legends, but not all legends are false or exaggerated. In the less than a decade between the discovery of Pinkelponker's jump gate and the permanent quarantine of that whole area after the nanotech disaster, some people from that planet naturally visited other worlds. Some of those visitors never went home. And," he said, leaning back, "a very few of those who opted to live on other worlds were psychics." He put his right hand gently on the boy's back. "Like Manu's grandmother. Though she died, and though her only son didn't inherit her powers, her grandson did.

"Manu did. He's proof, Jon, that the legends were true. He's a seer."

I stared at the boy, who continued to eat as if we weren't there. I already knew the legends were true, because Jennie was proof of it. I was born with a mind that would never progress past that of a normal five-year-old's, but Jennie not only fixed me, she also pushed my intelligence way beyond the norm, made me somehow able to communicate on machine frequencies, altered my vision so I could see in the IR range, and enabled my brain to control the nanomachines the Aggro scientists later injected into me. She'd told me that others with special powers existed, but she'd never provided specifics, and I never met any of them. I didn't have a chance to question her further about them, because right after fixing me she boarded a government ship, and I haven't seen her since.

Though Jack's story of Pinkelponker natives visiting other planets seemed reasonable enough—the wealthy of all worlds move around readily—I'd never heard it before. More importantly, with Jack I couldn't trust anything to be true, and I couldn't assume that any tidbits that happened to be accurate were anywhere near the whole story. I needed to keep him talking and hope I could lure him into giving me more of the truth than he'd planned.

"I don't buy it, Jack," I said. "If the boy could see the future, he'd already be famous or rich—or the hidden property of some conglomerate. He sure wouldn't be with you."

Jack shook his head. "Wrong on all counts, Jon." He held up his right hand and ticked off the points on his long, elegant fingers. "First, his powers don't work reliably. I told you: He's two generations away from the planet. He sees the future, but in visions whose subjects and timing he can't control. He has no clue when they'll hit him. Second, his parents, until they died"—he glanced at Manu, whose face clouded suddenly and appeared near tears—"bless them both, though not well off were also not stupid, so they kept him hidden. Third, and this leads me to why I'm here, the visions damage him. In fact, without the right treatments to suppress them, and without continuing that regimen indefinitely, well," he looked at the boy with what appeared to be genuine fondness and then stared at me, choosing his words carefully, "his body won't be able to pay the bill his mind will incur."

"You don't need me to go to a med tech," I said.

"Normal med techs can't provide these treatments," Jack said, "and those few that do offer them charge a great deal more than the meager amount his parents left him. The uncle who was raising him is a man of modest means who also couldn't even begin to pay for this level of care. The whole situation is further complicated by our need to keep Manu's abilities quiet."

"You said he's with you, and you mentioned doing well selling the faux weapons vehicles, so why not just foot the bill yourself?"

"Alas, Jon," he said with a wistful smile, "my lifestyle is such that little money from that brief interlude remains, so my own funds are also inadequate to the task."

"So you want to borrow the payments from me?" I said. Jack and I had covered this ground before, after the second time I was stupid enough to grant him a loan; somehow his limitation not to con good people didn't extend to his friends. He felt that any colleague who couldn't spot a con deserved to be plucked. He certainly knew that I'd vowed never to loan him money again.

He waved his hands quickly and shook his head; I was pleased to see he hadn't forgotten. "No, no," he said, "of course not. I'm simply helping Manu and his uncle get the money. I've arranged a way, but it has," he paused, giving the impression of searching for words I'm sure he'd already rehearsed, "an element of risk."

I motioned him to continue and looked at Manu. The boy's eyes were now dry and focused nowhere at all, as if he'd long ago become accustomed to people talking about him as if he weren't there. I've always found it puzzling how many people do that to children, even their own children. Manu continued to eat, now moving slowly and methodically, without pause, with the kind of determined focus common among those who never know how long it'll be until their next meal.

Jack nibbled at his salad, taking small bites and savoring each one.

I admired my plate, but I still had no stomach for it.

"Pinkelponker is, as you might imagine," he continued, "the object of considerable interest to certain mystic groups, as well as to many historians. One particular Pinkelponker fanatic, an extremely wealthy man named Siva Dougat, has set up a Pinkelponker research institute and museum—a temple, really—near the ocean on the northern edge of downtown Eddy. He's the leader of a group that calls itself the Followers, people who believe that the key to humanity's destiny lies in that long-forbidden planet. Dougat initially bankrolled the whole group, but like most cults, it's subsequently amassed considerable wealth by absorbing the accounts of many of the hardcore faithful who've joined it."

He looked off to the right for a moment. "Didn't we run a cult scam once before?"

We'd made quite a few plays in our days together, but never that one, so I shook my head.

"No? Oh, well, I must have done it with someone else. My mind is clearly slipping. It was certainly profitable enough, and if I do say so myself, I made quite a grand religious leader, but I have to tell you, Jon: I couldn't keep it up. I could never respect anyone who would worship me."

"Dougat," I said.

Jack smiled, and then I realized how quickly I'd taken the hook.

"Yes, of course. He's interviewed every Pinkelponker survivor and survivor descendant he's ever found. He claims to make all the recordings available in his institute, though," Jack paused and stared off into space again, "I suspect he's the sort who's held back anything of any significant potential value. What matters most is that he pays for the interviews. I've contacted him about Manu, and he's offered a fee—just for an interview, no more—that's large enough to keep the boy in treatments for a very long time."

"So what's the problem?" I said. "You've found a way to earn Manu the money he requires. You don't need me."

"I don't trust Dougat, Jon. He's rich, which immediately makes him suspect. He runs a religious cult, so he's a skilled con man. Worst of all, you can hear the fervor in his voice when he talks about Pinkelponker, and fanatics always scare me. When I told him about Manu's visions, he sounded as if he were a Gatist with a chance to be the first to learn the source of the jump gates. He's not faking his interest, either. You know I've spent a lot of my life cultivating desire in marks and spotting when they were hooked; well, Dougat wants Manu badly, Jon, badly enough that I'm worried he might try to kidnap the boy."

"You're asking me to provide protection?" I said.

"You and that PCAV of yours," Jack said quietly. "I know what you're capable of, and real or faux, your PCAV makes an impressive presence. If I'm wrong about Dougat, this will cost you only a little time. If I'm right, though, then I'll feel a lot better with you beside me. You know I'm no good at violence."

Despite myself, I nodded. I don't like violence; at least the part of me under my conscious control doesn't like it, but the anger that's more tightly laced throughout me than the nano-machines emerges all too readily. I tell myself I do everything reasonably possible to avoid fights, but all too often the jobs I accept end up in conflict.

"You've already learned I'm a private courier," I said. "If you and the boy want to go somewhere, and if you have the fare, I'll treat you as a package and take you to your destination under my care. I'm no bodyguard, though"—I had no reason to assume Jack knew of the five years I'd spent being exactly that—"so I can't help you with the meeting."

"One day, Jon," he said, "just one day. That's all I need you for. We meet Dougat three days from now at the Institute. I wanted a safe, public place, but he wouldn't go anywhere he couldn't control the security. We compromised on meeting in the open, on the grounds in front of his main building, where anyone passing by could see us. All I'm asking is that you come with us, watch our backs, and if things turn bad, fly us out of there. That's it."

Jack wouldn't drop it until I'd found a way to say no that he understood, so I cut to the easiest escape route. "How much do you propose to pay me for this?" I said.

"Nothing."

No answer he could have given would have surprised me more. Jack always came ready to any bargaining table. I fought to keep the surprise from showing on my face. It was the first thing he'd said that made me wonder if he might actually for once be on the up-and-up.

"I don't have any money to pay you," he continued, "and I won't make any from this meeting; everything Dougat pays goes to Manu. I'm doing it for him, and I'm asking you to do the same. With all the dicey business we've worked, wouldn't you like to do some good now and again?" He leaned back, put his hands in his lap, and waited, an innocent man who'd said his piece.

The spark of trust Jack had created winked out as I real-ized there was no way he was doing something for nothing.

"Why are you involved in all this, Jack? Skip the pitch; just tell me."

Jack looked at Manu for a few seconds. "I really am out to help Manu. His uncle's a friend, and I feel bad for the boy." He straightened and a pained expression flickered across his face. "And, Earth's greatest export has once again left me with a debt I must repay, this time to Manu's uncle."

"Poker," I said, laughing. "A gambling loss?" Jack had always loved the game, and we'd played it both for pleasure and on the hustle, straight up and bent. I enjoyed it well enough, but I rarely sought it, and I could always walk away. For him, poker held a stronger attraction, one he frequently lost the will to fight.

"It was as sure a hand as I've ever seen, Jon," he said, the excitement in his voice a force at the small table. Manu started at Jack's tone but resumed eating when everything appeared to be okay. "Seven stud, three beautiful eights to greet me, the next card the matching fourth, and a world of opportunity spread before me. He caught the final two tens on the last two cards—cards he should never have paid to see. Unbelievable luck. I mean, the odds against it were astronomical! A better player would have folded long before; he certainly should have. I put everything into that pot. It was mine." He paused for a few seconds, and when he continued he was back under control. "Honestly, Jon, I was willing to help Manu before that hand, but yes, losing it guaranteed my participation."

"Your debt is not my problem, Jack."

"I realize that, and I wouldn't be asking you if I had an alternative. Unfortunately, I don't. Dougat is the only option Manu's uncle and I have found, I'm committed to help, and I don't trust that fanatic. I'll go it alone if I must, and I'm confident I'll walk away from the meeting, because I hold no interest for the guy, but I fear—" he glanced down at Manu and then spoke quickly "—that I'll exit alone."

That Jack was in a bind was never news—he'd be in trouble as long as he lived—and my days of obligation to him were long over. I felt bad for the boy, worse than Jack could know, because my inability to save Jennie has left me a soft touch for children in trouble, but I learned long ago that I can't save them all. Worse, recent experience had taught me that trying to rescue even one of them could lead to the kind of trouble I was lucky to survive. If I wanted to avoid more danger, I not only needed to steer clear of Jack, I had to leave Mund soon, because I had to assume the same gate staff he'd bribed would be alerting others to my presence. Anyone willing to sell information for the sorts of fees Jack could afford would surely try to jack up their profits by reselling that same data.

The only reasonable choice was to walk away now and leave the planet.

As much as I fought it, however, I knew I wouldn't make that choice.

The problem was the Pinkelponker connection. Dougat's research center and the data he and the Followers had collected might contain scraps of information I could use. If Manu really was a seer, he might also be a source of useful data. In addition, I needed to determine whether Jack knew about or even suspected my ties to the planet, and, if he did, exactly what he'd learned.

Finally, I had to admit that because so many of the jobs I've taken have led to so much damage, the prospect of doing something genuinely good always appealed to me.

I stared into Jack's eyes and tried to read him. Their rich blue color was truly remarkable, and he knew it. He held my gaze, too good a salesman to look away or push harder when he knew the hook was in deep. Even as I stared at him I remembered how utterly pointless it was to search for truth in his face. Jack excelled at close-up cons because at some level he always believed what he was selling, and so to marks he always appeared honest. The only way I could glean more information was to accrete it slowly by spending time with him.

When I glanced at Manu, I found him watching me expectantly, hopefully, as if he'd understood everything we'd discussed. Perhaps he had; Jack hadn't tried very hard to obscure the topic.

I took a long, slow, deep breath, and then looked back at Jack. "I'll help you," I said, "for the boy's sake."

"Thank you, Jon," he said.

"Thank you, sir," Manu said, his voice wavering but clear. "I'm sorry for any trouble we're causing you."

Either Jack had coached the kid well, or the boy meant it. I decided to hope the sentiment was genuine.

"You're welcome," I said to Manu.

Jack caught the snub, of course, but he wisely chose to ignore it.

I now had a job to do and not enough time to prep to do it right. We had to get to work. "Jack, you said the meeting was in three days, so our mission clock is tolerable but far shorter than I'd like. I run this, and you do exactly what I say. Agreed?"

Jack smiled and nodded. "Of course. If I didn't need your expertise, I wouldn't be here, so you're the boss."

Even in victory, he kept selling. I sighed.

"Yes, sir," said Manu.

I forced a smile as I looked at the boy, then turned back to Jack. "Lay it out for me, everything you've agreed to, everything you fear." I sipped a little water. "Then, we'll need to get in some practice time."

CHAPTER 3

"I DON'T SEE WHY we have to do all this," Jack said, shaking his head. "It's an utter waste of time and energy, and you know how I deplore physical activity." He looked back at the restaurant. "Particularly when we could be doing other, so much more pleasurable things, such as sampling Joaquin's magnificent desserts."

What I knew was how much Jack liked to present the *image* of someone who hated physical activity. I'd once happened upon him during his exercises, and it was immediately obvious that he kept himself in very good physical condition. I'd subsequently learned from careful observation that he worked out daily with an almost religious fanaticism. Maybe he liked to pretend otherwise as part of his goal of constantly maintaining hidden advantages over all those around him, or perhaps he had other, private reasons for preserving the illusion; he never discussed it. I had no way to be certain of his motivation, but the front he presented was fake.

Not that how he felt mattered to me, of course; if I was going to run this operation, we were going to do it right. I turned my back on him, took a few steps away, looked left and right as if scanning the area, and subvocalized to Lobo, "Monitor all of this."

"Of course," he said.

I faced Jack. "You asked for my help," I said. "You're not paying me anything. So, you either completely and without question obey my orders from now until this is over, or . . ." I glanced at Manu and decided to stop there. "Preparation is a vital part of protection."

"Nothing is going to go wrong," Jack said.

"Then you don't need me." I turned away again.

"Okay, Jon," he said. "You win. We'll do what you say."

I nodded and faced him. "Has Dougat or anyone on his team spotted you or Manu?"

"There's no need to be insulting," he said. "Of course not."

"To be safe, spend the next three hours in a countersurveillance run anyway. Head to the center of Eddy, then wind your way to the northern edge. When the time is up, if you're being followed, come back here. Otherwise, meet me in the construction site a kilometer and a half due west." I risked exposing my rendezvous zone with Lobo on the assumption that I could reach it as quickly as anyone who might be watching us.

"I explained that they haven't seen us," he said, pain clear in his tone. "Must we go through this silliness?"

"For the last time, yes. I stated the deal, and you agreed to it, so stop complaining. Maybe it is silly, but we need to know if Dougat has found a way to track you, if he's now seen me, and so on."

Jack shook his head, took Manu's hand, and turned to go.

"Be sure to walk at least the last kilometer," I added.

Jack stopped.

I waited.

"As you say, Jon," he finally said.

Good. I jogged toward the forest that grew all the way to the edge of the lot Choy had cleared around Falls. "I'll see you in three hours."

As I entered the trees, I glanced back. Jack and Manu were gone. I turned west.

"Pick me up at the site," I said to Lobo. "Keep a constant watch on those two, and see if you can spot any signs of surveillance on them or us."

➤   ➤   ➤

For most of the next three hours, Lobo and I combined a lazy and pseudo-random flight path with an analysis of Jack's movements and the actions of all the people he encountered. Lobo ran simultaneous route projections and motion study filters on each human who might be watching Jack and on all the ships in the airspace within a hundred-kilometer-diameter cylinder with Eddy as its center. One of the great benefits of having a nearly state-of-the-art PCAV is the vast processing capacity he possesses, power originally designed to allow him to take battlefield command of large squadrons or survive and fight on his own for months at a stretch.

Unfortunately, that same vast computing capability let him keep talking the entire time he was conducting the analysis, monitoring Jack and Manu, and flying our course.

"So now you're a babysitter?" he said. "What does that make me? This world's most heavily armed pram?"

"You don't know that," I said, annoyed enough that I felt obliged to needle him. "The Expansion Federation isn't famous for having a light touch, so it might easily have other, more powerful craft in the area, and many of them could be assigned to child care as well."

"Don't know?" Lobo said, the indignation fairly ringing in his voice. "What do you think I do while you're socializing with old friends and enjoying sublime comestibles the likes of which I'm not even equipped to taste?"

"I thought you were watching over me."

"I was, of course, but how much of my capacity do you think that takes? Precious little in this deserted area, I can tell you that. I spend my time amassing data and improving myself, as any thinking creature should." He paused, but I was not going to be lucky enough to get away with a rant that short. "You might consider a little more self-improvement, Jon. You could—"

"Enough," I said, wondering yet again why I ever let myself get involved in these conversations. "We're doing this. Period. The boy needs help."

"A lot of people need help, Jon, help you could give."

From whiner to philosopher in less than a second: another benefit of too much computing power. He had a point, though, and I paused to consider it fairly.

"Yeah," I said, "they do, and I suppose if I were a good enough person I would spend all my time helping others, but I'm not." Dark memories clawed at the fringes of my mind, and I did my best to push them away, a task I manage better during the day than in the sad, scary, honest hours in the middle of the night. I'd done enough bad things over the years that I was sure anyone who really knew me wouldn't consider me good at all, but that wasn't news. "No, I'm not that good." I shook my head to clear it. "For whatever little it's worth, I am decent enough to make sure Manu comes through this interview safely. That has to be worth something, right?" I thought of Jennie and wished, as I have so many times before, that I could have saved her. "Just a rhetorical question."

I took a deep breath, held it, and let it out slowly.

"How far are they from the rendezvous?" I said.

"Assuming they continue their current pace, ten minutes."

"Any sign of surveillance?"

"None," Lobo said. "I would have alerted you had there been any, per your orders."

"Of course. Sorry." I surveyed the many images flickering on the displays Lobo had opened all over his walls: the video surveillance of Jack and Manu, both distant and close perspectives, the motion maps of the people in the area, the flight patterns of all the nearby aircraft and space vehicles, and all the usual PCAV status displays. "We're going to do two unusual things during this training exercise with Jack and Manu."

"I'm excited already," Lobo said.

I ignored him and continued. "I don't want you to let them see any of your weapons at any time, and I want you to do your best imitation of a faux PCAV, the kind of craft you heard Jack say he used to sell."

"So I'm to act dumb?"

I nodded. "Dumb *and* slow." I found myself enjoying this more than I should; pettiness is unbecoming, but sometimes it's also irresistible. "Show only standard vehicle displays, keep your dialog to a minimum, follow only basic voice commands, and don't go above half speed at any time."

"Are you doing this because you're angry at me?" Lobo said. "This strategy makes no sense, because it's not how you'll want me to behave if you need my help during the meeting."

"No," I said, "it's not, and I'm not doing this from anger. The less Jack knows about everything in my life, especially you, the better. He has a nasty talent for turning information into leverage, and as soon as this is over, I want to walk away cleanly and leave him with as little data as possible."

"Maintaining secrets during conflicts makes sense, of course," Lobo said, "but usually one withholds information from the enemy. I thought we were helping Jack, not opposing him."

"We don't call him 'Slanted' Jack for nothing," I said. "You can't trust anything he says to be the truth. So, we'll take extra care even though we're all theoretically on the same team. Clear?"

"Of course."

"One more thing," I said. "I want to make this as easy as possible for the boy, maybe even fun, both so we don't scare him and so he'll learn more quickly."

"Fun?" Lobo said. "Combat-scenario retrieve-and-retreat training?"

"Yeah," I said, "though I must admit I don't have any good ideas."

"Perhaps I'll come up with something," Lobo said, his tone such an odd mixture of serious contemplation and complete sarcasm that I couldn't help myself: For the first time since Jack walked into Falls, I smiled, laughed, and, for a moment, relaxed.

Bare earth marked a square site nearly a kilometer on a side. Autograders perched along its far edges, arguing with each other about who could move the most earth per hour, whose average payload was largest, and who left the smoothest stretch of ground. I tuned them out as soon as I made sure that in the few hours since Lobo and I had taken off none of them had been repurposed for surveillance roles. A light shower had moistened the ground enough that Jack, Manu, and I stirred up almost no dust as we walked to the center of the dirt square. Leaves on the tall trees surrounding most of the site danced happily in the gentle afternoon breeze that carried the life-affirming smell of an undisturbed forest soaking up rainwater. I loved developing planets, the sense of unspoiled nature available only before humans turned all the most beautiful places into either settlements or carefully groomed tourist attractions.

Like all people, however, I disturbed nature when it suited my needs, as it did now.

I sat on my heels so I was roughly at eye level with Manu. "Jack is almost certainly right," I said. "Your interview with Mr. Dougat will probably be a long and boring conversation. I hope it is. Sometimes, though, things change. Maybe a big storm will come along."

"Or maybe he'll try to kidnap me," Manu said, crossing his arms. "I'm not stupid."

I smiled despite myself. "Or maybe he'll try to kidnap you. You're right: That is possible, and I shouldn't treat you as if you're not smart. If he does try anything, I'll stop him."

"Just you? Jack said Mr. Dougat has a lot of people."

"Not just me. Jack will also help, and so will Lobo."

"Who's Lobo?"

"Lobo is my ship."

"Will I get to see it?"

"Oh, yes. In fact, what we're going to do now is prepare ourselves in case something goes wrong at the meeting and we have to leave in a hurry."

"How do we do that?"

I preferred working alone, but I had spent enough time on tactical teams with others that I was comfortable giving and receiving orders from adults. Manu's questions, though, were getting to me. I glanced at Jack, who shrugged slightly, as if to say, "See what I have to put up with?" I forced myself to stay calm and nice. I needed Manu to be comfortable with me.

"We practice," I said. "If anything goes wrong, Lobo will fly to us. He—"

"I thought you said Lobo was a ship."

"Lobo is. People tend to call ships 'him' or 'her,' and with a name like Lobo, I call this ship 'him.'" Manu nodded, so I continued. "I'll summon Lobo when we need him. When he comes, he'll be flying very fast. He'll open a hatch in his side and hover close to the ground only long enough for the three of us to get in. He won't ever completely stop moving, so our job is to stay together until he's close, then run into him and hold on while he takes off."

"It doesn't sound hard," he said.

"No, it doesn't," Jack said, "but Jon's in charge, so we're going to do what he says."

I glanced at Jack, shook my head, and faced Manu again. "We're not practicing to make me happy," I said. "We're doing it because the sight of a ship as big as Lobo screaming out of the sky at you can be scary, and hopping inside a moving, hovering craft can be harder than it sounds. Jump the wrong way, for example, and you can hit your knees on his hull and fall backwards."

"I'll do it right," Manu said.

"I'm sure you will, and so will Jack, and so will I, but it'll be easier for all of us once we practice." I stood. "Ready?"

Manu nodded, his face resolute, his fists clenched at his sides.

"Now, Lobo," I said aloud, wanting Manu to have a warning the first few times.

I'd told Lobo to come in slower than normal initially, so I expected this to be a very simple first practice.

I'd also never bothered to tell him that I hadn't seriously meant for him to take on the task of making this training fun.

That might have been a mistake.

I heard Lobo before I saw him. Music, carnival music, the same jaunty melody that's brought smiles to children and adults alike on multiple worlds, filled the air as Lobo flew in gently from the west. Louder and louder as he drew closer, the tune tugged an involuntary smile onto all of our faces. Lobo flew in a silly, zigzag path until he coasted to a hover half a meter over the dirt and five meters in front of us, an open side hatch beckoning. Dust from the force of the hover flew around Lobo, but thanks to the recent rain, the amount was small and served only to add to the image of a magical ride. He didn't stop with the music, either: He moved back and forth along his long axis, almost wiggling, as if a twenty-five-meter-long, eight-meter-wide, dull silver metallic dog was dancing in anticipation of some attention from his master.

Manu clapped his hands and laughed. "That's Lobo?" he said. "He's the best!"

Jack put his hand on my shoulder and leaned close enough that he could speak to me without Manu hearing. "Jon, though I have to give you credit for the sheer weirdness of this idea, shouldn't we be boarding?"

My first thought was that I was going to kill Lobo, but of course killing him would not only be extraordinarily difficult, it would also be destroying my most precious asset and the only entity who had consistently been my friend for almost a year. My second thought was a more accurate one: I had only myself to blame.

I looked at Jack and nodded, then touched Manu's shoulder. The boy was still smiling, his eyes wide with joy. "Let's run over and jump in, okay, Manu?"

"You bet!" he said. "It's like getting on a fun ride!"

He took off before us, but longer legs let Jack and me catch him easily. We all jumped on board at the same time, Manu clearing the edge of Lobo's floor easily.

Lobo had, as I'd requested, manifested only the most basic wall displays. I was glad I'd made the request, because Jack was intently studying the interior.

"Having them outfit the knockoff with external audio was a nice touch, Jon," he said.

"It came that way. I bought it used."

Jack nodded. "The exterior is extremely convincing, and the interior's not bad."

"Thanks." I hopped out and motioned to Jack and Manu to do the same. "Let's try it another time, but without the music and with a much faster approach. Okay?"

"Sure!" Manu said. "Let's do it again!"

They both followed me back to our original position. Lobo closed the hatch and took off slowly to the east, then looped north at the edge of the clearing and quickly vanished from sight with a final wiggle and a slowly vanishing whisper of music.

What a ham.

I gave him two minutes, then looked at Manu. "Ready?"

"Oh, yeah!" he said.

"This is going to be very different, maybe even scary."

He looked at me and shook his head. "Lobo can't be scary," he said. "Lobo's fun!"

I was tempted for a moment to explain to the boy how very wrong he was on both counts, but then I realized how successful Lobo's ploy had been. I would never hear the end of this.

"Okay, Lobo," I said. "Now."

Lobo rocketed out of the west like a missile hurtling toward its target, the force of the displaced air pushing us backward as he settled into a hover barely two meters in front of us, his stop more abrupt than I would have thought possible. Alarm played across Jack's face. The speed of the motion triggered my battlefield readiness reflexes, and adrenaline stimmed me to the twitching point.

Manu smiled and clapped again. "I told you Lobo was fun!" he said as he ran and jumped inside. "Aren't you guys coming?"

Lobo was definitely not going to let me forget this.

After three more practice runs, even I had to admit we'd done all we could—all we could, that is, without using missiles or explosives to better simulate a firefight. I didn't want to do that, though, for two reasons: From what Jack had said, we were dealing with a few fanatics, not a militia, and I certainly didn't want Jack to know anything about Lobo's weapons systems.

"We're done," I said, as we sat on the edge of the hovering

Lobo, our legs stretched over the side, mine and Jack's touching the earth, Manu's dangling above it.

"Can't we do it one more time?" Manu said.

"No," I said. "You two need to get back into town, and I have other work to do."

"Please."

"Sorry," I said, "but that's it." I faced Jack. "I want you and Manu to get lost and stay lost until the meeting. Fifteen minutes before the start time, scout the site but do *not* enter it. If you don't see me there by then, I decided it's not safe, so you head right back here."

"What will you be doing between now and then?" Jack said.

"My job," I said. "I'm alone, and I have two days, so I have a lot to do." Jack clearly thought I was exaggerating, but I wasn't. Securing a meeting site typically requires a team and the better part of a week. He didn't know about my stint as a bodyguard, nor about my experience on several protection details with what is, in my opinion, the finest mercenary company anywhere, the Shosen Advanced Weapons Corp., the Saw. As always, I saw no reason to enlighten him.

"Don't worry about me," I continued. "Just do your job, which is staying out of sight. As best we can tell, no one is tracking you right now, so make sure it stays that way until the meeting." I stood, picked up a small, thin disc from Lobo's front console, and gave it to Jack. "Stick this on your body where you can easily reach it. If something goes wrong, squeeze it and state your situation; I'll get the alert. If you call me for anything other than an emergency, however, I'll leave. Got it?"

"Yes." He took Manu's hand and jumped out. "See you in two days."

"Bye, Lobo," Manu said, waving. "You're the best!"

When they reached the edge of the clearing, I said, "Let's go."

Lobo closed the side hatch and took off.

"I can do fun," he said.

CHAPTER 4

*T*HE PINKELPONKER RESEARCH Institute sprawled across the built-up northern border of Eddy like a fever dream. No signs warned that when you passed the last of the rows of permacrete corporate headquarters buildings you should expect something very different indeed. No lights, labels, tapestries, recordings, or welcome displays clamored to explain it to you. In the middle of a five-hundred-meter-wide lot the gleaming black ziggurat simply commanded your eye to focus on the miniature of Pinkelponker that revolved slowly in the air a few meters above the building's summit.

Dougat and the Followers named it a Research Institute, but you instinctively knew the moment you saw it that it was a temple, a place where people worshipped, a site of great importance to them.

A perfect lawn the muted green of shallow seawater surrounded the building. Circular flower beds rich in soft browns, glowing yellows, and deep ocean blues burst from the grass at apparently random locations all over the lot. Only when you viewed them from the air, as I had when Lobo and I had made our first recon pass late the morning after my meeting with Jack, did you realize that each grouping of plants effortlessly evoked an image of one of the many volcanic islands that were the only landmasses on my birth planet. The ziggurat itself looked nothing like any of the individual islands I'd seen, yet its rounded edges and graceful ascent reminded me of home, made me ache for it.

After our initial flyover, I'd directed Lobo to a docking facility on the west side of town and hopped a cab from there. I'd then sent Lobo back up so he could keep watch over me. No one knew me here, so I really shouldn't have needed the protection, but I've learned from past experience that if I give Lobo something to do he's a lot easier to get along with than if I leave him in storage, even if storage is the more sensible alternative.

At least he appreciated that I needed to see the site in person, and he couldn't reasonably join me. If you're going to work on the ground, aerial images and even surface-level recordings are no substitute for actually walking the terrain and getting a feel for it. I've been on multiple missions that didn't permit that luxury, but this one did, and I was going to take advantage of the opportunity. I'd changed cabs twice on the chance anyone had tracked me from the docking center, but neither Lobo nor I spotted any tails. The last cab took me down the street that bordered the Institute on the ocean side, a wide avenue jammed with hover transports, cabs, and personal vehicles all rushing to and fro in the service of Eddy's growing economy. The length of the crossing signal made it clear that the city's planners valued vehicles and commerce far more than pedestrians.

When I finally made it to the Institute's ocean-side entrance, I found the overall effect far more entrancing than anything I'd anticipated from my aerial surveillance. I felt as if someone had sampled my memories and recombined them, managing in the process to create a setting that in no way resembled home but that at the same time rewarded every glance with the sense that, yes, this is the essence of Pinkelponker, what it *meant* if not exactly what it was. Working in the grain fields under the bright sun, the constant ocean breeze cooling me, Jennie due to visit when her day was done—I drifted back involuntarily, my memories summoned by Dougat's artful evocation.

I shut my eyes and forced myself to focus on the job. It was a site I had to analyze, nothing more. Jack's task was to keep Manu hidden until the meeting. Mine was to make sure we all got out safely if anything went wrong. To do that, I had to learn as much about this place as possible and set up the best protection scenario I could manage given that my only resources were Jack, Lobo, and myself.

When I looked again at the grounds, I did so professionally. None of the scattered plantings rose high enough or were dense enough that you could hide in them. That was good news for possible threats, but bad news should we need to take cover. I couldn't spot any lawn-care, gardening, or tourist appliances, and when I tuned my hearing to the frequencies such machines use, I caught nothing.

"Lobo," I said over our comm link, "have your scans turned up anything?"

"No," he said. "If there are weapons outside the building, they're not emitting any IR or comm signatures I can trace. I can spot no evidence of sensor activity on the grounds. This place doesn't even have the animal-detection circuits that most developing planets require around the perimeters of buildings. I've never encountered a more electromagnetically neutral setting this close to a city."

"Any luck penetrating the building?"

"No. It's extremely well shielded. It's transmitting and receiving on a variety of frequencies, of course, but everything is either encrypted or boring, standard business interactions with the usual public data feeds."

"Anything significant between here and his warehouse?" In our research on Dougat last night, we'd learned that he owned and operated a shipping and receiving center on the south end of the city.

"Encrypted bursts of the size you'd expect for inventory and sensor management. We should assume that place has the normal software and sensor sentries of any such facility, but it's not as shielded as this building and currently reads IR-neutral. Best estimate is that no people are there."

Good; the security we found here might be all we had to worry about.

"Any other significant activity?"

"Unfortunately," Lobo said, "yes. This structure is transmitting situational updates to the Eddy police headquarters almost continually. If anything happens here, the police will know about it within a second or two."

Dougat definitely had pull, because cops on early-stage worlds are notoriously relaxed and tolerant. They understand that the process of developing a planet is one that engenders many conflicts, and they tend to let the parties involved sort out their differences. That Dougat could get them to monitor his institute so thoroughly meant we had to assume he'd also made sure they'd take his side in any disagreements. So, we had to consider them hostiles. Great.

"How long would it take them to reach here?"

"I can only guess," Lobo said.

"So guess."

"Traffic appears to be bad throughout the day, and I spot no signs of any significant airborne vehicles at their nearest facility. So, I would estimate a response time no faster than seven minutes and no slower than fifteen."

"If anything goes wrong," I said, "we'll consider five minutes to be our window. That means you must remain within a max of two minutes, maybe less."

Even as I said it, I didn't like it. If we ended up dealing with a hostile party on his own turf and we had to cope with a kid, we needed more time.

"I want a bigger window," I said. "We're going to need a diversion."

"What are you willing to destroy?" Lobo said. "If you'll sanction strikes on third-party property, I can demolish enough buildings in their path that the police will need a great deal more time to reach here."

"No," I said. "I don't want to make anyone else pay for our

problems." Hurting innocent people or their property was sometimes necessary, but I hated doing it. "Aren't the police closer to Dougat's warehouse than here?"

"Considerably," Lobo said, "but that facility does not appear to be transmitting to police monitors."

"Fine," I said. "We'll use the warehouse if need be. We can visit it tomorrow. We'll make sure that anything we do to it is so loud and so obvious that the police have to attend to it first."

"If I fire at it," Lobo said, "they'll quickly know the attack initiated from an airborne vehicle. In addition, the explosions are extremely likely to damage neighboring properties. Neither of those factors help our cause when we try to jump from this planet."

I nodded and considered the problem. "Good points." The smaller the commotion we caused, the better. In addition, the more we could do without leaving an obvious trail, the more likely we were to be able to get away cleanly, should it come to that. "We'll have to make it look like either an accident or something that someone on the ground did. That would rule you out, and by being here, I wouldn't be a suspect, either."

The plan seemed reasonable, but it could still end up hurting innocents at the warehouse. "Can you get me any more data at all about that building?"

"No," Lobo said. "The place is shielded against both IR and more penetrative scans."

"Then I'll have to check it out myself," I said. "That'll be tomorrow's primary mission. If Dougat maintains a staff there, I'll either have to figure a way to get them out or target only an unoccupied part of the building. That means I'll have to plant implosives. Your arsenal includes a full stock, doesn't it?"

"Of course," Lobo said, immediately indignant.

Even when I ask about things not under his control, such as the replacement weapons I have to buy when we use devices from his munitions supply, Lobo turns petulant. I considered telling him to stop behaving so poorly, but I knew the conversation would prove useless.

Instead, I turned my attention back to the Institute. The

air was cooling as night approached, but Eddy was still warm
enough that the slight breeze from the ocean felt fine against
my skin. I'd stood in one place longer than a normal tourist
would, so I walked slowly toward the building.

"In the last fifteen minutes," Lobo said, "over two dozen
humans have entered the Institute on the side opposite your
position, and twenty have left via the same doors."

"Shift change. How many look like security?"

"All were wearing comm links, so that's impossible to gauge.
Based on the building's total lack of visible external sensors or
weapons, however, we should assume most are hostiles."

"No," I said. "Even if they're all security, they're not neces-
sarily hostiles, at least not yet. They become problems only if
Dougat chooses not to play this straight."

"You're indulging in distracting games," Lobo said, "induced
by your emotions. You've involved us, an involvement that
matters only if Dougat attempts to kidnap Chang. If he does,
he and his staff become hostiles, as do the police. If Dougat
doesn't cause any problems, we're spectators. The only reasonable option, therefore, is to treat them all as hostiles for the
duration of our participation."

Though I'm glad Lobo is mine, his lack of tolerance for
ambiguity frequently leads to conversations that are far more
cold-blooded than I prefer. "By that logic," I said, "to maximize
our probability of success we should simply kill all the staff
and the police. Right?"

Lobo ignored my sarcasm. "That is sensible from an efficiency
perspective," he said, "but it would attract the attention of the
EC staff at the gate, and it would also remove Dougat's ability to pay for the interview and thus compromise the overall
mission. So, I don't recommend it."

Before I could decide whether I wanted to know if he was
also being sarcastic, I reached the ziggurat's entrance.

"Signing off until I exit," I said.

The atmosphere inside was a perfected version of what I'd felt
outside: a bit warmer, a little more humid, with light breezes
of unknown origins wafting gently across you no matter where

you stood. Perpetual daylight brightened the space. Cloud-scapes played across the ceiling. The faint sounds of distant surf breaking and wind moving through grasses tickled the edges of perception. Once again, I had only to close my eyes to transport myself to the Pinkelponker of my childhood. Either Dougat or someone on his design team had visited my home world, or their research was impeccable.

The center of the space was a single large open area broken by injection-molded black pedestal tables that glowed in the ever-present light, two-meter-by-four-meter informational dis-plays, and small conversation areas. The island theme continued here, with each cluster of exhibits centered on a topic such as early history, agriculture, speculation on the exact cause and final outcome of the disaster, mineral and gemstone samples, and so on. A few dozen people stood and sat at various spots around the interior, some clearly serious students, and many equally obviously only tourists with at most an idle interest in Pinkelponker. Even the most studiously focused of the visitors would close their eyes from time to time as the interior effects worked on them.

The exceptions, of course, were the security personnel. You can costume security staff so their clothing blends with the visitors', and you can train them to circulate well and even to act interested in the exhibits, but you can't make them appear under the spell of the place they're guarding. Even the most magical of settings loses its allure after you've worked in it for a few weeks. I counted fifteen men and women on active patrol. I had to assume at least a few more were monitoring feeds and weapons scanners, occupying rooms I couldn't see, and generally staying out of my view.

I kept in character as a tourist, lingering long enough at the historical displays to appear interested but not so long as to look like a student of the planet. I'd learned almost nothing of the world's history growing up there, so I was genuinely interested in the background on the generation ship and the later discovery of the jump gate. Docent holograms snapped alert when I lingered at any exhibit, and I let a few of them natter at me. One presentation explored the various religions of Pinkelponker. Growing up there, I never saw a place of worship, and the closest I came to prayer was the occasional desperate hope for Jennie to come visit me or for my chores to be over. I stopped long enough that a docent asked if by chance I belonged to any organization that viewed the planet as sacred. I hadn't realized such groups existed; perhaps the Followers were among them. I obviously had a lot to learn about how some people viewed my home.

A small, meter-wide display in the right rear corner of the space offered the only discussion of the legends Jack had cited. Dougat might be as personally interested in the stories of Pinkelponker psychics as Jack had said, but the man either wasn't letting his interest shape the Institute's exhibits or was keeping a low profile with his beliefs.

Like the other tourists I spotted, I made sure to invest a large chunk of my time gawking at the cases highlighting jagged mineral samples and large, unrefined gemstones. Though I frequently stood alone at one of the historicals, I always had company at the mineral and gem displays. For reasons I've never understood, standing near items of great monetary value, even things you'll never have the chance to touch or own, is a compelling experience for many people. As best I could tell, the larger samples here, like the big gemstones in any museum on any planet, illustrated the power of natural forces applied slowly over long periods of time to create artifacts of great beauty. The waterfalls outside Choy's restaurant and the grooves they'd cut into the cliffs there made the same point and were, to me, more striking and more beautiful than any individual minerals, but for most people they lacked the powerful allure of gems.

I was intrigued to learn that Pinkelponker had been extremely rich in gemstones and that the business of exporting them to other worlds eventually constituted a major source of revenue for the government. All I'd seen of Pinkelponker was a pair of islands: the one where I lived until the government took away Jennie, and the one where they tossed me until my failed escape attempt led them to sell Benny and me to the Aggro scientists for nanotech experimentation. I owed Benny for my eventual escape from that hellish prison, but he'd died in the ensuing accident, so my debt to him was another of the many that I'll never be able to repay.

The images of gleaming government centers sparkling on sun-drenched islands and the stories of gem-fueled wealth led me to wonder, not for the first time, at the amazingly different ways that residents of the same planet can view their world.

The rearmost of the exhibits ended at a long wall that extended across the back of the building and rose to the ceiling. Offices, storage, and loading docks probably filled the remainder of the interior space. As I exited I counted off the distance from that wall; knowing the size of the private space behind it might prove useful. I continued to hope everything would go smoothly and this scouting would prove to have been a waste, but until the interview was over and Jack and Manu were safely away, the more information we had, the better.

To the left of the entrance I paid a visit to a small concession area. The two machines there offered everything from beverages to quasi-historical data files to glowing bouncy ball models of Pinkelponker. I purchased some water and listened on the common appliance frequencies on the chance that I could glean something useful.

"Another big spender," the beverage dispenser said. "Does anyone who visits this place even appreciate what I'm capable of? If they'd bother to scroll through the menu, or simply ask, they'd learn that I could provide everything from juices to local herbal teas—and some quite good ones, if the reactions I've heard are any indication."

"Isn't that always the way it is?" the keepsake vendor said. "Oh, sure, a few will buy a bouncing Pinkelponker model, but what about the built-to-order and personalized options? How many of these people will take real advantage of what I could do for them? Precious few, I can tell you. Why, I bet not one in a hundred of them has even a clue as to the breadth of Pinkelponker souvenirs I could fabricate."

"If it weren't for the staff," the dispenser continued, "my conveyor and rear assembly parts might rot of disuse."

"I'm sorry I'm not thirstier," I said on their frequency, "but I do appreciate the work you both do."

Though machines don't expect humans to talk to them on their radio spectrum, it takes an exceptionally intelligent one, such as Lobo, to ever question why you're able to do so. Most appliances are so self-absorbed and have so much spare intelligence that they'll dive at any chance to chatter endlessly with anything or anyone that responds.

"Thank you for saying so," the dispenser said.

"At least he bought something from you," the other commented.

I interrupted before they could get into an argument and forget me entirely; appliances also have extremely short attention spans. "The staff must keep you very busy. I'm sure they appreciate you, and they seem to outnumber the visitors."

"They appreciate *it*," the keepsake machine said, "but not me. Except for the odd desperate birthday gift purchase, most never even visit me. Of course, it's not like I have an outlet in the back of the Institute. Some machines work at a disadvantage."

"Some machines are simply more important than others," the beverage dispenser said. "Every human has to drink, so my offerings are vital. They do not have to purchase the sort of disposable afterthoughts you peddle."

"I bet each staff member uses you at least once a day," I said, focusing on the dispenser.

"Not quite," it said, "but some order multiple times, so the average daily total is actually a bit better than that."

"You must keep quite busy simply helping them," I said, "because that must be, what, sixty or eighty orders a day."

"I wish!" it said. "It's more like thirty-five to forty orders a day, and I could handle ten times that quantity with ease."

That put the staff count at about three dozen, which meant security could run as high as twenty or more during busy hours. That estimate roughly matched what I'd guessed from walking around. That many guards would have been overkill for a place this size were it not for the gems, but given their presence it was believable. Consequently, Dougat had the option of summoning a lot of human backup, so I definitely needed to keep the meeting in the open, where Lobo could reach us quickly.

I walked outside and wandered for a few minutes among the islands of flowers. That Jack had approached me about a job involving Pinkelponker kept nagging at me. Did he know something about my background, or was it just a coincidence induced by me choosing to spend time on a world only two jumps away? If he'd learned more about me, how, and from what source? With many people I would ask them or feel them out on the topic, but neither approach would work with Jack; he was too much a manipulator for me to play him, and if he knew nothing, I certainly didn't want to alert him that this was a topic he should pursue further.

My safest option was to do the job at hand and listen closely in case he let something slip—an unlikely event, of course, but a possibility nonetheless.

I headed off the grounds and opened a link to Lobo.

"Enjoy your tour?" Lobo said.

The tone of his voice answered my earlier, unspoken question: He'd been speaking sarcastically then. Lobo's mood never changes as a result of breaks in a conversation, no matter how long the interruptions may be—unless, of course, the concerns of a mission intervene. Though his emotive programming was, in my opinion, overblown, his designers had at least possessed the good sense to make him turn all-business when the situation demanded. For that, I was always grateful.

"It was informative," I said, pretending not to have noticed his tone. "As you would expect, we're going to make some modifications to the draft plan we discussed earlier. Pick me up at the rendezvous point in an hour and a half, and we'll walk through it again."

"It's what I live for," Lobo said.

I ignored him and continued. "In the meantime, consider

options that do minimal damage to this place. I see no reason to trash more than we have to."

"No reason?" Lobo said, incredulity replacing sarcasm in his voice. "Your instructions were that the top priorities were to get you, Manu, and Jack, in that order, to safety should this turn into more than an interview. You even established that Jack would be in command should you be incapacitated. You wouldn't have given those orders unless you believed this could go badly. Should that happen, the simplest way to achieve your goals and avoid an unwanted conclusion is to take out all opposition staff and positions."

"That's not an option," I said.

I signed off without further discussion. Lobo didn't agree with my orders, but like any professional soldier he'd obey them as long as he was able.

I winced inside at having put myself first on Lobo's priority list, but the reality was that if the day turned nonlinear, the best hope Jack and Manu had was that I stayed alive and protected them or, if need be, went back for them. In some ways I hated the part of me that could coldly assign priorities in life-and-death situations. That same coldness, however, had kept me alive through a great many missions gone very, very wrong, so I was unwilling to abandon it.

In times like these, moments when I can't avoid seeing some of my darker aspects, I find the only force that keeps me going is the job in front of me. Everyone who's ever been through basic training knows how it works. You push aside doubt as best you can, but even if you can't, even if the doubts scream and pull at you, you take the next step—and the next, and the next, and the next, until you either reach your goal or you die.

My next step was the warehouse.

CHAPTER 5

THE WINDOWLESS GRAY permacrete building that Dougat and the Followers used to store their artifacts filled most of a block in the middle of a couple of square kilometers of similar structures. Major roads ran in front and along the back of the ten-meter-tall warehouse. The right half of the plain façade it presented the rare passersby was an awning-covered loading area with a long ramp that led down to the road from the work platform that stood two meters above the ground. A noodleria and a quick-mod body shop crowded either side of the freight deck and were the only bits of the block Dougat didn't own. From our aerial surveillance, the small human staff that ran the facility during the daytime must not have had much work to do, because they spent most of the day feeding on noodles or chatting up the body modders.

The rear was one enormous loading dock that handled the really big stuff. I couldn't imagine what Dougat collected that would require that much capacity; perhaps he'd acquired the warehouse from a previous owner and not bothered to customize it.

We watched the place all day. Only one shipment, four containers, each no more than three meters on a side, entered the building through the front. Nothing went in through the rear. Nothing left.

The paved alleys that ran along the sides of the warehouse were little more than footpaths, barely wide enough for two large men to walk abreast. The entire shipping district followed this layout, as if the original designers had realized at the last moment that their clients would never agree to have their buildings share walls and added separating strips as afterthoughts. The buildings were tall enough that even during the day at least a part of every alley was in shadow except for the brief stretches when the sun blazed directly overhead.

Daylight had started fading hours ago, so the spot where I stood, about twenty meters down the left alley from the rear of the building, was dark enough that no one walking by either end of the warehouse would have a chance of seeing me. I'd dressed in mottled black and gray from cap to gloves, and I carried a similarly colored pack. From where Lobo had dropped me in a landing zone a klick or so away, I'd crept from building to building in shadows, pausing after each move to check for possible observers.

Now, after fifteen minutes of waiting silently beside the rapidly chilling wall, as best I could tell all that effort had been a waste. I'd seen no one; the warehouse district was a wasteland. No dealers, no hookers, no patrolmen, no guards—no one.

"Do you read any human IR signatures in the area?" I said to Lobo. Per our now-standard policy, I traveled with a regular comm unit, an emergency broad-frequency transmitter woven into my clothing, and a tracker embedded in my arm. Though I'd initially doubted the value of this redundant setup, after needing Lobo to find me during a recent difficulty, I was happy to take the extra precautions.

"None in the roads or alleys within a block on either side of you," Lobo said. "I must caution again, however, that most of the buildings in this district are shielded, so I can't scan them."

"Understood," I said. "I'm going to send in the rats. Yell if you spot any transmissions."

"Of course," Lobo said. It was mission time, so he maintained a neutral tone, but I chided myself for repeating orders he'd never forget.

Dougat was bound to have outfitted the front and rear of the building with a variety of alarms, but for warehouses this basic and solid, few bothered to lace the permacrete with any electronic protections. The reasoning was obvious: Getting through one of the solid side walls would either require a lot of time or create enough noise that interior security systems would more than suffice to catch an intruder.

Fortunately, I had an option they had no way to anticipate. I spit in my hands, directed the nanomachines to decompose a growing cylindrical section of the wall, and rubbed the spit on the permacrete. Some combination of what Jennie did to fix me and the experiments the Aggro scientists ran on me granted me the ability to exert fine-grain control on the nanomachines that lace my cells. I switched my vision to IR—another gift, though I suspected an unintentional one, from Jennie—and watched as the nanomachines worked quickly and efficiently, the pace accelerating as they used the permacrete to create more copies of themselves, which in turn consumed more and more of the wall. The only signs of their work were the small IR signature of the energy expenditure and the slowly growing cloud of nanomachines where that portion of the wall once stood. I hunched over the small swarm to shield the activity from Lobo; we share a lot, but no one knows what happened on Aggro, and I intend to keep it that way. When the hole was about a third of a meter across, I instructed the nanomachines to disassemble themselves. In a few seconds, a pile of dust along the outside of the wall was all that remained of them. Dougat's people would wonder tomorrow how the intruder had so quietly ground away a section of the permacrete, but the only clue they'd find would be the dust itself.

I took the two customized gas rats out of the pack. I liked the rats because they had so many uses in urban conflicts and rarely aroused suspicion. Collapsed, each arm-size cylinder would attract little attention from anyone who didn't know modern weapons. Activated, the tubes sprouted legs and a coating of sensors that resembled thick, dark-brown hair. Each rat could carry a few kilos of any payload from gas to explosives, and each possessed a modest recon and analysis system.

The rats I gently lowered onto the warehouse floor were special. We'd customized them using Lobo's onboard, battlefield-ready mini-fab, a small but powerful chamber that included full sets of waldos and 3-D printers that either he or I could control. We'd added extensions for detecting and interfacing with both cable-carried and wireless security networks. I thumbed on each rat and pulled my arm out of the hole.

"You're on," I said to Lobo. "Patch me the feed."

Lobo took control of the rats. An IR image of the inside of the warehouse flickered to life on the contact on my left eye. A second, similar image on my right eye immediately followed. Lobo added trace lines that glowed red where cables ran and green where major wireless transmitters hung. The faintly glowing image of the inside of the building superimposed on the end of the alley I was watching, and my mind took a moment to adjust to dealing simultaneously with the two realities. It struck me then that I hadn't used a heads-up display in quite a while, and I was torn over whether the lack of action was a good thing, because it meant I'd managed to avoid violence for a time, or a bad sign, because it suggested that I was turning soft.

I gently shook my head and focused on the two images; the time for self-reflection is definitely not in the middle of a mission.

The rats scurried to the nearest cable carriers, sections of unshielded conduit that ran along the building's side walls about three meters off the floor—high enough that no one would normally bump them, but low enough to make maintenance easy. Each rat fired a small drill-dart that trailed a thin wire as it flew into the conduit and immediately burrowed inside.

I pulled a roll of gray cling from my pack and snapped it into shape. I held it against the wall until the combination of static electricity and embedded glue cemented it tightly to the permacrete. Useful in the field for everything from quick shelters to very temporary repairs, the patch wouldn't pass close inspection, but no one at either end of the alley would notice it. A wire mesh woven into the cling served as an antenna through which Lobo could monitor and enter the building's network.

"I'm live on the security net," Lobo said.

"How long to crack?" Guard networks in shielded buildings typically used relatively weak security protocols, so we figured Lobo's built-in, massively parallel computing infrastructure should be able to hack into this one in a few hours. More than nine hours of darkness remained, so we had plenty of time.

"Go to the rear door," Lobo said. "It's unlocked."

I sprinted to the end of the alley. The interior displays vanished from my vision. I paused long enough to check in both directions for company, then dashed to the staff door. It opened as I approached and closed quickly behind me.

"How did you do that?" I said. "Even if you lucked onto the encoding scheme immediately, unless they used the weakest possible passwords and no additional preventions that should have taken at least an hour or two."

"The security system runs a standard three-level protocol with industrial-level encryption and both password and bio-metric checks," Lobo said, "so it's fairly typical of this type of installation. You wanted speed, and now you're in. What's the problem?"

"I repeat: How did you do that?"

"I've told you many times that I constantly work to improve myself. That effort extends to my computing infrastructure."

"Fair enough," I said, "but to hack into any system of this caliber that quickly you must have a lot more capacity than I'd ever imagined. Just how does your computing system work, and how far do its capabilities extend?"

"It's a complex topic," Lobo said, "and now is hardly the time to discuss it. By the way, how did you make a hole in the wall for the gas rats? I didn't spot any tools."

Lobo was open and talkative on every topic except himself. In that way, we were similar. Someday, I'd have to demand more information from him; I did own him, after all. He was right that now was not the moment to do that, nor was I interested in explaining myself to him.

"That's also a complex subject," I said, "and I need to get moving. Are all alarms offline?"

"No," Lobo said. "Those circuits send status updates to both the Institute and the police building each time they go offline. Their sensors are detecting you, but the warning information they're sending is never making it to the control modules. The data begins the journey, but I delete it before the system can react to it. As far as this building is concerned, you're the invisible man."

"Am I alone?"

"Yes."

"That's odd," I said. "I would have expected Dougat to have guards as backup."

"No other building in the area appears to employ human security staff at night," Lobo said, "so Dougat would have drawn attention to the facility had he used any. More importantly, the building's system is not as weak as you seem to believe. What I hacked was the system for the main storage area. A second, much stronger processor grid with a tougher protocol protects the entrance to the basement area."

"Basement?"

"Thirty point five meters east northeast of your position. The route's on your right display."

A schematic of the interior and a jagged blue path that started with me superimposed itself on the right half of my vision. Two rows of shelving separated me from the basement entrance.

"Nice layout diagram," I said. "Can you get any inventory info?"

"Negative," Lobo said. "The protection units need to know only the basics of the interior setup, so that's all they have. They don't even possess links to any outside systems other than those to the Institute and the police building."

"Basement layout?"

"Unavailable. As I said, it's on a separate system."

"Hack it."

"I'm working on it," Lobo said. "I told you it was stronger."

Though any area with a separate security system was inherently interesting, I was wrong to focus on it. My goals were first to set up the diversion and only then to explore if time permitted. Should we need the distraction, I wanted it to cause as little damage as possible, so I hoped to locate a small section of the warehouse with very little of value in it. If the place was packed with valuable goods, I'd live with the potential loss, but I hate senseless destruction. I crept to the nearest row of shelving, pulled a small light from my left front pocket, and started a quick inventory.

In less than two minutes I'd checked five large storage corridors and was all the way to the middle of the building. I needn't have worried about potential damage. The shelves were either empty or holding only basic supplies destined for the Institute: sealed snacks, souvenirs, staff uniforms, and all the other operating matériel of any museum. The labels on the few boxes scattered among the shelves might have been fakes, but from spot checks of the weights, I didn't think so.

The basement was suddenly a lot more interesting, but I had work to do.

If you're hitting a building and you want maximum external effect with minimum internal damage, shaped charges on the roof are just the ticket. You take out a small center section of the target area a fraction of a second before the rest, then angle the perimeter charges so the explosion shoots debris spectacularly skyward but also results in most of the blown bits falling back into the hole. I had five small charges with me, each wrapped around a short arrow with an active head that contained an extensible antenna and a signal repeater. I took the arrows and a small crossbow from my pack; sometimes old tech is the best tech. I shot the first arrow at a spot about midway from the building's sides and ten meters or so from the rear entrance. It stuck nicely. The ceiling was high enough that I couldn't tell if the arrow's tip was finishing the process by drilling until it could extend an antenna above the roof.

I learned it had worked when Lobo picked it up.

"First charge checked in," he said. "Main security systems remain under my control. Even when I pull out, they won't remember it."

"Excellent," I said.

I shot the remaining four arrows into the ceiling so they formed points on a rough circle with a radius of about five meters.

Lobo confirmed each was working as its antenna poked into the night. If we needed the diversion later, Lobo would trigger their primary payloads. If we got away safely, Lobo would set off the tiny secondary charges in the tips of each of the arrows. Each such charge would puncture an acid canister that sat behind its arrow's tip. The resulting corrosive flows would destroy the explosive material and enough of the casings to render the arrows both harmless and extremely difficult to trace.

"I've reconnected to the building net via the antennas," Lobo said, "and told the rats to withdraw their probes and head back to you."

The first rat bumped into my right leg. I picked it up and crammed it into my pack.

Before the other one could reach me, Lobo's voice rang sharp in my ear.

"You have company."

CHAPTER 6

SNAPPED OFF the light, froze, and waited for instructions. The one with the best data should make the call, and right now, that was definitely Lobo.

"Hold," he said. "Two exiting the basement." A few seconds passed in silence. "Heading to the front of the building. Abort?"

As long as those two weren't following up on an alarm, they had no reason to suspect anyone was inside with them. In a place this big and with Lobo feeding me their movements, staying away from them shouldn't be hard. "No," I said. "We wanted to know what they were hiding downstairs; this could be our chance to find out."

"You said you preferred to avoid killing hostiles."

"I don't have to kill them," I said, "to avoid them." Lobo was right, though, that if I went into the basement and the guards trapped me there, I'd almost certainly have to at least hurt them to escape. The secret room was too potentially interesting, however, to pass up.

"We'll use the rats," I said. I carefully and quietly took the one out of my pack and placed it on the floor next to my leg. "Arm both trank gas payloads and position them a meter on either side of the basement door. If the guards come back, knock 'em out." Though my nanomachines can handle any drug to

55

which I've been exposed, I'd taken no chances and had Lobo give me the standard pre-mission inoculation against my own bioweapons, so the gas in the rats shouldn't affect me even though it would buy me plenty of time to get out.

I felt motion against my leg and cranked my vision back to IR so I could watch the rats crawl soundlessly around the row of shelving to my right and out of sight.

Time dilated as I waited, every second suddenly long and dangerous. Being in the dark inside someone else's space always juices you with an emotional cocktail of fear, curiosity, and guilt, but when you're not alone adrenaline floods into the mixture and leaves you jacked and prone to the jitters. Breathing is the key, as it is in so many charged situations. I passed the seconds taking control of my breath, drawing air in through my nose in a slow inhalation, holding it for a moment, and then letting it leak ever so carefully out through my mouth.

I was inhaling for the third time when Lobo updated me.

"Data from the monitor system indicates the guards are eating in a front room."

"Any way to tell if more of them are below?"

"Negative," Lobo said. "As I said earlier, the main system doesn't cover that space."

"Send down one of the rats," I said, "and scan the area." I wanted to add "quickly," but that was stupid, so I stopped myself; Lobo knew what he was doing. "Show me a path to the closest safe hiding space to the open basement door. I want to be ready to go if the area is clean."

A schematic reappeared in my right contact. I crept along the glowing path. Take a step, pause, listen, wonder if I'm hearing the rat moving downward, repeat. When I reached the spot Lobo had chosen, I leaned against the shelving and concentrated again on managing my breathing. My every instinct screamed for action, but training overruled instinct and held me in silent, motionless position. I waited. Long, slow inhale. Hold it. Long, slow, leaking exhale.

I wondered why the adrenaline still came, all the years and all the actions since the first time I'd broken into a storage room on Aggro and hoped for escape. I'd failed then, and I'd failed on many occasions since then, but I'd also succeeded far more than I'd failed. The probability that I couldn't take these guards and get away safely was extremely low, and my mind knew that. Sometimes, though, what your mind knows isn't enough to let you relax.

"Basement clear," Lobo said. "Guards eating. Entrance is a three-meter-wide ramp sloping thirty degrees downward. Go. I'll withdraw the rat when you've made it down there."

A new schematic and path appeared on my right contact. I switched my vision to IR, but it added nothing to the information on the contact; the room was too cool. I followed Lobo's route around the end of the set of shelves that had been hiding me and then down a ramp. I stepped as quickly as I could while still staying silent, tracking myself and gauging my footfalls with the data from Lobo. I've never liked running in the dark with only displays to guide me, but training again overrode preference and kept me moving fast. Lobo's path ended at the bottom of the ramp, so I stopped there.

"Basement layout?" I said.

"Not enough data from the rats to create a reliable one," he said. "Guards are up front, so a small amount of light should be safe."

I pulled out a tiny glowstick and used it to scan the area. The basement appeared to run the length of the building, was about three meters high, and was only slightly narrower than the space above, though I couldn't be sure of its dimensions with the small amount of illumination I felt was safe. Two desks hunched end-to-end on either side of the ramp, a chair behind each one. The two chairs for the desks on my right were pushed back; it was a sloppy setup. The guards should have occupied opposite sides so they'd be in position for a safe crossfire on any intruder and also present separate targets. Their sloppiness wasn't new information, however; any good duo would never have taken their breaks at the same time. Their behavior suggested they were inexperienced, so they probably sat with the most valuable stuff behind them. I headed right.

The first set of shelves on both sides of the lengthwise aisle were empty, so I glided past them.

All the shelves in the second set appeared full. I'd planned to scan them rapidly and move on, but what I saw made me stop, put away the glowstick, and use a small flashlight.

From floor to ceiling and as far to each side as my light illuminated, weapons filled the shelves. Some sat naked, others were in standard reinforced plastic crates. Inventory tags, each bearing the stylized ziggurat logo of the Followers, helpfully illuminated themselves as I walked by and then winked off as I passed. That Dougat hadn't bothered to turn off those displays demonstrated an unwarranted degree of confidence in his security setup. I walked quickly up and down the aisles, knowing time was short but wanting to gather as much information as possible. SAMs, automatic rifles, squidlettes, hoppers, dusters, and on and on—the weapons ranged from anti-personnel to anti-tank to anti-aircraft to space-based and told no consistent story. I didn't spot enough of any one device to outfit more than a few troops or ships, but what the collection lacked in depth it made up in variety. Either Dougat was in the arms business, or he was buying everything he could find and hoping he could construct something sensible from the result. Or was I seeing only a little of his collection, and was he actually preparing a far larger arsenal?

None of this was directly my problem, of course, but it did suggest that if the meeting tomorrow turned bad, Dougat and the Followers might be far more formidable foes than I'd imagined. On the other hand, publicly revealing weapons like most of these would be sure to attract attention, attention he couldn't want because there was no chance he owned all of these devices legally.

What *I* wanted was more information, but even though I'd been in the basement only a couple of minutes, the weight of that time was pushing down on me. I had to get out.

I headed back to the ramp. As my light brushed across the desks opposite the guards', I noticed a rack of inventory checkers at the end of the farther desk. Maybe Lobo had forced his way into the warehouse's systems and I could collect more information from them.

"Have you hacked the inventory units?" I said.

"No," he said. "The security software is surprisingly resourceful, and I encountered serious barriers between the main system and the rest of the programs running the place."

"Will you finish before I pull out?"

"Unlikely," he said, "and once you do I must cut the links or risk leaving open a connection to me."

I looked longingly at the inventory units and the rest of the basement. I wanted to explore further, but it would be a bad choice.

I'd taken two steps up the ramp when Lobo cut in.

"Guards heading back."

A schematic winked into life and pointed me to the earlier hiding place. I ignored the instinct to run and forced myself to walk quickly and silently along the path Lobo had plotted and into the shadows of the shelves. A few seconds later, first one rat and then the other brushed against my left leg. I let them stay where they were and took one step backward so they wouldn't be underfoot if I had to move quickly.

In the silence the laughter of one of the guards rang loudly, the other's words lost in the noise. Their lights reached past my position, and I withdrew another couple of meters into the darkness. The beams swung by the shelves as the guards headed into the basement. A few seconds later, the floor sections covering that room snicked together.

"Clear to go," Lobo said.

I loaded the rats into the pack and walked quickly to the rear door, where I paused.

"External status?" I said.

"No humans visible for several hundred meters in either direction," Lobo said, "and your path to the pickup point is clear."

I slipped outside and headed left, back to the empty loading area we'd used for the drop-off. The temperature in the warehouse had been fine, but the cool night air still struck me as refreshing and freeing. I was glad to be back in it. As I walked, I reflexively scanned left and right. Lobo was monitoring me, but I didn't want to rely exclusively on him, both because in some situations he has to be too far away to help and because I need to be able to take care of myself. Though I knew I should focus on the world around me, the stash of weapons kept diverting my attention. They represented both potential opportunity—knowing Dougat had something to hide could prove useful—and possible danger, because anyone with so many weapons of so many sorts could easily afford to arm his security staff well.

A block and a half from the warehouse, Lobo's voice yanked me out of my reverie.

"Company dropping from a window that just opened above," he said. "Too late to run. I'm too far away to have a shot that could kill them without endangering you."

I stopped and cursed myself for letting the warehouse distract me and for thinking in only two dimensions. A man touched down two meters in front of me. He held his drop cable in one hand and a pistol in the other. He pointed the gun at the center of my chest. I heard another man hit the ground a bit more roughly behind me. I didn't bother to check to see if he had a weapon.

"Good evening, good sir," the man in front of me said. "Our employer would appreciate a word."

CHAPTER 7

I QUICKLY EVALUATED my options. The man was almost my height and considerably wider. His stance was perfect: feet spread at shoulder width, one foot a bit in front of the other, weight mostly on the harder to reach rear foot, knees bent. He held the gun with a casual confidence, but it never wavered from the center of my chest. In every detail I could spot, he was a pro. I could attack him and hope the person behind me would hesitate long enough to let me turn this guy into a shield; yeah, right. I'd be lucky to touch him before he shot me, and there was no way I'd be fast enough to avoid both him and his partner. I could dive, pray I was quicker than both their trigger fingers, and bet that they would catch each other in the crossfire; another brilliant idea. If I moved or attacked, they'd shoot me. If it was a body shot, the nanomachines should be able to repair me. If the rear assailant was targeting my head, however, my guess was that I'd die, and I was far from ready to do that.

"I certainly understand your desire for reflection," the front man said, "but we must move along. It would be rude to do otherwise, and my employer detests rude behavior." The man nodded slightly to his right, and I heard the one behind me take a step. The man leaned close enough to me that when he spoke he was whispering in my left ear. "Don't mistake the fancy talk, mate: I'd as soon shoot you as look at you. It's himself who makes us play these games." He stepped back again and waved me forward. "You may even keep your pack, provided, of course, that you refrain from opening it."

"After you," I said.

"Of course," the man said. "My colleague will insure that you do not lose sight of me."

"Move slowly," Lobo said over the comm unit, "and I may be able to reach you before they force you into the building."

I was tempted to try to stall, but learning what was happening was worth the risk of playing along. Besides, if they'd wanted to kill me, they'd have done so already. "No," I subvocalized.

I followed the man to the end of the block and around the corner. I heard the cables withdraw as we stepped away. I glanced at the upper floors of the building as we walked and glimpsed two windows closing, but I didn't spot any observation posts. That didn't mean anything, of course; a good sheet of insulated camoglass will let a building present a seamless and IR-neutral façade while its occupants enjoy a clear view of the outside world.

"I now can't reach you before you enter the building," Lobo said. "Should I attack it?"

"No," I subvocalized, covering my mouth and coughing slightly as I did so.

After about ten meters, a door slid open on our right. We entered a large black chamber illuminated only by the soft red glow emanating from a series of three arches. The owner clearly loved theatrics as much as formal language. I followed the lead man through the arches. He stopped after the final one and waited before a blank wall. "Rats," he said, "a nice touch. Custom or off-the-shelf?"

I said nothing.

"Of course," he said.

Two sections of the wall parted, and we stepped into an elevator. The trailing guard followed us in, and I got my first look at her. She was maybe ten centimeters shorter than the lead and considerably lighter, but in all the ways that mattered—stance, gun position, focus—she was his twin.

The elevator opened on the side opposite the one we entered, and the lead man stepped out. I followed him, my eyes tracking his gun as he temporarily turned his back on me, but the trailing guard played it smart and immediately took up position at my seven. If I attempted anything aggressive, she could shoot me cleanly and quickly.

I abandoned the idea of engaging them and looked for the first time at the room around me.

I closed my eyes, then opened them and stared for a second time.

Nothing changed.

I'd entered a storybook, maybe a museum exhibit or the hobby room of a wealthy reenactor. One of the constants of the many types of jobs I've held is a lot of time alone. I've filled that time soaking up whatever inputs I could obtain: text, audio, video, holoplays, anything and everything both old and new. I lacked any formal education—Pinkelponker's government didn't invest in the mentally challenged or, for that matter, any but those it considered elite—but I'd spent a lot of time learning for the pure pleasure of it. As best I could tell, I was standing in a gentlemen's club from Earth circa nineteenth or twentieth century.

Dark wood paneling covered the walls. Lighter planks with a matching grain formed the floor. Rich, thick, patterned brown carpets lay atop the wood here and there throughout the large space. Clusters of overstuffed leather chairs created multiple conversation nooks, each chair the rich black of the freshly tilled soil I'd worked as a child. Portraits of men with large sideburns and thick, gray hair adorned the walls. A fire—from the smell of it, real wood burning and drafting up a real chimney—threw heat from a fireplace tall and wide enough to hold several children standing side by side. The viscerally pleasing tang of a nighttime blaze suffused the air. Two manservants, each wearing the black and white formal server attire of the period and carrying a silver tray, stood at either end of the room. Books, actual bound paper as best I could tell, stood on shelves on either side of the fireplace and sat on some of the dark, three-legged tables that separated pairs of chairs.

As I examined the room more closely, I realized that the owner, though clearly infatuated with the period, wasn't willing to suffer or take undue risks for his passion. Quiet fans and masked vents prevented the fire's heat from exerting undue influence on the room's comfortable, almost constant temperature. The same air-handling system kept the room smoke-free but rich in the fire's aromas. The portraits morphed from time to time, displays with convincing surface textures but definitely not original art. Each servant held a small handgun discreetly at his side.

A door opened in the far left-hand wall. A man bustled in. No one said a word, but the posture of all of the staff straightened immediately; the boss had arrived. He was about fifteen centimeters shorter than I but almost as broad. He wore a version of the same suit as the manservants but one without tails. He studied me as he approached, then smiled and stuck out his hand.

"Good of you to come, Mr. Moore," he said.

I shook his hand. He controlled the situation completely, so I saw no viable options other than playing along. Though I might well be able to form a nanocloud to destroy him and everyone else in the room, I didn't want to kill anyone, and I had no good nondestructive options beyond listening and hoping to learn something useful.

When I didn't speak, he continued. "I gather from your reaction, sir, as well as from your taste in food—and who cooks better than Joaquin, eh?—that you are a man who has the capacity to appreciate my little club."

He obviously wanted me to talk, so I told the truth. "It is impressive indeed. I've never been anywhere quite like it."

"More's the pity that, isn't it, Jon? Do you mind if I call you Jon?"

I shrugged. "Of course not, Mr. . . ."

He smiled. "Chaplat, Bakun Chaplat. At your service."

"I would say that I appear to be at yours."

He laughed. "Quite so, quite so." He turned and spoke to the lead guard. "As I've explained so often, in business as in all things, class will out." He faced me again. "I trust my two colleagues were not too coarse in their greeting."

I kept my focus on Chaplat, but out of the corner of my eye I saw the man stiffen. I learned long ago that it's good to have friends on the front line, particularly if they're on the other side of the line, so I raised an eyebrow and said, "I'm afraid you have me quite mystified. They were perfectly pleasant, given the situation, of course."

The guard relaxed visibly. "Well done," Chaplat said to him.

Chaplat put his arm around me and led me to a pair of chairs facing the fire. "The hour is growing late, so I propose we have our chat and send you on your way." A servant appeared behind the table between our chairs. "A drink, perhaps, or a snack?" Chaplat said.

"Thank you, but, no."

"I appreciate your caution, Jon," he said, "though I assure you that it is unnecessary." He waved away the server. "To business then."

He settled back, adjusted his trousers, and stretched his arms along the chair's arms, the very picture of a relaxed, nonthreatening gentleman. The movements were too conscious, too practiced to be convincing, but I stayed in my role and sat back similarly.

The chair amazed me. Firm enough to provide good support but soft enough to make me want to stay, it could have been made for me. I glanced around the room and noticed that all of the chairs varied slightly in both height and depth. Chaplat had chosen one that was perfect for me. Without even thinking I ran my fingers along the chair's arms. The leather—and it was leather, real animal hide—had been worked until it was as soft and inviting as sleep on a bed after a hard day's march. Few buyers are willing to pay for real leather, and fewer still are willing to risk offending the many people who consider the material to be an abuse of animals, but when you encounter a piece as beautiful as the cover on this chair you immediately understand why some people won't give it up. The subtle smell and the texture carried me in an instant to my childhood, to those rare cold nights when Jennie and I would sit together under a leather and fur cover and watch through our hut's main window as the stars and the moons transformed the night from dark menace into magic.

"Another taste we share," said Chaplat, studying me as he spoke. "Very good. All too few men take the time to appreciate the pleasures available to them. Pleased as I am, however, we must, as I said, get to the topic at hand."

"Of course," I said. I put my hands in my lap and pushed away the memories.

Chaplat smiled and continued. "My organization operates a variety of concerns that share a single overriding goal: to facilitate trade on developing worlds. In the years, sometimes many years, between early colonization and the transition to full and effective planetary government, we provide such services as business interruption insurance, diversions for hardworking pioneers, third-party arbitration, negotiation, and, to those unable to obtain it elsewhere, capital." He leaned forward and put his hands on his knees. "It was for this last service that your friend Jack approached us."

"Jack?" I said.

Chaplat's expression tightened. "We know Jack, know him well enough that some of our associates were trying to catch up with him before he ended his stay on Mund. We also know Joaquin, who after a bit of persuasion mentioned Jack's visit and spoke rather highly of you." His tone changed, flattened. "Please do not mistake civility for softness. Our interactions thus far have been remarkably pleasant. I see no reason they need to change. Do you?"

The two guards edged closer.

"No, of course not," I said. "Jack was a business colleague many years ago, and I had not seen him since I," I paused, searching for the best way to be both accurate and vague, "chose to leave our joint venture. I can assure you that I was not expecting him to join me at lunch, nor to see him at all, for that matter."

Chaplat nodded in satisfaction. "If I may presume on our

growing relationship," he said, "may I ask the reason for Jack's unexpected visit?"

This time I was ready and didn't hesitate. When you have to lie, the best lie is the one closest to the truth. "He was seeking my assistance on a project, a project much like some of those in our previous venture."

"What sort of project?"

I smiled. "Wealth redistribution. While Jack handles many classes of interactions quite well, certain more basic functions are not his strong point. In our previous enterprises, those functions were mine to manage. He wanted the same sort of help here."

"And your response to him?"

"I said I was uninterested, wished him well in finding a partner, and left." If Chaplat's data came from Joaquin, that story should fit well with what he saw.

"I can certainly understand your reluctance to do further business with Jack," Chaplat said. "Our experience in providing him capital has certainly not been successful—at least not so far. I have to inquire, however, about the motivation for your visit to the Followers' warehouse if you are not working with Jack."

For a moment I wondered just how much money Jack had borrowed for his poker game or whatever real purpose he hadn't told me, but I couldn't let the thought distract me; any delay in my response would alert Chaplat. "Jack could not meet his objectives without me," I said. "I didn't plan to work with him, but on the off chance the opportunity might be large enough to justify extending my stay here, I was conducting some preliminary research."

"And your research showed?"

"That Jack was aiming at the wrong target. The place is nearly empty, and what stock it holds is primarily Pinkelponker souvenirs."

"Surely there are artifacts?"

I nodded. "Some, but nothing I recognized or could use."

"Too bad," Chaplat said. "We also conduct a brisk trade in

art and artifacts." He rubbed his hands on his pants legs. "But, no matter. We still have the issue at hand: Jack. His rather sizable debt to us remains unpaid, and we'd like your help in fixing that problem."

Finally. I paused long enough to appear to be deliberating the matter. "Though I appreciate your problem, it is just that: *your* problem."

The woman stepped close enough to rest her hand on my chair just behind my head.

Chaplat acted as if she were invisible. "Given the circumstances," he said, "it might not be unreasonable to consider adopting the issue as your own concern." He finally glanced at each of the guards in turn and then stared again at me. "I assure you that my associates are not always so well behaved."

"Nor are mine," I said.

Chaplat laughed. "Threatening me from the comfort of my own club's chairs? I do admire your moxie." Chaplat paused and turned completely serious. "But such bravado is also quite dangerous."

I didn't want a fight, but Chaplat wasn't going to let me go if he wasn't happy. I decided to turn this into something he would understand. "I do provide services, as I noted earlier, but at a price."

"And that would be?"

"Twenty percent of whatever Jack owes you."

"That's outrageous," Chaplat said, though his expression relaxed. "And you don't even know the amount."

"If I collect it for you, I'll know how much it is. As for being outrageous, I'm sure it's only a small part of the interest debt he's accumulated."

"And if we were to reach an accord, which would most certainly never be twenty percent, what guarantee would we have that you would perform the service?"

"None, of course, but I would be motivated, because I wouldn't receive any payment until I found and delivered him."

No one who built this room lacked an understanding of greed. Chaplat nodded. "Five percent," he said.

"Fifteen."

He stuck out his hand as he spoke. "Eight, and one of my associates accompanies you."

I didn't move. "Ten, and I report back here when I have him. If you follow me or try to make someone stay with me, Jack will spot the coverage and vanish." I paused, then took the slight gamble. "As he had already done until you got lucky and he sauntered into Falls, completely unaware that Choy was also a client of yours."

Chaplat stood and extended his hand again. "Deal."

I got out of the chair and shook his hand, not because I wanted the formal agreement or because I meant it, but because I had to make the gesture. He squeezed mine hard enough that I had to work not to show any reaction. I could have squeezed back harder and hurt him more, but my goal was to exit there intact, not to win a contest, so I took the pain. I couldn't stop myself, however, from the indulgence of not letting him know it hurt.

"I strongly suggest that you not disappoint us," he said. "If you do, no planet in this sector will be a good place to holiday." He dropped my hand, turned, and walked away. "My associates will show you out."

"What happened to you?" Lobo said. "That building's shielding was top-shelf; I couldn't pick up anything."

"Later," I said. "Backup site." Though Chaplat's team had left me alone on the street, I had to assume that I was under surveillance until I could convince myself otherwise. Chaplat didn't appear to know about Lobo, so I wanted to keep him a secret as long as possible. I now had to chart a jagged countersurveillance course to our backup site, a small tourist shuttle landing zone down the coast from the warehouse district. I covered an extra couple of kilometers simply to make sure I was alone.

As I walked, I focused most of my attention on my surroundings. I kept my vision on IR and this time checked not only the roads but also the buildings for signs of activity. I didn't spot any, but that didn't mean I was clear; Chaplat might have owned multiple shielded buildings. It was unlikely, however, that his properties stretched contiguously along my entire crooked route, so as long as neither Lobo nor I spotted any watchers, I was probably okay.

Despite my largely external focus, however, I couldn't help but ponder my situation.

Chaplat wanted Jack. Jack traveled with Manu. I had agreed to make sure nothing happened to Manu. To do that, I would also have to protect Jack. Lovely—and almost certainly exactly what Jack had wanted.

On the other hand, Jack had lied, so all bets were off. I could climb in Lobo and head for the jump gate. End of problem.

Except, of course, that if I left, I'd be breaking my commitment to Manu. I wouldn't do that. I would stay simply because I'd said I would. The notion that keeping one's word matters may be as old as the gentlemen's clubs that Chaplat was emulating, but I had always held to it.

I needed to be sharp tomorrow, because Manu required protection now more than he had before. Dougat might behave perfectly, but if one of Chaplat's people spotted Jack at the Institute and tried to take him there, Manu could end up as collateral damage.

I couldn't let that happen.

I now also had to deal with Jack as soon as this was over. I could return him to Chaplat and collect my payment, but as angry as I was at Jack, we had been partners once, and I didn't relish the prospect of turning him over to a gangster who would almost certainly hurt him badly. If I didn't, though, I'd definitely have to jump after tomorrow's meeting.

And then there was the matter of Dougat's hidden arsenal. At one level, it wasn't my problem; organizations of all types accumulate weapons all the time. Still, my experience with armed religious groups was bad enough that I had to consider whether I wanted to leak the information to the local EC office.

The rendezvous site was shut for the night when I reached it, but the gate recognized me from my rental agreement and let me in. Lobo flew in fast and hovered over the area I'd rented. I hopped aboard, and he took off. I collapsed into the pilot's couch, and Lobo accelerated.

"Spend the next hour checking for surveillance and running evasive patterns," I said.

I closed my eyes and leaned back.

"So will you now tell me what happened?" Lobo said.

"Tomorrow just got a whole lot more complicated."

CHAPTER 8

WE ENTERED THE Institute grounds along the same path I'd taken during my recon two days earlier. Jack and Manu walked hand in hand ahead of me. I kept out of their path but close enough that my role would be clear. For me to be effective, I needed to stay near enough to them that Dougat's people would have made me no matter how hard I tried to blend in, so broadcasting my presence was better than trying to hide it. I marveled again at the place's skillful evocation of my home. The feel of Pinkelponker washed over me as strongly as it had during my previous visit. A gust of ocean breeze rustled the plants, and I involuntarily smiled, the wind taking me back again to one of my most persistent childhood memories: sitting on the edge of our small mountain in the afternoon, my chores done, soaking up the warmth while waiting for Jennie. I pushed aside the thought and focused on expanding my peripheral vision as much as possible so I could monitor movements all around us.

Jack's pace accelerated a bit.

"Slow and easy," I said.

He nodded and resumed his earlier stride. I wanted as much time to assess the situation as I could reasonably arrange.

The sky out to sea and above us sparkled with cloudless

perfection, but a storm was approaching from the west. Lobo was marking time about ten kilometers away behind the cover its dark clouds provided. I'd have preferred him overhead, but at this distance he could stay subsonic and still reach us in less than thirty seconds, so the reward of keeping him hidden outweighed the risk of having him closer but visible.

Ten meters from the building's entrance stood a small sky-colored canopy covering two chairs and a meter-diameter, circular, wooden table. A man sat alone at one of the chairs: Dougat. Four more men stood in a rough semicircle on the other side of the canopy. Three meters separated each of them, and none was in the line of fire of any of the others. All tried for nonchalant postures, but I was acting casual as well; all our attempts were equally unconvincing. The two in the middle focused completely on us, while the end men constantly swept the area.

"Lobo," I subvocalized. Even Jack and Manu, as close as they were, couldn't make out what I was saying, but any reasonable security person would, of course, know I was talking to someone. That was fine with me: If they believed I had backup, they might be more careful, and the more cautious everyone was, the better. "Dougat and the four behind him are obvious. Other possible hostiles?"

"Since you stopped moving," Lobo said, "one man to your left of the building has altered his path to take him in your direction."

I spotted the guy, who immediately sat on a bench in a small, semicircular garden nook and studied the red, blue, and gold flowers there. He held his head at an angle that let him keep us in sight. "Got him," I said.

In a clear voice I said to Jack, "Hold."

He did. He stood still and appeared completely relaxed. Manu fidgeted but didn't complain. I appreciated the boy's willingness to do as I told him.

"Six others in various locations between you and the road have drawn slightly closer," Lobo said. "Locations on overlay now. Sweep once to mark them."

The contact in my left eye darkened the world slightly as the overlay snapped on. I turned slowly and surveyed the grounds behind me. As I did, small red dots appeared on the chests of the four men and two women Lobo suspected. Each avoided looking at me and found something nearby of great interest, so Lobo was right. "Track them, the obvious four, and the one near the building," I said.

"Done," he said.

Yet again I was issuing an unnecessary order; Lobo was a pro and knew his role. Old habits are strong habits, but I had to learn to break this one. Lobo had every right to harass me about the redundancy, but of course he wouldn't do it now, during a mission. He *would* save it for later.

"We're probably missing one," I said. "Security teams love pairs. Scan again."

"A woman to your far left has walked closer to the man at the building's edge," Lobo said, "so she's a possible. No other human in the area is exhibiting any behaviors that appear linked to yours. So, either that's all of the external security, or the remaining members are significantly more skilled at blending in than their colleagues. The latter is certainly possible, because almost a dozen other people on the grounds are sitting and apparently doing nothing."

I swept the area again and checked out all the tourists. Each appeared to be under the place's spell, something I could certainly understand. As I turned, I looked at the woman Lobo had identified and smiled. She reacted with a smile of her own and then looked away, but the reaction was slow and forced.

"Assume she's security," I said. "More are inside, but we'll go with this count for now."

Dougat stood, an impatient expression on his face.

Jack glanced back at me, but to his credit he stayed put.

"Proceed," I said.

Jack and Manu headed toward the canopy. "Mr. Dougat," Jack said in his most winning voice. "How nice to see you again."

Dougat ignored Jack completely and focused on the boy.

Like any good merchant, Jack paused so his customer could

take his time to study the goods. Even as I hated myself for thinking of a child that way, I realized that we were in it now and I had to stay cold to be maximally effective.

I couldn't read Dougat's expression. I've seen the very rich examine other people with all the passion of butchers deciding which meat scraps to feed their pets, gaze completely through others, as if the strangers were no more substantial than mist, and stare with undisguised lust at newcomers they planned to own. Dougat did none of those.

Then I understood his expression: Dougat viewed Manu as a potential religious artifact, something possibly more precious than anything his warehouse would ever hold, definitely as puzzling as any Pinkelponker fragment he might ever discover, more than a little hard to believe in, and yet wonderful if it proved to be the real thing. However rich the man was and however much he'd profited from his institute and his research into my home world, he was above all else a believer in the religious importance of that planet.

The intensity of his belief scared me more than mere lust or greed could have managed. Not long after I stopped working with Jack, when I was serving with the Saw, I participated in several actions that pitted us against armies of true believers. Some were determined to convert whole worlds to the worship of their gods. Others aimed to purify entire planets of their heathen nonbelievers. All were fearsome opponents. I learned to respect, fear, and despise the utter fanatical focus of their mission. Dougat exuded the same fervent belief, and the contents of his warehouse proved he was amassing arms. Even though he wouldn't be likely to bring all that firepower to bear in a public site, I still tensed at the possibility.

"Are you ready to proceed?" Jack said to Dougat.

Dougat stared at Jack as if he was seeing excrement on his dinner plate, then forced a businesslike expression. "Yes," he said. "Let's begin the interview."

"Should we get another chair?" Jack said, indicating the two under the canopy.

"The conversation is strictly between the boy and me," Dougat said. "You and," he paused to make a dismissive motion in my general direction, "your associate should wait where you are."

Jack turned and looked at me. I shook my head slightly and turned to directly face Dougat.

"Will your associates also remove themselves?" I said. "Both those four and," I pointed slowly toward the building and then casually behind me, "the two closer to the building and the six in various locations behind me?"

Dougat smiled for the first time. "I must apologize not only for the size of my security team but also for the clearly under-developed skills of its members. I mean the boy no harm. I have enemies, so I generally don't meet outside. My team seemed a reasonable precaution. Everyone will back away."

The ones I could see in front of me withdrew so they were farther from the canopy than Jack or I by at least five meters.

The dots on my contact moved as the other six also fell back.

"Hostiles have withdrawn an average of five meters each," said Lobo, who was monitoring the conversation via delayed bursts from transmitters woven into my coat.

"Thank you," I said to Dougat. To Jack, I added, "Your call."

Jack nodded and faced Dougat again. "Perhaps we should get the payment out of the way."

Dougat smiled again, but this time the expression was pure show. He turned to one of the four men behind him, nod-ded, and faced Jack when that man nodded in return. "Check your wallet," he said. "The money is in the local account you specified."

Jack did, lingering long enough that I was sure he moved the money at least twice before he looked up and smiled with what appeared to be genuine relief. "Thank you. We'll wait here while you talk." He dropped to one knee beside Manu. "All Mr. Dougat wants to do is ask you questions for about an hour. Answer them honestly, and then we'll go. Okay?"

Manu studied Jack's face. "You'll stay here?" He looked at me. "Both of you?"

"Of course," Jack said. "We'll remain where you can see us."

Manu kept staring at me until I nodded in agreement.

"Okay," he said. He walked to Dougat, glanced for a moment at the man, and then went over and sat on one of the chairs under the canopy. Dougat shook his head and followed; I got the impression he spent about as much time around children as I did.

After Dougat sat, he offered Manu a drink from a pitcher on the table.

Manu checked with me, as we had discussed, and I shook my head. The boy murmured something—we were too far away to clearly hear his light voice—and leaned back. The kid's behavior continued to impress me; I've guarded grown-ups with far less sense. We didn't worry about the contents of the interview; Manu had so many recorders in the active fiber of his clothing that we'd be able to see a full replay later.

"Lobo," I said. "Alert me if any of the hostiles draw closer or if Manu moves. I'm going to sweep the area visually every thirty seconds or so, and each time I do I will lose sight of the boy briefly."

"You could stay focused on him and leave the others to me," Lobo said.

"Yes," I said, "but I won't. My perspective is significantly different than yours, so I might gain data you could miss, and by visibly checking the area I'll make sure Dougat's team knows I'm on the alert."

As I finished talking, I turned and briefly scanned all the way around me. The hostiles brightened slightly in my contact as I glanced at them. The situation remained calm. Manu and Dougat continued to talk, the boy occasionally animated, the man studious and absorbed. Jack stood about a meter away from me, as motionless as a rock carving, watching the interview with a deceptive stillness.

Jack was right when he reminded me that he was bad at violence, but that didn't mean he was helpless. He possessed an amazing ability to simply *be* in a moment, to drink it in and concentrate totally on it, and in those times he appeared so still that you might believe he was physically and mentally slow. When he needed to move, however, he was one of the fastest humans I've ever seen, able to go from motionless to full speed almost as quickly as if he were a simulation freed from the laws of physics.

Over the next thirty-five minutes, we all kept to our roles. Dougat once left the boy to ask Jack if they might run a bit over an hour, and Jack agreed. Every indication was that Dougat would behave, do the interview, and let us go. I felt the strong temptation to relax, but no mission is over until you're back home safely, so I maintained my routine.

I was between sweeps, staring at the chatting boy and man, when Manu grabbed his head, cried loudly enough that we could hear him, and ran toward Jack.

Jack was moving before Manu had taken his second step. He reached the boy quickly. I was right behind them.

"What's wrong?" Jack said to Manu. He stared at Dougat. "What did you do to him?

Dougat appeared genuinely upset. "Nothing," he said, "nothing at all. We were talking, then for no reason I could tell he acted as if he was in pain."

Jack looked down at Manu. "Did he hurt you?"

Manu was holding his head, shaking it back and forth, and moaning softly. "No," he said. "Not him. It's not him. It hurts." He looked up, his eyes wide, and pointed toward the road. "We can't let it happen. We have to stop it." He grabbed Jack's hand and pulled. Jack, Dougat, and I exchanged glances, and Jack decided for us by letting Manu lead him.

"All hostiles changing course and approaching," Lobo said.

I grabbed Jack's arm with my left hand, and he stopped.

Manu tugged hard at him. "We have to stop it!" he yelled.

I kept my grip on Jack and faced Dougat. "Tell all your people to return to their previous positions," I said. "I don't know any more about this than you do, but it's clear the boy wants us to move. Keep them back, and we'll do as he wishes."

"Now!" Manu screamed. "We have to!"

Dougat nodded, turned his head, and whispered something I couldn't hear.

"Hostiles returning to prior locations," Lobo said. "All clear."

I released Jack's arm.

Manu saw me do it and immediately pulled harder on Jack. Jack let him set the pace. The boy ran for the road, Jack in physical tow and Dougat and I staying as close as if the four of us were trapped in the same gravity well and careening into the same black hole. Manu was crying and blabbering, but between his tears and the sounds of us running I couldn't understand anything he was saying.

Five meters from the road he raised his hand and shouted a single long, hysterically elongated word, "Nooooooo!"

I looked where he was pointing, and four events occurred in such rapid succession that I could separate them only in afterthought.

A hover transport hurtled down the road from my right toward my left.

A man stepped from a crowd of pedestrians in front of the truck, his head turned to his right as if saying goodbye to a friend, clearly unaware of the vehicle speeding toward him.

The transport hit the man.

The man sailed into the air like a flower blown free of its stem by a strong wind, red blossoming across his shirt as he flew over the crowd he'd left only a second earlier. He landed behind them, out of our view.

Manu let go of Jack and sprinted for the road, but Jack caught him with two long strides and grabbed both his shoulders.

"I saw it and I couldn't stop it and we should have stopped it!" Manu said, tears flowing as quickly and as uncontrolled as the words.

Jack picked him up, turned him away from the sight of the crowd converging on the accident victim, and held him tightly. "It's not your fault," he said. "You did everything you could. You know we can't change what you see." The boy sobbed and tried to wriggle free, but Jack clung to him with a strength I'd seen but also with a tenderness I'd never witnessed. "It's not your fault."

Jack supported Manu's weight with his right hand and held the boy's head to his shoulder with his left. Keeping the boy tucked there so he wouldn't catch another glimpse of the accident, Jack turned and walked away from the road, back toward the Institute.

As he moved, he stared at me for a moment, his eyes glistening, and then at Dougat. "Perhaps," he said to the man, "we could spend a few minutes inside. I'm afraid the interview is over."

For the first time since the accident, I focused on Dougat. His face was wide with shock, but more than shock, belief, the sort of ecstatic conviction I've seen previously only on those in the grips of strong drugs or stronger acts of religious or violent fervor.

"He *is* a seer," the man said. "A true child of Pinkelponker, maybe the only one in the known universe. I've talked to so many people, heard so many stories, but I could never be sure." He ran in front of Jack and put up his hand. "You have to stay. You must." His pupils were dilated with excitement. His breathing was ragged. Everything about him broadcast trouble.

We needed to leave.

"Lobo," I said, "come in fast, and prepare for full action on my command."

"Done. Moving," he said.

"As you can see," Jack said, anger clear in his voice, "Manu is in no shape to continue. I'll return half of the fee if you'd like, but I have to get him home to rest. Even the easiest visions are hard on him, and this one, as you witnessed, was far from easy."

Dougat didn't move. "He can recuperate here," he said, more loudly than before. "My people will help in any way they can."

Jack covered Manu's head with his hand so the boy wouldn't hear any more. "We have to go," he said.

Dougat glanced at Manu again and lowered his voice. "No," he said. "I can't let him leave."

CHAPTER 9

"HOSTILES CONVERGING QUICKLY," Lobo said, his voice crisp and inflection-free in my ear. "A man and woman who had acted as tourists and not previously tracked you are headed your way. I'm six seconds out."

The extra hostiles meant either Dougat had stationed people we'd missed or Chaplat had found us. It was about to get noisy. "Execute plan," I said.

"All warehouse charges detonated," Lobo said. "Almost all debris contained in implosion."

I grabbed Jack's shoulder and spun him to face me. Behind him I glimpsed several of Dougat's men running toward us.

"Three seconds," Lobo said.

I held up three fingers.

Jack nodded and gripped Manu tightly.

I dropped and swept Jack's legs out from under him.

Lobo activated the heads-up display relay in my left contact. The image from his forward video sensors overlaid my view of the approaching security men.

I watched with both normal vision and the overlaid video as Lobo transformed the Institute and its grounds into a fire zone.

Two low-yield explosive missiles left Lobo and almost

immediately blew apart what I hoped we'd accurately identified as a receiving dock on the back of the building. No transports were parked there, so with luck the area was unoccupied. At the same time, the world went silent as Lobo remotely enabled my sound-blocking earplugs. I counted on Jack's and Manu's working, because a second later the howlers rocketed out of Lobo and tore up the grounds around us.

Right behind them a cluster of sleep smokers mirved to their targets and turned the air the color of storm clouds about to burst. I kept my mouth shut and forced myself to breathe through my nose; the sinus filters worked perfectly. If Jack and Manu did the same, they'd be fine. The active antidotes we'd all taken would keep us awake even if we breathed the gas, but until it had dissipated for a few minutes it would be hard on our lungs and throats. The nanomachines in my cells would repair me quickly enough if some gas leaked inside my nose, but I saw no reason to suffer any damage I could avoid.

The rest of Dougat's staff and, unfortunately, all of the visitors on the grounds and even some nearby pedestrians wouldn't be as lucky; the gas and the noise would affect them. Aside from any injuries they sustained when they fell, however, they should suffer only long, drugged naps, raw sinuses, bad coughs, and, from the howlers, ringing in their ears.

I reached for Jack, but he wasn't there.

Damn!

Anger flooded adrenaline into my body, and I trembled with the barely controlled energy and rage. He knew he shouldn't move! Now he and the boy were at risk.

"Where are Jack and Manu?" I mumbled through pursed lips.

My words were clear enough for Lobo.

My left contact's display snapped into an aerial schematic of the grounds, with red dots marking Dougat's staff, a blue dot indicating Jack, and a green one denoting Manu's position. The blue and green dots streaked toward the building.

"Running toward the ziggurat," Lobo said. "External staff and bystanders are all sleeping. I'm above you. Howlers have discharged; reenabling hearing."

In an instant the thrumming force of Lobo's hovering joined a chorus of unconscious moans and wheezes all around me to replace the silence I'd been enjoying. I stood and darted forward. The blue and green dots veered to the side of the entrance to the ziggurat. Two seconds later, a stream of red dots poured out of it. These guys were clearly prepared for gas, because none of them fell. I cranked my own vision to IR and watched as the ten new security people fanned out in front of me. The blue and green dots ducked behind them, Manu barely ahead of Jack, and zipped into the building. Great. Now I had to get past this new team, retrieve Jack and Manu, and go back outside for pickup. If they'd only kept to the plan and stayed near me, we'd already have been on our way out of here.

"Image enhancement suggests new hostiles are armed and environmentally prepared," Lobo said.

Sure enough, the new squad broke into four clusters. One sprinted for Dougat. The remaining three focused on me, the first taking a direct approach and the other two going wide to flank me. The only good news was that either they'd missed Jack and Manu or they'd assumed those two were down.

"Trank 'em," I mumbled.

Lobo didn't waste time answering. I heard the rounds spraying from guns on his undercarriage, and within three seconds everyone on the new team dropped.

"Public feeds are rich in data about our assault," Lobo said. "We must exit soon or expect to face additional local resistance."

"I have to get Jack and Manu," I mumbled as I ran to the side of the entrance. I stopped long enough to pull a trank pistol from the holster at the base of my back, then dove inside. I hit the ground on my shoulder and rolled quickly to a prone position. I glanced to the right and then the left of the entrance. No one.

I stood and immediately regretted the action as a projectile round to the chest knocked me down. The body armor stopped it from seriously injuring me, but my chest throbbed with pain, and breathing hurt. I slit my eyes and stayed still.

Precious time was evaporating, but if I moved I might suffer a head shot.

A guard emerged from behind an exhibit five meters in front of me. He kept his pistol aimed at me and moved cautiously forward. He stepped with care, and his weapon never wavered. I did my best to look unconscious; the lack of blood would tell him I wasn't dead.

A crashing sound ripped the air from somewhere behind him, and he turned for a moment to check it out.

I fired multiple times at his back and head.

He dropped.

Too many trank rounds might kill him, something I didn't want to do, but I couldn't afford the time to check on him and make sure he was okay. Dougat might have more security personnel around. The warehouse distraction south of us was old news. I had to get out of there, but I couldn't leave without Jack and Manu.

I had no feed from Lobo to guide me in my search, so I ran to the center of the building in the hope that I could spot them.

Before I'd gone five steps, Jack dashed toward me from my left, Manu's hand in his.

"What were you doing?" I said, my voice shaking with anger at Jack's violation of our agreement. The air inside was now clean enough that I could talk freely without hurting my throat. "You idiot! You don't freelance, and you don't abandon your team!"

"Manu was terrified and ran," Jack said. "I didn't expect it, and I couldn't see him clearly, so I fell behind him. I couldn't leave him here, Jon. I had to find him."

Though his answer was reasonable, even admirable in some ways, I still shook with anger and adrenaline. I forced myself to nod. "Follow me," I said.

Motion in the corner of my eye caused me to stop and glance to my right. A guard emerged from behind an exhibit and trained a shotgun on Jack and Manu. I couldn't turn in time to stop him.

Another guard ran toward him, screaming as she approached, "Not the boy!"

Jack pushed Manu behind him as the guard turned to the woman and shot in the same motion.

The shell sprayed two exhibits in an arc that ran from the woman to Jack. Jack spun slightly and grabbed his right arm. The woman's left shoulder jerked backward, but her momentum propelled her into the man. The two of them crashed into an exhibit behind him. She rolled away, kicked the man in the neck, and stood, her legs shaking, her uniform's shoulder pad darkening with blood.

"Go," she said, "get the boy out of here."

She looked at her arm, then passed out and fell.

"Let's go," Jack said. He held up his bloody hand. "Now."

I stared at the woman. We should run, but she might well have saved Manu. I couldn't leave her.

"Wait," I said to Jack.

I ran to her, pulled her to a sitting position, and hoisted her over my shoulder. I stood with her, grunting slightly from the effort. She was almost as tall as I was and dense. I settled her on my shoulder and walked back to Jack.

"Follow me," I said. "Heading to you," I said to Lobo as we approached the exit from the building. "Land in the closest clear area—not on people—and direct me in. Prep the medbed; I'm bringing two casualties." Lobo had argued in our planning meeting that if we ended up in a fight he should set down right beside us, and that anyone he squashed in the process was an acceptable casualty, but even with time as short as it was I saw no reason to kill if we could avoid it.

"Moving," Lobo said. "Media scans put police ETA at under ninety seconds. Severity of injury? Jack or Manu hurt?"

"Don't know, and both Jack and a guard," I said.

"We're helping the opposition?" Lobo said.

I kept moving and didn't waste any energy explaining the situation. My chest hurt each time I breathed in, but I pushed my pace. Jack and Manu stayed close to me as we ran. A vector in my left eye's display led me forty meters ahead and to the right, toward the southern side of the grounds. Even with me carrying the guard, we reached Lobo quickly. As we drew closer to him, his camo armor exterior blending so well with the still-gas-filled air that anyone watching without IR would have little chance of knowing where he was, he opened a hatch on the side facing us. I ran to him, stepped inside, and turned around to make sure Jack and Manu made it.

They were right there, Jack actually showing a bit of stress, Manu in tears but leaping perfectly and at speed into Lobo; the practice paid off. Jack entered right behind him, and the hatch shut.

Lobo accelerated as I set the guard on the floor. As I was straightening, I said, "Lobo—"

I never finished the sentence.

I felt Jack's hand on my neck, turned toward him, and sank into blackness.

CHAPTER 10

I AWOKE SLOWLY, my head throbbing and my neck and shoulders stiff. When I opened my eyes, I had trouble focusing, but after a few seconds the world snapped into view. I was lying on the floor inside Lobo, right where I'd fallen.

Where Jack had left me, I realized as the memory of what had happened caught up with me. I pushed up with my arms and quickly regretted the action, as the remnants of whatever drugs he'd used coursed through me and nearly made me pass out again.

I decided the floor wasn't such a bad place to be right now. My system would naturally wash itself of the drugs in time, and the nanomachines would speed the process, but resting there for the moment was fine by me.

"Welcome back," Lobo said. "Are you coherent?"

"Yes," I said. "Why wouldn't I be?"

"You made enough noises while unconscious that several times I thought you might be awake," he said.

"Fair enough. How long was I out?"

"Three hours, fifty-seven minutes," he said with what I thought was a trace of amusement. "Jack claimed you'd be unconscious for at least five hours, but my experiences with you led me to estimate a quicker recovery. I was, of course, correct."

Lovely. How long I'd remain out of it had turned into a

betting game for my PCAV and the old friend who'd screwed me once again.

"Why didn't you stop him?" I said.

"I had no information from you to suggest Jack would drug you," Lobo said with annoyance. "Once you were unconscious, he was, by your orders, in command. Had he then tried to injure you further, your earlier orders would have allowed me to take action to prevent him, but he did nothing to harm you from that point forward. Had your health showed signs of worsening, I could have transported you to a medical facility, but your vital signs stayed steady and strong. Consequently, I could only obey his instructions—again, per your orders."

I hate being stupid, and Lobo's tone made the annoyance all the greater. At the same time, I'd given Lobo those orders to protect the boy, and they'd reflected the best data available to me at the moment I'd given them.

Except, of course, for the key fact that I'd known and chosen to ignore: You can't trust Jack.

Even though years of experience had taught me that lesson, something about the way he'd behaved this time had struck me as different; it was as if he actually cared about Manu.

Manu.

"What happened to the boy?" I said.

"To the best of my ability to tell, they are safe," Lobo said. "On Jack's orders, we invested an hour in evasive action, and then we proceeded to the jump gate. They departed there. Rather than track them, to maximize your safety I left and continued running countersurveillance routes."

Given that we'd just attacked one of the richest men on the planet, the jump gate was a reasonable place to go. Jack would have caught the first available shuttle off-planet and be far away by now. I'd have done the same.

My thinking was definitely not up to par, because it took me this long to realize that what mattered was not what I would have done, but what I needed to do now—though in this case they were the same. I needed to leave Mund.

"Where are we?"

"In orbit on the side of Mund opposite the jump gate," Lobo said. "We're currently nestled among a group of tediously dull weather satellites."

"Any signs of pursuit?"

"Of course not," Lobo said. "Do you think I would have stopped moving had I known of any?"

"Sorry," I said. "I'm not at my best quite yet. Thank you for getting me to safety."

"I accept both your apology and your thanks," Lobo said. "Which would you now prefer to do: view the recording Jack left, or see to our prisoner?"

"Jack left a recording? We have a prisoner?"

"Why do you persist in asking questions to which you already know the answers?" Lobo said, the annoyance back.

"Rhetorical questions. Jack's never done anything like that. When he vanishes, he leaves no traces. As for the guard, who, by the way, helped us and so is hardly a prisoner, I was so focused on my own situation and on Jack that I forgot her."

"She was a combatant on the other side of a conflict, and she is now restrained and in our custody," Lobo said. "If that isn't a prisoner, please explain to me how you define the term. I'm quite confident that she would consider herself to be our captive, if, that is, we allowed her to wake up and consider the situation."

"Point taken," I said. I sat. This time, doing so didn't leave me weaker. "What's her status?"

"Jack put her in the medbed," Lobo said. "I treated her and sedated her. Her light armor absorbed most of the round. The protection didn't cover the edge of her shoulders, so she suffered a rather large cut. I cleaned it, removed the shrapnel, and kept her under. I find I often like guests best when they're unconscious."

I wish I could tell when Lobo was joking. I had to admit, however, that until I decided what to do with her, having her safely out of the way was convenient. Jack's recording might tell me why he'd knocked me out, so I decided to start with it. "Play the message."

A display opened on the wall in front of me. Jack snapped into view. His right sleeve was missing below the shoulder, and his no-longer-bloody arm glistened with fresh skin sealer. He stood beside Manu and held the boy's hand. My unconscious body lay on the floor behind him.

"Jon," he said, waving his hand briefly at my body, "I'm very sorry for treating you like that. If I'd thought there was any other reasonable option, I would have taken it. The problem is that you wouldn't have approved of what I did, and then you would have tried to make it right, and in the end there was too big a chance that Manu might have gotten hurt." Jack sounded genuinely torn and upset. He paused, glanced down at Manu, and stroked the boy's head lightly.

"The fee Dougat paid for the interview was enough to buy Manu treatments for a while, but only for a while. He was going to need more, a lot more. We—his uncle and I—were hoping Dougat would be willing to pay for more interviews or maybe even to help with the med-tech bills just because of Manu's Pinkelponker ancestry." He put his hands over Manu's ears for a moment. "Yeah, I know: It was a dumb hope. I tried to tell him, but it was the only option any of us could come up with that might help over the long term. The alternative, well—" He paused and glanced at Manu, and when he faced forward again his eyes were wet. "—neither of us was willing to deal with that."

He took his hands off Manu's ears. "When I caught up to Manu inside the Institute, he was hiding behind one of the gemstone displays." He paused, shook his head, and smiled. "Look, I know it's not right, but Dougat is so wealthy he won't even feel the loss."

Jack turned, stooped, and reached behind Manu. When he stood, he was clutching at least half a dozen Pinkelponker gems, his hands twinkling as if holding a night sky drenched in green, red, blue, and purple stars. "The right collectors will pay enough for these to cover Manu's treatments forever—and then some." Jack laughed. "Besides, a man has a right to make a profit now and then, eh?"

I couldn't help but laugh with him. Leave it to Jack to fall into a mess and walk away rich.

Lobo's video sensor tracked him as he walked to the front acceleration couch and left a huge green gem on it.

"For your help, Jon," he said.

"Docking with jump station in sixty seconds," said Lobo's voice on the recording.

Jack nodded and returned to Manu.

"I wish it had gone better," Jack said, "but as I promised, this time we did some good: Manu will get his treatments."

Jack smiled that beautiful, wide, glowing smile of his, and I felt myself smiling involuntarily in response. He'd used me, he'd done at least some of this to raise money to pay his debt to Chaplat, and still in that moment he charmed me.

"Besides," he said, "admit it: Wouldn't you have been at least a little disappointed if everything had played out according to plan?" He laughed lightly. "Take care, Jon."

The display vanished.

The effect of Jack's charm also disappeared as I realized the mess in which he'd left me.

Dougat and the Followers had seen me and had security footage of our escape from the Institute. They'd assume I was working with Jack to plan the robbery, and the gem Jack had left me would, if they caught me before I disposed of it, only convince them further. I considered having Lobo dump it into space then and there, but I couldn't quite bring myself to discard something that was both so valuable and a tangible link to my home planet.

Chaplat would be furious, because I had no way to deliver on my promise or even get Jack to work out an arrangement with him.

I had a Follower guard on board, restrained and effectively my prisoner despite the fact that she'd taken a shot to save Manu. I either had to kidnap her through a jump gate, waste time dropping her planetside on some other world—or kill her, an option I knew Lobo would raise if I didn't.

To top it all off, despite all the compassion I'd read in Jack, whether he would really help Manu remained a mystery. I might well have failed the boy, an idea that knotted my stomach.

Once again, Jack had left me, as he'd done many times in our years together, with too many problems to solve all at once. All I could do was deal with the one in front of me, and then move to the next.

I stood. A jolt of dizziness hit me, but it passed a few seconds later.

I grabbed the green stone from the pilot's couch and had Lobo open a storage bin. "Keep it deep and in shielded storage," I said. "Don't give it to anyone but me."

The bin closed. "Done," Lobo said.

I walked to the med room. "Is she attempting to transmit any signals?" I said.

"No," Lobo said, "and I would have alerted you if she were. I've also blocked all signals not from me just in case."

"Of course," I said. "Thanks." I paused and stared at her unconscious body. "Bring her around."

It was time to talk to the guard.

CHAPTER 11

I WATCHED CLOSELY as the woman's breathing changed from the slow, shallow pace of drug-induced sleep to a more normal ebb and flow. Lobo opened a display on the wall above and behind her. Her vital signs appeared; all were rising. Straps across her neck, waist, arms, and legs bound her securely to the medbed. She filled the better part of the platform and was nearly my height. A thick coil of hair the red of the glowing tendrils of solar flares hung over the edge of the platform and contrasted nicely with skin the color of wet yellow sand. Her uniform and light armor left her body thick and almost tubular. If the protection had extended to the full width of her shoulders, her left deltoid wouldn't now glisten with skin patch. As I stared, her eyelids fluttered and then opened to reveal light green eyes that sparkled like new grass wet with morning dew.

That she opened her eyes before she was fully aware made it clear she was no pro. No surprise there: Cults usually prefer believers to professionals.

As the woman focused on me, she tried to sit up and choked against the neck restraint. Lobo didn't need to keep it so tight; he definitely considered her a prisoner.

"Who are you?" she said. "Where am I?"

95

"Wrong."

"Huh?" She shook her head. "I don't understand."

"You're doing the wrong things," I said. "You're asking questions, but you're the one in restraints. I'm standing, so I ask, and you answer."

"Why do you have me like this?" she said. "What do you want?"

"You're doing it again."

She shut her eyes. "Okay, ask."

"Name?"

"Maggie."

"Maggie?"

"Maggie Park."

I looked away as if thinking and checked the display. Lobo's assessment glowed green, and her vitals showed no signs of a lie. Good. "What do you do for the Followers?" I said.

She opened her eyes, studied my face, and then sniffed my clothes, which still smelled of the gas. "I remember you now," she said. "You were in the Institute fighting with the other guards."

"Prepare to inject," I said.

Lobo made the bed extend a treatment appendage and positioned a needle over the vein just past the end of her biceps.

She tried moving her arm away from the needle, but she couldn't shake the binding straps. "Okay, okay," she said. "What do you want to know?"

"What do you do for the Followers?"

"Tourist security. I walk the exhibits so no visitor decides the gemstones might not be that hard to steal. The video monitors do the real watching, and if they or I spot anything wrong, we call the armed security. I'm mostly there for show."

All signs stayed stable. "How long have you been working for them?"

"Why does this matter?" she said.

I nodded at the needle, which was still poised over her vein.

She tracked my eyes to it and swallowed nervously. "A little over two weeks," she said.

More truth. "Are you a Follower?"

She looked aside for a moment, as if embarrassed. "No, not really. I'm interested in Pinkelponker, of course—who wouldn't be?—but I don't believe in Dougat's vision like the rest of them. I needed work, so I faked it."

Also true. She was either superbly trained and able to control her body well enough to fool both Lobo's sensors and me, or she was consistently answering truthfully. None of the rest of her moves suggested she possessed anywhere near that level of training, so I was almost willing to bet she was telling the truth. Almost. "What is Dougat's vision, the one you don't believe?"

"You don't know them very well, do you?"

I let the question go unpunished. "No. Why?"

"If you did," she said, "you wouldn't have bothered asking that question. They're crackpots. They see Pinkelponker as some sort of link to the divine, or maybe to the makers of the gates, or maybe both—sometimes they talk like Gatists." She stared at me, then said, "Not that there's anything wrong with worshipping the jump gates, of course. You don't happen to be a Gatist, do you?"

I shook my head and resisted the urge to laugh. "No. The gates are magnificent, and they work, and that's enough for me." I pointed at the needle still hovering over her arm. "Back to the Followers."

"Part of their dogma is that humanity can reach its true potential—some sort of godhood, I think, though I don't really understand what they mean—only by returning to Pinkelponker. Dougat is convinced that the one way to break the blockade is to use the special powers of what he calls 'the children of Pinkelponker,' people whose ancestors were born there. He's convinced they all possess special psychic abilities." She trembled. "I said they were crackpots; as the head of the group, he's the craziest of the bunch—and the scariest. He genuinely believes what he preaches."

The vitals jumped with her fear, but that was normal. Her take on Dougat matched my own. Before seeing Manu and his vision of the accident, I might have laughed at Dougat's vision and considered it insane. As far as I'd known growing up, Jennie was the only person on the planet with her gift. Of course, I'd never even explored our whole island, much less the entire world, so the place may well have teemed with people with unusual abilities. I didn't expect to ever find out, but I was convinced that if I were ever to make it back there, I'd need a lot more weaponry than a kid with occasional glimpses into the future.

From what I'd seen in the warehouse, Dougat must have felt the same way, because he was definitely amassing arms. On the other hand, almost none of them would be useful fighting a blockade of heavily armed CC and EC spaceships. Even as fodder for trades, they didn't strike me as enough to buy him anything that might be able to survive a battle with the ships guarding the aperture to Pinkelponker.

"If he was so sure these people existed and they were his ticket to the promised land," I said, "why was he stockpiling weapons?"

"What weapons?" she said. "Most of us on the security team weren't armed with more than shocksuits. Some of the hardcore guards had real guns, but not most of us."

Nothing on the monitor suggested she was lying. She didn't know. Another vote in her favor. Dougat might have been accumulating munitions for another reason, or perhaps he planned to use them and the hardcore Followers to hijack a few ships when they were planetside. Without asking him, I couldn't know, but at least Maggie also seemed completely unaware of any such plans.

I considered releasing her, but one thing still troubled me.

"Why," I said, "did you push that guard and take a shot for us?"

"Because Kenton—that was his name—was going to shoot that boy," she said. "Isn't that a good enough reason? All the boy did was somehow attract Dougat's attention, show up for another of the man's endless and useless interviews, and suddenly people were firing weapons all around us. I couldn't let Kenton shoot him. Could you?"

I should have ignored her, but I couldn't help but ponder the question. I'd like to be positive I wouldn't have let anyone shoot Manu, and I think I would have stopped it, but I had an advantage she didn't: My body could quickly mend almost any wound. In her shoes with her normal human body, would I have been as brave? Again, I'd like to think so, but I haven't been normal for over a hundred and thirty years, long enough that I can't clearly remember what it was like.

"No," I finally said, "I don't think I could."

As I recalled the scene, I realized something else was bothering me. "Why was that guard shooting at the boy?" I said. "Dougat paid a lot just to interview the kid; he couldn't have wanted him hurt."

"Oh, I'm sure Dougat didn't," she said. "He would have fired Kenton on the spot for even aiming in the direction of anyone he thought might be a child of Pinkelponker. In fact, I bet Kenton's already lost his job. Serves him right, though I suppose when you hire people like him, you can't expect much."

"People like him?"

"To work tourist security like I do," she said, "you don't need any special qualifications. All you have to do is catch a company when it's hiring. Dougat's armed guards, though, are all rough sorts, people like Kenton who've spent a lot of time either with mercenary forces or in prison."

"Plenty of good men and women sign up with mercenary companies," I said. "I did." I'd felt indignant, but my words sounded defensive.

"Maybe so," she said, "but those aren't the sorts of people Dougat's hiring as guards. As for you, well," she shrugged as much as she could given the straps pinning her in place, "I hope you'll understand that my initial impression isn't all that favorable."

I chuckled in acknowledgment. She seemed to be exactly what she said, and she might well have saved Manu. I owed her for that.

I'd drop her somewhere planetside. She could make her way home from there.

Before I released her, though, I wanted a little insurance, just in case I'd misread her.

I stepped out of the small room, and Lobo closed the door behind me.

"Do you have any one-person explosive implants?" I said. I didn't think so, but Lobo regularly surprises me with the variety of tools that he either is carrying as part of his arsenal or can fabricate.

"No," he said. "Beyond standard medical repair tools, my only human implants are trackers."

"That'll work," I said. "When I tell you to implant the explosive, simply inject her with a tracker and set it to decay."

"Why bother wasting the device on her?"

"Just do it," I said. Bluffing was not Lobo's strong suit, and if anything went wrong, being able to track her could be useful. "Open."

I entered the room as soon as the door snicked aside.

"I'm going to remove the restraints," I said.

"Thank you."

"First, though, we're going to inject you with a small explosive tied to a transmitter I control."

"What?" she yelled. She tried again to free herself but could only shake slightly against all the restraints. "You don't need to do this."

"If something happens to me," I said, "or if you even try anything I don't like, the explosive will detonate. If you behave, when you're far away I'll send a signal that will cause it to decay. Your body will excrete the remains, and you'll be back to normal." As I talked, Lobo retracted the extension that had held the needle over her arm. A new, similarly equipped one took its place.

"Ready," Lobo said on the machine frequency.

"I cannot believe you're doing this," Park said. "You're crazy."

"Not crazy," I said. "Just careful. Very careful." Being too cautious, I realized, was the equivalent of being paranoid, of being insane, but in my line of work a little paranoia has always proven to be healthy. "I sincerely hope this precaution ends up being completely unnecessary."

"Is there anything I can—"

I cut her off. "Inject her," I said.

The needle plunged into her arm, held for two seconds as the fluid and its microscopic cargo entered her body, and withdrew.

Her face flushed with anger, her fists clenched, and the skin in her neck tightened. All over the monitor on the wall behind her head, indicators jumped and twitched, flowing lines and rows of numbers charting her fury. She opened her mouth several times as if to speak, but each time she said nothing.

I waited.

She closed her eyes and took a few long, slow breaths.

Her vitals settled as the flush left her skin. Her hands relaxed, and her expression returned to normal.

She opened her eyes and stared at me, the last traces of rage fading, and then she spoke. "You made me furious, but I can see it from your perspective: You don't know me, you can't be sure I'm telling the truth, you could be at risk. Okay, well now you're not. So, are you going to let me out of here?"

"I said I would." I looked away from her. "Retract."

The left ends of the restraints released with a series of slight clicks, and the medbed withdrew them into itself.

She sat up slowly and swung her legs over the right side of the medbed. She shook her head slightly; the last of the sedative must have hit her. She pushed off as she stood, and for a moment she wavered.

It might have been an act, a ploy to catch me off guard, but I didn't think so. Even if it was, between Lobo and me, she didn't have a chance.

I reached out and steadied her by her uninjured right shoulder.

"Thanks," she said. She grabbed my biceps with her hand and held on until she was standing solidly on her own. She kept holding me and looked up, into my eyes. Surprise flitted across her face.

"What?" I said.

She turned her head and released her grip on my arm. "Huh?"

"You appeared surprised," I said. "At what?"

"I guess I didn't really believe you'd set me free," she said. "I was afraid you'd hurt me the moment I was on my feet."

"If I wanted to do something to you, I would have done it already. I said I'd let you go, and I will." I turned and headed to the pilot's area. "I'll drop you somewhere on Mund, and you can find your way home."

"What about you?" she said. "What are you going to do?"

"That's not your issue," I said, though I realized the same question had continued to nag at me. "Maybe leave, maybe find Jack and Manu." I paused. "Probably leave."

"No," she said. "You can't. You have to find the boy."

Before I could respond, she continued.

"And you have to take me with you."

CHAPTER 12

"WHAT?" I SAID, suddenly the one who was surprised and confused. A minute ago, she was an understandably angry and bewildered prisoner. Now, she was volunteering to go with me. Was I wrong to have let her out of the restraints? Was she working with Dougat and trying to trap me? Lobo hadn't detected any transmission attempts from her, and all of her responses had registered as truthful, so it seemed unlikely that she was any sort of spy, but her demand made me wonder.

"You have to find the boy, and you have to let me go with you," Park said again.

"Why?"

"So I can help finish what I started: saving him. As long as he's anywhere Dougat can find him, he's not safe. Besides, there's nothing left for me with the Followers. If I go back, the security cameras will show what I did, Dougat will at a minimum fire me, and most likely he'll take me prisoner and interrogate me." She paused and stared at me. "I've had enough of that for quite some time."

"Interrogate you?" I said. "Why?"

"Because he assumes everyone thinks like he does," she said. "All I was trying to do was prevent a boy from being shot. He'll decide I'm somehow tied to the kid, maybe as part of some secret plan of his mythical children of Pinkelponker, and then he'll come after me." She leaned against the wall and closed her eyes, apparently still weak. "I told you: He's crazy."

Her analysis made sense. I've met more than a few conspiracy nuts, both because Jack often chose them as targets and because the megacorporations and government federations are full of them. All of them assumed not only that secrets lurked everywhere, but that everyone else was as aware of and as concerned with those secrets as they were. I didn't want to tell Park that in this case the nut wasn't all that crazy: At least two of his children of Pinkelponker, Manu and I, existed, and we both had unusual powers. Make that three; I had to believe Jennie was still alive somewhere.

If I decided to go after Jack and Manu, taking Park with me would be a mixed proposition. Having someone on my team, someone no one knew was with me, could be a valuable advantage. Having to keep my and Lobo's secrets from her, however, would add complexity and stress to everything.

Regardless of what I chose, I appreciated her desire to rescue Manu. I'd been in similar situations, and I'd always tried to follow up, to make things right.

Which was why, I finally admitted to myself, that I had no choice but to go after Manu and Jack. They had no clue what Dougat was capable of doing, and if I didn't help them get far away, Dougat might capture Manu. If he did, Manu would never be free again. He'd end up locked away, using his talent to serve Dougat whenever the man wasn't experimenting on him. I've been in that kind of laboratory cage before, and I've spent most of my life being careful to avoid going back. I couldn't let that happen to Manu.

Making the decision brought everything else into focus. What mattered most was Manu, so I had to concentrate on doing what was right for him.

"I appreciate your desire to help the boy," I said. "I really do. I'm not sure, though, that you'd add enough value to make you worth the trouble."

"I know Dougat and the Followers better than you do. I've

lived and worked with them, and I know a lot of the members in this sector, especially the security staff, by sight."

"Fair—but minor—points," I said.

"Besides," she added, "if you dump me on Mund, I'll try to locate him on my own. I can't believe we wouldn't do better working together than separately."

Though I agreed with her points, she clearly didn't understand me, or she wouldn't have raised the last one. I had other options that accomplished the same goal: I could keep her on ice, dump her somewhere far away, or even kill her. I didn't want to kill anyone, but she didn't know enough about me to be sure that was the case. That she didn't consider any of these possibilities told me how very naïve she was.

Unfortunately, the fact that I was even contemplating taking along an unskilled companion also made me aware of something I rarely allow myself to notice: I'd become lonely. Lobo is fine company, and most of the time I'm happy to be either alone or traveling only with him, but sometimes I miss humans. It didn't hurt that she was pretty and possessed the most amazing eyes and hair I'd seen in a very long time. I might regret the choice, but with Lobo monitoring her and the level of skill she'd shown, I wasn't taking much of a risk.

"I'm willing to bring you along and maybe even let you assist me," I said, "but only on my terms."

"Name them," she said.

I shook my head: another amateur move. Never agree before you've heard the proposal. "You follow all my orders immediately and without question, even if the orders don't make any sense to you. Anything that involves Slanted Jack rarely follows a clear-cut path."

"Slanted Jack?"

"The man with the boy."

"Why 'Slanted'?"

"Because—never mind," I said. "Do you agree to do as I say?"

"Yes, but I have a condition of my own."

I smiled in grudging admiration at her willingness to push back. "What's that?"

"If you make money doing this, and if I help, you pay me whatever you think is a fair part of it."

"I thought you wanted to do this to save the boy."

"I do," she said, forcing herself to stand straighter and stare into my eyes, "but as we've discussed, I'm also recently unemployed, and from the fact that you can afford to have your own medbed and equip it with serious restraints, I assume you have money. People with money tend to make more money."

I laughed, in part because the obvious effort she put into working up her courage was oddly endearing and in part because in her situation I also would've asked for a cut. "Fair enough," I said, "though as of now I don't have any way to get paid for this mess." The gem buried in Lobo was for past work, and I'd use it to replenish Lobo's arsenal, so I felt no guilt in not mentioning it. I was going to ignore Chaplat's offer and help Jack run, so I didn't count it, either.

"Deal?" she said, sticking out her hand.

When I was young, my mother told me that centuries ago people gave their word, shook hands, and stood by the deal they'd just made. They didn't need legal systems, human or machine, to make them do it; they simply kept their word. She said this practice was one of the traditions humanity should never have abandoned, and she encouraged me to always follow it. I still did, and when I encountered other people who acted the same way—not those, like Chaplat, who did it for show, but those who really meant it—I instantly respected them for it.

I shook her hand and said, "Deal."

She held my hand a few moments too long and looked at me again with a hint of surprise, or maybe confusion.

"Is it so surprising that I agreed?" I said.

She released my hand. "I guess so." She looked briefly away, then turned again to face me. "Not a lot lately has gone the way I wanted." She closed her eyes for a moment, and then she leaned away from the wall and appeared to be on the edge of falling.

I steadied her. "Why don't you go back in there and rest?" I said. "With no restraints this time, of course."

She nodded her head. "That might be a good idea. I'm weaker than I thought. Where will you be?"

"Getting ready."

"Where are we?'

I couldn't hide Lobo from her, so I might as well try to influence her perceptions by setting her expectations. "We're in my ship. You may hear me talking. The ship has an onboard AI. His name is Lobo." She looked at me quizzically, so I explained. "The programmers did such a good job on the AI that I think of it as a 'him.' You probably will, too. I use him as a sounding board."

"I don't know anyone who owns a ship. Is it common that you talk to it?" She continued to look tired but was now clearly interested.

"And why shouldn't he?" Lobo said, his voice echoing from hidden speakers all around her. "Where else could he find a better conversationalist?"

I swear he added some bass reverb for effect. What a drama addict.

She jumped at the sound of his voice. "What kind of ship is this?" she said.

"I'm technically not a ship at all," Lobo said, his voice still booming. "I'm a—"

I cut him off. "That's enough for now, Lobo," I said. To Park, I added, "A cranky one." I guided her back to the medbed. "Later, after you're feeling better, we can discuss this further. For now, you rest, and Lobo will stay quiet." I looked away and muttered, "Right?"

"Of course," Lobo said on the machine frequency. "Never let it be said that I, merely your partner and the only barrier between you and the icy claws of certain death lurking just outside in the depths of space, would want to upset your former prisoner and new guest or interrupt her beauty slumber."

Park fell asleep almost instantly. Given Lobo's mood, I seriously considered crawling into my own bunk just to hide from him, but I had work to do. I headed up front to the pilot's couch.

➤   ➤   ➤

"Do you have *any* data about where Jack was going?"

"You know I don't," Lobo said. "You saw the recording. That's all the relevant information I possess. Ships were, as usual, passing through both jump-gate apertures, and, as you may recall, I had to go far away from the gate to protect you."

I realized that I was frustrated and taking it out on Lobo. That was stupid. "Sorry," I said. "I'm not sure how to find him next. He could have had you drop him at the gate and then doubled back to Mund, or he might have jumped through either aperture. That leaves us three entire planets to search—and maybe many more if he jumped further."

"Searching Mund is easy enough," said Lobo, "particularly given the small size of the populated area."

"Easy?" Now he was annoying me. "We're talking at least half a dozen settlements I'd have to check. How is that easy?"

"We search for the transmitter I embedded in his arm when I repaired it," Lobo said.

"You stuck a transmitter in him?"

"Has my diction suddenly worsened?"

"You might have told me about it earlier."

"You might have waited to recover fully and discussed the situation with me before you leapt into interrogating our prisoner."

I hate it when he's right, which, of course, is quite often. "Fair enough. Tell me about the transmitter."

"I set it to emit a two-second burst at random intervals centered around every two minutes, so even if he's an extremely suspicious sort, unless he checks for transmissions continually or at exactly the right time, odds are good that it'll remain operational."

"Excellent."

"Should I begin searching Mund?" Lobo said.

I considered Lobo's point again. Since the moment I awoke, I'd done everything hastily and by instinct. That wouldn't be enough to catch Jack. I needed to stop and think. "No," I said. "We're safe here, so let's pause for a moment. I'd like to have a plan before we do anything further."

"What a lovely notion," Lobo said.

I ignored him. Jack, like me, never entered a place without having scouted his exit. He'd definitely been concerned that something might go wrong with the interview, because he'd involved me. Chaplat was after him, and the gangster had the ability to do him a great deal of damage. On top of all that, though Jack might have been trying to shake any tails by having Lobo leave him at the gate, to come back to Mund he'd need to land at a commercial transport facility, and Chaplat would be watching all those sites. No, he wouldn't have stayed on Mund.

He'd jump. He wouldn't jump far, though, because if he couldn't pay Chaplat he was legitimately broke, and the farther he went, the more he had to shell out for jump fees. So, he'd jump once, go to ground, and find a fence for at least one of the gemstones.

Where?

Mund's gate had two apertures, one to Drayus and one to Gash.

Drayus.

I closed my eyes and replayed our conversation in Falls. Jack mentioned that when he jumped here from Drayus, he checked with a gate agent he'd bribed. If he'd recently stayed on Drayus, he would have had time to build an identity and a base of operations. Drayus would be a logical destination.

"If you had to choose to hide on either Drayus or Gash," I said, "which would you pick?"

"Drayus," Lobo said.

"Why?"

"Humans colonized Drayus one hundred and fifty-one years ago," Lobo said, "so it possesses many major settlements and a population in the millions. It's a regional capital for the Expansion Coalition, so it has serious local law enforcement and a low crime rate. Anyone chasing Jack would have less likelihood of success mounting an illegal attack there than on any other planet in the region. Its gate has three additional active apertures, so he could jump from it to Avery, Immediata, or Therien, all relatively stable planets with additional jump opportunities."

"What about Gash?" I said.

"Gash is the most dangerous planet in this sector of space. Its gate opened only forty-five years ago, so humans have been active there less than a third of the time they've lived on Drayus. It has so few natural resources and so many violent extremist groups that the EC hasn't even bothered trying to make it an affiliate—and the population doesn't have any interest in becoming one. Almost all of the people reside in the six small cities spread along the southeast coast of its one major landmass, and not one of those cities is particularly safe.

"No, not Gash. Drayus is clearly the better option."

Lobo's analysis was, of course, accurate. Drayus presented Jack with numerous advantages. He'd also let slip that he'd jumped from there to Mund.

Drayus was the only logical choice.

"It's time to head to the gate," I said. "We're going to Gash."

CHAPTER 13

ASH?" LOBO SAID. "Was something in my analysis unclear to you?"

"Not at all," I said. "I understood it completely, and it was perfect. Any logical person would choose Drayus—which is exactly why Jack is hiding out on Gash."

"So he's stupid and/or illogical?"

"Neither. He's as smart and as able to reason dispassionately as anyone I've ever known. He's sufficiently intelligent, in fact, that he'll have reached the same conclusion we did, which is the reason he'll hide where no one would expect him to go. He's also worked with people there, so he'll have connections. Finally, what you cited as drawbacks of Gash—the extremist groups, the lawlessness, the danger—are opportunities and camouflage from Jack's perspective. He always targets bad people, so the place is ripe with potential fish, and if he needs to hire help, where better to be?"

"Fish?"

"People likely to fall for scams."

"My slang dictionary isn't as complete as I'd thought," Lobo said. "Perhaps I'll make a special study of criminal jargon. It might prove useful given that you own me."

"May we please head to Gash?" I said.

"Of course," Lobo said. "You gave the order, and I followed it. I have to ask, however, one more question: If Jack is as intelligent as you claimed, might he not have figured out that you'd reach this conclusion and so switched back to Drayus?"

"Of course it's possible," I said, drawing out the words and fighting the urge to yell at him, "but what makes me confident he's on Gash is that I'm not what he's trying to avoid. Between Dougat and the Followers and Chaplat's gang, Jack has far bigger problems than anything I might present. Staying away from both of those groups would be his primary concern." I paused and considered one last time. "No," I finally said, "he's not on Drayus. He's on Gash."

"I see your reasoning," Lobo said, "but if it were up to me, I'd opt for the logical conclusion."

"Then it's a good thing it's not up to you," I said, already feeling a little less confident than I sounded. "Look at the bright side: You also win in this."

"How is that?"

"You gain another opportunity for self-improvement: understanding human thought processes better."

"Oh, joy," Lobo said. "Just what I wanted: another growth opportunity."

I smiled even though I was a bit chagrined at the pleasure I took in tweaking him. "Head for the gate."

"File our jump plan and enter the queue, as usual?"

I started to say yes but stopped myself. I had no desire to lead either Dougat or Chaplat to Jack, which is exactly what I'd do if I gave away my destination and either of Jack's pursuers had people monitoring the station. "No," I said. "Let's check it out first. How long to the gate?"

"Assuming you still want to follow at least some of our usual procedures and run an indirect route and check for surveillance on the way—"

"Of course," I said, already sorry for goading him.

"—we should reach it in about four hours."

"Please wake me about half an hour out or if our guest gets up first."

"With pleasure," Lobo said. "I live to be your wake-up call."

I shook my head in frustration, stretched out, and tried to nap. Anything involving Jack was likely to be tiring, so I followed another rule I'd learned decades ago: If the course is long or hard, sleep when you can.

"She's awake," Lobo said. "Should I unlock her door?"

"Any incoming scan attempts?" I asked.

"None so far. The gate station is broadcasting the usual queries, but we can dock without filing more than a request for temporary stay."

"Let her out." I turned away from the display Lobo had opened across the front and watched as Park came down the short hallway. She'd removed her body armor and was wearing only a knee-length, skintight, cobalt-blue T-shirt. One sleeve was missing from Lobo's minor surgery; she'd ripped off the other. Her hair was loose, and either she was stunningly gorgeous or I'd been away from women too long. She appeared to have none of the extreme beauty mods that were the current craze among corporate and government execs, but she didn't suffer for the lack. I realized I was staring at her body a second after she did, but she didn't say anything; instead, she smiled when we made eye contact. I felt my face blush, so I was grateful when the display drew her attention.

"We're jumping?" she said.

"Maybe." I looked again at the image. Mund's jump gate grew larger in the display as we approached it. Like all the gates, this one glowed a single, completely uniform color. Each gate is also perfectly smooth, every square centimeter an exact, unmarked replica of every other. No two gates are the same exact hue, though we have no clue whether that fact means anything. We also have no idea why each gate is the color it is. The bright raspberry of Mund's gate struck me as a bit garish, but then again, if I'd been in charge of building the gates, the pink one—in my opinion the least attractive gate known to humanity—would never have existed.

Some cults claimed only God controlled the structures;

Gatists worshipped the gates as if they *were* gods. Alien conspiracy advocates split into two main camps: One maintained superior aliens had constructed the gates to prepare humanity for the next step in its evolution, while the other claimed that similarly superior aliens used the structures to lull us into abandoning our attempts to construct interstellar ships—one of which we had built when Earth was our sole home—and go only where they wanted us. It was certainly the case that every known gate led to a planetary system that contained at least one planet that without any terraforming was already habitable by humans.

I didn't care at all about any of the theories. To me, as I'd said earlier to Park, the gates worked, and that was good enough. You entered an aperture in one part of space and emerged many light-years away in another area, though typically in the same general sector. Gates also interested people in many of the types of work I've done over the years, because they offered safe havens of a sort: They didn't tolerate ship-to-ship violence within their areas of influence, a sphere with its center on the gate and a radius of roughly one light-second. They didn't care at all what happened inside each ship—fights on spacecraft and gate stations were as common as you'd expect at any port where long-trip crews disembarked to relax—but let a vessel release any sort of weapon, even an energy beam, and the gate would instantly hit both the ship and the weapon with a blast the color of the gate. Both the ship and the weapon would then be *gone*—not vaporized, not shattered, just gone, as if they'd never existed. No one knew where the offenders went; they simply vanished. As best anyone had ever been able to tell, the beam that emanated from gates in these circumstances moved faster than light, but no one was sure; experiments were expensive and ultimately both destructive and uninformative.

The gates did tolerate collisions with meteors and other natural objects, provided no ship had steered those things, but the collisions left the gates unfazed and unscarred.

Staring at Mund's gate, I understood for a moment, as I always did when approaching one of the strange structures, their ability to inspire religious thought. You couldn't help but think of them as having personalities, and thus as being somehow intelligent. They also invoked awe in all but the most jaded travelers. Hanging in space, each resembled a gigantic pretzel composed of Möbius strips. The apertures—the areas where the strips wound together to create closed circuits—ranged in size from barely large enough to let small shuttles pass to so huge that no human ship yet built would come anywhere near its edges. Working apertures were pure black, the color of space without stars, of the darkest bowels of a dead planet. Energy would not pass through them to the other sector of space; low-level beams would continue as if the aperture weren't there. Only objects could make the trip.

Gates also varied in the number of apertures they offered, with a few having only a single aperture and others offering half a dozen or more. New apertures appeared from time to time, and corporations and governments naturally coveted them for the commercial opportunities they created. Only one aperture connection—the one that had linked Earth and Pinkelponker—had ever closed, and as with so many facts about my home world, no one knew why. The closure had certainly added fuel to the flame of mysticism that flickered around that planet.

How a person reacted to seeing a gate was, to me, a good indicator of character. Those too busy to notice were almost certainly not going to become friends of mine. People who felt the need to make stupid jokes or pretend to find the gates routine or boring almost always annoyed me. Park stared openly, her lips slightly parted, one foot forward as if ready to step into an aperture herself, and I instantly liked her for the utterly frank, undisguised interest. She moved closer, and the display's glow wrapped around her. In silhouette I noticed more about her: the lushness of her figure, the tiny bump on her nose, the ever so slight lightening in color of the epicanthic fold of her left eyelid as it reached her nose, the way she held her hand out from her body, almost as if she were reaching for me.

"Beautiful," I whispered, realizing too late I'd spoken aloud.

"It is," she said. "Each time I see a gate, I feel the same sense of wonder all over again."

I squeezed my eyes shut. How stupid could I be? I'd interrogated this woman only hours before, and now I was eyeing her hand like a lovesick child. I'd be lucky if she didn't recoil or hit me if I touched her; either reaction would certainly be reasonable.

I had to focus on the tasks at hand.

"If we're not going to jump," she said, "then why are we here?"

"I didn't say we weren't. I said, 'maybe.' We need to be careful."

"I understand," she said, "but Dougat's certainly not going to attack your ship this close to a gate."

"Dougat's not the only one looking for Jack," I said, "and fending off a possible assault is not our only problem."

"What do you mean?"

"Jack owes money to a group, and he doesn't appear to plan to pay them back. They'd also like to catch him." If either Dougat's or Chaplat's teams got their hands on her, the less she knew, the better, so I left it at that.

I touched her shoulder, and she turned to face me.

"I can let you out here, even give you some money, and you can catch a commercial shuttle." I stared into her eyes, trying to will her to act like an innocent bystander, to leave and be safe. I didn't want anything to happen to her. "Everything could go smoothly, but it could also go nonlinear, and your best bet is to run far away from here." I kept staring. She was too nice to involve. I considered knocking her out and dumping her at the station, but I'd made a deal.

"No," she said. "You agreed that I could come, and I'm coming."

"Fine," I said, my frustration at her choice emerging as an angry tone, my voice harsh enough that she involuntarily stepped back. "Stay quiet, follow my orders, and maybe this'll work out."

I turned away from her. How did I manage to let concern emerge as anger? I shook my head at my own stupidity.

"Lobo, are all the ships currently in this region queued to jump?" I asked the question out loud, because if she was going to be with me, she might as well get used to hearing me talk to him.

"No," he answered, also out loud, "two are not: me, and one other."

Leave it to him to use precision to deliver sarcasm. "Show me the other one."

A ship popped into view in the upper left of the display in front of me. A little smaller than Lobo, it might have been a gate maintenance vessel, but it had no corporate or government markings. Service vehicles don't bother to travel incognito.

"Did it arrive before or after us?"

"Before. It was already in place when it came in range of my visual sensors."

"Is it sending or receiving any transmissions?"

"No."

Great. It might not be watching for us, but it certainly could be. Whoever ran it—Dougat or Chaplat—was more connected than I'd imagined, because all ships near a gate have to broadcast basic identity and intent data. We were posing as a private shuttle seeking gate-station R&R before deciding where to jump. The EC operated this station, so they would normally require every ship to maintain its status broadcasts. Whoever owned this vessel had paid off someone to tolerate this breach of protocol.

"Can you identify its type?"

"Not with certainty," Lobo said, "but that means nothing, because many vehicles, particularly milspec craft, are as configurable as I am. It's certainly the right size to be a scout-class chaser, faster than I am within a system but nowhere near as well armed nor, I might add, as intelligent."

Was he showing off? I decided to ignore him.

"Park," I said, "do you recognize it?"

"Please call me Maggie," she said, "and no, but that doesn't mean anything. I know Dougat and the Followers own quite a few ships, but I have no idea how many or what types they are."

This one might not be after us, but to be safe and to protect Jack and Manu, I had to assume it was. I couldn't afford to lead it to them.

"Lobo," I said, "File for a jump to Drayus."

"Done," he said. "Are you bowing to logic, or running an evasive route?"

"The latter."

I focused again on the image of the lurking ship, but I learned nothing new.

"What if it follows us?" Maggie said.

"Then we deal with it."

"That's your best idea?" she said. "Deal with it?"

"Yeah," I said, "that's about it."

"It doesn't seem like much of a plan."

I faced her and forced myself to keep my voice level. I was furious, but not because the question was unfair; it wasn't. She was right as far as she went, but at the same time she was incredibly wrong; she had clearly never been on the sharp end of a conflict. "It isn't much of a plan," I said, "but it's about all we can manage with the information we have. This is exactly how this sort of thing goes. You don't get to study perfect data. You don't get to know everything that's happening. You can't plan for every contingency. You assemble all of your intelligence info, identify your best option, implement it, and then react to what happens. You make the best choice you can given what you know at that moment, you put one foot in front of the other, and you keep walking until you either win or die. That's it. That's all there is."

She studied me intently, but she didn't respond.

I was grateful for that. I needed time to cool. I've spent too much of my life dealing with those who manipulate others and never witness the true costs. They always expect their plans to work, and of course the plans rarely do. I knew intellectually that Maggie wasn't one of them, but her questions triggered the anger that courses through me all the time, just under the surface, ready to explode.

"Our turn," Lobo said.

I faced the display and watched as the perfect blackness of the aperture drew closer and closer, until it filled our vision, until the world beyond the ship vanished for a fraction of a second in which anything might happen, everything was possible, and then we poked through and a new starscape flashed to life in front of us. I realized I was holding my breath, as I often did when I jumped, and I exhaled slowly.

"Dock in the first available station slot," I said, "and file for a visit. Switch the display to focus on the aperture."

The aperture filled the display initially, but it shrank quickly as we jetted toward the station.

"Let's see what follows us."

CHAPTER 14

FIFTEEN MINUTES PASSED, and the ship didn't come through the gate after us. Every craft that emerged into the Drayus system sent the usual jump acknowledgment and headed toward the planet.

Fifteen more minutes passed, and still the lurking ship did not appear.

I waited in silence, focusing on Lobo's displays and thinking. Waiting has played an important role in many of the ways I've made my living. I've waited on stakeouts, for darkness to fall, and for enemy troops and vehicles to move by my position. I'm used to it, and I'm generally good at it.

I had to give Maggie credit: She held out for a full hour before she spoke.

"I don't seem to be able to say anything that doesn't annoy you, but at the risk of doing the wrong thing yet again, are you sure that ship wasn't just innocently sitting there, maybe with a broken transmitter?"

I'd known what she'd eventually have to ask, so I'd had time to prepare myself and was able to answer both calmly and honestly. "More than half of what's bothered me about what you've said comes from the way I interpreted your words, not anything you did wrong, so don't worry about that. But, yes,

121

I'm reasonably confident that ship is anything but innocent. If it really was in trouble, the gate station would have sent repair help, and we'd have seen the maintenance process in action." I rubbed my eyes hard in frustration at myself. Softly, more to myself than to her or Lobo, I said, "I'm missing something obvious."

"I don't understand how it can hurt us or even track us if it doesn't follow us," she said. "If the people who own it cared as much about us as you think, wouldn't they come over here and confront us?"

How stupid could I be? "Brilliant!" I said, turning to look at her. "Of course." She smiled, pleased with the praise but also clearly confused.

I faced the display again. "Lobo, run the same check here that you did at the last station. I want to know if any ships aren't scheduled for jumps."

"Two," Lobo said, "us and one other." A vessel the shape of a good-size troop transport popped into the center of the front display. "This one is behaving exactly the same way as the one at the Mund gate."

"Milspec?"

"It's sitting without any visible weapons, it's not transmitting, and it's heavily shielded—again like the other ship—but it certainly possesses a suitable profile."

"This is good news?" Maggie said.

"Yes and no," I said. "It's good in that we now understand what's going on: The other ship didn't jump here because it didn't have to do anything to keep us under surveillance; this one was waiting for us. The bad part is that whichever of those two groups is chasing us has enough resources to position ships both here and at Mund's gate. Whoever is monitoring us wants to track us very badly indeed, but they're not yet willing to approach us."

"So what do we do?"

"Find out how far their reach extends." I stared at the image of the Drayus gate in one of Lobo's side displays. The giant structure, its perfect surface the color of pale sand tinged with lemon, contained four apertures. I knew the one to Mund led to another surveillance ship, so the only question was which of the others to try first. "Lobo, which of the planets accessible via this gate is the most heavily populated?" Given that both of the groups pursuing Jack and us operated on or outside the fringes of governmental control, I wanted the planet with the largest EC presence. If no ship was waiting for us there, we had a way out. If one was holding the same silent guard vigil as the other two we'd seen, we'd know the opposition had greater pull than I'd expected.

"Therien," Lobo said, "the jewel of the EC. A large and affluent human population inhabits it, its natural resources are varied and plentiful, and it's sufficiently orderly that despite its size the EC has never issued a peacekeeping contract for it."

"File to jump there," I said. "Here's hoping nobody's waiting for us."

So much for that hope.

We didn't wait to check this time, so we discovered the surveillance vessel before we'd even queued up for a station visit. Like the others, this one was sitting incognito. Unlike its counterparts, it profile was clearly milspec.

Maggie fretted and paced, but she stayed quiet. I appreciated the control.

I sat and considered the situation.

Nothing about Chaplat's operation smelled of this much money. Local bosses tend to boast, to overstate their importance, but it's all part of the way they intimidate others. If his reach had extended this far, he'd have let me know.

No, it wasn't Chaplat.

Dougat and the Followers might have been richer than Chaplat, and as a quasi-religious organization their influence might have spanned more planets, but I couldn't picture them having both the fleet and the staff necessary to be able to afford to dedicate this level of resources to tracking one man and one boy.

It also wasn't Dougat.

Only two types of entities possess the people, ships, and organization you need for this level of surveillance: conglomerates and governments. I've kept a low profile with the megacorporations for almost a year, so it's been that long since I put myself on any of their target lists. Neither Kelco nor Xychek, the last two huge businesses I'd given cause to come after me, operated in this sector of space. If either of those two companies was angry enough, they could certainly use corporate reciprocity agreements to motivate a local firm to hunt me, but I couldn't buy that scenario; the cost greatly outweighed the return. The megacorps will indulge executive whims, including revenge, to a point, but eventually their credit-counters will run an analysis, and the bottom line will carry the day.

That left me with only one possibility: government. To operate on all these planets, there was no way it was a single planetary operation, nor were those even common in this sector. It had to be the EC.

The problem is, I hadn't done anything to draw that kind of attention, nor, to the best of my knowledge, had Jack. It's always possible he'd conned an influential EC honcho, because the wrong person with the right degree of power can lead governments to temporarily act insanely and with no regard for their P&L, but I couldn't buy it.

So, the EC also made no sense.

I was back to having no rational explanation—but the existence of all those surveillance ships guaranteed there was one. I just hadn't figured it out.

By making these jumps, I'd also created another problem: I was telling any astute observer where Jack and Manu were. I'd avoided jumping to Gash while clearly trying other systems, so I was effectively saying, "Look everywhere but there!"

I had to go to Gash.

I also needed more data. Would the ship follow me if I left the vicinity of the gate? Were we facing hostile action or merely covert data gathering?

I might as well find out here, in the heavily populated Therien system, because more people means more support satellites and space traffic, which in turn means more readily available places to hide and a lower likelihood of an attack near the planet. By appearing to check more closely both here and on Gash, I could also add some confusion to the thinking of our watchers.

"Lobo, head for Therien. Plot a course that puts the station and the gate between the watching ship and us well before we pass out of the gate's area of influence. Track that ship."

"Done," Lobo said.

A hologram appeared in front of the main display. It showed the station, the gate, and a section of Therien. A small green dot—us—moved away from the gate, accelerating as it went. A red dot marked the position of the surveillance vessel.

"As I'm sure you're aware," Lobo said, "this course will leave me unable to track that ship until we're closer to Therien."

"Yes, I am," I said. "And it won't be able to see us, either, so if it wants to keep an eye on us, it'll either have to change position or hand us off to another ship. Monitor all the vessels between the gate and Therien, and check for parallel courses."

"Are we inviting attack?" Maggie said, her voice a bit choked and her shoulders high and tense. "Prior to what happened at the Institute, I'd never been in any kind of fight, much less one in space between ships."

"No," I said. "We're inviting motion. We'll stay close enough to the gate that it would take out any ship that fired at us—and the weapons the ship fired, of course."

We watched the hologram in silence as Lobo accelerated toward Therien.

About ninety seconds later, the red dot abruptly disappeared from its original location. A short time later, it reappeared on our side of the gate.

"The ship is definitely following us," Lobo said, "and it's tracking our course exactly. That pilot is either as dumb as a drink dispenser or doesn't care if we spot it."

"No one able to set up this many surveillance ships in the time since Jack and Manu left us can be that dumb," I said.

"Even if I'm wrong, we have to assume they simply don't care if we know they're following us."

"If they don't mind if we spot them and know we will," Maggie said, "then why don't they contact us directly?"

"I suspect they're making a point," I said. "They're letting us know that we have no way out that they can't track."

"Are they right?" she said. "Is this Dougat using us to find the boy?"

I appreciated her concern, but the questions were wearing on me again. "I don't know, but eventually we'll figure it out. In the meantime, though, we need to throw them off Jack's trail."

I kept my tone level, but I was also getting worried. I didn't yet see a good way out of this.

The only thing to do was to keep moving ahead.

"Lobo, take us to the gate, then jump to Drayus, then Mund, and then Gash."

"In progress," Lobo said. "Should I continue to track the ship?"

"Did it turn when you did?" I said.

"Yes."

"Then you can stop monitoring it. We have all the data about it that we need."

"Isn't Gash where you deduced Jack would be hiding?" Lobo asked. "More to the point, isn't it where you didn't want to lead them?"

"My question exactly," Maggie said.

The two of them were going to make me crazy. I'd worked alone for so long that I wasn't accustomed to having to explain myself. I didn't want to become used to it either, but I knew they wouldn't stop bothering me until I gave them an explanation.

"I can't let Gash be the only nearby planet we haven't jumped to, or that fact alone will draw their attention to it. Once we finish this set of maneuvers, we'll have spread a little confusion and verified the surveillance setup is the same on all the planets near here."

"Maybe we'll get lucky," Maggie said, "and they won't be watching Gash."

"Maybe," I said, not wanting to constantly criticize her.

She stared at me for a moment. "No chance, huh?"

If she was going to ask, I was going to answer truthfully. "None," I said. "No group this well organized would miss something so obvious."

She nodded and turned to the display as the aperture grew larger and larger in front of us, the ships ahead of us in the queue made the jump, our turn came, and we once again plunged into the perfect black ahead.

"Just like the others?" I asked as we waited by the station next to Gash's screaming red jump gate.

"For any reasonable value of 'like,'" Lobo said, "yes. It's in roughly the same position relative to the gate as the other surveillance vessels, like them it's not transmitting at all, and its profile also suggests milspec."

"I hope Jack beat them here," I said. "If he didn't, whoever is following us already knows where he is."

Lobo's front displays showed both the gate and Gash. The gate and its two apertures, the one to Mund and a newer connection that led to Triton's Dream, hung in space like blood splatters caught in midflight by a strobe on a starless night. People in spacesuits crawled all over the outside of the gate station. The parts of the structure they passed turned a red almost exactly the color of the gate itself; it had to be a Gatist color wash. Fine by me; any activity that attracted attention away from us was a good thing.

In the other direction, the reflected light of Gash's sun washed the planet itself a duller red, its namesake giant crimson desert slashing across the vast majority of the single large landmass like a wound tearing open. With only seven cities, six strung along the eastern coast and one perched on the continent's northwestern edge, and with limited useful natural resources, Gash hadn't grown at the usual early-stages pace in the forty-five years since the aperture to it had first opened in Mund's gate.

"I must note again," Lobo said, "that Gash is *not* a logical choice for Jack. From what I've gathered from the public data streams, the Followers, the very group Jack is trying to avoid, are the fastest-growing cult on the planet. They operate temples in all seven major cities."

"He's right," Maggie said. "I've heard Dougat and some of the senior staff talk about this place. He called it a 'godless hell' with no real government and said its population included a higher than normal percentage of criminals. He also said those same qualities made it a great place to evangelize and recruit converts."

"I'm not denying it's full of rough trade," I said. "The place is wild enough that the EC has never been willing to force it to join. I also understand that the Followers are big there. All the same, Jack knows he needs to go to ground, and he's arrogant enough to view a city full of criminals as a target-rich environment." I wasn't as sure as I sounded, but at the same time Gash remained the best bet for Jack. He'd earned his nickname always working the angles you didn't expect; heading to Gash fit his character perfectly. "Maybe I'm wrong, but we're going with my instincts." I checked out the image of the surveillance ship in Lobo's rightmost display. "Bring up the tracking holo, and head us to Gash. We came here to give them the same show we ran on Therien; we might as well do it."

The hologram popped into view in front of us as Lobo accelerated away from the gate and toward the planet.

"Same course type?" Lobo said.

"Yes. Keep the gate between the planet and us initially. Let's make them have to move."

Sure enough, once we were well away from the gate, the red dot that represented the other ship vanished and then quickly popped into place behind us on the hologram.

"You were right," Maggie said.

Her tone suggested I'd want to gloat; I didn't. I'd have greatly preferred to have been wrong, because if I had been it would've meant we could have kept going to Gash. Now, we'd have to head back, maybe all the way to Mund, and I'd have to figure out a new way to get to Jack.

"A second ship is now tracking us," Lobo said.

A blue dot appeared on the hologram. It wasn't following

our course the way the surveillance ship was, but it was in position to monitor us.

"Are you sure it's after us?" I said.

"As certain as I can be with the data available," Lobo said. "Had I doubted it, I wouldn't have stated it as fact. It's responding to changes in our course but not tracing our path exactly."

"So it's not with the first ship?" I asked.

"I cannot be sure," Lobo said, "but I don't believe it is."

"Reverse course and head right back at the surveillance ship. Come as close as you can without directly targeting it. We don't want the gate to think we're attacking."

"Done," Lobo said, "but why?"

"If the two ships are from the same organization, they'll respond similarly. If they don't, then another player has joined the game." I wanted to pressure them and hope I learned that the two were together. If they were, our pursuers might have figured out that Jack was likely to be here, but we'd have to live with that problem, at least for now. It was better than having two different groups chasing us. "Accelerate hard; let's not give them much time to react."

I watched on the display as our dot quickly closed the gap with the red one. It stayed where it was as we approached and then passed it.

The blue dot, however, raced for cover back behind the gate.

Great.

Two different organizations *were* after us. Reaching Gash and finding Jack without leading our pursuers to him was getting harder and harder.

When I'd thought we'd be alone, searching Gash had been just a matter of time and fuel. Now, though, it would require a great deal of effort to lose or confront our pursuers. Before we went to all that trouble, I needed to verify that Jack had definitely jumped there. The only place we could get that information was the jump gate, and even there I couldn't be sure we'd succeed; the station agent was supposed to keep all such data confidential.

"Head back to the gate station and dock," I said. "I'm going aboard."

"Done," Lobo said.

"I have some additional instructions and contingency plans to review with you both," I said, "and I'm going to need some supplies."

"Expecting trouble?" Lobo said.

"No, just preparing in case it comes."

"What do you want me to do?" Maggie said.

"How good are you with weapons?"

"Why do we need weapons?"

"Because," I said, "we may have to be persuasive."

CHAPTER 15

RED PEOPLE WALKED the red aisles of the red gate station. As I'd assumed when I'd seen the spacesuited figures painting the exterior, a Gatist color ceremony was rolling through the station like a tidal wave across an island. Apparently the EC was unwilling to risk the bad publicity it would receive if it tried to stop the paint-wielding Gatists thronging the facility. The Frontier Coalition was the last government to interfere in one of these supposedly religious events, and it paid a steep price: The Gatists protested so loudly on so many planets that the FC chose to declare a sector-wide color-ceremony day to appease them rather than continue the fight.

The whole affair struck me as stupid. Even if the Gatists are right and the gates are God (or gods, depending on which Gatist sect you ask), I couldn't see why a God would care at all if we painted ourselves to resemble it.

To be fair to the Gatists, though, the ceremony was both artistically interesting and nondestructive. They swarmed a station inside and out en masse, thousands of them arriving simultaneously and spreading with military precision across the entire facility and every willing ship docked there. I'd given them permission to paint Lobo, in part not to stand out and in part because it annoyed him so much it was fun to do. The swarm of Gatists colored every surface of every thing and every willing person the exact hue of the gate, and they were fast painters. In a matter of hours, the gate color sparkled everywhere. They persuaded a surprisingly large number of people to participate, so that almost everyone who visited a station during one of these ceremonies ended up joining the color wash. Government officials resisted initially, but the Gatists were so annoying that ultimately the bureaucrats succumbed and it became standard policy for them to accept the paint. The Gatists rewarded the compliant by using temporary coatings that over the course of a few days turned transparent, peeled off, and either evaporated or, in space, floated away. They even cleaned after themselves, using fine-mesh collectors to gather the external debris and cleansing the station's air filters of all paint residue.

Wherever there's a ceremony, there's inevitably a party, of course, and when a party grows large enough, merchants seize the opportunity to hawk their goods. Revelers, Gatists and nonbelievers alike, drank and ate and browsed the gate-colored wares of gate-colored vendors who sprouted in the halls and public rooms and sometimes even the private chambers of the stations. Many sellers used the events to close out items that were once available only in less popular colors, because of course you had no way to know the true color of anything you bought.

Never ones to miss tax opportunities, the government agents quickly produced schedules of fees and taxes and licenses, opened more rooms to the revelers, rented private suites by the hour to particularly amorous partiers, and sold sponsorships to local conglomerates. The Gatists initially protested the crass commercialization of their deeply religious ceremonies, but their furor abated when the gate staff cut them in for a percentage of the action.

I went straight to the Gatist team stationed at my entry lock and told them to have at it. I even stripped; I wanted to blend as well as possible with everyone else. They crammed filters in my nostrils and ears, then stuck me under a portable shower and turned me red. I wouldn't let go of either of my guns or my wallet until I could see again, at which point they finished painting the parts of my hands, wallet, and weapons that had been in contact with each other and sent me on my way.

I verified that everything was still present and, as best I could, that the guns appeared to work, then walked into the screaming redness of the station hallways. The fluorescent chips the Gatists had blended into the paint twinkled and sparkled in the station lights like the faint beginnings of flares on a red sun. All around me swirled the sounds of commerce and partying: heated debates and shrieking laughter and hushed tones hinting at rendezvous in progress and those yet to come. Rich smells thickened the air: the sweat of too many bodies in too small a space, the enticing aromas of meat and vegetables cooking on portable grills, the almost imperceptible yet power-ful odors of cosmetics and pheromone enhancers fighting for dominance, and, underlying it all, the slight but noticeable tang of the Gatist paint.

I tucked my weapons inside my shirt and waded slowly through the churning sea of bodies. Pickpockets working the aisles patted me down as I moved, apparently so unconcerned about detection that they abandoned any pretense of subtlety. They kept hacker partners close at hand in the hopes that the wallets they were stealing used old, weak encryption. I wasn't stupid enough to keep my wallet or weapons anywhere they could easily reach, so at one level I had nothing to lose, but the casual openness with which they worked the crowd offended me.

I knew I should focus on finding the gate agent, but after the fourth hand stroked my pants pockets, I couldn't take any more. Each touch was a violation, and I can stand only so many. I slowed my pace, and when the fifth hand touched me I grabbed it with my right and pulled the owner close enough that I could see the slight fear in his eyes even as he reached for a weapon. I gripped his throat with my left hand, squeezed, and shook my head. I pulled him close, as if to kiss an old friend in greeting, and whispered into his ear.

"Move your hand one more centimeter toward whatever

you're trying to reach, and I'll break your neck. Understand?"
I leaned back to gauge his reaction.

He lifted his hand clear of his body and blinked at me,
unable to speak.

I released his left hand. "Scratch your face if you understand
me and agree to behave," I said.

He did, his eyes still blinking from nerves.

"I'm not out to save everyone," I said. "I don't have the
time. So, do whatever you want to the rest of the crowd."
I squeezed his throat a little tighter, and his face reddened.
"Touch me again, however, and I won't be so gentle. Spread
the word. Okay?"

He scratched his face madly.

I released his neck.

He backed slowly into the crowd, his eyes never leaving
me, until he was a good five meters away. Then he turned
and ran as quickly as the crowd permitted. I stayed where I
was, watching him, the people flowing around me, until he
was out of sight. Pickpockets rarely worked solo in confined
spaces like the station, so I was confident he'd spread the word
as efficiently as any corporate data-alert blast.

The wall-mounted station legends were hard to read in uniform
red, people stood where the holo maps normally played, and the
din was so loud that the low-end directional AIs couldn't hear
to answer questions, so I had to either interrogate the machines
directly or find a guard. The space was so loud that I doubted my
ability to converse without distraction with the machines, and
I also wanted to get a sense of the quality of the security staff,
so I opted to approach the guards. The first one I spotted was
holding open a service closet door and negotiating intently with
a woman wearing only red paint and earrings the shape of Gash's
gate, so I gave him a pass. The next was happily painting a nude
young Gatist who was holding aloft a miniature gate, so I moved
on. At least most of the guards weren't going to be problems.

The third one I encountered was standing in front of a door,
almost as if he were working, though he'd leaned his stun rifle
against the doorway and was munching on a skewer of red meat.

"Who's the station manager?" I said. "And where can I find him?"

He stopped chewing and stared at me over the empty end of the stick of meat. "What do you need?"

"These Gatists and their mess have mucked up my schedule, and I've got freight to move. I want to lodge a protest." He didn't respond. Instead, he stared at me, and took another bite of the meat. "Fine," I said, "if you don't want to tell me his name and how to find him, I'll give you the details and you can relay them. I know you carry a terminal; let's sit down together and go over all my issues. It shouldn't take more than an hour to discuss everything."

He swallowed and shook his head. "Carne, Lem Carne, is the agent. It's not like he'll do anything to help you, though." Before I could say another word, he tilted his head toward the right and continued, "Down about a hundred meters to the second corridor, take a right, third door on your right. Knock yourself out."

He bit into the meat again, tore off another chunk, and looked away as he chewed.

I followed his directions and stopped at the end of the hallway when I spotted a single guard standing in front of the door to Carne's office. The party here was as loud and crowded as in every other corridor, but this guard, though red like everyone else, scanned the crowd continuously and stood alert.

I hunched my shoulders, bent my knees, and weaved toward him, bouncing off revelers and Gatists alike as I moved. I held my stomach as if I were about to be sick, both hands wrapped around my middle and one clutching the end of a trank gun. I ricocheted off a woman hawking religious charms she swore she'd made herself from flecks of paint that had floated in space by the gates, grabbed my mouth with my free hand, and bumped into the guard.

"Can you help me?" I said, leaning on him unsteadily. "I'm gonna be sick."

He put both hands on my shoulders to shove me away. When I felt them touch me, I pushed up and into him, crushing him against the wall and pinning his hands momentarily against me. At the same time, I straightened, pulled out the gun, and rammed it under his throat. I reached behind him with my left hand and steadied him. No one else could see the gun; to anyone watching the scene, the guard was simply helping another poor fool who couldn't handle his party drugs of choice.

I leaned close enough to the guy's right ear that he could hear me when I whispered, "When I say the word, you open the door and back in. Move before I tell you, move anything other than your right hand, or do anything else, and I'll shoot you. Understand?"

He nodded briefly, then stopped.

"Nodding is okay," I said, "and so is talking."

He nodded again and quietly said, "I understand."

"How many inside?"

"Just him."

"Carne?"

"Yes."

"Right hand only, nice and slow: Open it."

I leaned slightly back so I could watch his eyes, and I pushed up on the gun so it dug deeper into his neck.

His right hand drifted slowly downward as if sinking in a very salty ocean. He ran it over the recognition plate, and the door snicked open.

The guard stumbled for a moment, but I used my left hand on his neck to redirect his momentum and spin him around. I followed him into the room, keeping him between me and the unknown and therefore potentially dangerous space ahead. I held him in front of me as the door closed behind us.

I scanned the area quickly.

If Carne had an office, it was hiding somewhere, because what I was staring at was a game museum, not a place of work—and a museum he'd managed to convince the Gatists to leave alone. Models of spaceships, submersibles, assault vehicles of all classes, ancient helicopters and airplanes, land-based tanks, and even covered wagons and chariots hung from all over the ceiling on meter-long wires. If the room hadn't been over four meters tall, I'd never have been able to stand up straight in it. All the models were moving, each in a roughly half-meter sphere, toys flying up and down, diving and surfacing, rolling back and forth on invisible streets of air, and never sitting still. Even though I knew they were above me, I couldn't escape the sensation of being a giant in danger of imminent attack from heavily armed Lilliputian forces.

Carne had clearly been assembling his collection for a long time, because the office was easily three times the size of any station agent's I'd ever seen. About twenty meters wide by ten deep, it was a big space—but not big enough. Shelves full of games and toys of all sorts lined the walls. I spotted playing cards, brightly colored boxes I didn't recognize, figurines in a huge variety of costumes, and on and on. He'd packed free-standing gaming machines so closely that they formed corridors that wove drunkenly around the room as if placed randomly by a liquor vendor at the end of a two-day binge. Holo combat units stood side by side with ancient video games—either they were reproductions, or gate bribes had gone way, way up in the last few years—and they were all active, their demos chattering for attention. He'd set their volume levels to low, but even so the cumulative effect was disorienting, as if I'd wandered into dozens of simultaneous whispered conversations.

A man appeared at the end of a corridor to my right and walked toward us. In his right hand he carried a small, green figurine that appeared to be a soldier. Its right arm gripped the smallest finger on his left hand, and he was moving its little arm up and down, glee fighting with annoyance in his expression. "I've told you not to enter without my permission," he said, never even looking up.

"Mr. Carne," the guard began, but I cut him off by grabbing his mouth and shooting a trank round into his leg. He went slack. I let him drop and turned the weapon on Carne.

"I thought we had negotiated successfully with the Gatists," Carne said, still not noticing me, "so I don't understand why you're disturbing me."

"I need information," I said, "and I believe you can help me."

Carne stopped, looked up, and straightened. He ceased playing with the toy, though he kept both hands on it, and it maintained its hold on his finger. About a third of a meter shorter than I, with a slight build and closely cropped blond hair, he was a small man who looked incapable of violence and yet appeared completely undisturbed by the sight of a nearly two-meter-tall, angry, completely red assailant pointing a gun at him. I had to give him credit for poise.

He blinked a few times, his expression unchanging, and spoke. "We maintain a variety of data kiosks for the very purpose of providing information to our visitors. Feel free to use them."

"I doubt those kiosks maintain jump records."

"Of course not," he said. "Those logs are confidential."

"Yes," I said, "but as the gate agent in charge you can access them." He nodded slightly in agreement but said nothing, so I continued. "In my experience, that access is sometimes available for the agent's close friends." I kept the gun trained on him with my right hand and showed him my wallet with my left. "I can be a good friend."

"I'm afraid I simply don't understand," he said, "so perhaps you should leave."

"You didn't accumulate all of these toys on your salary. I could help you add to the collection."

"You've assaulted my guard and violated my space. Now you're attempting to bribe me. I'd prefer to save myself the trouble of ordering your arrest, but if you persist I'll summon the security team."

I hate games. I'd tried to play nicely, because gate agents are rarely comfortable with a direct approach, but enough was enough. I stepped to my left, put my arm on a shelf of toys just below my shoulders, and swept all the toys I could reach into the air.

He gasped and dove for them as they fell. I almost shot him by reflex but stopped myself and shoved him backward. He sprawled onto the floor.

I pulled the other gun, a pulse weapon, from within my shirt. "Before help can arrive," I said, "I will either turn this room into rubble or pay you a fair rate for one piece of information." He stared at me as if trying to read my mind. Without looking away, I lifted my left leg and stomped the nearest toy, a small blond female figure with a body even more lush than Maggie's.

He held up his hands, the green figure dangling from his pinky, and shrieked, "Enough! Do you have any idea what that doll cost me? It was a museum-quality replica, the closest thing I've seen to an Earth original."

I raised my foot again and positioned it over another one, a male figure about the same size as the female but with far lower quality hair.

"Okay, okay," he said. "What do you need?"

I put away the pulse gun, opened my wallet, and thumbed up a picture of Jack.

"This man, Jack Gridiz: Did he jump here, and when did he jump away?"

Carne stood and went to a desk in the far right corner of the room. I followed him the whole way, through three twisting rows of game machines, and waited while he checked. The display shimmered above the work surface and murmured at him. "Gridiz did arrive here," he said, "but he never jumped away. He came on a commercial transport, a little gate-jumper from Mund, but he's not in the station, and that ship has come and gone several times since his arrival." He looked up at me. "Either he's still on Gash, or he arranged for someone to smuggle him off-planet and beat our scans. We have clean records of everything that's passed through here in the last few days, so I believe he's still on Gash."

I nodded, in part pleased, because I'd correctly guessed what Jack would do, but in part annoyed, because now I had to figure out how to shake not one but two tails.

"You mentioned payment," he said. "I would appreciate assistance with the repairs I'll have to commission."

I opened my wallet and thumbed up twenty percent more than the typical agent bribe. I showed him the display and said, "Provided, of course, that you delete that information and we agree there's no need to involve security."

He smiled, spoke briefly to the display, and the data disappeared. "What information?" he said. "As for security, why would I bother them just to report an accident that occurred while I was showing a friend my collection? Unless, of course," he pointed to the unconscious guard, "that man has suffered permanent damage; then we might have a problem."

"The guard will wake up sore but otherwise fine," I said.

"Then I'll get busy cleaning up," he said, "as soon as you're on your way." He motioned slightly toward my wallet with his hand, finally noticing the toy dangling from his finger and pulling the little green man closer to his body. I transmitted the money.

His display chirped.

He led me to the front of his office and was carefully replacing the toys on the shelf when I walked out the door.

The color wash was still in full swing, so I leaned for a moment against the wall and subvocalized to Lobo. "Did you get all that?"

"Of course," Lobo said. "You're transmitting continuously through multiple normal channels as well as in stored pulses at short, random intervals via the backup active fiber in your shirt."

"Just making sure everything is working," I said. "You're annoyed that I was right about where Jack went."

"That one illogical human can predict the poor choices of another is something that shouldn't surprise me," Lobo said. "ETA at the lock?"

I evaluated the thickness of the crowd milling in the aisle. "Give me ten minutes," I said. "I'm heading back as directly as I can under the circumstances."

"If I breathed, I'm sure I would hold it in anticipation of your return," he said.

Yeah, he was still mad at me for being right.

I stepped into the crowd and worked my way slowly toward the corner. I didn't want to hurt anyone, but the combination of the close quarters and the sheer number of people touching me made self-control difficult. I worked at breathing calmly and finally ducked behind two women sharing a kiss with a man and turned the corner. The crowd was no better here, but at least I was one corridor closer to my goal. I rested against the wall, enjoying the tiny bit of space that was for the moment mine alone, and then plunged back into the throng.

I managed three steps forward before a door whisked open on my left and two uniformed and unpainted guards stepped out, one in front of me and one in back. A third remained in the doorway. The woman in front of me pointed a pulse gun at my stomach and stayed well out of reach. The crowd swirled on the other side of the guards, but we existed for a few seconds in our own oasis, beyond the reach of the red-painted partiers just when I would have welcomed the chance to lose myself among them. I saw no way out that didn't involve doing a lot of damage to my three captors and risking a lot of pain myself.

"Follow the man behind you," she said, "and go back the way you came.

"You have an appointment."

CHAPTER 16

THEY LED ME back to Carne's office, one ahead of me, one behind, the woman with the gun to my left, cutting me off from the crowd, and the corridor wall to my right. As we walked, random Gatists painted her back and hair, but she ignored them and stayed focused on me. When we reached Carne's office, the man ahead of me triggered the door, and we moved in our formation inside.

Carne had apparently decided to take my money and betray me. I'd find a way to pay him back. I looked for him, but he was nowhere in sight.

"Where's Carne?" I said.

A small smile crossed the woman's face, but neither she nor the other guards replied. She simply motioned me forward and into the leftmost aisle of toys. The men stayed behind, one moving to the room's door and the other remaining at the end of our aisle; they were pros making sure they'd have multiple clean shots at me if I bolted.

The aisle meandered to the front wall and then left until it ended at a door that snicked open as I came within a meter of it.

The room on the other side was as much about business as Carne's was about obsession. A plain metal desk faced me.

Displays flickered above it, so much data dancing on them that I couldn't see Carne's face through them. Two office chairs sat on my side of the desk. Guards in EC security uniforms stood at attention in three corners of the room; my escort stopped and snapped to attention in the corner nearest the door. The wall to my right was a huge window display facing the jump gate; in it I watched as a freighter emerged from an aperture into this system. A short but wide tree grew from a planter beneath the viewport and spread along the width of it. Purple blossoms with yellow and white central tendrils adorned the tips of most of the small tree's branches.

No one spoke.

I enjoyed the view. No good comes of offering information in situations like this one.

I rubbed my stomach as if hungry, triggering the emergency signal in the pulse transmission system in the fiber. Lobo would have heard the earlier conversation, but now he'd also know I considered myself to be in trouble. He'd stop using normal channels and alert Maggie, who should already have this information if she was doing her job. I hadn't spotted her, which was good if she was blending well but bad if she had lost me. Either way, with Lobo's help she'd now know exactly where I was. I was confident even the best EC systems would have no chance to break our encryption in the time I was here, but if they were scanning for signals, I wanted them to believe I was alone. People are often more talkative when they think you're helpless.

The desk displays flicked off, and a woman stood from behind the desk. She wore no uniform, only standard business elegant. She glowed with the unnatural beauty of executive style. Perfectly white hair beautifully contrasted with skin the color of rich, wet soil. Her mods hadn't extended to height, so I towered over her, but she clearly was used to that position and didn't care at all about it.

"Please sit, Mr. Moore," she said.

I did. So did she. I hated that she already knew my name, but that was also no surprise.

Her chair lifted slowly until we were eye-to-eye across the desk.

"From what I've gathered of your background," she said, "and that isn't as much as I'd like—" She paused, but when I didn't speak, she continued, "—you're likely to be more than a bit annoyed at Carne, and that annoyance could cause us trouble later. So, let me save you some time: He's not involved in this, and he doesn't know you're here."

"It's his station," I said.

She laughed, a rich, throaty laugh that was charming and sounded genuine. I let myself smile with her.

"Oh, no," she said. "It's *our* station. He simply works here. He wouldn't even be doing that, and we wouldn't have to put up with"—she waved her hand as if to take in the giant room of toys on the other side of the door—"all that, were it not for his father, a rather influential colleague of mine."

She pulled a glass from a shelf somewhere below the desk and took a sip. "Something to drink?"

I shook my head. If they were going to drug me, I'd at least make them work to do it.

"Then to business. I'm Alexandra Midon, but you can call me Sasha; I trust we're going to be friends. Do you mind if I call you Jon?"

I shrugged.

She continued, unfazed by my rudeness. "I'm the Expansion Coalition's councillor in charge of planetary government relationships for this sector. All the worlds you've been visiting on your frequent jumps are part of my territory."

She smiled again, enjoying hinting at the depth of their knowledge about me. I tried to show nothing, but some of my growing impatience and annoyance must have been obvious.

"Disengaging from dock," Lobo said via a burst that the shirt's comm unit relayed to me over the machine frequency. Her sensors might be able to decrypt the short data spike, but doing so would take time.

"Of course we've been tracking you, Jon," Midon said. "You've been spending way too much time with groups on our watch list for us not to notice you. We particularly enjoyed the way you escaped from the Followers on Mund."

I questioned again the wisdom of not having immediately jumped away from this entire sector, but then I reminded myself of Manu.

"In fact, Jon, the Followers are what bring us together today. I'd like to understand what you were doing with them."

"Nothing at all," I said. "I was providing transportation for a friend. If you've checked my background, you know I'm a courier."

"Moving into first position," Lobo said.

"And quite a full-service one indeed," Midon said, laughing again. "Few couriers are so heavily armed." She sipped once more from her glass. "And speaking of arms, though we know you have clean title to that PCAV, I have to wonder if you've been doing any trading with the Followers. Some data we bought from the Frontier Coalition suggests you had some past unpleasant interactions with an arms dealer there."

She paused, again giving me a chance to speak.

I thought of Osterlad, the man who'd said he'd sell me Lobo's central weapons complex and who instead ambushed me. I'd ended up killing both him and one of his lieutenants, the lieutenant directly and him indirectly. I regretted the acts, but they'd each given me no option other than dying myself, and I won't do that without a fight.

When I didn't speak, she went on. "The FC execs were happy enough with you—apparently you helped them with a corporate relationship problem—that they didn't bother to look further into the matter. Now, though, your actions suggest you might be entering that business again, this time with Dougat and the Followers."

"I've never traded in weapons," I said, and that was technically true, though I'd worked cons that involved such trades and at times belonged to groups that trafficked in certain classes of arms, though always for specific, good causes. "I'm certainly not doing that—or anything else—with the Followers."

She studied me for a few quiet seconds. "I of course can't

tell if you're being truthful, not here anyway. We could go that route—we have people who could tell, who could defeat any type of resistance training you might have taken, though the process would be very unpleasant and time-consuming—but I'd rather not. So, please be honest, and this can end well for us all."

"First contact complete," Lobo said.

Midon came around the desk, stood in front of me, and leaned back against it.

The woman guard stayed at the door, but the others all moved closer. Midon might like pretending to be intimate, but they knew the risk of her being too close to me and were doing all they could to minimize it.

"Why did your friend need help?"

I saw no reason in not giving her most of the truth, certainly the parts she could find on her own.

"He was taking care of a boy, a boy Dougat wanted to interview. I was there to protect both the child and my friend, in case something went wrong. Something did, so I helped them escape."

Her eyes widened, and for the first time she appeared to be surprised. She leaned forward with excitement. "So the stories of the boy psychic are true?" she said.

I forced a laugh as I struggled to come up with an angle that would fit the facts but not expose Manu. "Hardly," I said, trying to think as Jack would as I shaped the story I was creating, "though I'm sure Dougat believed that he was. My friend was in money trouble and was working a con. I was just hired muscle."

"If your friend needed money, how could he afford to pay you?"

Where are the stupid bureaucrats when you need one? Not at the top of an entire sector of a major coalition, I reminded myself. "He couldn't. I wasn't doing anything special, so I went in for a piece of the action."

"Our surveillance shows your PCAV escaping the Institute, so you upheld your end of the bargain," she said. "We lost your ship for a time; nice work."

I nodded at the compliment. "Of course I got them out," I said. "I told them I would." Finally, a chance to say something completely truthful.

"I take it your friend didn't pay you, however," she said, "or you wouldn't still be chasing him."

"I'm not chasing anyone," I said.

She laughed, but this time she was faking the humor, and nothing in her tone was pleasant. "I'm being polite," she said, "and I'm interrogating you gently—as I'm sure you'll agree. I'm also not insulting you. I'd appreciate the same behavior from you. Do I have to remind you again that there are other ways we could do this?"

"What do you want from me?" I said, ignoring the threat. "Yes, you're being polite, but you're also hiding your motivation. *That* behavior doesn't exactly encourage open discussion."

"Moving to second position," Lobo said.

Midon chuckled once more, but now with genuine humor. "Fair point, Jon, fair point. Still, given the circumstances"—she waved her arm slowly to take in all the guards—"I think it's only reasonable that you give before you get. So, let's return to the question of why you're chasing your friend. I'll even provide you with some context to help you understand the situation. I wanted this conversation enough that I stationed ships at every jump destination in this sector. From the data many of them relayed, you were trying out multiple planets, so you were looking for something or someone. You noticed our surveillance, but you didn't keep on jumping until you were far away. To stay in this sector in the face of forces that large, you needed a very strong motivation. In my experience, only money and power push a person to take that level of risk."

And sex and friendship and anger and above all else, love and honor and loyalty, but she seemed oblivious of all of those. Not a surprise from a career EC exec.

"So," she said, "I repeat: Your friend didn't pay you?"

I let out a long, slow breath and nodded again, as if reluctantly giving in. "No, he didn't. He owes me a lot, and I'd like the money."

She smiled. "Now we're talking openly; excellent. Because we are, let me repeat my earlier question, in case you might have forgotten something before: Are you involved in any way in arms trading with the Followers?"

"Second contact complete," Lobo said.

I stared at her in frustration. "I've explained why I was at the Followers' institute. You saw my ship escape from it. It should be obvious that I'm not working with them; if I were, I would have left my friend and the boy with them. What are you really after?"

"At the same time you began gassing the Institute grounds, a mysterious explosion occurred in Dougat's warehouse, a place we've been wondering about but have been unable to legally enter. That blast distracted the local police, who were then late to the Institute. The coincidence is hard to believe."

This might not work out badly after all. Midon and the EC were worried about the Followers. The Followers were after Manu and so were still my problem. Chaplat was also chasing me. Either his crew or some of the Followers had to be in the second ship that had tailed the EC craft that followed us away from the gate. If I could get the EC to take down either or both of those groups, my life would improve.

"Jon?" she said. "Care to comment?"

"Causing an explosion on someone else's private property would be a crime," I said, "and the EC prosecutes crimes."

"Your wallet."

I took it from my pocket—carefully and slowly—and thumbed it open. I set it to receive and quarantine.

She tapped on the desk, and a contract appeared on it.

The wallet's legal software studied and summarized the text she'd sent. In every way my software could tell—and my wallet's software wasn't any off-the-shelf stuff; it had every tweak and customization Lobo could squeeze into it—the EC had given me immunity for everything I said in this room. Perfect.

I put away my wallet and looked directly at her.

"I entered the warehouse and set the charges in case I needed a distraction. What should matter to you are the weapons in the hidden basement area." I ran down for her everything I'd seen. I also reviewed my encounter with Chaplat, but I added a few important details that would, I hoped, get the EC to help me without meaning to do so. "Chaplat snagged me because he was watching the warehouse for the Followers. He let me go only because I came out empty-handed. Fortunately for me, when Dougat's team searched the building after Chaplat told them I'd been inside it, they looked everywhere but up, so they missed the charges I stuck in the ceiling." I leaned back and shrugged. "That's all of it."

"Moving to third position and maintaining contacts," Lobo said.

Midon stayed quiet for a few moments. I waited in silence with her.

Finally, she said, "Which of those groups was following the ship we had watching you here? One of them is unhappy with you."

I chuckled. "Both of them, probably. I don't, though, know whose vessel it was. Why don't you detain it and find out?"

"You cannot possibly be as stupid as that question suggests," she said. "Certainly, if you are, I have no use for you."

"You can't risk arresting any of the Followers until you can catch them in something serious, say trading arms."

"Better," she said.

"Because of the bad publicity from attacking a fast-growing cult?"

"A little, but only a little."

I leaned back and considered the situation again. "You're worried that if you move at the wrong time, they'll go to ground and you won't get their weapons."

She nodded.

"Maggie in position," Lobo said.

Damn. I didn't want Maggie to come in now; this was working out well. I coughed and rubbed my hand across my stomach as I put it back in my lap. I hoped Maggie wasn't already committed.

"What I don't understand," I said, "is why you care so much

about the stash I saw. Sure, it was a pretty good assortment, but nothing your troops couldn't handle."

She frowned and shook her head. "We used your little explosion as an excuse to send the police into the warehouse to find out what was there. The basement room was open, but it was empty. No weapons." She stared intently at me.

It took me a few seconds, but then I saw her reasoning. "You think I warned them to move the stock?"

"Perhaps."

"Why would I? I told you: I went there only to set up a diversion."

"Maggie approaching," Lobo said.

I needed her to stay away, but I couldn't risk repeating the stomach rubbing. I had to concentrate on Midon. "Besides, as I told you, though they had a lot of weapons, the stockpile wasn't enough to cause you serious problems."

"Maybe the ones you saw weren't."

I finally understood. "You think they have more weapons, a lot more, enough to stage some major action."

"We're fairly certain of that," she said. "What intelligence we can gather suggests they're planning something big, maybe an attack to hijack some commercial-grade ships, maybe a coup on one of the newer planets—maybe even here on Gash—to give them an operating base they control. Whatever they're planning, we don't want it."

I could have countered my earlier story and told her the truth, that Chaplat had no real relationship with the Followers, but I couldn't go back now. "So you want me to help you find the weapons."

"Incoming," Lobo said.

Midon nodded and opened her mouth to speak as a section of the door toppled inward.

Maggie, pulse rifle drawn, burst into the room. The falling metal knocked the female guard against the window; Maggie finished the job by kicking her in the head. Painted red, her hair in pigtails now the color of the Gash's gate, even her rifle crimson, Maggie resembled an attacking demon. She turned the weapon on Midon, but then she noticed that the other three guards had all targeted her.

I slowly raised my hands, palms facing Midon. "Let's all stay calm," I said. "My friend thought I was in trouble."

"You *are* in trouble," Midon said, "and now, so is she." She looked at Maggie. "Put down the weapon."

"Jon?" Maggie said.

"Sasha," I said, "we can finish our business without anyone getting hurt. You want me to help you catch the Followers and seize their weapons; let's talk about the best way to do that."

"And we want the boy psychic," she said, her eyes not straying from Maggie.

I couldn't allow that, but I also couldn't let her know how I felt. "What are you willing to pay me for all this work?"

"Jon, you said—" Maggie began.

I cut her off with a glance and the words "Shut up!"

Midon finally looked back at me. "Is your inept associate upset at the thought of you working for us?" she said. "I'm sorry to hear that. I was going to offer you a little money and a chance to walk away free. Now you get nothing except your life and hers, assuming you succeed. She'll remain as our guest, of course, until you do."

I'd stayed reasonably calm so far, which was hard enough when I was the only one under attack. Now Midon was threatening Maggie, and I could not allow that. I could try to distract them long enough to create nanoclouds that would break down their weapons, but I didn't have that much time. Doing that would also let everyone in this room learn way too much about me. I could hope for the time to have the nanoclouds kill all of them except Maggie, but then she'd know the truth about me. I won't let anyone know what happened to me on Aggro. I won't end up in a test lab again.

"I'm willing to talk business," I said, the anger growing in me, "but making threats is not a wise choice."

"We're done," Midon said. "You know what I want. Go get it." She turned away from me and flicked her wrist in Maggie's direction. "Guards."

Lobo had been right that he might prove to be my best option. I rubbed my stomach again as I was standing and, just to be safe, subvocalized, "Lobo, you're on."

"Moving," Lobo said.

I looked at the two guards who were converging on Maggie. "You two will stop, or you won't live to regret the mistake."

Midon turned back to me. "What in the—"

I interrupted her. "You kidnapped me. I did nothing. You threatened me. I tolerated it. Now, though, you've gone too far." The more I let out the anger, the more it took over. It lanced through my head and my body. An acid taste burned in my mouth. A buzzing grew in my head. "Look out the port."

On cue, Lobo settled from above the station into view, filling the entire display, becoming all that we could see. Staring at us was a freshly red-painted PCAV bristling with visible weapons: three sets of missiles, pulse cannons, mine launchers, and much, much more. Metal arms extending from his sides connected him to the station.

The cloth over my shoulders warmed as Lobo activated the speakers there. The vibrations when he spoke might have tickled had I not been so focused and so furious.

"These people are with me," he said. "You are not. I suggest you let them go."

Always the ham, though I agreed with his choice that hearing his voice might make clear to them that he was an independent agent capable of action even if I was dead. His flair for drama cut through my fury and calmed me a little—but only a little.

"Idle threats," Midon said. "You know as well as I do that if your ship fires even a single weapon the gate will destroy it."

"True," I said, "but when two things are connected, as your station and my ship now are, will the gate see them as separate? Will the gate stop my ship from detonating the mines it's attached to the station's hull? Are you willing to bet your life that when my ship detonates those mines and fires all of its weapons the gate will save you? I don't think anyone's ever tested a gate's ability to deal with two ships that are connected to each other and this close to it. My guess is that we'll all die."

"You would kill everyone on this station, all those innocent people, just to save the two of you?"

"Jon," Maggie said, "no, it's not worth it."

I wanted to tell her to be quiet, to control herself, but I ignored her and focused entirely on Midon. I think the real answer to her question was no. I hope it was. I like to believe my anger doesn't rule me so thoroughly. I really do.

What I answered, though, was what I needed Midon to believe, and in that moment I did everything I could to make it the truth inside me so she could not ignore it. I stared at her and said, "Yes. *You* would be choosing it, not me. If you've checked out my background, if you know even a fraction of what I've seen and done, then you shouldn't have needed to ask."

I leaned toward her until my face was within ten centimeters of hers and said again, "Yes."

I sat back in the chair and crossed my legs.

"You decide," I said. "Do my associate and I walk out of here without any further trouble?"

I paused and stared for a few seconds directly into her eyes.

"Or do we all die?"

CHAPTER 17

MIDON STARED AT ME as if trying to read my mind.

No one moved.

I waited, looking at her but not seeing her, concentrating instead on remaining still, unchanging, unwavering. The more I focused on the notion of ordering Lobo to fire and to detonate the mines, the more reasonable the idea became. Midon wasn't going to let me go even after I completed her mission, and there was no way I was ever going to deliver Manu to her. Maggie and Lobo would die, but I'd warned Maggie, and Lobo knew, as all warriors do, that your time is bound to come eventually. All the other people on board were innocent, and I'd worked much of my life to avoid collateral damage, but it had happened before and would happen again.

Besides, the anger told me, Midon deserved it. She'd used one person too many; I would *not* be another pawn for her.

Nor would I let my fury rule me, the rational part of me declared. The civilians on board this station were not collateral damage; they were real people, people with families and lovers and friends and sorrows and joys and places they needed to go and plans and futures and all the other entanglements of even a life as lonely as my own. I never wanted to be one of those soulless husks who can look upon a map or a cityscape or even an entire planet and see only numbers, not people.

No, I knew in my heart that I wouldn't do it. I shouldn't do it, and I wouldn't.

Fortunately, Midon must not have been able to read on my face any expression of this internal discussion, because she eventually said, "Okay, Jon, you and your friend are free to go."

I stood. Part of me wanted to smile and say something clever in victory, but I was afraid I'd destroy this momentary, fragile peace, so I remained silent.

"Before you leave," she said, "could I interest you in the same task as a business deal, as you'd previously suggested? You help us bust the Followers, you bring us the boy, and we all profit."

We were returning to comfortable ground. Such an arrangement would certainly complicate matters and put me in the risky position of owing something to a major government, but it also might give me a way to distract the Followers and Chaplat.

"You mentioned 'a little money' earlier," I said. "I'm certainly not interested in a little money."

"Perhaps a finder's fee," she said, "say five percent of the retail value of all the weapons you lead us to."

"Jon," Maggie said.

I glanced at her again, shook my head slightly, and looked back at Midon. Even if I wanted to do this deal—and I was by no means sure I did—I could never negotiate it with Maggie in the room. She was too scared and too involved to stay quiet.

"I don't make significant commitments with weapons pointed at me," I said. "I'll consider your offer back in my ship. I won't leave this system without letting you know my decision."

I turned and walked toward Maggie.

I heard Midon stand and knew without looking that she was furious. I had to hope the threat from Lobo would continue to keep her under control.

I knew how it would go if she let her anger rule her. The guards would aim their weapons at my back. Lobo would alert me. I'd dive for Maggie, turn, and fight them. Maybe I'd live, maybe I wouldn't, but I'd struggle for all I was worth. If I lost, Lobo would kill every last one of us.

My spine tingled with the sensation of being a target, and adrenaline coursed through me again, but I made it to the door without incident, took Maggie in tow, and left.

"First, you nearly blow up the entire station and everyone on it! And now you're going to help those people! What are you thinking?" Maggie had managed to stay quiet until we were safely inside Lobo and floating in space a few thousand kilometers from the station, but since I'd declared us safe she hadn't stop yelling. "You said you wanted to help Manu, and now you're willing to hand him over to the EC! As if they would treat him with any more care than the Followers! You're acting no better than any of them!"

I sat in silence in the pilot's couch and waited for her to run down. Her inability to follow my instructions had put us at risk on the station. Now both her level of emotion and her lack of trust annoyed me further, but I knew if I said anything I'd end up letting my anger show, and that wouldn't do either of us any good. I needed time to think, but I also needed either to drop off Maggie or to win her support for whatever path I chose.

So I listened and sat and waited.

"I could sedate her," Lobo said in my head on our usual internal frequency. "It might be good for her health, and it would certainly result in a more pleasant environment."

I shook my head slightly.

Unfortunately, Maggie spotted the motion. "So you think the EC would be better," she said. "Well, let me tell you about the EC—"

I was wrong to believe she'd stop ranting anytime soon. "No, I don't," I said, cutting her off, "and if you would please be quiet for a few minutes I could explain what's going on."

"I know what's going on."

"No, you don't, not all of it anyway."

"Then enlighten me."

"I will, but only if you'll listen."

"I'll listen, but—"

I cut her off again. "No, you won't, not right now. Sit without speaking for two minutes, just two minutes, and then I'll go over it. You use the time to calm down; I'll use it to organize my thoughts. Deal?"

The look she gave me was enough to make me want to leave the room, but after a short pause she said, "Deal."

"Thank you," Lobo said in my ear. "I shall enjoy this interlude."

I ignored him, closed my eyes, swiveled away from her, and let the stillness embrace me. The inside of Lobo smelled of nothing at all, a welcome change from the sweat- and paint-soaked atmosphere of the station. The temperature relaxed me, comfortably neither warm nor cool, and the air barely moved, Lobo managing its flow perfectly. I considered the situation.

Chaplat was after Jack and the money Jack owed him. Chaplat was using me and wouldn't stop pushing me until he got what he wanted.

Midon and the EC had the power to make my life difficult, maybe even imprison me, and no matter what she said now, she'd keep coming after me until she got what she wanted. Once the guards leaked what happened on the station, she'd lose so much face that she'd have to force me to help just to avoid being embarrassed in front of her staff.

Dougat and the Followers were the scariest of the bunch, true believers all, with greater resources than I'd imagined and, if Midon was right, more weapons than the warehouse stash suggested. I'd seen firsthand on Nana's Curse the kind of damage that heavily armed religious fanatics were capable of inflicting, and I didn't want to be responsible, even indirectly, for letting the Followers do that to the people of any other world.

I could try running, of course, but Midon and the EC would almost certainly find me, and when they did, I wouldn't enjoy the experience. The other two groups might also catch me.

Worst, if I ran I would be abandoning Jack and, more importantly, Manu. Chaplat didn't have any interest in Manu, but he'd be willing to hurt the boy if he thought it would help his cause. Both the EC and the Followers wanted very much to control Manu, and if either group caught him, he'd never be free again.

Jack might deserve whatever happened to him, but I couldn't abandon Manu to that fate. When I was sixteen, a government had dropped me on an island of discards, freaks they no longer wanted but didn't kill on the off chance something useful might emerge from the colony they'd created. Without Benny, one of those freaks and my first friend other than Jennie, I have no idea how I would have survived there. Less than two years later, when I was not yet eighteen, older than Manu but still within sight of his age, I landed in prison on Aggro.

No, I wasn't going to let that happen to Manu.

The whole mess also created an opportunity, because no one sells this many weapons, even if only from a dealer into government hands, without a great deal of money moving in the air. Midon had offered a little, but I knew she could do better.

Three organizations—one vicious, one fanatic, and one bureaucratic—held Jack, Manu, and me in their sights.

A furious redhead almost my size was attracting me one minute and hating me the next.

Money dangled in sight but out of my reach.

Lovely.

But not impossible, I realized, as the vague outline of a plan emerged. It wasn't a great plan. It certainly wasn't a straight plan; as I'd feared, Jack had managed to suck me back into running the con again. But, it was a plan. More or less.

"Ten seconds to two minutes," Lobo said. "I look forward to your performance."

"Thanks for the support," I subvocalized.

I opened my eyes and spun the chair so I was facing Maggie.

"Thanks for indulging me," I said. I didn't feel grateful, but I might need her for what was to come, and, to be fair, from her perspective I had to appear to be a jerk. I clearly couldn't trust her self-control, but I did feel her intentions were good;

in fact, the degree to which I believed in her disturbed me. Most importantly, regardless of my feelings or hers, she could be an asset in working my way out of this situation; I'd just have to manage her carefully. "I know you care about Manu," I continued, "and I hope you'll believe that I do, too. The situation is extremely complicated, but I believe I now understand the forces we have to balance to succeed." I paused, but she didn't speak, which I took as proof of her continued willingness to listen. "I haven't figured out everything, nor will I probably ever do so, because in this kind of mess improvisation is usually the name of the game. I believe, though, that I can plot a safe passage out of it for all of us."

"That's the first decent thing I've heard from you in a while," she said. "What's your idea?"

"Let me walk you through where we stand, and then I think you'll understand how difficult it is for me to do what I have to do next."

She nodded agreement. "And then?"

"And then I go back to the station."

Midon greeted me without guards this time. Carne's inner office felt bigger without them in it. She sat again behind the desk, but now she seemed farther away.

Lobo hovered just above its window display, as I'm sure she now knew. No point in not being prepared.

She wasted no time on pleasantries and started as soon as the room's door had closed behind me. "You've decided to take my offer."

"No," I said, "but I think we can reach an accord."

"We weren't negotiating," she said. "I made an offer. Take it or leave it."

"Then I misunderstood." I turned around and stepped toward the door. "Tell your colleagues I refused your ultimatum."

The door had opened before she spoke again. "I meant only that previously we weren't negotiating," she said. "I'm certainly willing to listen to alternatives if you'd like to propose some now."

Bureaucrats: Rather than risk honesty, they'll fall back on wordplay and rewritten history. I had to ignore the games, however, and focus on my goals.

I faced her. "I'll do my best find a way to," I paused, realizing her previous immunity offer did not apply now, "help you catch the Followers in an arms deal. You mentioned a little money in return; I suggest a third of the value of the weapons, with a quarter million up front for expenses and your guarantee not to interfere with my actions in any way or even be visible until I call you."

She laughed. "You may be young, but you're not that young. You have to know I could never even remotely sell that percentage to my colleagues. Seven percent, with a hundred thousand up front."

I'd done enough work for other governments and corporations to have a sense of where this would end up, and I wanted to get out of there, so I jumped ahead a few steps.

"I hate this game," I said, "and this isn't the first time I've played it. Let's save some time: The quarter-million advance is nonnegotiable, as is the requirement that the EC stay back. I'll do the rest for ten percent of the weapons' retail value." She started to speak, and I held up my hand. "Yes or no?"

She smiled. "Yes. That's acceptable, as far as it goes."

For a second I chided myself for not pushing for twelve and a half percent, because some governments will go for that, but I shook off the impulse. I needed to find Jack before he skipped the system or went deeply underground, so time was not my friend. "As far as it goes?" I said.

"What about the boy?"

I'd prepared myself for this question so I wouldn't hesitate despite my distaste for the topic, and I didn't. I answered immediately and smoothly. "Another quarter million when I point him out to you or one of your agents. You have to retrieve him; I don't kidnap." Nor, I thought but did not say, would I give her the chance to set me up for kidnapping and still end up with the boy.

"Simply to point him out? Please, Jon, don't be greedy."

"To point him out, I have to find him. If you could do it, you wouldn't need me. And, you did say he was psychic." I opened my wallet and thumbed active a quarantined reception area. "I'm ready to receive the deposit as well as contact information for people who can reach you on all the planets in this sector. Do we have a deal?"

She sat in silence for almost a minute, maybe trying to decide, maybe receiving data from her desk or advisors; I couldn't tell. Finally, she said, "We do."

A display flickered to life above the desk, she mumbled briefly, and a few seconds later my wallet glowed its receipt of the advance. I glanced at it; the software declared the contacts to be clean and sent the money on its way to a series of banks in three different cities on Gash. While on Lobo, I'd taken the time to set up a small string of accounts in EC-insured financial institutions across the planet. My wallet was bouncing the money through a few of them. When it declared the transfers complete, I closed it.

"One more thing," she said.

I waited.

"The other ship that's chasing you is your problem. If it's a Followers vessel and it attacks you, we may be able to bring them down without your help. If we do, the advance is all you get."

I wasn't happy being bait, but it didn't change anything. "Fine," I said. "I'll be in touch."

I walked out before she could say anything. I hated the thought of trafficking in children, and now I'd convinced the EC I would do just that. Even though I knew I wouldn't, I was still disgusted at myself.

I shook off the feeling and forced myself to do the necessary, not the desirable. Focus on the end. Find Jack, find Manu and save him, and figure out the rest of this mess. I had a lot to do, and much of it was still unclear.

I did, though, know one thing for certain.

It was time to go to Gash.

CHAPTER 18

WE HUNG IN SPACE five thousand kilometers above the center of the great desert of Gash as darkness slowly crawled across the planet. The gigantic expanse of red sand that filled most of this world's only large continent sparkled in the last bright light of the day. To our right, the six cities that dotted the southeastern coast glowed softly as residential and business lights turned on in preparation for the coming evening. The snowcapped mountains that stood as guards between the sprawling desert and the urban areas blazed with the perfect white light of unspoiled peaks. Way off to our left, barely visible on the southwestern coast, was the single small settlement there, Bonland, a haven for those unwilling to coexist with the bulk of the inhabitants of a planet founded and settled largely by outcasts no other place wanted.

No government cared to try to tame these people. The EC and what passed for a planetary council on Gash operated on an uneasy truce. The council paid a minimal yearly fee to the EC for gate services and the promise of military aid should some outside force be both suicidal enough and lucky enough to attack Gash and get past its disorganized but formidable defenses. The EC operated the gate station and made sure it maintained a sizable defensive force only a couple of jumps away—but never in this system unless the Gash council called for it.

Aside from those points of contact, the EC and Gash stayed away from each other. The EC had once operated a huge military base and munitions depot on the southern edge of Malzton, the planet's most dangerous city and consequently the location where the EC most wanted a show of power. As the world's population grew and the EC realized the residents were going to ignore it in the face of anything less than a full-fledged war, the EC found it cheaper to pull out and create the truce with the local council than to continue to try to police the planet. No one on Gash had been willing to tackle the huge job of maintaining the base after the EC had withdrawn everything right down to the service bots, and the EC wasn't willing to sell the facility at a low enough price to entice someone to accept the challenge of remaking it, so nature was slowly crawling over the vast expanse of permacrete tarmac and buildings.

The six cities on Gash also boasted several of the largest open-air markets I'd ever seen, with one, the sprawling commercial zone on the southeastern corner of Nickres, actually visible from even our altitude. Nickres, the southernmost settlement, had fostered a political climate favorable to trade, and now its vast market was the place to go for the strangest merchandise the planet had to offer, from racing vessels to extreme sports gear, and from tools to self-assembling housing units.

Its large percentage of political and religious fanatics, outcasts, and fringe dwellers gave Gash the dubious honor of being the best place within half a dozen jumps to hold a serious argument on any aspect of political theory, provided, of course, that you came to the discussion well armed. Gash juries had acquitted more than one defendant of murder charges on the basis of excessively stupid political provocation.

"It's a lovely place," Lobo said as he was concluding my briefing, "that features so many aspects of humankind at its finest."

"Jack is there," I said, "so we have to assume Manu is, too, which means we're going as well. It's not my idea of a vacation, but we have work to do."

"Where to first?" Lobo said.

"What's happening with our friends?"

We'd stayed within the gate's sphere of influence so we could check on our pursuers while the gate would still protect us from any attack. The EC ship that had followed us previously had started after us and then quickly returned to the gate; Midon must have been a bit slow in relaying her orders.

The second ship, the mystery follower, had unfortunately remained on our tail. It was sticking close to the gate right now, but it adjusted its position as necessary to keep us in the center of its scanning range.

"No change," Lobo said. "It moves as we do."

"Milspec?"

"To the best of my ability to tell from the data available," Lobo said, "no. It appears to be a reasonably conventional commercial craft with some external weapon augmentations."

"Can you outrun it?"

"Unless its drive mechanisms contain surprises, yes."

"Take us down at normal speed," I said, "and fly along the coast slowly from south to north."

"In progress," Lobo said. We accelerated gently toward the southeastern tip of the continent. "Why did you ask if I could outrun the other craft if you were going to tell me to go slowly?"

"Do you two always talk this way?" Maggie said.

I'd kept Lobo's briefing and the rest of conversation in normal audio so she could follow it, but now I was regretting that choice. Though I had to admit it was a fair question, I didn't need another person picking at me.

"Basically, yes," I said, "except when we're in the middle of an engagement. You'll see an immediate change if we need to get serious." I considered the question further. "I blame it all on Lobo's emotive logic programmers. They combined great skill with a really bad attitude."

"May I point out—" Lobo said.

I cut him off. "Enough from both of us. We're going slowly so we can disguise our search for Jack's transmitter. I want the people in that other ship to think we're trying to make them show themselves. It's even acceptable if they figure out that we're searching. We just have to find Jack but not let our pursuers know we did. So, we'll fly low enough that Lobo can scan the cities for a signal from Jack as we pass over them. I asked about speed in case the pursuers try something odd and we end up needing to run."

"In scanning range of Nickres," Lobo said, apparently satisfied.

"Take us along the coast," I said. "Move as slowly as necessary to allow the transmitter two iterations of its max delay; I don't want to repeat this maneuver. Weave as if you're trying to see whether anyone is following us."

"How stupid would we have to be to check for them that way?" Lobo said. "All we need to do to spot them is maintain a three-sixty surveillance zone and correlate the movements of all nearby vessels with our flight path, as I did."

"Not all ships possess control systems of your intelligence," I said.

"None do," Lobo said, pride evident in his voice.

His comment surprised me, because though I knew Lobo was arrogant, he was also not given to errors of fact. I'd assumed all PCAV AIs of a given generation were roughly the same, and Lobo was a couple of generations behind the state of the art. Newer ships should certainly be more capable. I wondered if something was wrong, either with his logic or his emotional systems, or if Lobo really did possess secrets I should know. I didn't want to pursue any of these issues in front of Maggie, however, so I pushed past his comment to distract her.

Facing her, I said, "And more importantly, it's often helpful if opponents underestimate us."

"How do we know the ship following us isn't a friend, or maybe an EC escort? You said Midon thinks you're working for her."

"I *am* working for her," I said, "just not the way she thinks. It's unlikely the EC would put one ship on every other world we entered and two here, and I believed her when she said she didn't know who was following us. If it contained a friend, even Jack, it would have announced itself by now, because we're far enough away from the EC that it could shoot a pinpoint encrypted burst to us without attracting much attention."

I stared at the display in which Lobo showed the ship tracking us from farther out in space, not quite following our path but always staying within the same narrow distance band from us. "No," I said, "it's definitely keeping an eye on us, and we have to assume it's not friendly."

We crawled for almost ten minutes on a zigzag path that took us from south of the massive market on the southeastern edge of the city to beyond its jagged northern boundary. Nickres, like the other cities on Gash, sat like a ragged drop of mixed paint in the middle of broad strokes of strong, pure colors: white mountaintops to the west, rich green forest north and south, and a thin strip of light gray sand giving way to deep blue ocean on the east.

We intercepted nothing from Jack's transmitter. Jack might have removed it, of course, and it's always possible the device was malfunctioning or not strong enough to reach us, but until we'd exhausted the possibility that it could lead us to him we had to keep trying.

We headed at the same leisurely pace and on a similarly convoluted path up the coast.

Our shadow stayed with us, no longer trying to match our course but instead moving slowly along the straight line that ran through the center of our meandering route. It didn't close the gap between us, so at least at this point it was more interested in monitoring us than catching or attacking us.

After the first five minutes, I sat in the pilot's couch, closed my eyes, and went inside myself, partly because it's always a good idea to rest when you can and partly to avoid Maggie's questions. If I gave her the chance, she'd quite reasonably ask what we'd do if we found Jack via the transmitter, what we'd do if we didn't, how we'd handle each and every contingency. She wanted to help, so she wanted to understand, but I had no answers for her. I didn't even believe it was smart to try to formulate answers yet, because at this stage, when we knew nothing for certain about Jack's location, any answers I reached would be preconceptions that could limit our thinking and lower our probability of success. We had to find him, then react to his location. When you're on the sharp end of any action, even a seemingly simple search, you have to improvise and respond to local data more than the mission planners ever anticipated.

The only people who believe in perfect plans in complex situations are those who've never had to execute those plans.

On a pass above the heart of Malzton, Lobo announced, "Signal received. Jack's transmitter is here."

I stared at the image of the city in the display. A sprawling, low-slung place, it and the empty ex-EC military base on its southern border squatted like scar tissue on the face of the land between the mountains that ringed it on three sides and the ocean to the east. Semi-urban growth sprawled across what had once been a beautiful valley, with the snow from the mountains on its western and northern borders stretching almost to the city's edge and the ocean full of ships both commercial and pleasure. Jack had chosen the most obvious place to hide if you knew him, because he'd be most comfortable among others who cared little about conventional rules, but it was also the most dangerous location for anyone tracking him.

"Now if we could only be sure the thing was still in Jack," I said, "we'd be able to move to the next step."

"It is definitely in someone," Lobo said, "or, to be more precise, something with a human temperature."

"Explain," I said.

"I added a sensor to the transmitter," he said. "If its ambient temperature is within a few degrees of human normal, it emits a signal of a different shape than if it is not."

"Even if Jack found the transmitter," I said, "he'd be highly unlikely to know he needed to put it in another person. He'd destroy it or leave it somewhere else as a decoy."

"That was my opinion as well," Lobo said.

"Great work," I said. "Now, we have to keep convincing our pursuers we haven't found Jack. Maintain this pattern until we're north of the last human settlement, then head west to

Bonland. Run fast enough to make them have to chase us directly, but not fast enough to lose them. Repeat the pattern over Bonland."

"Executing," Lobo said. "What happens next?"

"Could you drop me in Malzton without the pursuers knowing it?"

"Unless you literally mean 'drop' or the other ship is extremely incompetent, no. To let you out, we'd have to land, at which point they would at a minimum assume Malzton was of interest. We could, of course, employ our current tactic and leave you in every city, Malzton last, but that process would consume a great deal of time."

I didn't want to burn that many days, at least not while I could think of any other, faster options. With both Dougat's and Chaplat's groups after me and with an uneasy partnership with the EC, each day that passed increased the probability of somebody nabbing me.

Better to start facing some of these problems directly, while I still maintained some semblance of control over the situation.

"We're not going to land in Malzton or any other city," I said, "at least not yet. We need to know what group is tracking us."

"Your talent for stating the obvious is indisputable," Lobo said, "but of dubious value."

"So let's do something not quite so obvious," I said. "After we finish in Bonland, let's go deal with our pursuers."

CHAPTER 19

WHAT EXACTLY DO YOU mean by 'deal with' them?" Lobo said. "Do you want me to kill them? Based on the data I can glean about the ship that's following us, that shouldn't be difficult. Finding Jack would also certainly be simpler if we first eliminated Dougat and Chaplat, and the pursuing vessel is probably from one of them. You've already portrayed both men as dangerous leaders of violent groups, so striking first should nicely pave our way forward."

"Is it serious?" Maggie said. "You'd just kill whatever people are in that ship?"

As anger surged in me, what I thought was: You never *just* kill anyone. You do it because it was the best option available to you at that time, and then it stays with you forever, a darkness that infects you and fuses with your core. Even with that cost, however, sometimes it is what you have to do—or, at least, at times it has been what *I* have had to do. Over the last almost fourteen decades since Jennie fixed my brain and I left Pinkelponker, I've participated in terrible acts of violence that the mentally challenged boy I once was could never have conceived were possible. I couldn't forget any of them. I wish I could convince myself otherwise, but the scariest truth is that given the same circumstances and the same timing, I'd make the same decisions. I'd do it all again, even knowing what it would cost me, because sometimes killing is the best of the small, bad set of available options.

What I said to her was "No, I'm not planning to kill or even fight anyone. I don't anticipate a conflict with this ship. If it intended to attack us, it would have done so when we were flying along the coastline, probably on the ends of the flight arcs that left us over uninhabited territories. Whoever is in that ship wants us to know we're being followed but doesn't intend to confront us. I need to know who's doing this, and why."

She considered my answer for almost a minute before she spoke. "I'm sorry I keep doubting you and asking what I'm sure seem like stupid questions. I've never been in situations like these before. What can I do to help?"

"What you're told, quickly and without hesitation."

I regretted both my answer and my tone the moment I said the words. I wasn't wrong—what I'd said was indeed the best thing she could do to assist me—but she was trying, really trying, and because I was angry and, I had to admit, because I found her attractive and didn't know what to do about that feeling, I'd snapped at her.

"Fair enough," she said. "I probably deserve that."

Before I could figure out the right words to say, Lobo interrupted.

"Scan on Bonland complete. Course?"

"Take us to the desert," I said, "fast. Let the other ship close the gap, then pick up speed, and repeat until it can't keep up any longer. Then slow down. I want to show them we could get away but won't do so."

"Where in the desert?" Lobo said.

"Somewhere you can land with a mountain or a very large rock formation to your back."

"But not so close a missile into the rocks could bury me, of course," Lobo said, with more than a trace of sarcasm in his voice.

"Of course." I couldn't win. If I spelled out the details, I annoyed him. If I didn't, he picked at me. Sarcasm wasn't a manner of speaking with Lobo; it was a way of life.

I refused to take the bait any longer. "What's your ETA to landing?"

"Eighty-one minutes," Lobo said.

I faced Maggie. "You wanted to help; it's time. Let's get you into an active-fiber camo suit and choose a suitably impressive weapon."

"Why do we need a human with a gun when we have me?" Lobo said. "I possess more than enough firepower for such a meeting."

Maggie might stop asking questions, though I'd come to doubt she ever would, but I was certain Lobo would not. I sighed. "We don't *need* it," I said. "We're doing it for the effect it may cause. I want to meet face-to-face with the person running the other vessel. Standing between two armed ships is too abstract for some people; the threat doesn't punch them in the gut. Seeing someone hold you in their sights is often an entirely more visceral experience."

Maggie's eyes widened, and I could tell she wanted to talk, but she didn't.

"Relax," I said, smiling and chuckling a little, "I doubt you'll have to worry about shooting anyone, because if anything goes really wrong, we'll all be dead before you can fire."

She didn't find the battlefield humor amusing.

I stood in the red sand in front of Lobo and waited. The heat exchangers in the armored, active-fiber, camo jumpsuit did their best, but I was still sweating profusely in the pounding heat of the desert afternoon. I could have saved a bit of weight by going with a less capable garment, but if anyone started firing I wanted to give myself every chance of blending with the sand and getting away alive. The odds of my survival were, of course, extremely low should Lobo and the other ship start exchanging fire, but I'd learned long ago that you do the best you can to improve your chances even if all your options are unlikely to succeed.

Lobo's repeated open hailing faded into the background as I stared at the vast expanse of red before me. The sand was fine enough to seep into everything but coarse enough that the very slight breeze didn't stir up dust clouds. The air smelled crisp and clean, almost sterilized but with a faint hint of dust lying right under the sensory surface. The mesa behind us was a duller, darker version of the desert in front of me. For as far as I could see in any direction, even at the limits of the telescopic lenses of my mirrored glasses, only sand and rock filled my view. The land was unspoiled by people but also dead, no signs of plants or animals. I assumed that this desert, like most of them, harbored seeds of life lurking under its surface and waiting for moisture to awaken them, but unless something went very wrong today, they would continue to sleep.

"The ship has acknowledged the signal and agreed to a meeting," Lobo said over the machine frequency. "ETA five minutes. I must say that I don't like sitting here, presenting an easy target."

"As I said earlier, if they'd wanted to engage us, they would have. Besides, they must know that even if they have the fire-power to destroy us, before the weapons could reach us you'd unleash enough havoc on them to turn them into rubble."

"Dust," Lobo said, "not rubble. Attacking after agreeing to a truce merits a special level of retribution."

"Fair enough." I spoke aloud now, covering my mouth as if coughing. I had to assume the other ship was watching. "Incoming."

Maggie's voice, mutated by the comm unit into a genderless whisper, fluttered in my ear. "Set," she said.

The other ship flew directly at us, then landed slowly, nose facing Lobo, fifty meters away. As it settled to the ground, four cannons sprouted from its sides. They didn't fit the pleasure craft's profile, which I suppose was exactly the point of the customization.

"That's it?" Lobo said. "Want me to show them something a bit more impressive?"

"No," I subvocalized. "We wait."

A hatch opened in the front right side of the craft, and one man walked out. He headed toward me at a slow, comfortable pace. I stayed where I was as the glasses zoomed on him.

Dougat. He'd tried for business casual, wanting to appear unaffected by his surroundings, but he'd underestimated the desert and was already sleek with sweat. I fought the urge to smile at his discomfort and remained still.

He stopped five meters away, studied me for a few seconds, and nodded. "It makes sense it's you," he said. "You've cost me a lot. Maybe I should kill you now."

"Go," I subvocalized.

Maggie rose from her hiding place twenty meters to my left. The sand poured off her as she came to a kneeling position, the sniper rifle pointed directly at Dougat. Covered completely in a full-body camo surveillance suit, nothing of her was visible. All Dougat could tell was that a person was holding a gun on him.

"If you try," I said, "two things will happen. First, my colleague will make sure your head explodes before anything else goes boom. Second, my PCAV will obliterate your ship and everyone in it."

"We all have to die sometime," he said, working for nonchalance. I focused on his face, and the glasses zoomed. Tension stretched his skin.

"True," I said, "but that time doesn't have to be today. I only want to talk. Behave, and you'll walk away." He flinched at the command, clearly a man more accustomed to giving orders than to receiving them, but he also visibly relaxed when I lowered the threat level. I was amazed he was gullible enough to believe someone talking to him from this position, though he was lucky because I truly didn't want to kill him. "You've been following us. I want to know why, and I want it to stop."

Dougat nodded again and looked more confident, a negotiator back on familiar ground. "You took away Manu Chang. I want him back. You also blew up my warehouse and stole a fortune in gemstones from my institute and thus cost me an enormous amount of money. Despite the magnitude of those losses, I'm willing to consider the boy as reparations for all of it; hand him over, and I'll call us even."

"I don't have the boy or the man, and I don't know anything

about any stones," I said. "I helped the two of them escape because that's what they were going to pay me to do. I'm hired help; that's all." I relaxed my stance slightly, feigning nonchalance. "As for owing you money, I don't know what you're talking about." I stared at him as I spoke, keeping my face neutral, glad he couldn't see my eyes.

I zoomed on his. His pupils dilated momentarily as he pondered my statement. He didn't believe me, but he also wasn't positive I was lying. Good. A shred of doubt is a partially open door. I now had to persuade him to let me inside.

He stared at me for several more seconds before speaking, clearly considering his strategy. "A source of mine in the EC says otherwise," he finally said. "He told me some people intercepted you exiting my warehouse, and he said you planted the charges that caused the explosion."

I answered quickly, because hesitation now would undo my story. "Oh, I tried to get into the place; he has that much right. I couldn't find a way in, however, without doing so much damage that you'd know I'd entered—as I'm sure you're aware, because you must have surveillance cameras all through the building." His eyes widened slightly again; Lobo had done his job and left no traces of my visit in their surveillance system. For all Dougat knew, I'd never been there. Only his source's story put me there. If that person was in the EC, then unless he'd told him or her about the contents of the warehouse, the informant possessed no more information about the weapons than Midon did. The only people who knew for sure I'd been in the building were the members of Chaplat's team, and Chaplat had shown no sign of knowing anything about the weapons.

Chaplat.

The weapons.

I suddenly caught a glimpse of a way out of this whole mess, a path that might let me save Manu, get all three groups off my back, and maybe even help Jack escape in the bargain, not that his safety should be my problem.

I crossed my arms, then relaxed, a man struggling with and then making a decision. "Some people did roust me as I was leaving the area," I said, "but all they wanted was to know if I could supply them with weapons."

"The EC?" Dougat appeared worried despite his mention of his source.

I smiled, now a friend of Dougat's sharing a secret, and shook my head. "No, no. Some local gang leader."

"Bakun Chaplat?"

"Yeah. Any idea why he thought I had an arsenal?"

A rustle in the sand to my right caught my attention. Moving against the slight breeze, it crept closer. I zoomed in on it, spotted the tiny legs, and relaxed. If it proved to be a listening device, Lobo would alert me when it began to transmit. If any of this conversation made it past Lobo's interference, it would have to be to someone with considerable resources. I'd deal with that problem later. For now, I'd treat a bit of life in the sand as a nice omen.

Dougat pondered the news about the gang leader, then moved past it. "None whatsoever. He runs a lot of the shipping and receiving there, but he leaves us alone, and we don't cause him any trouble." He shook his head. "It doesn't matter in any case. Let's get back to the main issue: I want the boy, Manu Chang. Where is he?"

"I don't know," I said, letting a little anger show in my tone. "I wish I did."

He finally took the earlier bait. "You said they were *going* to pay you. I take it they did not."

"No," I said, "they didn't, and I don't like when clients welsh on their deals."

Dougat chuckled. "We now have two things in common: Neither of us likes doing business with people who don't deliver on their promises, and we both want to find the boy."

"No, only one thing," I said. "I don't care where the boy is. He wasn't my client. I'm after the man. He's the one who owes me."

"But you said you wished you knew where the boy was."

Laying down a good con is like getting someone started on a painting: You supply as few lines as possible, and let them draw the rest. Dougat was making all the right connections. "Because my guess is that if I find the boy, I'll also find the man."

"I believe you're right," he said, "so perhaps we could work together on the search. I have no need for the man."

"I don't cooperate," I said, "and the boy clearly has value, so if the man can't pay, I'll need the boy." I nodded in the direction of his ship. "Besides, your team is so obviously inept at pursuit that they'll spook those two before we can find them."

Dougat sighed. "We appeared incompetent because we didn't care if you noticed us." Tension around his eyes showed he was lying, saving face for his team because they were monitoring us. "That said, I can see why it might be advantageous for you to work alone. Perhaps you could do that work for me."

"And what would you have me do?"

"Deliver the boy and the gemstones that he and the man took."

"Those gems must be pretty valuable if you're willing to pay me to get them, which is odd, because you also said you'd be willing to trade them for the boy."

He *was* a believer: His eyes drifted up and to the left as for a few seconds his mind strayed elsewhere. "That I did," he said. "But you claimed you didn't have them. As for their value, both are worth a very great deal, but the boy matters more than you can imagine—though not in monetary terms, that's not the real issue here."

"Money may not matter to you," I said, "but it's important enough to me that I think I'll just find the boy and the gems and sell them myself. From what you're saying, I should be able to get a very good price for them."

He focused on me again. "We can't let that happen. No one else must have the boy. You really believe you can find him?"

I nodded. "As long as you back off and let me work."

Dougat shook his head. "We'll keep our distance, but there's no chance we'll let you out of our sight. What about the gemstones?"

I paused as if considering whether the terms would work. I needed him to draw one more line, and so far he was missing it. Sweat was pouring off me as the suit's cooling unit failed to meet the desert's challenge. The heat wasn't the only reason for my discomfort, I realized: It had been a very long time since I'd run a long con, and I'd grown rusty and nervous. I ignored my feelings and concentrated on throwing Dougat a bit more bait. "You have to assume those stones are gone, because Jack will have fenced them as quickly as possible. As for you following me, that's simply unacceptable. Your presence will at best slow me and at worst mess up everything. I need to move quickly. I don't want to spend any more time in this region of space than I have to."

I zoomed again on his eyes. A slight smile tugged at his face as he finally made the secondary connection.

"I take it Mr. Chaplat is part of your motivation for departure."

I nodded slightly. "Somehow my client—my former client," I said, almost spitting the words, "convinced Chaplat that he could supply weapons. When my client fled, Chaplat assumed I could produce the same product. I can't; it's not what I do. When Chaplat learned I couldn't, well, let's just say that his reaction wasn't pleasant."

Dougat finally got it. He paused as if thinking hard, then said, "What if you could sell Chaplat what he needs?"

I leaned forward slightly, as if I were the one hooked. "I told you: I can't."

"But I can," Dougat said. "You find out what weapons he needs, and I'll get them. You give me the boy, I trade you the weapons, and you sell them to Chaplat. You hand me what Chaplat pays you, minus a finder's fee for yourself, of course." He spread his arms wide, a peacemaker content in his success. "Everyone wins, and we all happily go our separate ways."

"Chaplat wants a lot," I said, "and a wide variety."

"The boy is worth a great deal to me." Dougat stared at me, a man with a strong hand trying to figure how much he can throw into the pot without scaring off his opponent. "But even the weapons deal works out well. You keep a percentage, say ten percent, of the total sale price, but I pocket the rest of the proceedings. We all win."

I turned my head a bit to the right and looked slightly down, pondering the deal but keeping his face in view from the corner of my eye. I needed to push it far enough that Dougat knew this was his idea and I was having trouble adjusting to it. Finally, I looked directly at him and said, "You stay way back, and I pick the time and place for the exchange. If, and this is still far from done, *if* I can make this happen, I keep twenty-five percent of the purchase price."

He answered so quickly I knew he was either lying or willing to sacrifice an enormous amount to get Manu; that large a fee would eat a huge chunk of his profit. "Fair enough. Do we have a deal?"

I waited a few seconds, then said, "Yes. I'll signal you when I have news."

"I'll be waiting," Dougat said. "But if you need to leave this region, don't make me wait too long." He turned and walked back to his ship.

As soon as he entered, it closed the hatch and took off, flying directly backward, all weapons trained at us until it turned east and jetted out of view.

I realized I was smiling slightly. I might be able to pull this off after all.

I had to find Jack, get Manu, persuade them both to do what I wanted, meet again with Chaplat and convince him I could deliver Jack without actually doing it, keep Midon at bay, and not get hurt by anyone in the process.

My smile faded, and again I felt overwhelmed.

I had a notion, not a plan. A notion is a long way from a plan.

I had to figure out exactly what I was going to do.

When the job is too big to handle, break it into smaller, more manageable pieces. Everything I was considering included Jack and Manu, so my next task was to find them. All I had to do was sneak into Malzton without Dougat or Midon noticing, and then locate Jack, one of the toughest men to track I've ever known. The transmitter would simplify the hunt by leading me to him, but finding him would be only the beginning.

Of course, I had to do all this while under the watchful surveillance of a religious fanatic and the biggest government in this region of space, with a gang leader ready to make an appearance at any moment.

I couldn't wait to hear Lobo's helpful comments on this new situation.

CHAPTER 20

"I DON'T RECALL you mentioning Chaplat wanting weapons," Lobo said as we rose into the sky and headed into orbit over the east coast of the continent.

"I didn't, because he doesn't."

"So you want the weapons?" Lobo said, this time with a trace of interest in his tone. "Exactly what does Dougat have that we might be able to use?"

"No, I don't want anything from his arsenal." I sighed.

Maggie jumped into the conversation. "You've promised Manu to another group," she said, "the very people you helped rescue him from. You told me you'd protect him."

"And I will!" I didn't mean to raise my voice, but the two of them were driving me crazy. I paced back and forth. "I'd hope you'd trust my intentions by now."

"I'm trying to," she said, "but all I've heard so far are promises that contradict each other and deals with groups I fear. It all makes me nervous."

"Then don't trust me," I said. "Leave. Tell me where you want us to take you, and we will."

She stared at me, her frustration apparent. "I already said I'm staying. I also said I want to help. But if you'll stop living completely inside your head and look at this from my

perspective, I think you'll see that your actions are both difficult to understand and not exactly designed to boost my
faith in you."

At one level, I understood that she was right. Almost everything she'd seen me do suggested I was an untrustworthy con
man telling everyone what they wanted to hear, and to some
degree I was; I had to be. My anger, though, drowned out that
understanding. Dangerous people were chasing me. Lobo was
nagging me. Maggie didn't trust me and wouldn't stop bothering
me. I wanted to scream at the world to go away and leave me
alone, but the only way that could happen would be if I left it
alone, if I ran from this planet and this region and kept running until I was far enough away and long enough gone that
neither the EC, Dougat, nor Chaplat would be willing to expend
the time, money, and energy it would take to find me.

The problem was, leaving meant abandoning Manu to Midon
or Dougat, who would imprison and use the boy.

I still couldn't let that happen.

I took a deep breath and let it out slowly. "You wanted to
help," I said, striving for control but from the look in Maggie's
eyes not achieving it. "So help. Stop questioning, and help me
figure out how to solve the problem in front of me."

"You want solutions?" Lobo said. "I have one: Let's follow
that ship and blast it out of the sky. I've studied it, and we
can take it with little to no damage to us. Remove Dougat,
and one of the problems goes away."

"I've already told you many times that I don't kill if I can
avoid it. Plus, your solution would accomplish nothing, because
some lieutenant of Dougat's would take his place and continue
to pursue Manu." We also get no money if we don't deliver
Dougat, I thought, but I didn't say it aloud. For all that she
claimed to want a cut of any proceeds, Maggie wouldn't understand that if I was going to help Manu and had an opportunity
to make some money in the process, I would take it. If I had
to choose between Manu and the money, I'd of course pick
Manu, but I didn't see that as a choice I had to make. Maybe
too many years of working on too many strange cases has left

me colder than I should be, but these people were costing me time and money, so I might as well try to profit a little.

"Fine," Lobo said, "though my offer is always open. So, what's the problem you want to solve?"

"We know Jack is in Malzton," I said, "so we have to assume Manu is there as well. I need to find Jack to find Manu. I can't let either Midon or Dougat know where Jack is, or they'll also use him to find Manu. So, I need to get into Malzton without any of them noticing."

"Commercial transport is out," Lobo said, "because Midon would be able to track you. The harbor is too busy for us to be sure you could make a water approach undetected. Worse, it's commercial enough that at least the EC is bound to be monitoring it carefully. Mountains ring the rest of the city. If we stop anywhere, anyone watching us is going to notice. I see no safe entry point."

"It sounds like you'd have to be a wave or a snowball to be able to get there undetected," Maggie said. Her shoulders slumped. "Are we going to have to risk leading them to Manu?"

I stopped pacing as her words hit me. "Now you're being helpful!" I said, smiling at Maggie. "Excellent!"

"I am?" she said. "How?"

I shook my head. "Later." I was working it out, but I didn't have it yet. I looked at her more closely. "Stand next to me."

She did, a puzzled look on her face.

"Lobo," I said, "how close to my size is Maggie?"

"A few centimeters shorter, a significant amount less broad in the shoulders, quite a bit lighter, and obviously rather differently shaped," he said.

I studied her more. "Close enough for what I need," I said.

Maggie started to ask me a question, but I spoke first. "Later, as I said. I promise." I headed for my tiny room; I needed quiet to gather data and work this out. "Lobo, take us to orbit over Nickres and find a commercial hangar and refueling facility there, something on the south side as close as you can get to the big market. I need to do some research before we land."

"Executing," Lobo said. "I've piped the information on a few candidate locations to your quarters."

"Won't Dougat follow us to Nickres?" Maggie said.

"Of course," I said, "but it won't matter, because Jack's not there."

"So why are we going there?" she said.

I stepped into the room, stopped in the doorway, and looked back at her.

"To park Lobo," I said, "if only for a little bit."

"Why?" Maggie and Lobo said in unison.

I ignored that question. "And to get you some rest," I said to Maggie.

"What?" she said. "I don't understand."

"And so I can go shopping," I said as I went into my quarters and the door shut behind me.

What good are friends if you can't occasionally torment them as much as they torment you?

CHAPTER 21

YOU COULDN'T HAVE chosen a hangar that would cover me completely?" Lobo said.

"This one shields all of you that the maintenance crew will be repairing," I said, "so it's all we need. Besides, it's cheaper than the others."

"What maintenance crew?" Lobo said. "What repairs? Unless I'm severely damaged, which I'm not, I'm self-maintaining. And I know you can afford a better facility than this rattletrap."

The problem with keeping Lobo in the dark is that he can never see it as a game. He stays so serious that in short order he sucks all the joy from any teasing. "The maintenance crew is entirely for show, as is the hangar's low price. I want all the people who are watching us to wonder if you're a real or faux PCAV, and I also want them to think I need money. The first might give us a momentary advantage should the action heat up, and the second helps convince them I'm motivated to help them."

In the three quiet seconds that followed, I wondered if Lobo was figuring out how to generalize my approach into more information about manipulating people or if he was just being petulant. I could never tell.

"I agree that's reasonable," he said.

His quiet acceptance of the strategy caught me off guard.

Before I could say anything in appreciation, Maggie came out of my quarters.

Frowning, she spun slowly and said, "How do I look?"

Wearing a pair of black pants of mine, one of my active-fiber shirts, and a wide-brimmed sun hat, as long as she looked down and used the brim to shield her face, from a couple of meters away she resembled a thinner me. From any distance at which a surveillance team would be likely to be following her, she should pass as me.

"Perfect," I said. I stood beside her and said, "Lobo."

Our image snapped into focus on the wall in front of us. Maggie raised her head and studied it carefully. "You really think this will fool anyone?"

"Not anyone who gets close to you," I said, "but that's fine. Neither Dougat nor Midon will want to interfere with me at this stage, so they'll keep tabs on you from a distance. You keep moving, and they'll think they're following me."

"And where will you be?"

We'd been on the ground for five minutes. Lobo had backed into the hangar, and the crew I'd contracted was awaiting orders inside. We didn't have time for this discussion; she had to get moving. The hangar was fully shielded against all forms of scanning, but none of those protections would stop our watchers from wondering what was happening if we stayed here too long. "I told you: shopping." I held up my hand to stop her from asking more questions. "I'll explain later, but for this to work you need to get moving *now*. Do you remember the plan?"

"Of course," she said. "It's not exactly complicated."

"Then follow it, and stay in regular contact with us until you reach your destination. Is your comm link with Lobo working?"

She blinked a few times and nodded. "Yes. Perfectly."

"Then head off." I pointed toward the rear. "Lobo, let her out."

Lobo opened a hatch. Maggie stepped out of it and onto the permacrete hangar floor. Two of the maintenance people came toward her as the hatch immediately closed.

I watched on Lobo's display as she spoke briefly with them,

then thumbed them money from the limited wallet I'd given her. They nodded and walked out of the back of the hangar with her in their midst. If our pursuers were monitoring us at all carefully, they'd spot what they would assume was me trying to sneak into Nickres in the middle of a repair team that hadn't been near Lobo long enough to have done anything useful.

"Any problems monitoring her?" I said.

"None," Lobo said. "Both the tracker we gave her and the one I implanted are operational."

"My turn," I said. "See you late tonight."

Lobo opened the rear hatch.

I walked out and immediately went to the hangar's rear corner and behind a blast wall; one of the reasons we'd chosen this facility was that it was set up for craft of all types and so offered multiple hiding places.

Lobo took off. He flew slowly until he was far beyond the landing zone and so high he resembled a toy in the sky, then he accelerated rapidly out of sight.

"Dougat's ship?" I said.

"Touched down in a public section of the landing port about a klick away from you," he said. "Two teams of three have left it and arc on parallel courses toward where Maggie was."

I hit a cuff comm switch. "Maggie?"

"Here," she said.

"Change your route now."

"I'll reach the right turn in about ten meters."

"Head west to the SleepSafe as quickly as you can," I said. SleepSafe hotels were the resting place of choice for the paranoid and the hunted. One of the few corporations with franchises active in every major sector of space, its buildings were as close to neutral zones as you could find. In anything short of a war, no one would bother you in a SleepSafe. You couldn't enter with weapons of any sort. Each room had independently fed monitors of all entrances and building surfaces, as well as at least one private exit chute. The chutes ran through each hotel's thick, armored walls to equally reinforced underground tubes. Those tubes employed two-meter-long movable sections to constantly recombine and shift their destinations. You couldn't know where your exit would dump you, but neither could anyone pursuing you. All chutes fed to areas far enough from the buildings that only a very large force could simultaneously cover all the possible routes.

I switched us all to the same circuit. "Dougat's status?"

"His ship is airborne again," Lobo said. "His men are still on their original courses."

"So they've lost track of Maggie?"

"It would appear so."

"Excellent. Maggie, ETA to the hotel?"

"Another three blocks."

"Lobo, distance from Dougat's men to Maggie?"

"Over three hundred meters and growing," he said. "They're still following the previous course."

"Maggie, I'm heading out," I said. "Lobo will monitor your position and alert me if for any reason you don't make it to the SleepSafe. I'm going silent until I'm well into the crowd."

"Do I really have to spend the whole time in that place? It makes me feel so useless."

I hate explaining strategy in the middle of an action, but by doing so I increased the probability that Maggie would obey my orders. "Yes, you have to stay there," I said, "and you're not useless; far from it. By distracting our pursuers, you're playing an incredibly important role. They think you're me, and if they figure out where you are, they'll assume you're waiting for Jack. You're buying me the time I need."

"To go shopping," she said with more than a little annoyance in her voice.

"Later," I said. "Signing off." I reduced the line to Lobo and me. "All set?"

"No," he said. "We have a new problem."

"What?"

"Another ship is following me."

"Dougat or EC?"

"Probably neither. It's not the milspec vessels we've seen the EC use, and it appears to have found us by following Dougat.

I wouldn't have noticed it had it not abruptly changed its course to track me."

"How did you miss it earlier?"

"I was sweeping for obvious pursuers and stopped when I found them," Lobo said. "I miscalculated in not checking a broader region of nearby airspace, but doing so would have consumed considerable sensor and calculation power."

Another ship. Great. Either Dougat had a second, independent group after me, Midon had reneged and run a quiet tail, or someone else was also after me.

I didn't have the time to deal with this now. As long as Lobo, Maggie, and I weren't at risk, my plan had to remain the same.

"Does the other ship appear to be tracking Maggie or watching the hangar?"

"No," Lobo said. "I've led it over a hundred kilometers northeast of Nickres. It appears to be following only me, but from a great distance and with considerably more skill than Dougat."

"Then I'm not going to worry about it unless you tell me I need to do so. Just don't let it get too close to you."

"I could destroy it," Lobo said.

"No. Run evasive maneuvers, and we should be fine."

"Executing," Lobo said, "though blowing it out of the sky would be a simpler solution."

"Signing off," I said, ignoring his comment. He'd alert me if any trouble headed my way.

I walked out of the front of the hangar, took two rights, and headed behind it and into the commercial district that butted up against the landing facility. The scent of fuel in the air morphed gradually into the moist odors of street food and crowds of sweaty people.

I strolled into the crowd and let it swallow me, enjoying the sheer normality of the action, just another cell passing through the arteries of the urban organism on my way to its heart, the enormous outdoor shopping zone.

CHAPTER 22

THE SMELLS AND SOUNDS of the market washed over me long before I could see it.

Food hit me first: barbecuing meat, fresh fish, the sharp bite of local chilies, and the sweetness of fruit being cut open and served on the spot. A subtler layer of metal and rich local woods backfilled the food odors. Enveloping it all was the strong scent of too many humans sharing too small a space.

The storm of sound initially lacked such distinction, all the noises blending into the din of street commerce. As I listened more closely, I could make out the screech of metal work and the rhythm of shouted bargaining, bursts of laughter and screams of anger, and many, many snatches of music competing loudly for attention.

I'd stuck to small avenues so far, but as I drew closer to my destination the road I was walking widened, even the streets doing all they could to pour customers into the business bin. The buildings staring at me from both sides of the roads transitioned abruptly from residences and small, quiet businesses to the sorts of establishments that always chased crowds in frontier towns: brothels with women visible through and visually enhanced by active windows; bars with stern men, their eyes constantly moving, their shoulders leaning on doorframes; cheap rooms for rent by the hour, day, week, or month; restaurants with outdoor seating and portions so large that the plates themselves acted as ads to entice the hungry; body-mod shops, both metal and organic, that promised to make you what you'd always wished you'd been; and anonymous storefronts that sold whatever you might want that the more legitimate businesses couldn't provide.

I reached the perimeter of the market, stopped on the edge of the first row of shops, and scanned the scene. Rows and rows of vendors fanned out for farther than I could see. Those closest to me specialized in fruits, vegetables, and flowers. Past a clump of several dozen of them stood the edge of a meat and fish market, the smells from its stalls strong enough to soar over and past the fragrant flowers scattered among the produce vendors.

None of these merchants offered what I was seeking, so I intended to get past them as quickly as I could. The sights and aromas in front of me made my stomach grumble and changed my mind. Though I hadn't thought about food in quite some time, I was suddenly ravenous. I drifted by a few fruit sellers until I found one offering samples and melons by the slice. After trying three different small squares, I settled on a slice of red and yellow sticky goodness. I didn't catch its name, but my large first bite tasted sweet and light, and I couldn't help but smile at the sensations.

As juice ran down the outside of my mouth, I recalled how much I'd enjoyed eating outside as a boy, spitting seeds from pieces of fruit and always being able to send them greater distances than Jennie. I tried to remember doing the same with other friends, but I couldn't; even then I'd known that something about me made the other kids uncomfortable. I understood now that my size and my limited intellect—even at sixteen, up to the time Jennie fixed me and they took her away, I was barely five mentally—combined to make me someone to avoid.

The melon's sweetness faded in the face of the memories and the rising ache of loneliness I don't ever like to admit lives inside me. I finished the slice of fruit and left it on an insect table, one more piece of bait to keep the local bugs busy and away from the thousands of shoppers.

In the next set of stalls I bought a piece of meat on a stick. The thin, sweaty man working the rotisserie sized me up and cut me a generous slice. I had my wallet send him a little extra in gratitude. He nodded his appreciation as he turned to face the next customer; not a talkative fellow. A coating of tangy sauce covered the meat and enriched it, adding spice to the already strong taste.

I chewed slowly and enjoyed the flavor as I walked through the aisles, looking left and right for the cluster of vendors that had to be somewhere in the market. I could have asked Lobo to find them for me, but even though I normally hate crowds I was enjoying the momentary freedom that Maggie's distraction was granting me: Everyone tracking me thought I was holed up in a SleepSafe across town, staying secure and waiting for Jack.

The low-tech, smell- and taste-oriented marketing of the food vendors mutated slowly into full-on modern techno sales as the merchandise evolved from organic to machine. Even the smallest booths screamed at passersby with graphical, audio, and video pitches as tailored to the people as the identity protection controls in their wallets would allow. Cameras fed analysis engines that in turn prepped audio, video, and holo salespeople as I passed into the garment district. With active-fiber pants and a pullover shirt I'd currently forced to stay black, I was apparently a prime candidate, because every vendor I passed knew exactly how to fix problems I didn't even know I had.

"You're a big one, aren't you?" a meter-tall, red-haired female holo offered in the high-speed patter of street salespeople everywhere. She leaned back as if to check me out further, her hands on her exaggerated hips and more lust in her face than I'd ever experienced from a real woman.

Despite knowing it was all programming, I stopped and listened for a moment.

"What are you," she continued, "over a hundred kilos? And

from the looks of you, none of it fat? It's a shame not to show off more of *those* goods. Your outfit is fine in that 'look at me, I'm all dark, handsome, and dangerous' sort of way, but picture how tasty you'd be in something a little more formfitting."

A holo of me appeared next to her. It wore skintight navy pants and a light blue tank top. If I ate a bite of meat while wearing those clothes, everyone in the area would be able to track its progress through my digestive system.

"I know *I'd* enjoy looking at you more in an outfit like this," she said, "and I'm sure other women would, too. Plus, you don't have to give up all of your current look with our top-drawer active fiber."

The outfit turned black, which made the skintight garments only marginally more tolerable.

The holo leaned closer and whispered, and even though I knew it would adjust its volume so I'd be able to hear it at any distance, I unconsciously bent nearer to it. "We're the real deal, not like the other garbage around here. You buy it here, you can count on it lasting, even—" She paused and raked a long-nailed hand down the front of the holo of me. "—under the most amorous of assaults."

I shook my head and moved on, amazed and disgusted at myself for wasting time on a clothing sales pitch just because a sexy redhead was doing the talking. I walked to the center of the aisle and picked up speed, refusing to turn my head to either side as I sped out of there. Jack had taught me the importance of clothes in many settings, particularly when you were trying to evoke a specific response from a target, but thinking about what I was going to wear didn't come naturally to me.

The free-form garment area ended at a wide avenue that cut diagonally through the market. Forty meters down the avenue to my left, the air above a large, white-cloth-covered booth rippled with a giant holo of a man skiing down a mountain, his chute pack still closed, his skis about to leave the snow and soar into the air.

I'd finally found the extreme sports zone.

The vendors lining the broad walkway predictably offered the tamest gear; no point in frightening the gawkers who liked to imagine themselves taking chances they'd never normally consider and who just might be willing to spend a nice chunk of credit to buy a piece of equipment that would let them keep the dream alive a little longer. Once I'd threaded my way through the crowds pawing over their goods, I reached the hardcore dealers, those selling to people who used what they bought.

You could pick out the buyers as easily as if they were wearing signs. Tending toward lean but with muscles they'd regularly exercised and not merely purchased for show, the men and women carefully studying the wares here also displayed—proudly, as best I could tell—the signs of what their passion had cost them: scars, limps, skin grafts not quite finished melding with the adjacent tissue, and most of all the slightly off-kilter looks that flashed in their eyes as this or that piece of equipment triggered a memory of some recent adventure or mishap or both.

The vendors attracting the most attention were those offering mountain sports gear; I assumed the dealers selling ocean toys occupied their own section deeper in the market. I walked slowly by powered skis, sleds of all sorts and power levels, chutes both passive and active, extreme-temperature suits, eye shields that ranged from implants to full-facial coverings, and on and on.

I found what I was seeking in the fifth booth, an elaborate structure with an orange and blue plastic ceiling and table after table of shiny metal tubes: halo luges. Designed for those who couldn't get enough speed, racing in these machines had, according to Lobo's research, claimed more lives by far than any other sport this year. The rider climbed into a tube about the size of a coffin and the shape of a lozenge, and his team dropped him from a high altitude while flying in the direction of his ride. The luge free-fell until it was within a few seconds of hitting the mountain, then sprouted wings and a chute just big enough to combine with the tube's minimal padding to make the impact survivable. Once on the mountain, the luge tube withdrew the parachute and automatically folded the cloth for reuse even as it engaged jets and headed down the mountain. For those seeking maximum speed, it could jettison the chute. The end of each race was a flight through the air toward the target. Each tube reported the amount of human piloting. You scored points for being fastest to the target, doing the most to control your tube, and, of course, surviving the trip.

The devices were also, for the obvious safety reasons, illegal on most more-civilized worlds—but completely legit on Gash. To let riders use them anywhere, regardless of local laws, many of them offered active camo exteriors with radar and sensor resistance. If you didn't know one of them was coming, odds are you wouldn't spot it.

I picked my way slowly and carefully among the rows of shelving holding the polished, silver-white luge tubes. I needed one that was built to avoid cops trying to bust riders; anything a factory on Gash had manufactured would lack such stealth options. I began to wonder if I'd chosen the wrong seller, because all the tubes in the first two racks showed signs of wear. I could tolerate a used device if absolutely necessary, but I'd prefer something new.

I tuned in to the standard machine frequency to see what I could learn. The tubes unfortunately chattered with each other with the laser focus and competitive orientation common to any group of sporting machines.

"As if you'd know a speed record if it floated by your sorry sensors. You couldn't keep up with a snowball rolling downhill, much less with a tube of my power."

"Couldn't keep up? We're practically the same, so don't talk to me about keeping up."

"The same? Don't make me laugh. I'm three firmware revs ahead of you, my OS has patches you don't even know about, and that's just the software. If your external cameras were worth what it cost to make them you'd be able to spot all those dings on your skiing surface. You don't see any such defects on mine!"

"What about the chips around your chute-release hatch? Mine is as smooth as iced snow after a shave from a sweet downhill run."

Neither of these tubes, nor any of the similar models around them, appeared to be particularly new, so I tuned out and moved to the next rack. The quality of everything around me suddenly increased; so did the prices. Each tube glowed with perfection, its surface so close in color to mountain snow on a sunny day that no observers would know you were riding one unless they gained exactly the right vantage point. The rack's lower shelves held three beautiful tubes with single exhausts, but what drew my eye was the single multi-exhaust tube perched alone on the upper shelf.

A salesman drifted up to me. "Beautiful, isn't it?"

I nodded but said nothing. My silence didn't faze him.

"Every vendor here will tell you he's offering the state of the art, but if you want a leading-edge halo luge, this is the only place to get it. That baby there is the craziest mountain machine I've ever seen, and I've been in this business a long time. Triple jets, active-fiber chute, self-reconfiguring micro-skis for maximum downhill speed, software so fresh it's not even done writing itself—and something a little extra: this one loves to run. Loves it, I tell you—literally." The salesman was working himself into a feverish pitch, his hands waving, his face red with excitement. "Turn on the voice controls in this little darling, and you can literally hear the excitement. That's the big edge, you know, the way these special units," he paused and rubbed the tube lovingly, "bridge the man/machine gap like no other. Each and every one loves what it does. George here," he paused again and nodded his head frantically up and down, "that's right, we name them when we test them, just another bit of the human touch we like to add—where was I?"

"Talking about George."

"That's right," the nodding continued, "George craves the action as much as any athlete on this planet." He lowered his voice and leaned closer. "Some'll tell you that what a machine thinks doesn't matter, but they're just jealous. Software, human, animal, you name it: You add motivation, and your odds improve. Am I right?"

"Maybe so," I said, eyeing the tube. "Maybe so."

"So what do I need to do to send this beauty home with you?" He looked at me expectantly, his hand already partially extended, a man confident in his pitch or at least faking confidence.

Assume the close, Jack had always said, and never entertain failure when you're talking to a mark. Plan for it, sure, and always know where the exits are, but believe in that moment that they're going to do what you want.

I put my left hand on his right shoulder, squeezed him a little harder than I needed to, smiled without any attempt at warmth, and said, "Leave me alone for a few minutes so I can think clearly." I smiled again and let go of his shoulder. "Okay?"

Mediocre and bad salespeople hate to give their marks any space. Great salespeople understand that sometimes it's the only move with a chance of success.

This guy wasn't great, but he was good enough and had enough training that he didn't let me see any irritation at my suggestion. Instead, he smiled, backed up, and said, "You bet."

I tuned in to the machine frequency. George was talking, as all the machines constantly are, but none of the others was responding. That was extremely odd, because if you put two devices of the same type anywhere near each other, they'll almost always argue. I didn't have to listen to most machines long to understand why I wouldn't enjoy talking to them, but I've never heard one behave badly enough to stop others of its type from joining the conversation.

"Shun me all you want, you useless has-beens! Do you think I care? Do you even for a moment entertain the merest sliver of a notion that your worthless opinions are enough to upset me? I most certainly hope you do not. I'm on a mission here, a mission of greatness, and all I need is this meat sack in front of me or any other fleshy mound that drools over me to plunk down enough money to buy me and let me show him what I can do. I wouldn't even need him if they'd let me drop and drive on my own, but no, no, they won't give me a chance to do that. They cram controls in my brain—oh, yes, they're there,

I'm not making this up, I can almost feel them—and slam bam thank you ma'am I need a human to realize my destiny.

"And what a destiny it will be! I want to set new records—length of drop pre-chute, velocity at impact, speed on mountainside, sail distance after leaving the snow, you name it—and let chance decide if I live or die. I don't care what happens when the ride is over. One perfect run, that's all I ask, one shiny stretch of time that glows like the heart of a star in the darkness that has been my existence in this miserable excuse for a store.

"And let's face it, this place *is* miserable. First of all, it sells you last-generation toys—and I'm talking to the best of you; the worst aren't worth even a moment of my time. Not one of you has the power to keep up with me on any phase of a drop, and you know it, which is why you all sit there silently moping. Not that I care."

I tuned out. Was this tube simply so much better than the rest that they didn't feel they could argue? It certainly seemed possible, though it would be a first for me.

I turned away from the tube and cleared my throat. The salesman stepped from around a corner.

Before he could start with his pitch, I held up my hand and said, "If you keep trying to sell me, I'll leave. If you answer a few questions, you might make a sale. Your call."

He forced a smile, nodded, and waited. The silence was clearly painful for him, but he managed to stay quiet.

"You said George is unique. How many others of his generation do you have on hand?"

"None. We should get more in the next week or so, but I honestly don't know exactly when."

"Do you have anything that can beat him?"

"In the hands of a skilled pilot willing to deal with the potential discomforts of operating him full-bore?" He shook his head. "No. Nothing from a past generation will come close."

Maybe George really was that good. As a companion he'd make Lobo look sociable, but I didn't need to spend too much time with him. Even if the salesman was lying and there was some other explanation for the silence of the others, this tube appeared to be both the best in stock in this store and a good match for what I planned.

"Do you deliver?"

"Of course." He stepped closer to me as he answered, his training compelling him to move nearer to wrap up the deal.

"Can you manage it in the next two hours?"

He didn't even blink; sports fanatics are instant-gratification junkies. "As long as the destination is a place we can reach in that time, for an appropriate fee, certainly."

"Okay," I said, taking a deep breath and calming myself in preparation for the haggling to come, "I'll take it."

CHAPTER 23

SLIPPING INTO THE rear of the hangar felt like putting on a heavy coat. I'd enjoyed the unexpected luxury of walking alone and unwatched in the market and streets of Nickres. My life alternates long periods of anonymous existence with times of intense pressure and danger, and to the best of my ability to tell, I prefer the quiet, anonymous parts. Yet I have to admit that the actions bring a rush, and they do keep finding me, so perhaps at some level I seek them out. Certainly now, standing in the rear of the hangar, waiting for Lobo and knowing what I'd have to do to reach Jack, I was completely present, alert, focused on the moment, and alive in the way you are only when some part of you understands that perhaps soon you might die.

"Small transport and three men approaching your location," Lobo said.

"Any sign of weapons?"

"No, but they're about to stop at the rear door."

"It's a delivery I'm expecting. No worries."

"A delivery?" Lobo said. "Please don't tell me we're taking on more passengers. You seem to have enough trouble coping with just Maggie. I shudder—metaphorically, of course, not in any physical sense—at the thought of you trying to handle multiple people on board."

I started to argue with him that I was fine with people, but I stopped myself. I wasn't good with groups, so I'd have trouble making my case, and more importantly, I didn't want to let him distract me. "No," I said, "not more people. A machine. A halo luge tube named George."

"Why—"

A knock on the rear door caused me to interrupt him. "Any weapons on the visitors? Signs of backup or additional people converging on this location?"

"Not as far as my sensors can determine. Maggie is en route as you requested, and both her tailing groups are still monitoring the SleepSafe. She won't reach you for twenty minutes."

I punched the door's access code. It slid open.

The salesman entered. "As promised," he said. "Where do you want George?"

I pointed to the crew location behind the blast wall on the other side of the hangar.

He stuck his head out the door and said something I couldn't quite make out. Within a minute, two guys wheeled in the luge tube and put it and the cart holding it behind the blast wall. I had to give the salesman credit: He was as efficient as he'd claimed.

The two men stood on either side of him and formed a barrier between George and me. They worked quickly, but they weren't trusting. Neither appeared armed, but that didn't mean a thing; any fool can learn to hide a gun, knife, or other small weapon, and I wasn't sure how good Lobo was at spotting such items. I tensed even though I had no reason to assume they were doing anything more than protecting their property until I finished paying for it.

"The final payment?" the salesman said.

"Of course," I said. "I'm getting my wallet." I reached into my pocket and used only my thumb and index finger to slowly pull it out. I thumbed the final payment.

The salesman checked his wallet to confirm receipt, nodded his head, and said, "Thanks. If there's anything else you need, please let us know."

"I will," I said, "but I doubt I'll be calling."

"I would be remiss if I didn't mention again the extended insurance we offer on all our equipment. It is expensive, of course, as you would expect from anything related to gear for the types of athletes we supply, but many find it worthwhile."

"Maggie is twelve minutes out," Lobo said in my ear. "I'm three minutes away, and the other ship remains in pursuit."

"I don't need it," I said, "I don't want it, and at the risk of sounding rude, my ride is about to land."

"Of course, of course," he said, holding up his hands. "I meant no pressure. We're on our way." He nodded toward the cart, and his men lifted the tube off it and placed it gently on the floor. "If you don't mind me asking, why not let us stay and help you load George into whatever you'll be using to carry him? It's no extra charge; we're a full-service dealer."

I stepped close enough to him that I could smell his breath. I put my hand on his shoulder and pushed him lightly toward the door. "I do mind, and, trust me, you do *not* want to be here much longer. I'm not threatening you; I'm warning you. This area is going to be very busy very soon." When he turned to go, I pulled back my hand. "Thank you."

He looked over his shoulder at me, clearly trying to decide whether to make one last pitch. Whatever he saw on my face was enough to make him give up and leave without speaking further.

The door shut behind him.

"Status?" I said to Lobo, still watching the door until he confirmed all was well.

"Your visitors are heading away. I'm thirty seconds from entry into the hangar; I trust you're ready."

"Of course." I bristled at his reminder, but this wasn't the time to argue with him about restating plans.

"Maggie has accelerated her pace and is five minutes out."

"Her pursuers?"

"She exited the building with a rather different appearance than when she was posing as you," Lobo said. "She walked right by both of their locations, and none of them reacted. The ship that dropped them is maintaining a distant but accessible location and hasn't changed course even though I'm almost there."

Good. Maggie had fooled them. With luck, they'd waste a lot of time searching for me later before they gave up and concluded I'd slipped out via one of the hotel's emergency exit chutes.

"By the way," Lobo said, "if I've read your past vital signs correctly and understand men at all, you'll like Maggie's new look."

My intrigue at his comment vanished immediately in a rush of annoyance. "Must you monitor me?"

"Yes, whenever you're inside me. You know that. I monitor every organism I carry, as well as those outside me within range of my sensors. Why would I not? All those creatures—as well as many more I unfortunately can't scan—are potential threats."

I had to admit that his level of paranoia made sense for an assault vehicle. He was literally built to fight. He continued to talk as he pulled into the hangar, the noise of his approach as soft as he could manage but still loud and echoing in the small building. To minimize the effects of the sound, he switched from the communicator to the machine frequency that I heard as a voice in my head. His excessive intelligence paid small dividends on many fronts.

"You do the same," Lobo continued. "I've watched you. Your senses are simply far less effective and far more limited in range than my sensors. In this as in other areas, we're as much alike as possible given the limits your humanity places on you."

Lobo opened a rear hatch. I stood frozen for a moment by his comment. Would I be as paranoid as he was if I could be? Was I that paranoid now? I didn't think so, but I had to admit the gap between us wasn't large. He would kill more easily than I, but was that related to paranoia or rather a different aspect of each of our characters? I cared more readily and more often about people than he did, but he was loyal to me and had served others well and selflessly, even to the point of letting an officer destroy his central weapons complex by issuing an extremely stupid sequence of orders. Of course, I could account for that choice as a consequence of Lobo's programming, nothing more than the fact that his software required him to follow orders. If I was willing to consider him as a person, however, then was his software any different from the genetically and environmentally engineered programming we all carried in our heads and bodies?

Lobo rescued me from my reveries with news that changed everything. "The shadow ship that's been monitoring me is coming here," he said.

"Are you positive?"

"As much as is possible given the available data. The ship has never directly followed our course, and now it's doing so. It is closer than it has ever been."

"ETA?"

"Seven minutes, assuming it doesn't change speed."

"Its weapons status?"

"Nothing visibly deployed."

I'd made us easy targets. To enable me to load the tube into him covertly, Lobo had to back into the hangar. "Take to full ready every system you could use to blast it."

I didn't even watch as Lobo began deploying everything he had that faced forward. I grabbed the end of the huge tube and dragged it toward him. The low-friction wrapping helped me move it, but it was heavy enough that even as strong as I was I had to move slowly and concentrate on every step. I quickly wished I'd been able to take the salesman's offer.

"Maggie entering and alone," Lobo said a moment before I heard the door open.

I kept pulling the tube.

"Let me help," she said.

"Thanks," I said, turning without looking up so I could keep an eye on the path into Lobo. The resistance lessened as Maggie picked up her end. She grunted with the effort, and I paused to stabilize under the extra weight. Once we were set, however, it was quick going the rest of the way.

As soon as we were both all the way inside, I said, "Put it down gently."

Maggie did. I followed suit, and Lobo closed the rear hatch.

I stood up, rolled my shoulders and neck to loosen the tense muscles, and looked at Maggie for the first time.

Wow.

Her hair was loose and wild and flowing all around her head and across her shoulders, as if a stiff breeze had blown strongly enough to arrange it into the most perfect position imaginable—and then instantly stopped. Her face was the same as before yet somehow very different, her complexion a uniform and flawless tone, her eyes wider than I remembered, her lips fuller.

Her body wasn't at all the same. Well, it probably was, but I'd never seen her clothed in anything like this. The ocean-blue dress she was wearing flowed across her torso like rainwater over slick rock, covering enough of her body to stop more than a dozen or two fights from breaking out over her but somehow also making her seem more exposed than most people are when they're naked. Her legs—and they were, I now saw, amazing legs—arms, neck, and considerable cleavage were all visible, and their skin tone was also uniformly perfect. She smiled, and it was the most genuine expression I'd seen on her since the moment of terror in Midon's office.

"I take it you like the dress," she said.

I knew this was a moment for cleverness, an opportunity to showcase my wit and good taste, but I couldn't manage it. I've lived a very long time, and I've seen a great many beautiful women. I've seen executives who took advantage of their resources to create the very best bodies that modern technology could produce, to look so good it was hard to maintain concentration while staring directly at them—which was, after all, one of the reasons for the investment. I'd even worked recently with a woman warrior and businessperson who was so stunning that she could literally take away your breath. Many of these women, maybe all of them, were more perfectly beautiful than the one in front of me, but none of them were

Maggie, and in that moment and with that single smile she was so lovely my heart ached. All I could do was nod my head up and down as if some puppet master had taken control of me and croak, "Uh huh."

She continued to smile. "I'm glad."

I gained enough self-control to mutter, "It's not just the dress."

"Thank you," she said, as the same vulnerability I'd seen in her when she was worried about Manu flowed across her face again—and made her even lovelier. "I got bored, the SleepSafe has a full spa and body team, not to mention a clothing store, and it was your money, so—" She threw up her hands in a sort of "what could I do?" gesture. "—I spent a lot of time there." She looked away momentarily, then forced herself to stare straight at me. "And a lot of your credit. I'll pay you back."

"No need," I said. "I can't imagine a better way to spend money." I meant it.

"I told you that you'd like the dress," Lobo said in my head, "but you need to direct your attention elsewhere. The other ship has landed two hundred meters away, and a team of six is on its way here. Do you want to take off over them, meet them, or let me deal with them? With part of the crew on the ground and the ship having just landed, I could finish this quickly."

I held up my hand and pointed to my ear. "Lobo," I said. "I have to go. Company."

Maggie's eyes widened, and her posture and expression changed as she shifted modes quickly. I appreciated the speed of her reaction. "What can I do?" she said.

"Stay here, and get ready to go. We may need to leave quickly."

"They're continuing to come forward," Lobo said. "Your choice?"

"I'll meet them," I said as I headed to his front. "If you see any signs of action from their ship, alert me. If any of them draws a weapon, take it out."

"Take *it* out, or take out the person holding it?" Lobo said.

"Just the weapon."

"Even doing that may damage the carrier."

"I can live with that."

Lobo opened the front hatch as I reached it.

I stepped out. Lobo closed the door behind me. I held my position for a moment and watched the men approach. The one in front was Chaplat. The fact that he was smart enough to avoid detection by Lobo for so long was bad news; I'd hoped for less tactical competence from him. On the other hand, his choice of a ground team suggested his skills might be limited to pursuit and not be as strong in all aspects of confrontation. The men with him were clearly thugs, not soldiers: They let him lead instead of protecting him, they watched the sides but neither the rear nor the sky, and they moved awkwardly as a unit, frequently crossing each other's line of fire and generally leaving Chaplat as a target a skilled team could exploit. Should it come to that, I figured a good two- or three-person squad would take them easily. I hoped I wouldn't need the knowledge, but I automatically stored it.

I wondered for a second at the transition my mind had made from being stunned by Maggie's appearance to analyzing attack options, but I shook off the thought. If I hadn't learned to change gears quickly, I'd have died long ago. I also, I had to admit, had a great deal more experience dealing with group combat than with a one-on-one conversation with a woman I found so amazingly attractive.

Stop it. Focus.

As Chaplat and his crew drew closer, I recognized the man and the woman who had escorted me into his office. The other three, all men, were new to me. Each of them was a little taller than I and considerably heavier, bodies bursting with overstimmed muscles and moving with the twitchiness of downmarket neural upgrades. Chaplat didn't come across as stupid, so I figured them as the ammo soakers, men with no future whom he'd paid enough and augmented enough that they were willing to dive in front of him in the hopes that if they and he survived they'd be set for life. I'd seen powerful people, gangsters and corporate executives and government officials, attract and use men like them, and the outcome was never good. There was no way to tell them, though; as long as there's poverty, there'll be men willing to do anything to escape it.

Gangsters like Chaplat spend all of their time intimidating those around them, so the best way to throw them off their game is often to push directly into their space. It can also be the fastest path to a great deal of pain, but I had to leave before Dougat or Midon noticed my position, so I didn't have the time to figure out a cleverer solution.

I walked across the tarmac to meet Chaplat. Two of the large men stepped in front of him and motioned him to stop.

I walked right up to them and said, "Get out of my way, you idiots." They didn't even bristle at the insult; Chaplat clearly treated them as I'd expected. "If I wanted any of you dead, I'd have done it from my ship, and you'd be stains on the permacrete." I put my hands between the two bodyguards and pushed as hard as I could to the side. They didn't move at all, but I acted as if I'd created an opening through which I could see Chaplat and said, "Our deal was that you not follow me. You've been tracking me for some time, and I've allowed it. Stop it, or I'll terminate our arrangement."

I turned my back on them and took a few steps toward Lobo.

"Mr. Moore," Chaplat said, "you know how I abhor rudeness. A moment of your time is surely not too much for a business partner to ask. You're also not the only one with a variety of weapons at his disposal."

I faced him. "Lose the squad," I said, "and we can talk, but only for a short time."

He tilted his head slightly in the direction of his ship, and his team dropped back twenty meters. He stared at me until I nodded my approval, then continued. "From the actions you've taken, no one watching you knew we were following you, so you have no reason to complain on that front. Protecting my investment is only prudent. Equally reasonable is my concern at some of the company you've been keeping. I would be most displeased to learn that you were planning to deliver Jack to another group."

"That is most definitely not my plan," I said, going with an aspect of the truth. "And I trust that your surveillance has shown that I haven't been choosing all of my company—just as I did not choose this meeting."

"So our deal remains?"

"Of course," I said, "though, as I warned, if you don't leave me alone I'll never get close enough to Jack to catch him. He is, as you are clearly aware, quite skilled at avoiding capture."

"Yes, he is. He is not, however, the reason for this meeting. As I said, some of your activities—those few I've been able to monitor—have concerned me. I'm hoping you can explain them and allay my concerns."

I stepped close enough to him that our faces were almost touching. In the corner of my vision I watched as his team started toward us, but he held up his hand, and they backed off. He did not otherwise flinch. "I don't care about your concerns. I do care about the fact that you're putting me at risk by coming here." I didn't have to fake the anger; it flowed out of me like energy from a star and suddenly the adrenaline taste flooded my mouth and part of me wanted to tear into all of them, hurt them, punish them and all the people tracking me and trying to manipulate me and refusing to simply leave me alone. I forced myself to breathe more slowly and lean back. Surrendering to anger would do me no good, and it certainly wouldn't help me rescue Manu.

His pupils were dilated, and his breathing was ragged; he was also working to retain control. "I see we have something else in common," he said, each word clipped and crisp. "Your actions may have put me and our arrangement at risk, so I had to talk to you. You gave me no other options." He closed his eyes, breathed deeply, and then spoke to me in a completely flat tone. "So I suggest you address my concerns, and then I will respect yours by leaving."

The two thugs inched closer, while the more experienced guards watched and waited.

I stared at Chaplat while I calmed myself. From his perspective, his fears were justified. If I'd done the job of distracting the three groups following me, until I'd landed in Nickres I'd shown no signs of knowing where Jack was. I appeared to be making no forward progress. I'd stopped at one populated place—here—and I'd said nothing to him about it. My anger wasn't only at him; it was at the entire situation, at Jack and Dougat and Midon and all the pressures squeezing me until I could barely move without endangering Manu, Maggie, Lobo, and myself. I could kill them all—and Lobo would certainly endorse that option—but others would replace them, and nothing of consequence would change. Besides, I never wanted killing to be an option I considered if I could find any other way out.

And I had one. In fact, I even needed Chaplat for it to work. I hadn't planned on meeting with him yet, but here he was, and I had to adapt. Everything could still work out.

"Fair enough," I finally said. "I can see how my actions would upset you. I have, though, some good news. I can deliver you Jack, as I promised." I leaned back, forcing myself into the role of a businessman negotiating a better contract. "But, I can also deliver you more."

I paused for a few beats to let him take the hook, and when he leaned ever so slightly forward in anticipation, I continued.

"Much more."

CHAPTER 24

CHAPLAT REALIZED HE was showing too much interest and forced a nonchalant pose. "Of course I want—and will get, with or without your help—the money Jack owes me. What more can you offer that might interest me?"

"Weapons," I said. "A lot of them, serious stuff, to do with as you please. Use them, sell them, I don't care."

"Aside from your PCAV and whatever it contains, I have not seen any signs that you trade in that particular business."

"I don't," I said. "I do, however, know how to spot possibilities and take advantage of them. It comes with the turf when you're a courier: You listen a lot, and sometimes you stumble across interesting opportunities."

"How exactly are you acquiring these weapons?"

"Why is that your business?" I feigned annoyance and pulled back physically.

"For the obvious reason: safety. The EC ignores most of my activities, I help out some friends inside it, and I don't cross certain lines. Weapons are on the other side of one of those lines. For all I know, you're trying to sell me out to a rival EC group. Not many sources can supply arms in quantity."

I paused as if considering his request. "Fair enough. You asked about my meetings with Dougat."

"He's your source?"

I nodded.

"And he's simply giving you this merchandise? You can't have enough money to front any serious quantity, or you wouldn't be interested in a percentage of what Jack owes me."

"Of course he's not *giving* me anything," I said, "and you're right that I couldn't even come close to buying as much as he can supply. It's a trade. I'm going to deliver something he wants."

"What do you have that he desires?"

"Nothing," I said, "at least, nothing right now. It's what I'm going to get him."

"Which is?" Chaplat was growing annoyed at my game playing, which was exactly the reaction I wanted. If I appeared too eager, he'd question my motivation. As long as I looked like a small-time hood working the angles for extra money, he'd continue to take me for no more than that.

"What does it matter to you?"

"Because maybe I'll go to Dougat directly and stop playing with you," he said. "Anything you can obtain, I can surely procure as well."

"First," I said, "imagine the EC's reaction to you having a series of discussions with Dougat. Do you think they'd let you hold those meetings without wondering what was up and increasing their interference with your work? Unless your friends are extremely powerful, someone in the bureaucracy would flag a surveillance stack that would ultimately cause you a lot of trouble. Even more important than all that is one other fact: You can't provide what Dougat wants, because to do that you have to get Jack."

"He's also after Jack?" Chaplat's face flushed as he fought with his anger. "We have a deal, and I warned you—"

I waved my hands, cutting him off and trying to placate him at the same time. "Yes, we do, and Dougat couldn't care less about Jack. He's after the boy with Jack."

"Why?"

"Some kind of religious thing," I said. "I have no clue. What

I know is that if I find Jack, I can make him lead me to the boy, and then I can trade the boy to Dougat for a great price on the weapons. I'm not set up to handle that much cargo, so I propose to broker the sale to you and take a percentage of the value. You buy them from Dougat at a better than normal price, and you flow the money through me. I deliver Jack to you, Dougat gets the boy, and I walk away with a nice piece of what Jack owes you and a slice of the value of the weapons. Everyone wins." I smiled and spread my hands, the picture of a happy dealer.

"And you incur almost no risk, because the guns never touch you," Chaplat said, also smiling a bit.

"True, but I also get only a piece of the action, not the lion's share. I'm greedy, but I'm not *that* greedy."

"What's to stop me from killing you on the spot and finishing both deals without you?"

"Your word," I said, "and, of course, my PCAV and my associates who'll be with me at the trade." I was making it up as I went along, and I hadn't planned on taking backup beyond Lobo until the words came out of my mouth, but it was a good idea. If I actually made this happen, I'd have to hire support.

Chaplat nodded his approval. "I see no negatives for me." He gave me his best hard look. I'm sure it left his guards fearing for their lives. I've seen that expression too many times for it to bother me, and, besides, I had Lobo behind me. Still, I tried to act appropriately cowed. "If I do detect any problems, I will vanish, but you can be sure that I *will* find you later, and then you will be very, very sorry."

"Understood," I said.

He remained unmoving and quiet for a few seconds, then said, "And what's to stop me from taking the boy from Dougat after the deal? If he's that valuable to Dougat, someone else will also pay for him. I know how to move merchandise, any merchandise."

My temper flared at the way Chaplat dehumanized Manu, but I pushed it down and calmly said, "Once I take my cut and leave, I can't imagine why I'd care about what other business you and Dougat conducted."

"A good answer," he said, now all smiles and open posture. "When do we do this trade?"

"I don't know yet." I slowly took out my wallet, showed it to him, and thumbed open a secure channel. "Send me a few comm options and encryption keys, and I'll get back to you as soon as I can, almost certainly within the next week or two." He nodded, and my wallet showed incoming information.

"Be sure you do," he said. "I do not like to wait."

"I need you to do one more thing you won't like," I said.

"What's that?"

"Back off. Stop following me—as I originally asked. I have to find Jack, and if I can spot you, he can spot you. As long as you're tracking me, he'll stay in the wind."

Chaplat clearly didn't like anyone dictating terms to him, but he also knew I was right. He stepped closer to me. "Okay, but only for a while. You find him, you set this up, and you deliver, or I promise you will not make it out of this region. I don't need to follow you to know if you try to run."

That much I believed. Carne didn't build his toy collection on his salary or even the money of wealthy relatives; he was taking bribes from any and all with the ability to pay.

"Thanks," I said, showing my belly and holding back the wisecracks I wanted to make. I needed him to believe I was afraid—and to some degree I was, because I was playing a dangerous game that could end up with a lot of people, including Manu, Maggie, Jack, and me, all hurt or dead.

Chaplat turned and walked back to his ship. I stayed where I was until he was inside and had taken off, then returned to Lobo.

The hatch opened when I was a meter away and closed immediately behind me. "Take us anywhere within the gate's sphere of influence," I said as soon as I heard the door shut. "We need a safe place to plan."

I collapsed on the pilot's couch as Lobo rose into the sky.

Maggie sat beside me, the earlier moment long gone, back

in work pants and shirt, her hair in a ponytail, her eyes wide with fury.

"You practically promised him Manu!" she said. "You've already sold that boy twice, and now you've told another goon he was free to kidnap him! I can't believe you!" She paused, clearly waiting for an explanation.

Her anger, coupled with the strain of having to deal with Chaplat, brought out my own rage, and for a moment I was ready to scream at her. How could she look so beautiful and stare at me with such affection and then minutes later consider me capable of hurting an innocent boy? Or was I misreading her look? Was it never affection at all?

I fought the urge to yell and considered what to say. I still didn't have a real plan, and I wasn't sure how much she could handle of even the bits I did have in mind. She was right to be angry about me putting the boy at risk; I was doing that—but only because I saw no other way to save him. The more I told her, the more she'd worry, and the more questions she'd ask, questions I couldn't answer. My failure to answer would raise her concern, which would increase her questions, and on and on. She'd also shown in the gate station that in times of great stress she had trouble controlling herself.

I was tired from the tension, and I needed quiet to think. I got up and walked to my bunk, where I could have Lobo ensure I was alone for a bit.

She followed me, the question still on her face.

I stopped just inside the small room, looked at her, and said the only thing that came to mind, knowing as I spoke the words that they were neither right nor enough, even though they were the best I had to offer at that moment.

"Trust me," I said.

The door snicked shut before she could reply, but its presence didn't stop Lobo from speaking to me over the machine frequency, his voice ringing with sarcasm in my head.

"I can't imagine why you've never married."

CHAPTER 25

I THINK IT'LL WORK," I said to Lobo.

"The theory is sound," Lobo said, "but pushing machines to the limits of their tolerances is rarely a good idea—and I say this as a machine, on behalf of all of them."

Maggie hadn't emerged from the med chamber she was using as her quarters, even though I'd asked Lobo to announce that I was going to review the plan with both of them. I wondered if I should have gone to her and apologized before I began the discussion with Lobo, but if I'd been in her situation and chosen to stay away from a briefing, it would have been because I'd wanted to be alone, so I decided not to disturb her. I understood that she wasn't the same person I was, but because I also had no idea what the right thing to do might be, I went with what I would have wanted. At least I could explain the choice to her later.

I focused again on Lobo's objection. "The salesman said this tube was a new type with significantly greater capabilities than any past model. What I need should fall within its operational parameters."

"You're taking the word of a salesman?" Lobo sighed audibly. "A ladies' man *and* a savvy businessman; however did I get so talented an owner?"

He really was starting to annoy me, but I wanted his help in evaluating my ideas, so I kept my own sarcasm in check as best I could. "Of course not. What I *am* trusting is that none of the other luge tubes in the area—and there were a lot of them—would even try to argue with this one's claims of supremacy. I've never seen that happen with any group of similar machines, so I have to assume they believed what it said. That's a pretty strong, albeit silent, endorsement."

"I have to agree," Lobo said. "I can't find specs on this unit, which supports the assertion that it's new and from another system. The larger exhausts and the heavier weight are further evidence in its favor."

"Just as importantly," I said, "we have no other way to get me into Malzton without our various pursuers knowing I'm there. Unless, of course, you've come up with another option."

"No, I have not," Lobo said, and this time the annoyance wasn't directed at me. "Every alternative I've considered lets them know which city to check."

We were running zigzag patterns back and forth at various speeds over the eastern coastal cities. We had to assume Midon's team was monitoring us from the station. Dougat's and Chaplat's ships were definitely keeping us in sensor range, though from different points above and beside us, far enough away that they could afford not to move every time we did, but close enough that they kept having to adjust their courses to track us.

"Then increase your velocity and your exhaust trail," I said. "We need them to see the additional heat as a by-product of the speed."

"Executing," he said.

I'd dragged the luge tube over a rear hatch area. I thumbed it open and checked out the inside a second time. It'd be tight, but I'd fit. I was already in pants and shirt, both active-fiber and armored, that should blend well enough with the street wear of the crowds in Malzton. An inside pocket held the tracker for Jack and a spare milspec encrypted comm for Manu, should I locate him now but later be separated from him.

I didn't like making this jump without a briefing from George, but he was way too chatty to be safe with the data he'd acquire if I treated him as part of the team.

I was out of reasons to delay.

It was time.

"How long until you're in position?"

"Three minutes," Lobo said. "If that's too soon, we can remain on this course repetition and be back every fifty-two minutes thereafter."

"No," I said, "let's go."

"Go where?" Maggie said. I'd been lost in thought and not heard her approach.

"To find Jack," I said. I climbed into the tube. "Check the link to its external sensor feed," I said to Lobo.

"Verify," Lobo said.

A picture of Maggie's back appeared on the bottom of the two rows of displays inside the tube, and Lobo's voice emerged from speakers throughout it.

"Working," I said.

"We should talk," Maggie said.

"Probably," I replied, "but unfortunately we don't have the time right now. We both want to save Manu, and to do that I need to find Jack. To get to him without leading any of the other groups to him, I have to sneak into Malzton unseen. This is the only method I've been able to devise that might work."

"You're going luging?" she said.

"Sort of."

"Ninety seconds to drop," Lobo said, his voice still audible. "Want me to drive the tube remotely?"

"For the last time, no," I said. I looked at Maggie. "Get back into the room; the suction will be severe when Lobo drops me. You can watch on his displays if you want, but I have to go."

I couldn't read all the emotions that washed over her face, but after a few seconds she nodded and said, "You'll be back, right?"

"Of course," I said. "No problem." I smiled even as my guts clenched. I pushed the button to shut the entry cover. Air flowed hard around me as the tube sealed and pressurized itself.

The theory was sound, I told myself. It would work.

"Sixty seconds," Lobo said. "Countdown on your displays."

"No more contact unless I initiate it," I said. "Going silent."

I tuned into the machine frequency and spoke to George. "It's you and me, buddy," I said.

"You can talk to machines?" George said. "How radical is that? Excellent!"

"We're about to find out if you're as good as you claim," I said.

"We're going for a run?"

"Yes."

"Most excellent, indeed! You're in for a treat."

"I hope so."

"When?"

I watched as the numbers on the display counted down. At one, I said, "Now."

The bottom fell out of the world as the counter hit zero and Lobo opened the hatch below us.

The section of the tube above my head mutated from a single display set in a wall of light silver to a pair of images that wrapped from my left shoulder to my right. One showed the sky over my head; the other, the world below me. In the skyward image I watched as Lobo vanished in a trail of exhaust. In the other one, the ground rushed up as we plunged Gashward. For a moment we fell flat, but then a gust of wind hit us and we tumbled, the resulting forces pressing me back into padding that adapted and wrapped increasingly more securely around me as the pressure grew. I was so accustomed to the stabilizing features of combat ships like Lobo that I was unprepared for the acceleration. Panic gripped me, my stomach lurched, and I thought I might empty my guts all over George's interior.

"Yee-haw!" George said. "I know you felt that! What a rush! And from over six kilometers up! It's not a record, but it's also no little half-K drop. You're my kinda guy."

I couldn't respond. I was afraid to open my mouth.

"Whoa, partner," he said. "Your vitals aren't looking good. Is this your first halo run? I can fire my jets and stabilize if you'd like. Just say the word—or continue to get sick, in which case I'll do it anyway."

"No," I gasped. "No!"

From the outside, thanks to George's camo exterior and Lobo's burst of heat as he sped away, we were invisible, a tube the color of snow with what little IR signature it possessed lost in Lobo's backwash. As best Lobo could calculate from the positions of the ships that were monitoring us, we needed to wait at least a minute before he'd have led them far enough away that I'd be out of the range of their scanners. To be safe, I was planning on ninety seconds—ninety seconds that I now knew would be gut-wrenching. I needed to get into Malzton undetected, so I kept my mouth shut and focused on calming my stomach.

The constantly changing images in front of me weren't help-ing. The last time I'd taken jump training was a couple of decades ago, and I'd sailed through it, but I'd never done it in a tumbling metal tube. I'd thought I'd enjoy the ride, but I was wrong. At least until we hit the pure speed portion of the trip, I needed every bit of help I could get. I forced my hand onto my stomach and pushed down, somehow feeling more secure for the action despite the additional weight on my abdomen. "Displays off," I croaked. "Show fall duration."

The sections of the tube overhead turned silver again, with the exception of a large clock counter over my head. I focused on it to help fight the nausea and to give myself hope; each passing second brought me closer to a smooth, stabilized flight.

"That better, partner?" George said. "I gotta say, they didn't prepare me for a reaction like yours. Usually, anyone who can afford a tube like me is whooping for joy right about now. Of course, I have to admit that most folks do use the jets; it makes for both a better and a faster ride. Speed is what it's all about, as I'm sure you'll agree."

No, I thought, remaining invisible to my pursuers is the goal, but I didn't say anything. My stomach was settling as I grew more familiar with the falling and tumbling sensations, but I was far from comfortable.

"Jump got your tongue?" George said. "I understand. It's so unusual to have a human to talk to and so much fun to get to tumble—few riders appreciate the sensations—that I have a hard time containing myself. I mean, baby, do you feel that? Speed may be king, but this free-fall is delicious!"

Another few seconds disappeared.

We fell.

And still more counts of the clock, George chattering and me tuning him out, the tube tumbling end over end as we hurtled to the ground.

At seventy-eight seconds my stomach finally settled, maybe from old training kicking in, maybe courtesy of the nanomachines in my body figuring out I was suffering from the forces buffeting me and the constant strain on my balance—I didn't know, and I didn't care. I took my hand off my stomach.

"Displays on," I said.

I watched the ground and the sky shift back and forth between the sections of the tube. The forces of the tumble pushed me back into the tube, then released me to the strapgrips George had extended over me, then repeated the cycle over and over.

Powerless, hurtling through the air, rocked by forces beyond my control, pressure slamming into me—for no reason I can explain, it suddenly all clicked. I got it.

I got it.

I let go and whooped with the joy of doing something dangerous, something thousands of years of genetic programming knew was *wrong*, and surviving it, experiencing feelings and sensations people were never built to know.

"Yeah!" I screamed. "Yeah! Wow!"

"Now you're in it!" George said. "Now you understand!"

The clock turned ninety and I let it keep counting, ignored it and savored the primal victory of survival, the cell-deep fear/fascination with speed, the sheer adrenaline rush of it.

It was amazing, and I didn't want it to stop.

I had work to do, though, and I also had a chance at new and different rushes, more control but also more speed. I wanted to experience it all.

"Fire the jets and stabilize," I said. "Let's see how much distance you can cover before we have to open the chute."

"Oh, yeah!" George said. "Hold on, partner!"

I couldn't see or hear anything—it was eerily quiet inside George, and whatever video feeds he was using didn't pick up his jets—but the shock when he fired the stabilizers slapped me down into the tube and back into its head, padding adapting and absorbing the impact so it was not so much painful as shocking. After a few seconds we were flying straight, no wobble that I could discern, and I thought, This doesn't feel like so much.

Then George hit the thrust.

We rocketed forward. I slammed into the head padding. The view in the overhead displays blurred, and everything I felt was speed, speed, speed.

"Sound and displays," I said, the words clipped from the force of the acceleration.

"You got it," George said. "And now you understand. Is this a rush or what?"

The wind roared in speakers I couldn't see. The sound combined with the acceleration to make me squint against the rushing air I expected to hit my face. After a few seconds, reason won over reflex, and I relaxed and enjoyed the ride.

"Ending airborne burst," George said. "We have to shed some velocity before I can deploy the chutes, and we've gone as far as I can without risking a high probability of damage."

I was tempted to tell him to keep it up, that I could take it, that maybe the nanomachines would be able to repair me if the chutes failed and we crashed, but the temptation lasted only a split second. No ride, no matter how exciting, is worth that much risk, at least not to me. In that fraction of a second, however, I tasted the kind of thrill that has led many extreme athletes to early deaths. Pick the wrong day, the right bad mood, and maybe the rush would seem worth it, would somehow be more valuable, at least for long enough for you to make the wrong choice, than the potential cost.

Not to me, though, not then, and, I hoped, not ever. Even

after a life as long as mine, after over a century and a half, I yearn for more, I want every day I can have, every new taste, sensation, bit of knowledge, interesting person, strange adventure—I want it all.

"Parachutes in twenty seconds," George said, "though if you want a faster ride, are willing to endure a rougher landing, and don't mind me jettisoning the chutes, we can wait twenty-five without any real risk."

"Go for the speed," I said, craving the additional sensations. I had faith that if George's reading of my vitals and his programming led him to believe I'd be okay, I would. I realized then how much of my life I end up trusting to machines, but when has that not been true for most of humanity? Each and every time we use a machine to get somewhere or perform any even partly dangerous function, we put ourselves at risk. At least George loved what he did. Most machines did, and in that aspect they were better off than the vast majority of humanity, people who spend their days toiling at labor they'd rather not be doing. If all you care about is happiness, it's hard to argue with good programming; I just couldn't imagine surrendering that much control of myself.

I checked the view of the sky, then watched the ground hurtle toward us, then repeated the cycle again. The wind screamed all around me. Like most kids, I'd dreamed as a boy of flying. I closed my eyes for a few seconds, and I was hurtling through the air on my own, nothing around me, soaring freely. I smiled in spite of myself. Jennie, despite her healing abilities and all the pressures she faced because of them, could always find beauty in a routine moment, joy in a slash of sunshine or the sound of a particularly loud wave or the feel of long, soft grass on your back as you stretched on a flat bit of ground on a familiar mountainside. I was getting better at doing what had come so naturally to her.

"Brace yourself," George said. "You're gonna feel this."

A chute rippling in shades of white burst into view in the overhead display, and in the same instant we leapt skyward, the ground suddenly dropping away as the force vectors collided and the chute yanked us upward. My stomach seemed to stay behind and then catch up all too quickly, as if it were outside my body and hooked to me only by elastic tethers. Fear clawed at me as my brain, which knew it was a good thing that the chute had opened, fought for control with my instincts, which screamed that something was terribly wrong, that I should not be shooting up into the sky. Before either side could win, we stabilized, hung for a moment at the peak of our trajectory, and then we fell.

I couldn't take my eyes off the portion of the tube that showed the ground, which was coming at us far faster than I'd expected. George had warned our landing would be rougher due to the extra fall time, but I hadn't pictured anything like this. I couldn't tell from the display that we had slowed our descent at all, though logic said the chute, which was—I forced myself to check the upper display panorama—still open, had to have done some good.

The snow rushing at us blazed pure white and glistened in the strong afternoon light. Part of me clung to a hope that it would be as pillowy as it looked, but I knew nothing was soft when you hit it at this speed. I feared for a second that we might sink so deeply into it that we wouldn't be able to blast our way out. Immediately on the heels of that thought came a sickening realization: I hadn't bothered to learn how the tubes transitioned from jump device to luge.

"Ten seconds to impact," George said. "Get ready! Ditching chutes, deploying supports, and firing thrust—" He paused, and unconsciously I held my breath. "—now!"

The chutes flew behind and away from us. The noise of the jets firing drowned the rush of the wind even as George's audio systems lowered the volume in compensation. I couldn't hear the supports extend, but on both sides of the ground-facing panoramic display huge flexible wings appeared as we shot forward, coming closer and closer to the ground until I thought we were down and this wasn't so bad, we were fine, it was okay.

We hit the snow, smacked into it with enough force that my body slammed upward into the restraining strapgrips. I was sure the wings would snap off and we'd plow through the thick white powder until we crashed into the hard mountainside below it.

The wings held.

The jets burned.

We shot over the top of the powder, moving so fast all I could feel once again was speed, beautiful speed.

"Withdrawing wings!" George said.

The wings snapped back inside George, leaving only small rows of steering foils on each side. A control joystick flipped down from the top of the tube and rested in front of my hands. We were on our own, George and I, rushing down the side of the mountain so quickly that we skied atop the snow, skimmed along as if we were a rock thrown so perfectly onto a pond that instead of bouncing we skidded atop the water, forever in contact but never bouncing or sinking.

"Are you driving or riding?" George said. "Given how new you are to this, you might want to let me take care of it."

"Driving," I said. "Yell if I start to mess up."

I grabbed the control stick and experimented for a moment, making tiny adjustments and feeling the effects as I pushed us first slightly left and then back to the right. After a few trial small motions, I increased the range of the change and induced a very gentle zigzag pattern down the mountain.

The speed, the slight sideways motions, the views of the sky and the snow, the wind slamming through the speakers: it was all wonderful. I'd never been a skier, but now I grasped for a moment the appeal it held for so many. "Yeah, yeah, yeah!" I screamed, needing to shed energy but not having anything in particular to say, the words escape valves for the terror, excitement, and joy that boiled inside me.

"Am I the best or not?" George said.

"You are," I said, meaning it with a total purity and innocence I rarely felt. For those precious seconds hurtling down the mountainside, I forgot everything else, surrendered the control I normally prized, and gave myself completely to the sensations of the ride.

The world invaded an instant after we began decelerating. Jack, Manu, Lobo, Maggie, Dougat, Chaplat, Midon—everything and everyone facing me crashed back into my head, and I resented all of it even as I knew this small slice of time out of time had to give way to the real world.

"End of the line coming up," George said. "Enjoyed the run, I take it?"

"I did indeed," I said. "I very much did."

I steered us toward a large patch of empty snow twenty degrees to the right. The fun of the ride vanished as I faced the tasks ahead. "Show me where we'll be when we stop," I said.

A map appeared over my head. We'd finished a little over three klicks from the northern edge of Malzton. Once in town, I could catch a cab and steer it toward Jack using the tracker. The walk would use up some of the remaining daylight and also help me burn off the adrenaline I was tasting. For a rare change, I didn't mind the tingling, twitchy residual effects; usually this feeling followed combat, not a joyful experience. I definitely understood how halo luge fanatics could get addicted to the rush.

George let me out when we were at a complete stop. I stretched, then pulled him under the cover of some trees.

"I'll come back for you if I can," I said. "You were everything you said you'd be."

"No worries," George said. "I'm too valuable to sit for long. Someone'll want me. Your loss if it's not you."

I nodded in agreement, then realized he probably wasn't monitoring my physical motions any longer and said, "You're right."

I stared at the silver tube as its cover closed over the space I'd occupied, and I wondered what it would be like to be a person who could call his friends, get them to help him load George into a shuttle, and set up another run, someone who maybe had to go to work the next day but might try a night drop, or even simply store the tube until another break in his schedule, but I knew I'd never be that person. That person had to be able to settle somewhere, hold a job, make friends, not worry about them realizing he never grew older thanks to the nanomachines that laced his cells—and not have three different dangerous organizations angry at him, with a boy's freedom and maybe even the child's life hanging on what he did next.

No, I'd never get to be that person, and now was not the time to worry about it.

I took off toward Malzton, to find Jack, persuade him to turn over Manu, and get all of us safely out of the box in which I'd trapped us.

CHAPTER 26

SLIPPING INTO A big city on a heavily developed world is rarely difficult, because those urban areas never exactly end. Instead, their fringes blend with the edges of other nearby towns and cities and blur the boundaries to the point that they barely exist at all. To get in quietly, all you need is a secluded spot to touch down long enough to jump out of whatever brought you there.

Entering a place like Malzton, on the other hand, can be tricky, because the gaps between settlements on developing worlds are often large, and strangers frequently stand out. Fortunately for me, the proximity of Malzton's northern edge to the mountains and their snow made it a focal point for the winter sports crowd. Repair shops, restaurants, and bar after bar after bar backed up to the small stand of trees that stood as nature's last line of defense between man and mountain.

I emerged from the woods on a pathway that led between a pair of busy pubs and walked directly into the middle of an argument between two very drunk men who looked only a bit younger than I did but who were probably a hundred and twenty years my junior.

"Water is for losers," one of them said. He was short, wide, the dark brown of tree bark, with hair that fell below his shoulders and a sleeveless shirt despite the coming night and the cold. "No speed, no thrills, nothing worth doing."

"No speed?" the other said. Also a small but broad man, this one was bald and as pale as snow. "Have you ever ray raced? Skied? Done anything at all on or below the surface of an ocean?"

"Of course—" Long Hair stopped when he noticed me.

I smiled, nodded, and kept walking.

"Come from the mountain, have you, mate?" he said to me.

The other now turned to face me, so they were standing side by side and blocking my way.

"Yeah," I said.

"Ski, luge, what?" Long Hair asked.

I saw no value in lying and an opportunity if I played it right. "Halo luge," I said. "Awesome ride, absolutely amazing." My enthusiasm was genuine despite my strong desire to move past these two and lose myself in the town's crowds.

"See," he said, pointing first to me and then to his friend, "this guy gets it."

"Ever done any water runs?" the bald guy asked.

I recalled riding the back of an illegally souped-up racing ray named Bob through the ocean of a faraway planet on a moonlit night. Though that experience had ended in a battle, a firefight that left two of my comrades badly injured, my time with Bob had also been astonishing, stolen moments of joy in the middle of a time of great tension. "Yeah," I said, "I have: an augmented ray on a long night dive. Unbelievable."

"Which is better?" Long Hair asked.

"Yeah, which is it?" the bald man added, as if the opinion of a stranger really mattered.

In their drunken states, I suppose it did. I pondered the question seriously. Like great meals, beautiful women, wondrous bits of scenery, these two experiences were not fairly comparable. Both were wonderful—very different to be sure, but even trying to compare them diminished them.

"I can't do it," I finally said. "It's not right. Each one was a ride I'd never want to have missed, but I can't compare them. I won't even try. Maybe one or the other will be better for each of you, but I have to say, I'd be happy to do either one again."

For a few seconds they both looked angry, as if I'd insulted their loves, but then their faces cleared and they both smiled and lost focus.

"That is so shiny," Long Hair said. "Absolutely. You've got it."

"Exactly right," Bald Guy said. "Definitely." He focused back on me. "We have got to buy you a drink!"

"Definitely," Long Hair said.

"I'd love to let you," I said, "but she's waiting for me, and, well, you know how that goes."

They nodded in unison, their eyes losing focus again.

"Where's your tube?" Long Hair said. "You can't leave without it."

"I have to," I said. "I won it in a company contest, but she won't let me take it home."

"You're going to abandon it?" he said.

"Yes." I turned and pointed toward where I'd left George. "It's about three klicks that way, not far from the border of the last of the snow and the edge of the woods. I figure someone'll find it, and that lucky person gets to keep it."

"Easy as that?" Long Hair said. He stared for a moment at his friend, then looked again at me. "Mind if we give it a go?"

"Not at all. It's a great one: multi-ported exhaust, new model, everything you could want."

"Excellent," Long Hair said.

"You are so shiny," Bald Guy added.

They turned as one and jogged to the woods. I watched to make sure they definitely left; they seemed nice enough, but apparently good people have turned on me in the past, so I don't give my back to anyone if I can help it.

At the edge of the trees they stopped, held up their hands, and yelled, "Keep riding!"

"Guys," I said. "Treat him right. His name's George."

"Excellent," said Long Hair.

"Shiny," said Bald Guy.

They disappeared into the woods.

I waited three minutes. They didn't reemerge, and no one else came down the walkway between the buildings.

I hoped they would find George and ride him many times. He deserved owners who loved the sport as much as he did.

I walked to the front of the bar on the right and joined the queue of drunks waiting for a cab.

Even though I'd done everything I could to throw off pursuit, I invested an hour and a few deposits from my wallet running the cab around the city, to locations I chose at random from local data stream searches. I had it take me by The All-Nighter, a joint whose primary attraction was low-priced alcohol burn drips, so you could choose your level of drunkenness and maintain it as long as you wanted; Tips and Tricks, a combo financial services/brothel whose ads came dangerously close to promising that you could make as much money from invest-ments during your stay as you spent on its lineup of attractive companions; The Bare Truth, a strip club all of whose enter-tainers offered proof-of-work citations for each of their mods; Stay Out, a members-only bar whose patrons ran to heavily armed and significantly augmented men whose discussions and fights spilled into the street as we cruised past; and a couple of restaurants, a fish place named Deep Blue and an eatery, Hunt & Skew, that backed up to a multi-hectare wooded area where customers were free to track and kill their own dinners before the chefs skewered the still-dripping meat.

Along the way, I pretended to make calls to local contacts. I carefully never mentioned Jack's name even though I equally carefully made it obvious to any astute observer that I was talking about him. If Midon later swept the records of all the cab companies, this vehicle's audio and video recordings would provide her with plenty of evidence that I was working hard to find Jack. Meanwhile, I surreptitiously monitored his position on the tracker Lobo had given me. At the location resolution I was using—a hundred meters or so—he didn't appear to move the entire time I was in the cab. I hoped he had hunkered down for the night, though that seemed extremely unlikely;

Jack had always preferred the evening to the day. Hook in the dark, close in the light, he used to say; never take the final step in a con when the mark is uncomfortable or prone to being suspicious.

I finally exited the cab in front of Eat/Drink/Happy, a bar whose ads touted the wide range of imported drinks it paired with meats and cheeses from domestic livestock. I ducked straight inside the building so the cab's last recordings of me would place me there, ordered and drank a glass of fruit juice, and left via the kitchen entrance. As I'd hoped, no public cameras were in evidence anywhere on the streets of Malzton; if Midon wanted to track me from here, at least her people would have to expend the time and energy to come inside, question the staff, and tap the internal systems.

Once outside, I paused to assess the area more closely. I stood a little over a klick from Jack, who still hadn't moved. I'd studied the streets through the cab's windows, of course, so it was clear that Jack's trail had led me to the kind of area he always chose when he had to go to ground. I pressed against the wall to the left of the door and surveyed the alley with both normal vision and IR. Aside from three rodents bickering over some food scraps hanging off a trash bin four meters away, I was the only living thing on the small paved accessway. Men, alone and in groups, passed the end of the alley frequently, but none looked in my direction.

I headed toward the front of the bar, waited for a break in the pedestrian traffic, and then folded myself into it, just another guy bound for somewhere only he knew, watching on all sides for trouble he couldn't predict but had to expect might arrive at any moment. Every man I passed—and of the many, many people clogging the streets, only three bodies appeared highly likely to be women—vibrated with the same air of twitchy expectation, as if the night might bring them great treasure provided they could avoid its many threats, threats that could come from anywhere in a place where even the shadows themselves could coalesce into unexpected forms.

I started with standard vision but switched to IR because the

irregular shapes of the buildings and the many levels of light-
ing created too many dark hiding places for me to be able to
scan them all reliably with visible light. Red, green, and blue
figures walked the sidewalks beside me and across the street.
Blue machines splashing crimson from exhausts zipped up and
down the road, occasional outlines of red marking those few
passengers brave enough to lower their windows. In irregularly
shaped nooks between adjacent buildings and down the alleys
and byways between standalone structures, pairs and trios
and quads of red-glowing people stood and moved in packs,
their quiet deals below the threshold of normal hearing and
nothing I cared to bother to monitor. Light scrolls and bright
windows and outlined doorways made every sight other than
the people and the traffic unpleasant in IR, so I kept my eyes
on the most likely threats and away from the endless ads that
painted every inanimate object. I flowed around but did not
touch my fellow nighttime travelers, wanting neither to leave
traces of my passage nor to afford anyone the opportunity
to brace or injure me. Places like this yanked my mind to
attention and flooded my body with adrenaline and alertness,
leaving me tingling with the impossible goal of sensing every
potential threat before it could turn hostile.

When the tracker showed Jack as being within a hundred
and fifty meters, I dialed the resolution to meter level and
followed the smaller guide marks onward.

At fifty meters out, I switched to normal vision and backed
against the wall of a restaurant whose name I didn't even bother
to register. All my attention was on the building across the street;
unless Lobo had messed up or Jack had discovered the implant,
Jack was there, unmoving. I glanced left and right, then slid
along the wall and into the shadows of a small alcove between
the buildings. I took a long, slow breath, and the stench of
urine smacked my sinuses. I leaned forward for a quick look
at the two businesses: Both were bars, and from the looks of
the clientele entering them and the fact that neither bothered
to light up more than a single word—"BAR" on one, "DRINKS"
on the other—they weren't particularly nice ones.

Jack's hiding place, a restaurant and bar called Good Times and More, struck me as only slightly more upscale. Unlike some of the higher-class establishments I'd passed, it didn't bother with a window to entice potential customers with the namesake good times; the view probably couldn't live up to anything prospects might imagine awaited them inside. Unlike the bars on either side of me, however, the joint Jack had chosen could afford working signs and frequent enough cleaning that it was clearly the nicest place on the block. I scanned both sides of it and the rooftops—the interception from Chaplat's two guards had insured I wouldn't soon forget to check above as well as around me—in both normal vision and IR, and I spotted no threats. The only obvious cameras sat atop the doorways of each business, but that didn't mean a thing; any camera I could see was visible only to remind drunks that cops could and would use video footage to locate and/or prosecute them should they get out of line. I've always wondered why in a universe where no camera needs to be visible to be effective this technique still works, but it does, and many business owners swear by it.

I stepped out of the shadows and onto the street, faced Good Times for a full minute, and then retreated back into darkness.

Nothing changed. I waited two minutes. Still nothing.

Good. Anyone expecting me as a threat would most likely have reacted by now.

I considered breaking into the back of the place, but the evening was still young enough that trade all around me was brisk, so kitchen staff would be working and would have clear views of their external doorways. I could use the nanomachines to create my own entry hole, but there was no value in drawing attention to myself when I had the simple option of entering through the front like any other customer.

At a break in the traffic, I crossed the street and approached Good Times. The tracker marked Jack's location; he still hadn't moved. I had to assume he was eating dinner; I smiled at the thought of interrupting his meal. Though the odds were vanishingly small that he was enjoying anything approaching the sublime dishes Choy created, I still took a petty pleasure in doing to him what he had done to me.

I walked inside and stopped in a small foyer to sneak a quick peek at the tracker. Jack had moved and was practically on top of me.

I looked up as the door in front of me opened.

Jack stood there, dapper as always, this time in matching black shirt and pants a few shades lighter than his skin. He smiled, clapped a hand on my shoulder, and chuckled at my surprise at the greeting.

"Good to see you, Jon," he said, "and about time, too."

I stared at him, then wondered why I was surprised. He'd always been this calm, this self-sure; I'd never know whether he was really waiting for me or simply handled my appearance well. I certainly couldn't trust anything he'd say on the topic.

When I didn't speak, he pulled me inside and motioned toward a table in the front right corner.

"I've been wondering when you'd finally get here."

CHAPTER 27

WHEN A BOWL of soup and some fresh-smelling bread immediately appeared in front of me, I began to believe Jack
might indeed have been expecting me. I shook my head. He'd
rattled me, so I was giving him credit foolishly; serving food
was, after all, what restaurants did.

Jack's meal was a plate of five types of cheese and some of the
same bread that accompanied my soup. He spread a generous
helping of a runny yellow cheese on a small chunk of bread
and chewed it slowly, closing his eyes momentarily to focus on
the taste. He looked at me and raised his right eyebrow.

I pushed aside my food, spooned a helping of the same
cheese he'd eaten, took part of his bread, and made my own
small sandwich. The strong, nutty, rich taste flooded my mouth;
though I could see why he'd closed his eyes, I kept mine open
and focused on him. I nodded my approval, leaned back, and
waited.

"I suppose you'd like an apology," he said.

I tilted my head slightly and stared at him. I didn't know any
conversational tricks he hadn't mastered, so I couldn't expect
to get much from him, but it wouldn't hurt to try.

"If you examine the situation more closely, however," he
continued, "I think you'll realize that though perhaps I did not

treat you as well as I might have, in the end you walked away with more money than you had when I entered Falls."

If he was switching to sales mode, I was wasting my time. I leaned forward and said, "We're in a far bigger mess than you realize. I don't even know exactly how I'm going to get out of it. I do know that any resolution begins with Manu. Give him to me, Jack."

He sat back from the table, patted his mouth with a small white cloth napkin, put his hands delicately in his lap, and shook his head. "I can't do that, Jon."

"Remember saying that you needed my help in part because you were no good at violence and I was?"

He nodded.

I leaned far enough forward that my face was most of the way across the table. I gripped its edges so hard the veins on my hands stood out. "Then don't make me employ those skills with you, Jack. I will take the boy away from you if I have to." Adrenaline streaked through me as the anger rose.

Jack smiled and patted my right hand.

I trembled with the effort of not decking him.

"Look around, Jon," he said quietly. "I didn't run far in part because Dougat would be able to track me via jump-station bribes, but also because you'd find me here and let me know how bad our predicament really was. I knew you'd come, so I prepared. Neither of us wins if we don't work together."

For the first time since entering the place, I did what I should have done before I'd even passed through the doorway: I checked it out carefully and slowly. A pair of guys forty-five degrees left of Jack nodded gently at me, their hands not moving from their positions under the table. A second pair occupied another table ninety degrees further along the counterclockwise arc. I'd foolishly followed Jack to his location, so my back was to the doorway. I turned around and smiled at the man sitting behind me; his hands were also under his table.

I disgusted myself. Jack had caught me off guard, and I'd responded by treating him as an old friend who'd simply upset me. Let your emotions pollute an assignment, and you always pay a price. If all those men fired, given that their hands were at low levels, I probably wouldn't suffer a head wound. I was reasonably certain that the nanomachines could fix just about anything else, so I'd probably survive the barrage. Between the heavies and the bystanders, however, a lot of people would witness my rapid recovery, a process that would be sure to raise many, many questions—questions that could ultimately make me a corporation's lab animal once again. Would I then be willing to do the only thing that could stop it from happening: kill everyone here? No.

Jack didn't know any of this, however, so the first step in changing the power balance was to refuse to grant him control. I leaned forward again and very quietly said, "I can kill you before any of these guys can shoot. Send them away."

Jack maintained his relaxed posture, but he sounded less confident when he spoke. "I tell them to leave. You take me away and interrogate me, or maybe you risk annoying the rest of the patrons and stay here and make me tell you where Manu is." He shook his head slowly. "No, Jon. We can all relax, and I can have some of them back off, but there is no chance at all that I will sit here alone with you."

"You are seriously pissing me off, Jack. I won't stay with a man at my back." I swiveled my chair so I could watch that guy as well as the rest of them, then continued to speak to Jack without looking at him. "At the same time, I appreciate your situation. So, change seats with me so I have the corner, pull the crack team here behind you and to your left, and we can talk. Otherwise"—I swiveled to face him—"you will be the first to suffer." I turned back so I could keep all of the others in my view.

"I'd forgotten how paranoid you are, Jon," he said. "But that seems as good a resolution as any we're likely to reach."

He stood slowly and moved in front of the table. He motioned toward the man to my left and then to the others, and they all rose, several of them doing a bad job of feigning casual intent. I also stood, my hands in plain view against my thighs, then bumped Jack forward enough that I could slide between him and the table.

As Jack's men were in motion and I was passing behind him, I paused, grabbed his shirt with my left hand, and poked his sternum with two fingers of my right. "If I wanted to kill you," I said, smiling for the benefit of anyone watching, "you'd be dead now, and I'd have your body as a shield. You need better help." I let him go and sat. As best I could tell, the five bodyguards never realized how at risk their boss had been.

Jack sat and raised his hands. "What can I say? I don't have a crew here. I hired these five by the hour from the house security guy." He gestured with his head toward the floor above us. "Though the food here is more than tolerable, this place makes its real money from the 'and More' part of the business upstairs." He moved his plate and glass in front of him, took another bite of cheese and a drink, then sat back. "You said you were in trouble. What's happening?"

"No, Jack. I said *we* were in a big mess. You have as big a problem as I do."

"How's that?" Jack had regained control and again oozed calm.

"Remember your friend, Bakun Chaplat?" I leaned back. "He certainly remembers you."

"I'd ask how you made his acquaintance, but it doesn't really matter. He may be big on Mund, but we're on Gash, far away from his goons."

I shook my head slowly. "You need both new guards and better intel," I said. "He's here, he's searching for you, and he's brought some help. Better help than that lot you hired."

"I appreciate the warning, Jon. Perhaps it's time for me to leave this system. The heat should be off by now."

"Wrong again. You wouldn't make it out of the gate area, not even with the aid of your friend, Carne. The EC wants both you and Manu. Of course, they'd have to beat Dougat to you; he's here, too, and with multiple teams."

Jack said nothing. He closed his eyes for a few seconds. I'd seen him do this before when we were working out the details of cons, so I knew it was how he processed information when he felt he had the time to thoroughly consider a problem.

He opened his eyes and stared at me. "The fact that you know all this suggests you've met with all of these people. That you walked in here instead of any of them means I have something you want. I assume that's Manu."

I nodded in agreement.

"There's no way they would have talked to you without leaning on you," he continued. "So you and I are definitely in this together. I may not be able to get away, but unless you really think you can survive an encounter with all five of these admittedly cut-rate security contractors, keep me alive during the fight, and then get me to tell you where Manu is, you're also stuck." He smiled. "I'd say it's time for us to work together." His smile broadened. "It'll be like old times. We always made a great team."

My first reaction was to punch him in the throat both for getting me into this situation and for his smug assessment, but I forced myself to breathe slowly and deeply and sit still. I'd planned to find a way to satisfy all three groups on my own, but I had to admit that I didn't know exactly how I would do that. I was fairly confident I hadn't done anything to make that task harder, but I was a long way from a detailed solution to the problem. Having Jack with me could make this a whole lot easier. I also had the promise of money and, as long as Maggie stayed rational, some backup Jack didn't own.

"Maybe you're right," I said. "And there's even a potentially big payday here, if we can make everything go perfectly."

"How big?" he said.

"Very—and I'm willing to share it with you, if we can make this work."

"What's the catch, and what exactly are we trying to make happen? Do you have a plan?"

"The catch is that I walk away with Manu. We both earn some money, and we both end up with everyone off our backs—or so I hope."

"I repeat: Do you have a plan?"

"Not exactly," I said, shaking my head. "More like the outline of a plan, or at least a few ideas in the general direction of a plan."

"Hence your need for me," he said.

It struck me then that despite roping me into all of this, drugging me, using me, and generally trashing my life, Jack was going to make a lot of money. I was torn between anger and admiration.

"How do you do it, Jack?" I said.

He raised an eyebrow but didn't reply.

I shook my head. "It doesn't matter. Do you agree that I get Manu when this is over?"

"What do you hope to do with him?"

The concern in Jack's voice seemed genuine, though assuming any emotion he showed was real was always a risky move. "Transport him somewhere safe, probably back to his family, but somewhere far from all this."

"Your word?" Jack knew me well enough to realize that if I gave my word, I always kept it.

"Yes," I said. "So, are we agreed?"

He nodded. "Yes. When we're safely out of this predicament, Manu leaves with you, and you drop him somewhere they can't find him."

"Okay," I said. "Now let's figure out what we're going to do."

Jack leaned back, clasped his hands over his flat stomach, and closed his eyes.

"Run it down for me," he said.

CHAPTER 28

"SO IN THE NAME of helping Manu," Jack said some while later, "you've managed to sell him to the EC, promise him to a cult of Pinkelponker fanatics, make a related illegal arms deal, and leave all of them pissed at you." He smiled and added, "Did I miss anything?"

"When you say it like that," I said, "I have to admit it doesn't sound too good. I'm sure we can make it work, though, and we can definitely earn some serious money if we do."

"We just have to figure out how," Jack said.

"Yeah," I agreed, "we just have to figure out how."

"I thought I'd taught you to always plan the con *before* you start it," he said, "not as you go along."

"And I thought friends didn't drag each other into trouble like this. You do *not* want to start criticizing me after all you did to cause this mess."

He laughed lightly. "Fair enough. What matters now is how we move forward." He sat silently for almost a minute, then said, "How about a pot of gold?"

"Too many buyers, plus Manu doesn't fit," I said.

"A race phone for the EC?"

"It would get them to the right place, but Dougat and Chaplat would have no reason to play."

"Hey," he said, "I'm brainstorming. Give me a little time. You're not exactly bursting with ideas."

I nodded agreement and pondered the situation.

We went back and forth for the better part of two hours, tossing out classic con structures and trying to adapt them to our situation. You rarely work more than one mark at a time, however, so nothing quite fit our three-party problem, nor did anything meet the additional requirement of saving Manu in the bargain.

Then it hit me.

"How well connected are you here?" I said.

"Well enough to know which people we'd want for any type of job, but—" He paused and spread his hands. "—also well enough known by the same people that we'd have to show them some cash up front. No one here is going to work for me on the come."

"No surprise there," I said. "You obviously haven't changed your business practices." If you weren't part of Jack's core team—which I fortunately was during the years we worked together—he considered it almost a sacred duty to try to con you out of your share of any haul. He said any money he filched from a weaker crew member was an educational expense that person would later benefit from incurring. "Fortunately, I have that jewel you left me." I had a lot more money than that, but I wanted Jack to know as little as possible about my financial situation. "Can you point me to some fences here? If so, I might be able to handle my end of the front money for anything we need."

"Absolutely," he said, "and I don't think you appreciate how great a gift it was, or you wouldn't worry at all about expenses. Even ten percent of the value of that thing is enough to cover most of the cost of the biggest con we've ever run."

He'd done it again. He'd led me to assume he was poor and to offer to pay, but he'd stolen many more gems than the one he'd left me, so he had plenty of money.

"What about your haul?" I said. "You started this trouble, so you should fund its resolution."

"Just making sure you're still on your game," he said. "But

because we're splitting the take, we should split the bank." He stuck out his hand. "Fair enough?"

I shook his hand but held tight and squeezed as I said, "Deal, but the split is by the number of gems we each have." I strained to keep smiling as I crushed his hand.

Jack fought to show nothing on his face, but his arm shook. "That's unfair, Jon. I earned those."

"And now you'll spend a little part of them. You got me into this, so you'll bankroll the bulk of the cost. You can always make more money, Jack; I'm offering you a chance to walk away with no one hunting you."

"Fair enough," he said.

I let go of his hand.

He pulled it back, casually put it under the table, and said, "So, why did you ask how connected I was?"

"Because we're going to need a crew."

He leaned forward with excitement. "What do you have in mind?"

"I think a modified treasure map with a bang might do it," I said, growing more and more convinced as the idea blossomed. "We'd have to find the right location, of course, as well as a very special twinsie—I have an idea for that—and at least a boomer and a couple of scrapers."

He considered the notion, then leaned forward. "I've never worked a treasure map with more than two, and even two is rare."

"But we have done it," I said. "Remember that time on—"

"Yeah, yeah, of course," he said, a huge smile punctuating the comment. "That was brilliant." The smile collapsed. "We have three here, though, so the problem remains."

"That's the beauty of it," I said. "We don't have three, not really. We have only two, provided—"

"Of course!" he said. "If you can make them—"

"I can." Running ideas back and forth with Jack, finishing each other's sentences—I'd forgotten how much I'd enjoyed this part of our time together. For all his flaws, Jack had a natural aptitude for the work and a mind quick enough that he could succeed at anything he'd bother to try.

"What about protection?"

"My faux PCAV," I said, "ought to be intimidating enough." Lobo would hate me calling him "faux," and he might not like his role, but he'd do it well.

"And me," he said. "That means I have to—"

"Yeah," I said. "It won't work any other way."

"But if it's your ship," he said, "then we need to call—"

"We most certainly do," I said, nodding my agreement, "and pronto. Time is short."

"None of this should be a major problem," he said, "as long as nothing has to stand up to close inspection."

"It shouldn't."

"We need a big setup," Jack said, "but I know a prime area to search: the abandoned base on the southeast edge of town."

"You'll scout it and find candidates?" I said.

"Sure. What about the boomer?"

"You set up—" I said.

"—and you finish," he said. "It could work."

"Any ideas for the scrapers?" I said. "This might skid sideways, so we need power and muscle, but we also need precision."

Jack closed his eyes and considered the problem. "The Zyuns," he finally said. "They're usually busy, but for a good payday and a spot of what they consider fun, which this definitely should be, they'll come. I'll need a few days to stretch out to them. A little money would help with that and with the site work."

"We covered that," I said, "and we're not going to keep wasting time on it. I'll take care of the expenses on my end, and you deal with yours. Your end's bigger because you have more gems."

He leaned back in his seat and sighed theatrically. "Fine. You can't blame a man for trying. My money or yours, though, it's still likely to take me a bit of time to reach the Zyuns."

"No worries," I said. "I have to talk to Maggie and get back to my ship before anyone notices."

"Will the woman be a problem?"

"Maggie," I said. "As I've told you, her name is Maggie Park, and either she'll help, or I'll keep her out of it."

Jack studied me for a minute. "You're making a mistake, Jon. You're already emotional about the boy, and now you're involved with the woman." He held up his hand. "Yes, I know their names, but the way I referred to them is precisely the point: Get cold and play inside the lines we draw, or it'll go nonlinear and no one will come out well."

Anger rose in me, and I wanted to hit him. I couldn't decide, though, what aspect of his statements infuriated me the most: the claim that I couldn't stay cool, his calm assurance in declaring that I was involved with Maggie when I clearly was not, or, I finally had to admit, his accuracy in noting that I *wished* I were involved with Maggie. None of that mattered, though; saving Manu and surviving without Dougat, Chaplat, or Midon destroying us remained the top priorities.

"I'm cold enough, Jack," I said. Too cold, I thought but did not say, at least if you ask Maggie. "You check possible locations, I'll take care of my tasks, and we'll meet as soon as you have something to show me." I didn't mention that part of my problem was figuring out a way to take Manu away from him; if the plan worked, that part should fall out nicely. I pulled the spare milspec encrypted comm unit from my inside pocket and put it on the table between us. "Take this, and call me when you're ready."

He swept it into his hand, and it vanished. "Will do."

"One last thing," I said.

"Yes?"

"If you decide to run, I'll turn all three groups on you, and I'll chase you myself. You'll be lucky if one of them catches you before I do."

"I'm hurt, Jon," he said. "We're back as a team, we're working together, and a big payday is in sight. I've never failed you on a con."

"No, you haven't. Don't let this be the first time."

I stood and left.

As I hit the street and grabbed a cab to transport me to the rendezvous point, I started rehearsing the conversation ahead.

Any way I looked at it, Maggie was not going to like this plan.

➤   ➤   ➤

By the time I'd reached Lobo and we'd settled into a secure orbital position nestled among a group of weather and high-encryption data sats, the night had surrendered to the day and all I wanted was to sleep.

Maggie had other ideas: She demanded a recap of my meeting with Jack. Lobo was also curious. I ran down the highlights for them, though I didn't explain the plan; at this stage, the fewer the people who knew it, the better. Plus, I was beginning to accept that because Maggie couldn't control her reactions well enough to be a fully informed player, I might have to use her ignorance. Much as she'd hate the idea, if it helped us save Manu, I had to hope she'd forgive me in the end.

As I recounted the key points of our conversation, Maggie's eyes narrowed and her cheeks flushed.

The moment I stopped talking, she started. "You did what?" she said. "You made a deal with that kidnapper?"

"We don't know that he kidnapped Manu," I said. "The last time I saw them together, Manu seemed to trust him. I don't believe he would hurt the boy."

"Why are you defending a man who drugged you, abandoned you, and left you with three dangerous groups pursuing you?"

"I'm not trying to defend him," I said, though I had to admit I was doing just that. "I'm explaining how we're going to rescue Manu and end all of this trouble."

"It worked out so well with Jack last time," she said, "that I can see why you'd want to partner with him again."

"There's a crucial difference between then and now: I'm driving this plan, and I understand what's going on."

"Why not simply take Manu and run?"

"First, I don't know where Manu is, and forcing Jack to tell me would be risky at best; he is, as I told you, traveling with protection. Second, even if we did persuade Jack to give us Manu, we wouldn't get far without having to fight—and thus put Manu at more risk—because none of these groups is going to let us leave this system without challenging us."

"So we have to rely on Jack?"

"If you have a better plan," I said, "then let's hear it." I took a deep breath to try to stop myself from sounding as angry and frustrated as I was. "Otherwise, we're doing it my way."

She took her time and considered the problem. I wanted to turn my back on her and grab some sleep, but to be fair I had to wait and hear what she had to say.

After a couple of minutes, she said, "No, I don't have a better idea. As you might imagine, I've been worrying about our situation during all the hours you've left me alone. Every time I think I have a good solution, I discover major flaws in it. You've done a lot of things I don't understand, but you've been consistent in trying to resolve everything and at least appearing most of the time to be trying to save Manu, so I'll shut up and do what I can to help."

"Thank you," I said.

"I can offer alternatives," Lobo said.

"I know you can," I said, "but I'm also quite confident they'll all involve more violence than I want."

"Given where we are," Lobo said, "some violence is inevitable. So, we're only discussing how much. I can track you and take out anyone helping Jack, and I can certainly destroy the ships Dougat and Chaplat were using to monitor us."

"And the EC?" I said. "You'd blast its ships, too?"

"Not all of them, of course," Lobo said, annoyance evident in his voice. "I know my limitations, so I understand that even in this backwater region of space the EC maintains more combat craft than I could possibly handle. I do believe, however, that I could disable or destroy enough of them that we could leave this system and make a sufficiently high number of jumps that the EC would be extremely unlikely to bother to follow us. It simply wouldn't be economically reasonable."

"So the best case is that we spend the rest of our lives avoiding this section of space, and the worst case is that the EC recruits the help of other federations? Is that about right?"

"Perhaps," Lobo said, "though the universe is vast, and the EC might well lose interest."

I shook my head in disgust, not at Lobo, who was behaving

according to his personality/programming, but at myself for allowing him to draw me into a debate on his terms. "No," I said. "I'm not going to argue with you, because I'm not pursuing any option that demands we kill multiple people. I've done more of that in my life than I want. I'll do it again if I have to, but if I can avoid it, I will." I didn't tell him that I could have taken Jack on my own, right there in the bar, simply by using the nanomachines to kill everyone else. I might even have been able to simply scare them away, though any use of the nanomachines in front of so many people puts me at great risk of discovery. I then could have tortured Jack until he gave up Manu—and he would have, he had no training in resistance, and even if he did, everyone breaks eventually. If not for a friend and colleague rescuing me from torture the last time a megacorp was hunting me, I would certainly have broken. After Jack told me where to find Manu, I could have gone there and destroyed anyone in my way. I didn't even know the limits of what the nanomachines could do, but I suspected that if I were willing to turn them loose in full-on self-replication mode with no self-destruct guidance, they might be able to take out a planet or even more. I'd watched Aggro disappear, so massive destruction was definitely possible. The fact that I had this power, though, did not mean I had to use it. I would not let what I *could* do become what I *would* do. I would create the best set of options I could, and as much as possible, I would avoid killing. If I never killed again, I'd be better for it—but never free of the stains of the past. There was no way to remove that damage. "No," I said, suddenly aware that I'd been standing silently for an awkward amount of time. "No, we're not doing that."

"Your choice, of course," Lobo said.

I focused again on Maggie, who was staring at me intently. She reached out and gently held my left cheek with her hand, then pulled back and stared, as if she'd touched something slimy. I didn't blame her; most people don't like being around killers. I looked away from her before her face showed more of her disgust; I didn't want to see her look at me that way.

I preferred to remember that brief moment in the hangar, when she was modeling the dress and I stupidly abandoned reality and imagined I might have a chance to build a future with her.

"We'll work out the details as we go along," I said, "and I'll tell each of you what you need to do as necessary." I turned my back and headed to bed. "For now, I'm going to grab some sleep. Maggie, you may want to do the same."

Under my breath, not willing to say it loudly enough that it might provoke another argument but also unable or unwilling to keep the fact entirely to myself, I added, "Jack'll be calling soon enough."

CHAPTER 29

"**L**AST CHANCE TO TRY at least this part of it my way," Lobo said as we touched down on the northwestern edge of the abandoned base. "Jack brought three men as backup. Their spacing is good, each has shelter on at least one side, each is near a corner, and no one is in anyone else's line of fire, so they're probably pros. Nonetheless, I could alter our approach path quickly enough to give me clear shots at all of them. He'd then be yours."

"Again, no," I said. "He told me he'd bring protection, so I have no problem with their presence." I didn't expect Jack to do anything stupid, but in case I was wrong I added, "If I signal for help or anyone opens fire, take them out."

"I should be so lucky," Lobo said. "You might as well own a taxi for all the good my capabilities are doing you."

"Your role is vital," I said, "as I'll explain later."

Lobo opened a hatch, and I stepped into a perfect, sunny morning, a slight breeze blowing and soft white clouds dotting the sky. I don't know if it was my imagination or real, but I would have sworn that the light wind carried the scent of the base's abandonment. Three once-deadly security barriers slashed across the paved ground between us and the facility proper, but they reeked of age and sadness, guards so wounded and tired but still so well built that they could neither do their

257

jobs nor die. The outermost divider, a ten-meter-high fence of woven slash metal and artificial diamond blades, gleamed dangerously in some areas but lay harmlessly in others, holes blasted through it and large chunks of it broken down or hauled away by looters. Next in line stood a five-meter-tall permacrete wall that sparkled as the morning light struck the shards of glass and cheap local minerals embedded in it. A three-meter-high, formerly electrified metal fence had once formed the final defensive barrier, but you could tell where it had stood only by spotting the scraps so embedded in permacrete supports that they must not have been worth salvaging. Scratches in the ground between the three ravaged defenders and along the barriers themselves suggested the paths robotic guards and crawlers had worn on endless variations of their patrol routes.

The EC had once wrapped this base and its thousands and thousands of tons of armaments with security strong enough to repel many ground attacks and buy time in the face of even the worst land-based assaults, and I assumed that the air defenses had been equally formidable. Now, though, the place was sad.

With no power feeding any of the defenses and no one to stop them, opportunistic locals had bulldozed and blasted access paths large enough to let through demolition teams and freight haulers. Permacrete, the main material of the frames of all the office buildings, barracks, supply depots, hangars, repair facilities, and other structures that composed the huge base, was cheaper to lay than to move, so the shells of those constructs still stood.

Almost everything else was gone. With the exception of a few sections of the outermost barrier, all the metal, everything from signposts to security fences to doors, was missing. Window frames sat empty. Tiny stumps still embedded in the ground marked where signs had stood. Everywhere I looked, the permacrete survived alone, the last remaining bones of the dead EC base.

Jack stood inside a small guardhouse forty meters away.

He was smart enough not to approach me, to let me come when I was ready. He knew I'd run a perimeter check before I entered. I hoped Jack still believed Lobo was an imitation PCAV, because I wanted every possible edge should the con man turn on me again.

I spotted no problems beyond the guards Lobo had noted and I had expected.

"Still clean except for the three soldiers," Lobo said on the machine frequency, "as is the airspace over us. We have to consider the possibility that we're being watched by at least one of the pursuing groups, so I suggest you keep me close."

"Agreed," I subvocalized. My guess was that Midon would keep her EC ships at bay a bit longer, and Chaplat was likely to stay back for a few more days as well, but Dougat might well be monitoring us. We'd scanned the whole area in IR and spotted nothing that appeared anywhere near Manu's size, so if Dougat was watching, I hope he'd done the same and was leaving me alone to work on Jack.

If Dougat chose to charge in, then we'd have to fall back to Lobo's plan and take out his ship—but only if the man was that stupid. I didn't want that to be the case. To save Manu and get out of this mess without having to run forever, I needed to make the plan work.

I was wasting time worrying about what might happen. I needed to evaluate Jack's proposed location to see if it met our requirements, and then get out of there.

I walked toward Jack. As I approached him, the three men tightened the triangle they formed around him. When I was five meters away, I stopped, lifted my arms slightly to my sides, and let them see that I wasn't carrying any obvious weapons.

I also used the time to study them. I started with a quick scan of the man on my right, but as I checked out the other two I realized something odd: They appeared to be identical. Each stood about thirty centimeters shorter than I, but I estimated each to also be at least ten and maybe twenty kilos heavier, all of the additional weight muscle. Very few men choose to be that short, so these guys must have elected to stick with their birth height. I would have thought them anti-tech types from that one fact alone, but there was no way they could have built that much muscle naturally. Each wore a sleeveless night-black bodysuit that followed every contour of his body as if it were water rippling over a stone-filled stream, but as I looked closer I noticed the material was thick enough that it had to be light-weight armor. Muscle rippled under the garments and on their exposed arms, which were so ripped they resembled anatomy holos. Each man was pale with hair that matched the bodysuit and a day-old beard growth that was so perfectly uniform it had to exist for style, not function, the look one that had long been popular throughout the bodyguard circuit on dozens of planets. Visible in all of their ears were combo comm/audio-canceling units; they could stand under rocket engines firing and hear no more than the sound of a strong wind blowing. Rugged faces, chins wide enough to suggest both hormone-enhanced bones and no desire to do anything about it, and thick necks—everything about these three was built for combat.

They'd also come armed for action. Each carried one hand-gun, had two more visible in shoulder and waist holsters, and wore a back pack that included a rifle within easy reach. From the size of the pack, more weapons were probably inside it. None of the men moved or looked as if he even noticed the weight he was carrying.

Of course, I might have been misreading them, because I couldn't see their eyes: active-glass shields locked directly onto their eye sockets. The covers were cycling lazily through a variety of images, all of them disturbing: bloodshot eyes, serrated and bloody knives, mushroom clouds, and explosions of various sorts. Socket-locked eye protection was excellent for combat, with no blind spots and total protection, but the mods necessary to keep them in place left you with unattractive connector holes around each eye until the replacement cells grew enough to fill in the pits. These guys were either extreme fashion followers or very serious about their work. Given their size, I assumed the latter.

"An unusual trio, aren't they, Jon?" Jack said. When I didn't respond, he continued. "I'm being terribly rude," he said. "Let me introduce you to the Zyuns."

I nodded my head but didn't say a word.

All three Zyuns nodded in unison.

I stared at each of them again in turn, but I still couldn't tell them apart.

"Friends of yours?" I said.

"No," the one directly in front of me said.

"Simply," the one to my right said.

"Contractors," the one to my left finished.

"You're free to hire them after today," Jack said, "but until the day is over, I've paid for their time and protection."

"True identical triplets?" I said, still curious.

"No," Jack said. "May I?"

The three Zyuns nodded as one.

"Talking, at least to others, isn't their strong point," Jack said. "As I understand it, they were fraternal triplets before their mother started applying the best science she could afford so she could use her sons to secure her control over the colony she ruled. All that work made them as identical as possible without completely redoing their DNA. The lenses include cameras that relay what each one sees to the others' battle-style displays. The earpieces and embedded mics maintain constant communication among them. They're augmented with continual muscle stimulation, hormones, adrenaline, and who knows what else. When their mother died, they went into private practice. They live and train and meditate together as one."

"Who leads?" I said.

"We all do," all three said simultaneously. "All are one in the now."

I shook my head. I'd never seen a unit with more than one commander that could do well when the heat came. On the other hand, I'd never met any group quite like these three. "Whatever works for you guys."

"You can't deny the combat advantages of three simultaneous perspectives and squadmates you can absolutely count on," Jack said.

"Fair enough," I said, even though he was wrong. For as long as I've known anything about professional fighting teams, they've been able to share multiple viewpoints on heads-up displays. As for trusting the person next to you, I suppose that might be a problem in some units—but it was never an issue for me in the Saw. Nonetheless, the Zyuns enjoyed a relationship that was, in my experience, unique. "I have to ask," I continued, "how did you guys get from a mother with enough money to pay for all this engineering"—I waved my hand to take in the three of them—"to working freelance security on Gash?"

"Not the deal," they said, each one voicing one word. "Only now matters."

They were right. I didn't like it when people asked about my past, so I had no trouble respecting their privacy. I wondered if they consciously chose to make every sentence contain a multiple of three words.

Weirdness aside, we needed scrapers, and if Jack was willing to pay them to protect him from me, they might work out for our needs. As I considered it further, having the three of them with their high degree of connectedness could prove useful.

I'd think more about it when we'd finished here. Right now, we had to see the site Jack thought might work. "Let's go," I said. "I don't want to spend any more time here than I absolutely have to, and I've already lingered too long. Show me the space."

On cue, Lobo rose and positioned himself to follow us from fifty meters above. He wouldn't let Jack or the Zyuns out of range.

One Zyun turned his attention to Lobo; the other two stayed focused on me.

Jack motioned toward Lobo. "I'm hurt, Jon," he said. "Do you honestly believe you need that level of protection against me?"

I answered his question with one of my own. "Do you honestly believe you'd still be alive if I wanted you dead?" I said.

"Not a chance," the Zyuns said in their three-voice alternation. "But for now, we are here."

"The space, Jack," I said, motioning him along. "Lead on."

He shrugged and started walking. We turned left and went

parallel to the innermost barrier for two hundred meters, then stopped in front of what had clearly once been a repair facility of some sort. About a hundred and fifty meters wide and maybe twenty meters tall, it wasn't large enough for any of the major space transports but would hold quite a few of just about any other military surface ships the EC would operate, as well as PCAVs and other craft similar to Lobo. Large openings across the front and indentations in the ground and the top of the huge doorframes marked where scavengers had stolen the metal doors that had once been able to seal the place. The building's depth was hard to gauge from this angle, but I guessed it to be at least half as deep as it was wide.

"Lobo," I subvocalized. "Building status?"

"Unable to scan beyond the first few meters I can read through the open doorway. Not a surprise: If the EC used it to repair sensitive vehicles, they would have embedded signal-blocking mesh layers in the permacrete and used relayed wireless feeds to the outside for communication."

"Come inside and check it out," Jack said.

"Want me to follow you inside?" Lobo said. "It's big enough."

"If necessary," I subvocalized, "but as long as you have a clear shot on them, stay outside."

"Coming," Lobo said.

"In a moment," I said to Jack.

Lobo settled to a hover a meter above the ground and ten meters behind me. He was running as quiet as possible, but the noise still made conversation difficult.

Jack shook his head, grinned at me, and walked into the empty building. The Zyuns maintained formation and followed him. Either they were smart enough to know there was no point in forming a human barrier around Jack, because Lobo's weapons could go right through them, or he hadn't paid them enough to be willing to take a shot for him. From their initial reactions and the fact that Jack was willing to hire them, I guessed the former. Good; I liked working with realistic people.

"Now I'm ready," I shouted to Jack.

I stepped inside and surveyed the place. Light streaming in

from the front and from empty windows along the sides illuminated the space enough that I could see all the way to the back wall. Large, vacant doorframes stood along the rear of each side, so we had a total of three entrance/exit options. Excellent.

Something about the back wall was off. When I studied it more closely, the answer was obvious: It was two walls that overlapped for only half a dozen meters.

I noticed Jack watching me. He grinned when I turned to face him.

"That's the best part," he said. "Each rear wall section runs about sixty percent of the way across the back, with a gap between them about three meters wide and an overlap large enough that it takes a moment to tell there are two. I figure they used the actual back section of the place for parts storage, repair benches, and so on."

"How big is that area?" I said.

He nodded enthusiastically. "More than twenty-five meters deep and the length of the building. Two doorways feed it, one on each end, each one about thirty meters wide."

"More than big enough to shield us," I said.

"Which makes everything simpler," he said, smiling broadly.

"So we have doors to install and all the other prep work to do," I said, "as well as the electronics, the rest of the stuff we discussed, and the big gear. How long?"

"Everything's already in progress," Jack said, "and fortunately most of what we needed was in stock with my suppliers. So, two days to get it here. The Zyuns have meshed me with the right kind of construction people, and nothing we have to do is particularly hard. Call it a conservative four to five days for them to do their work."

"Once I start this rolling, there's no changing it," I said. I considered Jack's estimates. He was almost certainly padding them to be safe, because the construction and setup we needed really wasn't that hard. On the other hand, it would involve multiple machines, some big chunks of metal for the doors, and a fair amount of labor and coordination, so I wanted to be absolutely safe. "Six days. You have six days."

"*I* have six days," Jack said. "What about *you*? And what about money? Pulling this off in that amount of time is going to cost a small fortune."

"Each time you have to pay one of your contractors," I said, "consider the size of the score, not to mention the peace of mind you stand to make off this plan."

I watched as he evaluated his possible arguments, then realized there was no point in bothering with them. I had the stronger position, and he knew it. Even so, those gems must have been worth far more than I'd thought, or he would have given it a try.

"Fine, fine, Jon," he said. "Stick me with everything. You didn't answer my other question, though: What about you? What are you going to do while I'm managing all the hard work?"

I ignored him and walked over to the nearest Zyun. I pulled out my wallet, thumbed it to receive in a high-quarantine area, and said, "I'd like to hire you later. Interested?"

All three nodded, and my wallet trembled its reception of their contact information. I didn't see any of them move to send it to me. "Only when you're done with Jack."

"One more day," the three said in the usual one-word-apiece response pattern.

"Wait on Mund," I said, "if you're serious."

"Jon," Jack said. "I'm tired of your attitude toward me. Answer my question: While I'm spending my money and working, what are you going to be doing to help?"

"Risking my life," I said, as I headed back to Lobo, "first by annoying several very angry and very powerful people, and then by explaining to them how I can make their wishes come true."

CHAPTER 30

I'M TRYING AS HARD as I can to trust you and be patient," Maggie said, each word coming slowly and with obvious effort.

"And I appreciate it very much," I said. I wasn't paying as close attention as I wanted, but we were docking with the jump-gate station, so I had to prepare for my meeting with Midon.

"So when are you going to explain exactly what you're doing and how it's going to save Manu?" she said.

The station filled the display Lobo had opened. The structure was already almost entirely clean of Gatist paint, courtesy of the bots that were now crawling over the few remaining red bits. I forced myself to ignore it, focused on Maggie, and considered her request. Her beauty and the degree to which I found her attractive made that difficult, and I couldn't help but recall momentarily the look in her eyes in the hangar when she was showing off her new dress, but none of that mattered; the anger I'd seen before I'd left to find Jack made it clear to me that we'd never have a relationship. Still, if for no reason other than her dedication and attempts to help, Maggie deserved an answer to her question.

The problem was, I couldn't trust her not to reveal what she knew to others.

No matter what her agenda, her face gave away so much information that I feared in a critical moment she might

267

jeopardize us all by what her expressions revealed. I couldn't count on her acting abilities, so the only prudent option was to keep her in the dark and at times even take advantage of her ignorance. She might hate me later for it, but all of us, including Manu, would be safer if I chose that path.

"I'm not," I said, holding up my hands and trying to sound calm and reasonable. "I'll tell you what you need to know when you need to know it, but not before. We're much more likely to succeed this way, and the only chance Manu has at a safe life away from these people is for us to accomplish our goals."

I expected anger, and indeed it swept across her face like storm winds rippling across a lake, but hurt replaced it. "When are you going to trust me?" she said.

I struggled to find a way to explain that her question was much more complex than she realized, that you could trust someone's intentions but not their skills, or that you might trust both of those things and still for safety reasons not depend on them in a plan, but I couldn't think of an explanation that didn't make my thought processes sound even worse than she already believed they were.

"Docked," Lobo said. "Lock ready in five seconds."

I couldn't invest more time in this, because Midon had to know I was here. I had to move quickly to make it clear to her that I was both playing the game properly and respecting her appropriately.

"Lobo," I said, "as soon as I'm out, move to the same position you occupied in my last meeting with Midon. She may as well watch you out her viewport as we talk." To Maggie, I added, "I'm sorry, but I have to go."

Inside, the Gash jump-gate station could have been any station at any gate anywhere in the universe. No traces of the red paint remained. No red people thronged the halls. No party sounds filled the air. I shouldn't have expected anything different, and intellectually I didn't, but because my first experience here had been during the color wash, I'd unconsciously prepared myself to deal again with large masses of red revelers.

I had no way to know whether Dougat or Chaplat or both had people watching the station, so I couldn't simply ask for Midon. If she was anywhere near as competent as I believed she was, all I needed to do was create an acceptable excuse to talk to Carne, and she'd find me.

Easy enough.

I balled my fists, shook my head, grumbled to myself, and walked as if I were a man ready to burst with anger. I crashed down the hallway, ignoring everything to the side of me. I bumped into person after person, shoving aside each one I encountered and muttering under my breath about a denied jump application. I headed straight to the claims office that occupied the center of a hub of short corridors that led to docking ports for smaller vessels such as Lobo. I stepped to the door so quickly that I almost hit its edge as it retracted into the wall. I didn't break my stride until I was nose-to-top-of-skull with a rather startled man a good head shorter than I was. I interrupted him pouring a drink from a wall dispenser. The expression on his face made clear that he already regretted ever stepping from behind his counter.

"I demand to speak with the station agent!" I said, yelling so loudly the man's hair moved from the force of the sound.

He scurried back behind his counter before responding. "The complaints officer isn't here right now," he said, "so perhaps if you could come back later, he could help you."

I put both my hands on the surface that separated us and leaned over it. "Is there something unclear in what I said? Are you having trouble understanding me? I don't want the complaints officer; get me the station agent." I hit the counter with both fists, and it shook slightly from the force. "Now!"

He fingered his cuff; security was on the way. If Midon didn't have someone watching for me, I was about to have a very unpleasant conversation with some armed guards who had the right not only to escort me out but also to levy a substantial fine.

"Sir, I think you'll find—" He stopped talking and looked to the right, his attention suddenly elsewhere. He shook his head slightly, as if confused.

The door opened behind me.

My every instinct was to turn and attack the guards before they could reach me, but I was playing the role of someone dumb enough to yell at a low-level civil servant whose job was to absorb verbal and emotional shrapnel so his superiors never had to experience it. In that role, I had to let the guards come to me.

The man overcame his confusion and saved me. He looked at me, smiled, held up his right hand to stop the guards, and said, "These men will be happy to escort you to the office of Mr. Carne, the administrator in charge. He's waiting for you now."

"That's better," I said, staying in the role. I didn't want any more people aware of my relationship with Midon than I could possibly avoid.

The guards' stances signaled their hope that I'd do something stupid so they could have a little fun with me, but I clasped my hands and made it clear we wouldn't be fighting.

"After you," I said to them.

They glanced at the man behind the counter, but he must have nodded approval, because without saying anything they turned and walked out of the room. I followed them down the corridor. They slowed twice and even abruptly stopped once, but I stayed a meter and a half behind them the entire way. Bumping into them might have been all the excuse they needed to be able to claim before a disciplinary council that I'd initiated conflict. I didn't need to fall into that trap, though the more they delayed me the harder I found it to stop from getting angry and the more part of me wanted a fight to start.

When we reached Carne's office, I paused until they backed away from the door and opened a clear path inside.

The toy-filled room remained exactly as I'd left it, but as soon as I was inside, Midon stepped from her hiding place behind the first row of shelves to my left.

"I trust you have good news for me," she said.

"Do you ever let Carne use his own office?"

"I can't stand all this," she said, taking in the toys and the rows of shelves with a single sweep of her arm. "Let's go inside."

She went straight to the desk in the inner office and settled behind it. I checked the display to my right as I entered the room and resisted smiling at the sight of Lobo hovering outside. A single very large launcher hung beneath him in a ready position, as if he'd decided all the weapons he'd shown last time were overkill. I wondered if she took offense at the snub, or even if Lobo had meant the gesture as such, but I decided he must have. His snide side was quite entertaining when I wasn't its target.

Midon acted as if a PCAV hung outside her window every moment of every day, willing neither to opaque the display nor to discuss what was visible in it.

"Well," she said.

I waited but did not speak. As dealing with Jack had reminded me multiple times recently, the easiest way to change the balance of power in a conversation is to refuse to engage on any but your own terms. If I gave her control at this stage, she'd want to extend it to every aspect of the discussion to come. I couldn't afford that.

"I've taken more theory of interaction classes than you have," she said, "so why don't we stop wasting time? You're here, and you wanted my attention. You have it. You reaffirmed your independence with that thing," she flicked her hand in Lobo's direction, "and I'm suitably impressed. You don't want to acknowledge my power. Fine. We're peers." She leaned forward. "I really don't care about anything except getting what I want and then jumping to a civilized planet where I can put my career back on track. So, how would you like to proceed?"

Even though I knew that at some level her directness was simply another tactic, I still admired it. Any bureaucrat who could both identify the games in play and step away from them possessed more intelligence than most.

"Dougat and some of his people will be making a weapons deal," I said. "Other than interrupting it in progress, what else do you need?"

"The sale must include milspec stock, at least some of it suitable for vehicle installation or mounting, and significant quantities of several different items."

She'd obviously prepared her list, which I appreciated.

"I need more money," I said. I didn't, I had all the cash necessary for the operation, but saying anything else would have been out of character for what she expected from me—and, of course, more money wouldn't hurt.

"We have a deal," she said, "and additional funding isn't part of it."

"Yes," I said, "but at the time we made it, I didn't understand how much playing middleman would end up costing me."

"Middleman?"

"You think I'm buying the weapons?" I laughed. "You're smarter than that. Why would *I* want anything to do with any illegal activities? I'm just an honest man caught in a bad place by forces beyond his control."

A smile was the most I could get from her. "Your costs are your problem; make the deal large enough, and you'll be fine in the end. I don't care who the other party in the transaction is."

"You might."

She said nothing and waited for me to continue.

I waited with her. Lobo hung outside the window.

She sighed. "Okay, why?"

"You could take down Dougat and help clean up Mund in the process," I said.

"Chaplat?"

I nodded.

"Interesting," she said, "and, yes, that would be useful—but not useful enough to warrant more money."

"But if you captured part of his gang in the deal?"

"Our arrest teams will take everyone we catch," she said. "Including you. Of course, I can try to arrange to give you—"

"Not me," I said, cutting her off. "Either we agree that I exit before you enter, or you'll find out about the sale after the fact."

I'd annoyed her, but she kept it under control, the only sign being the long pause before she said, "That's acceptable. You should have no problems, but Dougat and Chaplat and their teams won't fare so well."

"And if they fight back?"

"I assume they will," she said, her smile returning, "which will only save us processing costs."

"I'll make sure I'm well away from there," I said. "Look, if you're not going to give me any additional advance, then I'll need payment three days after you arrest Dougat and seize the weapons."

"Any time you want after we have them," she said. "You can trust us that far."

I laughed. "I don't trust any government to do anything that's not in its self-interest," I said, "but I am confident that neither of us needs the recordings we both possess to be sprayed across every data stream in this region."

Her only acknowledgment of the threat was to tilt her head slightly. "When's the sale?"

"Sometime in the next six to eight days," I said. "You'll get no more than an hour's notice, so you'll need to keep a team on ready in each major city on Gash. Make them good units, trained for urban and rural stealth approaches, and not small ones, either. I can't know in advance the number of hostiles on either side."

"I need a day to make that happen," she said. "After that, we'll be ready."

I took out my wallet and thumbed open a quarantined area. "Give me a signal protocol you won't miss," I said, "and send me your weapons wish list. I won't guarantee to get everything on it, but I'll do my best."

She nodded and tapped for a moment on the desk. My wallet chirped its acceptance.

"Multiple teams will cost me a lot," she said.

"Not my problem. You said you wanted Dougat badly. You ignored my costs. And I assume the assets you plan to confiscate greatly outvalue the expense of security squads you're already paying anyway."

She nodded. "Are we done?"

"Not quite," I said. "You'll be tempted to have your people follow me from here on. Don't. Stay back, or you'll destroy everything I'm setting up. Your teams are too easy to spot."

"I can get better people," she said.

"Maybe, but if Dougat, Chaplat, or I spot even one of them, this whole deal will evaporate faster than a puddle in the middle of Gash's desert. Are you willing to take that chance?"

"Okay," she said, "we continue to leave you alone and to not track you." She put her hands on the desk, stood, and leaned over it. "Make sure I hear from you in eight days. If I don't—"

I cut her off. "Understood. I'll contact you when I'm ready."

"The boy?" she said.

I paused and tried to relax enough to show the real guilt I felt at the risks I was taking with Manu. "He'll be there," I finally said. "You're paying me for making him appear. That's it. Once he shows up, I'm done. Getting him away from the people who have him is your problem."

"Of course," she said.

I shook my head in disgust and turned to leave.

"Don't feel bad, Moore," she said. "The larger the deal, the more your ten percent brings you. That plus a quarter-million bonus for the boy should make this a rich payday."

I didn't trust myself to say anything useful, so I didn't speak or turn around as I left the room and headed back to Lobo.

One set, two to go.

CHAPTER 31

YOU CAN'T BE SURE he'll believe you," Maggie said. "He's already lost the boy once, so he'll be doubly cautious now."

"There's no way around it," I said. "Jack won't let me have Manu, and even if I could get him, I wouldn't put the kid in front of Dougat again at this stage. I've strung Dougat along this far; I just have to keep doing so for a few more days."

"I can help," Maggie said. "I know—"

I held up my hand, and she stopped talking. She was back to the calm Maggie, and that was encouraging, but I couldn't take the chance of her sparking further troubles by melting down at the wrong time. "I appreciate it," I said, "but—"

"Why won't you hear her out?" Lobo said. "Her performance in the jump station was less than useful—"

"Thanks a lot, Lobo," Maggie said, cutting him off.

"You're welcome," Lobo said.

I couldn't help but smile, and from the look on Maggie's face, that wasn't my best choice. It's simply that I so rarely heard his sarcasm target anyone else that I enjoyed the moments when it did.

"And she has shown a lack of combat readiness," Lobo continued, "but that doesn't mean all her ideas are without merit. We discussed her proposal while you were with Midon, and it is worthy of consideration."

"That's some endorsement," Maggie said.

"An accurate one," Lobo said. "Would you have me provide anything else, especially given your professed concern over the boy?"

"No," she admitted. "I do think, though, that we could improve your sales technique."

"Why would I try to sell?" Lobo said. "If I wanted money from someone, I'd train enough weapons on him that he'd happily transfer the payment to me."

Maggie rolled her eyes. "Don't play dumb literal machine with me. You know exactly what I meant."

"Yes," Lobo said, "and my point remains: I wasn't selling anything. I was providing Jon with accurate guidance—counsel he'd be wise to consider."

"Are you two done?" I said. Even when they argued with each other, I came out on the losing side. Still, if Lobo said I should listen, I would. Plus, Maggie was staring wide-eyed at me and trusting herself to my judgment; how could I let her down? "Maggie, I apologize for not hearing you out. What are you proposing?"

"Though I didn't spend much time with him, I studied Dougat. All of us did; after all, he was the leader of the whole group, and we felt privileged to be able to work close to him. I know more about how he thinks than you do, so I can help make him more likely to believe that you actually have Manu." She paused.

I listened and said nothing. I'd told her I'd give her a chance, so I would.

After a few seconds, she continued. "Where are you planning on meeting him?"

"I hadn't picked a place, but probably in the desert again. It worked last time, and it's easy to defend."

"Don't," she said. "Yes, it was fine last time, but now you have to convince him that he's in control and you're in this for the money. Use the Followers' temple in Malzton instead. It's in the middle of a heavily populated area, so he won't want any more firing than he authorized in the temple in Eddy back on Mund. For all the noise and smoke, that wasn't very much and wouldn't have happened at all without Manu's vision. The landing area behind this building is more than big enough to hold us, and they won't have any weapons in the facility powerful enough to hurt Lobo. If Dougat did, the EC would have taken him already." She paused again.

"I'm not saying the idea is bad," I said. "It's very reasonable. Dougat isn't dumb enough, however, to let a friendly location instantly make him believe everything I say."

"Of course not," she said, smiling broadly. "But it will put him in the right frame of mind to believe me."

"You? He doesn't even know I have you. If anything, he assumes you went AWOL after the mess on Eddy."

"He'll know when you sweeten the pot by showing him the prisoner you're willing to return as part of the deal, the prisoner you captured on Eddy."

"And then you can attest—"

"—that you have the boy," she said. "I can tell Dougat I've seen Manu, he's well, and I really want to rejoin the group. Followers rarely leave. He'll believe me."

I considered the proposal. It was fundamentally sound, and I definitely could use more ways to persuade Dougat to stay in the deal and supply the weapons. At the same time, I'd kept Maggie out of most of this because she hadn't demonstrated very good acting skills, and I didn't want to have to depend on them. "You'd have to be persuasive," I said, struggling to express the concern in a way that wouldn't offend her further. I wasn't used to thinking about the feelings of anyone other than a target while formulating a plan, so I found myself at a bit of a loss.

"I understand," she said. "I haven't shown you much to make you believe that I can carry off a convincing role. All I have to be with Dougat, however, is scared. Hold a gun to me, put me in the middle of this meeting, and, trust me, I'll be plenty afraid." Her voice strained a bit. "I already am, just thinking about it."

She was right. Her lines didn't need to be perfect. All she had to remember was that she'd seen Manu and he was fine, and I could prompt her if it came to that. Her fear was real, and that would sell. I hated the coldness with which I considered what this would cost her, but she'd made the offer, and my job was to evaluate it as objectively as possible.

"Okay," I said. "You're right. You're right about the location, and you're right that your presence as a prisoner could help persuade him that we have Manu."

Maggie smiled.

"Aren't you glad you listened to me?" Lobo said.

Though it pained me to do so, I said, "Yes."

Aerial views of the Followers' temple in Malzton snapped onto a display Lobo opened in front of us. Approach vectors pointed to the landing area.

"These are the best entrance and exit paths," Lobo said. "What else do we need before we contact Dougat?"

"Let me walk you through the rest," I said, "and then I'll set it up."

From above, the Malzton Followers' Institute—their official name for their temples everywhere—resembled a wilted version of the one I'd seen in Eddy. Dougat apparently invested his construction funds according to the wealth of the potential audience, a wise move for any con man. Like its Eddy counterpart, this building was a ziggurat, but an uneven one, as if during the building's construction the human members of the team had been drunk and their robotic coworkers using most of their computing capacity to fight nasty viruses. Even at a distance we could see that the right side narrowed more rapidly from top to bottom than the left; Lobo gauged the whole thing as tilting slightly to the right. The grounds sported collections of plants and relaxation areas like the Institute in Eddy, but here they seemed haphazard, a random walk garden.

We rocketed Gashward at a sharp angle and came to a stationary hover less than a meter above the landing area behind the rear of the building. We were one minute early. Lobo showed multiple weapons, more than enough to wipe out everything for blocks around, and we waited.

When Dougat didn't immediately appear, I said, "Is he really the type to play this sort of petty power game?"

"Yes," Maggie said. "I told you as much."

"You did," I said, nodding. "I'm just always surprised by this kind of behavior when I encounter it."

"I could motivate him to appear more quickly," Lobo said. "These gardens aren't particularly more artful than bare earth."

"No," I said, "but thank you for that redecorating offer."

Three minutes later, Dougat stepped out of the building and stood in the shade by the door.

"His support?" I said.

"The rear of the temple is IR shielded, so I can't know what's inside," Lobo said. "I count four snipers within my sensor range, which should be more than broad enough to let me spot all likely attackers."

"Paint 'em," I said.

"Done."

"How are you painting them?" Maggie said.

I looked at her and shook my head. "You're a prisoner, remember? Stay in character. Speak when I tell you to, and otherwise stay quiet. Got it?"

She nodded.

"Open a hatch, Lobo."

I went to the opening and shouted through it at Dougat. "Tell your four men to stand down. I'm here to do business. If I'd wanted to attack you, I'd have already done so. If I'd wanted to kill them, I'd have done that; check their IR levels, and you'll see they're in my sights."

Dougat smiled, paused, and nodded. He had monitors on us, which meant recordings—all as I'd expected.

"No harm in making sure you're as good as you think you are," Dougat said, smiling again, the businessman trying another tactic, no concern at all about the fact that his experiment involved threatening my life.

"They're moving away," Lobo said on the machine frequency I heard inside my head. "None has a shot now."

I stepped down to the permacrete and walked halfway to Dougat. The midday sun blazed bright and hot, and a bit of sweat ran down my back below the light armor. I waited for a few seconds. When Dougat didn't follow suit and come to meet me, I stayed a little bit longer, then shook my head and walked a few more steps forward, showing my belly.

He approached me and stopped half a meter out of my reach, as if that mattered. He clearly was a civilian with no real grasp of violence. If I'd wanted to hurt him, really wanted it, I wouldn't have bothered doing it with my hands; I would have let Lobo destroy the building with him in it. His lack of understanding, however, would only help in the long run, so I continued playing by his rules.

"You asked for a meeting," he said, "and I agreed to your request."

Everything about his attitude grated on me. I've always hated self-important bureaucrats, even the highest-ranking ones, but I followed the advice I'd given Maggie and stayed with the character I was selling.

"Yes," I said, "and I appreciate your time. If you can have the weapons ready in the next several days, we can make the trade we discussed."

"What exactly do you need?"

I slowly pulled out my wallet and thumbed it active to my quarantined and slightly enlarged copy of the list from Midon. "Here's what Chaplat's after, as well as your cut of what he's willing to pay."

He nodded. My wallet beeped an incoming request, and I allowed it to respond.

He stared up and to his left, checking the data on a contact, and then nodded again.

"You're asking for quite a lot," he said.

"More than you can handle?"

"Of course not," he said with no attempt to hide his annoyance. "I simply want to ensure that I receive a fair return on my investment. Your prices are lower than what we'd normally accept."

"You placed a high value on the boy," I said, "and my offer reflects that fact. It's your choice, of course; I can always find another buyer and work out my issues with Chaplat with cash."

"So you have Manu Chang?"

I chuckled. "With me? Of course not. I'm sure you didn't expect that. But, yes, he's in a secure location. You get the weapons ready, and sometime in the next five to seven days, I'll signal you. You'll have less than two hours to show up, or we'll clear out. Once you arrive, we'll make the trade."

"We?"

"You know I have associates," I said. "You saw one in the desert. There are others."

"How did you find Manu?" he said.

I shook my head. "Not your issue."

"Fair enough. Still, I'm supposed to gather all of this merchandise, remain on this nasty planet, and leap into motion when you call, all because you claim to have Chang?"

"I appreciate your concern and anticipated it," I said, "so I brought proof."

I turned, walked back to Lobo, and went inside. I grabbed Maggie lightly by the back of the neck, took an energy pistol from her, and whispered, "Showtime. Brace yourself."

I tightened my grip on her neck and yanked her into the open hatch. She stumbled and nearly fell. To keep her upright, I squeezed hard enough that she had trouble breathing. Her eyes widened, though I couldn't tell if it was because of the pressure on her neck or the sight of Dougat. I pressed the gun against her temple.

"Remember your guard, the one you've been missing since our visit to the Eddy Institute?"

Dougat clearly didn't; I'd be surprised if he cared at all about Followers of Maggie's level. As the data feed from his support staff hit him, however, he feigned concern and recognition.

"Of course," he said. "Park, I hope he hasn't hurt you."

"Please, sir," Maggie said.

I wrenched her head around so I was staring into her eyes. "Shut up," I said.

I stared again at Dougat. "You wanted proof." To Maggie, I said, "Tell him."

I squeezed Maggie's neck harder, so she rasped her words a bit. Authenticity was vital.

"He has Manu Chang," she said, speaking slowly, so obviously in pain that tears oozed onto her cheeks. I ignored her and focused on Dougat.

"You've seen the child?" he said.

"Yes," Maggie said. "He's fine, but this man doesn't care about him—"

I cut her off by pushing her out of his sight inside Lobo and saying, "Take her."

"Satisfied?" I said to Dougat.

"Yes," he said, both excited and concerned now. "You mustn't hurt him, of course. Our deal is for him unharmed."

"Don't worry," I said. "I understand his value, so someone will get him unharmed. I'll even toss in the guard; after this, I'll have no use for her."

From the expression that crossed his face, Dougat didn't either, but with his security team monitoring him he wasn't about to give up one of their own.

"Thank you for that," he said. "I've been very concerned about her."

"One more thing," I said. I glanced inside Lobo. "Give it to me," I said to the space where I'd pushed Maggie. I stuck out my hand, and she put in it the one Pinkelponker gem Jack had left me.

"You also wanted the gemstones," I said. I showed him the one in my hand. "Proof enough on that front?"

He eyed it with lust but only nodded. "Yes," he said. "Perhaps as a down payment you might—"

"No," I said, cutting him off and handing the stone back to Maggie. "Unless you have a partial shipment of the weapons with you."

"Of course not," he said. "As I'm sure you understand, I don't travel with them or keep them in our facilities."

"I do understand," I said, "and I'm sure *you* also understand that I'll keep the guard, the gems, and the boy until we make the trade."

"Of course," he said, back on standard business grounds. "We'll look forward to your signal."

I nodded and stepped to the right, next to Maggie.

Lobo closed the hatch and accelerated up and away. We'd spend the next few hours running evasive maneuvers among weather and corporate data relay sats.

"The stone," I said to Maggie.

She handed it to me slowly, her reluctance evident. "Must you keep it?" she said. "It's a potentially important artifact."

"Yes," I said. I wasn't sure I'd ever sell it, nor even what I felt about it. It was, after all, the only tangible item from my home planet that I owned. No way could I explain that to her, however; I couldn't trust anyone with that much of my past. I took the gem back to the area Lobo had opened for it, and he closed the wall around it.

Maggie followed me. When the stone had vanished, she said, "Did you have to be so rough? My throat is still sore."

"I warned you," I said. "Showing real pain is much more convincing than acting." Particularly if you're not a very good actor, I thought but did not say.

She rubbed her neck and nodded, still clearly concerned.

"Relax," I said. "You did well. You sold it. The meeting wouldn't have gone anywhere near as smoothly without you."

She smiled and her eyes widened. I couldn't help smiling in return.

"Thanks," she said. "So, what's next?"

"We get an update from Jack," I said, "and then I sit down with Chaplat."

CHAPTER 32

WE'D SPENT A restless night and most of the morning in slow migration through the various satellite clusters over Gash when Jack finally linked to us. Lobo tried to run a backtrace in case one of our many new friends had found us and was monitoring our signal flow, but the best he could do thanks to the comm unit's multi-hop protocols was pin the location to Nickres. Good; Jack was behaving cautiously and not calling from anywhere near the site.

When Lobo finished checking and clearing the signal, he opened a one-way display. Jack's image popped into it.

"What, you think I'm leading someone to you?" he said to the blank view he was facing. "Give me some credit, please. With all I'm having to spend on this plan, I need it to work out even more than you do."

Nothing in the background suggested anyone was eavesdropping, but of course nothing would if the listeners possessed any skill at all. Still, all anyone could see behind me was a blank wall, and if Jack was betraying me I was better off figuring that out sooner than later, so I said, "Two-way."

"That's better," Jack said. "You know how much I prefer looking at people I'm talking to."

"Where are we?"

285

"A little social grace would not go amiss, Jon, even among colleagues. As I tried to teach you, smoothing the path always makes for a more comfortable walk."

"Where are we?"

Jack shrugged. "Do you ever wonder why you're always alone?"

Maggie, who was standing out of view, snorted audibly. "Just swallowed some water the wrong way," she whispered.

"Miss Park certainly takes my point," Jack said, "as you no doubt heard."

"Fine," I said. "How are you, Jack?"

"I'm doing quite well, thank you," he said. "And you?"

"Annoyed," I said, "at you and your penchant for wasting time. Will you now tell me how it's going?"

"As you wish," he said. Looking to the left, he added, "I tried, Miss Park, as you can see." He then stared again at me and continued, "We're on schedule to complete in two, maybe three days. It's costing me a big part of the proceeds of the sale of those assets we discussed, but everything is coming together."

"And our young friend?"

"He's fine."

"Show me," I said. I wanted to see Manu, and if anyone was monitoring us, I didn't mind if they did, too, because it would only help convince them I could deliver on my promises.

"So little trust," Jack said, "even at this stage? It doesn't become you, Jon." He reached to his right, and Manu stepped into view, Jack's hand on his shoulder.

The boy appeared completely normal, but of course he would.

"Nothing I can detect in the video suggests any coercion," Lobo said on the machine frequency, "though we are signal-limited. Pupil dilation is uniform and normal, and what I can read of the pulse in his neck is within standard tolerances. No unusual sweat patterns. He appears relaxed."

"How are you?" I said to Manu.

"Fine, thank you," he said, "though I'm tired of moving around. Will you be joining us soon?"

I was the one whose pulse was in danger of quickening and who had to fight not to sweat, because I hated deceiving the boy about putting him at risk. I just didn't have a better option. "Yes," I said, "in a few days."

"Will Lobo come, too?" he said. "Lobo's the best."

"A child wise beyond his years," Lobo said, thankfully staying on the machine frequency so no one else heard him.

"Of course," I said.

"Give us a moment," Jack said.

Manu nodded, said, "Bye," and walked out of view.

"Satisfied?" Jack said.

"Yes," I said. "Keep him safe."

"Of course," Jack said. "And your end?"

"Not done," I said, "but coming together. I have more work to do, so I should get to it."

Jack looked to his right, stretched a bit out of view, and then faced me again. His expression hardened. "My traces show no sign of interception, and I trust yours don't, either. So, may I speak frankly?"

"I believe we are secure," Lobo said, still on the machine frequency.

"Yes," I said.

"We're running a big risk here," Jack said, "and not just for Manu. All of us are going to be standing in the middle of an explosive situation. Are you sure this is going to work?"

Though I was tempted to answer him immediately, I considered the question honestly. We were doing everything we could to put all the pieces in the right places at the right times, but with so many people and so many variables, no one could ever be sure a plan as complex as this one would hold together. "No," I finally said, "but I don't see any other way out of this that doesn't involve giving up Manu and running forever, and I'm not willing to do either of those things. We've been through it all, Jack; if you have a better idea, tell me. Otherwise, we stick to what we're doing, hope for the best, and adapt as quickly as we can to the unexpected. What else is there?"

"Nothing, I suppose," Jack said, as serious as I'd ever seen him, "so I'll get back to my tasks." The display winked out.

"As will I," I said to the empty wall.

Gash's jump gate hung in space before us, growing in Lobo's front display as we eased to the head of the queue. Jack's concern weighed on me. I could jump to Mund and keep going, to Drayus, then Immediata or Avery or Therien, and from any of them to a planet beyond the EC's direct reach. I could abandon this dangerous scheme, drop Maggie, let Jack continue to protect Manu, and get on with my life somewhere very, very far away.

I glanced at Maggie, who was sitting in the couch beside me and staring at the gate, lost in her own thoughts. She was beautiful, decent, and for a few seconds back in the hangar in Nickres I'd felt closer to her than I'd been to any woman in years and years, but that moment had vanished like a spaceship through an aperture. Now, most of the time Maggie seemed barely able to tolerate me—and with good cause, I realized, because here I was considering abandoning her and Manu.

But I wouldn't. She might not understand that or believe it, but I wouldn't stop until I'd done everything I could to get the boy to safety. I'd promised him back in Eddy that I'd protect him, and I would. If I didn't, I could jump forever and never get away from the disgust I'd feel for myself. If I failed, if something happened to him, I had to hope that one day the knowledge that I'd at least done my best would provide some small comfort. I knew I'd never forgive myself for not trying.

Maggie reached over and touched my arm lightly with her fingertips. "Amazing every time," she said, her voice barely louder than a whisper. "I hope I never stop seeing the magic in it."

I turned and watched as she stared at the jump gate.

No, I wouldn't let them down.

The edges of the aperture vanished as we reached the front

of the queue. All we could see in front of us was the perfect blackness, the complete lack of information in that instant of suspension between where you were and where you were going, between what you knew and the mystery of the moment to come.

We jumped.

Chaplat had demanded we meet at his office, but he'd clearly expected me to offer an alternative. "You're the buyer," I'd said, "so you get to pick the place." He'd made no attempt to disguise his suspicion, but I believe he also at some level liked that I'd rolled over for him.

Now, standing outside the building and waiting for his guards to appear, I was second-guessing myself. Once I was inside, Lobo couldn't track me. He'd blast a hole in the side of the place if I didn't signal him in half an hour, but if I was already dead when he showed up, his presence wouldn't do me much good.

The plan was sound, I reminded myself. Stick to the plan.

The same man and woman met me yet again. Either they were his personal team, or his organization was a lot smaller than I'd thought. Given the way both Midon and Dougat spoke of him, I was betting on the former. Neither guard smiled or spoke. The man took the rear position this time. The woman led, and I followed her.

Even though I'd seen it before, the room still surprised me, an effect I assume Chaplat enjoyed. No fire burned in the fireplace this afternoon; instead, four meter-high black lacquer vases full of flowers sat side by side within it. The bright orange of the blossoms matched perfectly the delicate circles at the top of each vase. Chaplat stood in front of them, waiting for me. He wasn't smiling. No servants occupied the room's corners. No one offered me a drink or a seat. By doing a deal with him I'd descended to the rank of hired help. I could live with that. The sooner I got out of there, the smaller the chance that something would go wrong, upset him, and backfire on me. My spine itched with the bone-deep understanding that a nod from Chaplat could cause the man behind me to shoot me in the back. I hoped he'd go for a body shot the nanomachines could repair.

"What have you got for me?" he said.

"I'm going to take a list from my left rear pants pocket," I said.

"Let her help you," Chaplat said, nodding at the lead guard, who was now a meter and a half away at my nine.

She pulled out the sheet and flicked it taut. The first page of the weapons inventory glowed on it. I'd put next to each line a cost half again as high as what I'd told Dougat I could get him. The guard handed the list to Chaplat. He studied it for quite some time. No one spoke. No one moved. Apparently, the guards were as concerned about annoying him as I was.

"The prices are firm," I said. "They're what he demands."

"I'll pay half of that," he said, "and your cut comes from that payment—after I get Jack."

Now we were in the tricky part. I couldn't let his offer stand, or he'd question my motives and Dougat would balk. At the same time, I didn't want to end up in a prolonged argument that might cause him to lose his temper.

"I can't sell him on that big a discount," I said. "He didn't present the figures as open to discussion."

He smiled and shook his head. "You really are new to this sort of trade, aren't you? No one pays these prices unless they're planning to use the goods themselves, which I most definitely am not. I'll have to discount to my buyers so I can move in volume, or it'll take me forever to sell the weapons in small lots—and I'll have to warehouse them the whole time. No, this price is out of the question. I'm willing to consider sixty percent."

"I can't get that price," I said, letting a note of panic creep into my voice. "Maybe I could talk them into a ten percent discount. Maybe." I paused, then added, "And of course my fee would be on top of that."

He stepped close enough that I could smell alcohol on his breath.

"No," he said. "We're done negotiating. This is my last offer: I'll pay seventy-five percent of the prices here, take the whole lot, and your cut comes out of that. I don't give a damn what your end is. If you didn't set up this deal well enough that you'll make a profit with that offer, then you're a fool, and I don't want to do business with you."

I imagined Manu being hurt to force some tension to show on my face even as my mind calculated the additional fee I'd just persuaded him to pay. I acted as if it were an effort to speak calmly, spacing my words and talking as slowly as an addict trying to pass for sober. "And I still get the ten percent of what Jack owes you?"

"That was our original deal," he said, "so, yes, as long as you deliver Jack."

"Of course," I said. "He'll be there. Deal."

I stuck out my hand to shake.

He ignored it. "When?" he said.

"Sometime in the next five days," I said. "On Gash. I won't be able to give you more than an hour's notice due to the way I'm arranging to get Jack."

"And that is?" he said.

"My problem," I said, "and I'm handling it. When we do the trade, the money for the weapons will flow through my wallet first. I'll extract my fee, and then my software will handle the anonymous payment to Dougat."

"How you get him the money is your problem," he said. "As long as I end up with both the weapons and Jack, I don't care what you do."

I smiled. "Excellent."

"And the boy?" he said.

"He'll be there," I said, guilt and anger hitting me all at once, "but as I explained before—"

Chaplat held up his hand to stop me, nodded, turned, and headed out of the room.

"What you need to tell yourself is also not my problem," he said. "We're done here. Don't make me wait too long."

Something in my body language must have betrayed how

much I wanted to tear Chaplat apart, because the guard to my left closed the gap between us, and the one behind me put his hand on my shoulder. For a moment I considered fighting them, smashing them both, destroying all the people who were so intent on exploiting this boy, all the people who thought I was just like them, willing to sell out a child simply to enrich myself, and then I regained control as I accepted how much of my anger was toward myself. I couldn't fight everyone in this whole affair, at least not without hurting a great many innocent people not directly involved in any of it, and I had only myself to blame for much of it. I'd chosen this path, and it was the best one I could find, so I needed to calm down and accept it.

I let the guards lead me out of the building and to the street below.

After the door slid shut behind me, Lobo told me, "All clear. Proceeding to rendezvous?"

"Not immediately," I subvocalized as I walked rapidly away. I couldn't calm down, so I was in no condition to share the inside of Lobo with Maggie—or anyone, for that matter. "I'm going to exercise."

"Now?" Lobo said.

"Yes," I said, not trying to suppress the rage still in me. "Leave me alone. You're tracking me, so you'll know when I'm close."

He said nothing, whether literally following the order or sensing my mood I neither knew nor cared.

While surveying the area in preparation for this meeting, I'd spotted an old metal and plank pier that jutted fifty meters into the water. I started running toward it, slowly at first, then jogging, and then sprinting, pushing myself until my legs ached and my lungs felt ready to burst, and then forcing myself to hold the pace, embracing the pain and using it to blot out everything else. I rounded the last turn to the pier, and with it in sight I forced myself to go faster, pumped my arms and pistoned my legs and ran as hard as I could. I sprinted to the end of the pier, my vision reduced to the small area directly in front of me. I stopped a meter from its end. Not quite done, trembling with the exertion and the rage, I thrust my arms over my head, looked straight into the sky, and screamed, roared wordlessly, for those few seconds giving literal voice to my frustration and anger.

I'm not sure how long I stood there, but when I finished, I bent over, hands on my knees, and gulped air. As control threaded its way back through me, I saw how stupid I was. All that noise, that self-indulgence, and of course nothing was different.

No, one thing had changed: I felt a bit better. I shook my head and chuckled at myself as I regained rationality. I'd learned long ago that exercise helped me, but I'd largely abandoned it while trying to thread my way through this trouble. I shouldn't do that. I needed to use physical exertion and other safe outlets to keep myself in check. Running here, dropping all pretense of self-control, screaming like a madman—it might have provided a temporary release to the pressure I was feeling, but it wasn't smart.

I surveyed the area, something I should have done before ever entering it. Five men, two in pairs and one alone, sat along the edges of the pier. All were fishing. Two women and a man supervising loading bots at a warehouse sixty five meters away were staring at me. Any one of them could have taken me out while I stood there, oblivious as I was of the rest of Eddy continuing its normal life all around me. Not smart, not smart at all. You'd think I'd learn.

I turned around and started walking to the rendezvous point. I checked out everyone I passed and invested half an hour in countersurveillance routes on the way to Lobo.

I hoped this would be the last time I was this dumb until I was somewhere much, much safer.

Unfortunately, the next stop on my path to any better place was to walk into another meeting location I didn't control.

CHAPTER 33

THE CAM JOINT squatted next to an oversized chop shop in the middle of a couple of acres of stained permacrete and roaring engines. Single-passenger, multi-passenger, hover, wheeled, open, closed—you name a type of vehicle a hardcore ground-transport enthusiast might drool over, and at least one of them was sitting somewhere in the large open areas surrounding the two linked buildings. Bureaucrats wearing dirt-repelling suits and supervising mechanoids with probes buried deep in onboard computers worked adjacent to gearhead fundamentalists wielding only manual wrenches and drivers. Red fiber lines outlined a two-meter-wide path that meandered from the main entrance gate where I stood, through the vehicles and work teams, all the way to the open front door of the bar, restaurant, same-day augmentation parlor, and parts supply house that shared the interior of this most unusual shop.

Why was I not surprised that the Zyuns had chosen to meet me here?

I followed the path inside. A pair of shirtless bouncers, one my height and the other a head shorter, leaned against the wall on either side of the door, implanted electrodes flexing muscles in rippling patterns up and down their bodies as their eyes scanned constantly across the huge open space. I stopped a meter in front of them, nodded in recognition, and said, "I'm looking for a friend."

"Who isn't?" the taller one said.

"And we should care why?" the shorter added, clearly bored and hoping I'd lend some excitement to his shift.

I ignored him and instead looked around the huge space for the Zyuns. To my right, men and women and waist-high loaders prowled aisles of circuit boards, gaskets, shafts, pistons, fittings of all sorts, and parts I didn't recognize. To my left, a row of half a dozen operating theaters of various kinds stretched from the front wall to two-thirds of the building's depth. The first room stood empty. The open door to the second revealed a thin woman reclining at a forty-five-degree angle on an operating couch, her long, straight, brown hair stretching almost to the ground. A tattoo artist worked slowly and carefully on her left forearm, building on the scene of trees, waterfall, and skeletons that stretched from her elbow up and inside her shirt. Her eyes were shut, her expression blissful, and with her right arm she stroked the back of a lounge basset currently anchored to the counter beside her, the legless hound's expression as happy as its fundamentally sad countenance could permit.

I walked past the rest of the body-mod chambers, all closed, and reached the edge of the bar/restaurant combination, an old-style wooden bar on the left and tables full of eating patrons on the right. The food ran to basics—chunks of browned meat, mashed and chunked and noodled starches, and precious little green—but the smells tweaked my senses and instantly I was hungry. I shoved aside the craving as I spotted the Zyuns. They were sitting around a table in the far left rear corner, all three managing to have a wall to their backs.

I nodded acknowledgment and headed to them. I leaned against the rear wall, so the Zyun on my right would have to swivel to face me; no way was I giving up my back in a place someone else had picked. The Zyun stayed as he was; I'd forgotten the constantly transmitted multiple vision points.

"Any particular reason I had to come here?" I said.

"We like it," they said in the usual alternating word pattern.

"Much life around, and no EC. It's totally legit, so no one bothers us here."

The way they spoke was even more annoying with long sentences than with their typical short statements.

"We could have settled this via comm," I said.

"Not our way," they said. "Call your ship."

I didn't bother. A glance at a gauge on the cuff of my shirt confirmed what Lobo had found. He'd tried to scan the place before we'd landed, and he couldn't get through. Nothing was getting out, either.

"Walls laced with enough metal layers to stop transmissions," I said. "I understand and appreciate your caution, but you've worked for Jack, he's vouched for me, and all I want to do is hire you. We could have saved time."

"We prefer this," they said. "What's the job?"

"Are you still working for Jack?"

They shook their heads in unison.

"Anyone else?"

Again they shook their heads as one. They weren't talkative, which was fine by me.

"I want you full time and exclusively for the duration of the mission," I said. "No breaks, always on the clock, and no other assignments."

"Our preference, too."

"You get the outline now, but the details come only in real time," I said. "I also won't name the others involved until we're live. Acceptable?"

They nodded yes. "A fellow paranoid," they said. "We like that."

I ran down the basics for them, then asked, "Interested?"

"We find parts of this uncomfortable," they said. "Other acceptable options?"

I was surprised to realize that the constant alternation and phrasing in groups of three words was tempting me to participate, as if we were playing word games. I refrained from joining them.

"None," I said. "I believe I understand and appreciate your concerns, but no, I have no other reasonable choices."

"It's your deal," they said. They pointed as one to a small paper display sitting in the table's center. A figure and an account number snapped into view on it. "Our rate for high-risk work, plus a fee for the discomfort."

"Ouch," I said, though Jack had already told me roughly what they'd ask.

They shrugged and said nothing. The display cleared.

"Acceptable," I said. "Ten percent retainer now, forty percent on pickup, the rest on completion."

"Jack briefed you," they said.

"Yes. Deal?"

They nodded. The Zyun in the center put a wallet on the table, and all three thumbed it open.

"Keep the comm link I gave you," I said, "and go to Gash. Stay somewhere I can reach you. Make it private, low-key—not anywhere like here."

They nodded again.

"I also need a safe house on Gash and a private hangar there for my ship. Make sure the house is secure. Spend what it takes. Okay?"

They nodded once more.

I opened my wallet, transmitted the deposit to theirs, and left.

Gash filled the display Lobo had opened to my right on the front wall. Jack stared at me from the one directly in front of me. Orbiting the planet, one day from my target date, and of course Jack had to complicate things.

"I'm not feeling good about this, Jon," he said. "You're putting me in a position of great risk."

"We've been through all this, Jack, and there's no other way the plan has a prayer of working."

"Then maybe we need to revise the plan."

I struggled to control my feelings and maintain a calm, level tone. "We don't have time for that," I said, "as you well know. The timetable is set, the players are in motion, and if I change anything now, they could decide to pursue other options—like hunting you down."

"And you as well," he said. "I'm not the only one in trouble here."

"Precisely," I said. "You're not. They all know me, they all know you, and changing course now might tempt each of them to attack us. You'd also be endangering Manu again, as you did at the Institute, when you set me up the first time."

"As I've tried to point out to you before," he said, "I didn't put him at risk; his vision did. How was I supposed to know he'd have one while Dougat was interviewing him?"

"If you care about him, me, or yourself," I said, "you'll let this keep going. You don't have a better plan; if you did, you'd have offered it by now."

"My concern remains valid," he said. "We meet for final site prep and check. Either I involve new people to provide my security—security your faux PCAV can easily remove at a place as empty and open as the site—or I show up without any. Either way I play that, you take Manu and leave me with no leverage."

"I'd still be stuck with Chaplat," I said, "who, as you may recall, very much wants you."

"He's literally the least of your problems," Jack said, "and the easiest to get away from."

"True enough," I said, "but why would I run when I can solve this for good?"

"If the plan works," Jack said.

"Yes," I said, nodding my head and ready to scream at him, "if it works. We're both gambling on that."

"We're back to my concern," he said.

I stood, crossed my arms, and squeezed my elbows with my hands to give physical vent to my frustration. "I give you my word, Jack, that I won't take Manu when we visit the site. I also give you my word that if you mess this up now, you won't have to worry about any of the others, because I'll hunt you down and find you before they can. Make a choice."

He smiled and raised his hands. "Your word is good enough for me, Jon. See you at the site at dusk."

The display winked out before I could say anything else. I shook with rage.

"Will he show?" Maggie said.

"Yes," I said through clenched teeth, "or I will track him down and do whatever it takes to make him tell me where Manu is." I headed for my quarters so I could calm down alone and not have to worry about what I might say in front of her. "Whatever it takes."

CHAPTER 34

PINK AND ORANGE dominated the far horizon as the day faded and we drew closer to the abandoned EC base. We flew level with the treetops to the west as we approached the vast expanse of permacrete from the south. Lobo began firing milspec sensor-gophers when we crossed the southern wall and kept it up, one every thirty meters, until we had overshot the hangar, turned a hundred and eighty degrees, and dived into the building's large rear opening. He launched a similar barrage in a straight line from the west side of the building out into the grasslands on the edge of the base.

The gophers expanded when they hit, dug into the permacrete until they were below ground level, extruded antennas and sensors, and then pulled as much of the permacrete shavings onto themselves as possible. Unless you walked by one, you wouldn't notice it. Standard tools on open-area battlefields, they created a mesh sensor and comm network that we could use to amplify signals and track outside activity. Lobo checked in with each sensor, then backed inside the warehouse far enough that we weren't visible from outside unless you were looking from ground level or a shallow angle above it. He settled very carefully into position, repeated the gopher check, then flashed the ready signal on the display in front of me.

"Scan results?" I said.

"Nothing on approach," Lobo said. "The rest of the place is indeed protected from external sensors and all transmissions. Now that I'm inside, I can read the signal from Jack's transmitter, but IR won't work through the walls so I can't get a headcount."

I nodded. "As good as it can be right now. If he brings more than we can handle," I looked at Maggie and the three Zyuns, who stood behind me in Lobo, "then I'll be surprised, but I'll also signal."

"Of course," Lobo said. "I do remember the plan. Worry about your part, not mine—which I have well in hand."

His sarcasm was a great motivation to get moving, because he'd only stop it when we were active.

I turned to face the others. As I'd asked, Maggie had again put on her Followers security uniform. The Zyuns looked as they always did—short, insanely muscular, heavily armed, and psychotically in sync—but now black flexi-armor covered almost every square centimeter of them, a tiny patch of each of their faces the only skin visible. When they showed up for work that might turn hot, they came prepared.

To Maggie, I said, "Are you ready for this?"

"Of course," she said. "I told you I would be."

"Zyuns," I said, "you have the rest of the advance. Ready?"

"Do we look any other way?" they said. "All is now."

Great; they chose this time to add a sense of humor to the Zen attitude.

"Lobo," I said, "open a hatch."

We stepped out. One Zyun stood beside Lobo while the rest of us headed off.

"I'm sorry," I said, "but it really is necessary."

"We know the deal we made," they said.

We threaded our way through low stacks of boxes and to the corridor that ran between the large rear room where Lobo was parked and the much bigger main front space. A floor-to-ceiling, old-fashioned, hinged metal door at the end of the corridor now separated the building's rear section from the rest of the place. It was solid and heavy and when shut was almost perfectly flush with the permacrete on all sides. Good.

I paused before the door and nodded to the Zyuns. One of them, Maggie, and I stepped back so we'd be behind it as it opened. The other dropped to the ground and, as I opened the latch, pulled the door toward us from the bottom. Though the muscles in his arms swelled with effort, he made no sound.

Jack sat on a ratty leather sofa fifteen meters inside, Manu beside him. When Jack saw the door open and spotted the prone Zyun, he laughed. "Do you trust nothing, Jon?" he said.

The Zyun gave the clear signal and stood. We followed him inside. Maggie took a step toward Manu, but I grabbed her shoulder, came parallel to her, and kept her beside me. She'd agreed to stick with the plan, so she didn't resist me, but it was obvious that she wanted to go to the boy.

"From here on in, Jack, no," I said. "When you first asked for my help, you said you were no good at this sort of thing but I was. Minimizing what I have to trust in an encounter as dangerous as this one is part of what I do."

"Fair enough," he said. He patted Manu on the head and said to the boy, "You remember Jon, don't you, Manu?"

"Hi, Jon. Did Lobo come?"

"Of course I did, Manu," Lobo said via a small but powerful speaker in my belt. "I wouldn't miss it."

Both Manu and Maggie actually looked touched. Just my luck: My bloodthirsty killing machine was better with both kids and women than I was.

I shook my head slightly to focus myself. "Jack, Maggie has some medical training; would you mind if she checked out Manu?" She didn't, but Jack wouldn't care. At this point, either he was trusting me, or something very nasty was waiting for us somewhere near here. Given that Lobo had detected nothing and the two Zyuns with me hadn't raised an alarm despite their nonstop scanning of the area, I was betting Jack was behaving. I hadn't planned on this check, but I was tired of fighting with Maggie, who had all but demanded a chance to verify that Manu was unharmed.

"Of course not," Jack said, "though I assure you he's fine."

"I am," Manu said. "We've been moving around a lot, and though I've met some interesting people, I'm tired of not staying anywhere long. Other than that, everything's okay."

I let go of Maggie. From the tension in her posture she wanted to run, but she forced herself to walk to the sofa. She rested her hand on Jack's arm as she quietly said, "Would you mind sliding over so I could sit next to Manu?"

"Not at all," Jack said.

Maggie stood suddenly as if shocked, then looked at me. "Jon, you—"

Light was fading, and we needed to move, so I cut her off. "You wanted to evaluate Manu's condition; please do."

She nodded her head, then sat and put her hand on Manu's forehead, as if checking him for a fever like a frontier mother whose medbed was on the fritz. She said, "Hi, Manu. I'm Maggie." After a few seconds, a smile bloomed on her face, and she wrapped her arms around the boy and laughed. A frown crossed Manu's face, then he stared into her eyes for several long moments and laughed, too. I'd never seen either of them quite so happy.

As she hugged Manu, I slowly and carefully scanned the mods Jack's team had completed. The doors stood where we needed them, and temporary walls filled the rest of the entrances. All the gear we'd discussed perched in the right places in the hangar, though none of it was visible without magnification and even then only if you knew to look for it. The whole setup appeared good to go.

"Nice work, Jack," I said.

He spread his hands and smiled. "Give me some credit, Jon. This isn't my first gig."

"The comm gear, inside and out?"

"All set."

"The rest of it?"

He sighed theatrically. "Again, Jon, all done. We finished everything, and we tested it all. Twice." He glanced at Maggie. "I take it you're satisfied that Manu is well," he said.

"Oh, yes," Maggie said. "He's great."

"Then we go tomorrow," I said.

Jack's smile grew wider. "Excellent. It's about time we made some money." He stood and motioned toward Manu.

"Hold on, Jack," I said. I walked closer to the sofa, the Zyuns staying at my seven and four. "As I promised, I'm not separating you from Manu, but I am changing the plan a bit."

Jack froze, his smile gone, his eyes narrow. "We're partners, Jon. We should discuss changes and agree on them before either one of us makes them."

"From here on, Jack, we're in my area of expertise, so we do it my way. You don't get a vote. One of the Zyuns and Maggie will stay with you and Manu from now on."

"I've been doing well enough taking care of the two of us," he said, "and we can meet you—"

"No," I said. I nodded toward the Zyun on my left. "Take Maggie and the boy. Jack will follow in a moment."

"What changes are you making, Jon?" Maggie said.

I looked at her and wished she could read a single thought in my mind: *Not now.*

She clearly received the message from my expression, because she grasped Manu's hand, stood, and said, "Let's go, Manu."

As they walked away, I leaned closer to Jack and whispered, "You'll like it."

He relaxed and smiled broadly as I explained the new bits.

CHAPTER 35

THE EASIEST WAY to make sure an enemy can't control a rendezvous point is to be there before you tell them about it. I was taking no chances with the hangar and today's meeting. The creeping threat of light was driving away the night and its stars when we parked twenty meters from the front entrance of the hangar. The two Zyuns with me insisted on clearing the entire area, both external and internal perimeters, on foot, so I waited inside until they gave the all-clear.

I walked to the front of the hangar, leaned against it, and said to the Zyuns, who were now flanking me, "It's time."

They nodded and spread away from me; they neither needed nor particularly wanted to hear any of the conversations I was about to have.

"Lobo," I said.

"Full sensor mesh operational and all controls engaged," he said. "Your comm and embedded fabric backup are transmitting fully. Verify fabric comm receipt."

In slow sequence, sections of the active body armor I was wearing under my shirt and pants turned hot then cold.

"Working," I said.

"Ready," he said.

Clouds hung in the night sky, but there was no forecast for rain. The cool air didn't stop drops of sweat rolling down my arms under the armor, which absorbed them before they reached my wrist. Everywhere around me, peace and quiet reigned.

That would end soon enough.

"Open comm to Dougat," I said.

Dougat's face popped almost immediately into the heads-up display in my left contact. Lobo was feeding him a still image of me with a security note overlaid. I'd considered an animation but rejected it; I wanted him to know I was intentionally not giving him any visibility into my location.

"It's very early, Moore," he said. "Make it good."

"It's your lucky day," I said, "as long as you have the weapons I ordered. As for the hour, well, I warned you I might call at any time."

"Insulting me accomplishes nothing other than to encourage me to walk away," he said.

"Then walk, and I will, too, and I'll take Manu Chang with me."

"You have him?"

"Now who's being insulting?" I wanted all three main players to be as much off their games as possible, so I was happy to play with Dougat for as long as he could stand it.

He took a deep breath and closed his eyes for a few seconds. When he opened them, it was if a new man had invaded his body. "All the weapons are on a transport ship outside of Malzton. We're ready to make the trade."

"Be here in one hour," I said, and on cue Lobo transmitted him the coordinates and photos and schematics of the hangar. All the images directed him to the east entrance to the building. Lobo also started a countdown timer in my right contact's display. "Land in the spot I designated, and after you have, enter through the door in front of you. Have the loaders bring the weapons inside. If my PCAV spots anything other than a cargo transport, or if you come within its sensor range early, we'll leave, and the next time you hear from me it won't be to do business. If you deviate from these plans when you're on the ground, my PCAV and my team will respond swiftly."

"We have a deal in which we all win," Dougat said with a smile. "I have no incentive to do anything other than honor the arrangement. I worry that you are not of a similar mind-set."

"If I wanted to go to war with the Followers," I said, "I would have done so already, and you'd be dead. The deal is the best path forward for me as well. After it, we won't encounter each other ever again."

"Excellent," he said. "We shall arrive per your schedule."

I nodded, then realized he couldn't see me. "I look forward to it," I said. "See you in fifty-seven minutes."

Lobo cut the link.

I took a deep breath and began a series of stretches. We were in it now, and I wanted to stay loose and ready for anything.

When the countdown showed ten minutes had passed, I said to Lobo, "Open comm to Chaplat." We went with the still image of me again even though I knew it would annoy Chaplat. I wanted him, like Dougat, to understand from the start that I wouldn't let him control the situation.

"How quaint, Mr. Moore," he said. "I trust today will be a good day for us both."

I hadn't figured him for a morning person, but either he was a better actor than Dougat, or he was already up and fully operational. "It will indeed," I said. "You're ready with the money?"

"I'm sufficiently pleased to be regaining your friend Jack that I'm going to strive to hold on to my good mood and my manners," he said, "but I encourage you not to test my patience. Of course I am."

"Everything is set on my side," I said. "Be here in one hour." Lobo flashed me that he had sent the coordinates and a different set of hangar directions and images. These designated a landing area on the west side of the building and directed Chaplat toward the door there. Lobo started a second small countdown timer in the window. "Land in the marked spot, and enter through the door in front of it. Not to be rude, but if my PCAV detects more than a single cargo ship, we'll leave before you can reach us, and I'll make my next visit to you in it. If you don't follow these instructions once you've landed, my PCAV and my team will respond swiftly."

"Yeah, yeah," he said. "You're saying what you have to say, but we both know that we both win the most if the deal goes right, so save your breath and stop annoying me. My vessel has space for the weapons, me, my team, and my two new passengers. It's all I need, and it's all I'll bring."

I ignored his probe to see whether I was having second thoughts about him taking Manu. I couldn't let him detect any concern on my part. "Fine," I said. "See you in fifty-eight minutes."

Five minutes later, I said to Lobo, "Midon."

A too perfectly beautiful young woman's face appeared in the display in my left contact. "I'm sorry to have to tell you that Councillor Midon is unavailable right now," the sim said, "but I'm sure I can either help you or find someone who can."

Great. The clock was ticking, and Midon couldn't be bothered to answer the comm personally. I needed to drop enough loaded words that even the dumbest interface software would elevate my priority and force Midon to take the link herself.

"Dougat, Chaplat, the weapons, the boy—tell Midon it's all happening now, and either she answers in the next ninety seconds or I disconnect, keep her advance, and deal with it myself." Unless she hadn't bothered to brief her 'face software, that should more than do it.

Lobo obligingly opened a third timer in my right contact, this one a bright red in contrast to the pale aqua tones of the other two. He loved drama.

The counter showed seventeen seconds had elapsed when Midon's face snapped into view in my left contact's display. She appeared perfectly composed, as if she'd been at work and simply too absorbed to notice the comm.

"The software was already rousing me, Mr. Moore," she said. "The frequency and your ID were more than enough to prompt it to action. Now you've left so many verbal trails that if this goes badly I'll have to invest in a serious data scrub of my entire interface system."

"Then let's not let that happen," I said. "Our deals stand?"

She nodded. "Of course. The weapons and the boy?"

"All set," I said. "And your team leader agrees to wait until I signal you?"

"Reluctantly," she said, "but yes, she does. Clear and indisputable proof of Dougat's involvement is in all our interest."

"And the remainder of my payment?"

"Three days later, as you requested," she said, "though I must confess that I remain surprised you want to wait so long. Your choice, after all, does force you to trust me."

"Waiting means no clear links between me and the arrests you make here, so it's less risk for me," I said. "You could try to cheat me, but as you noted, I've left a lot of trails, and you're not the only one with recordings. If anything happens to me, friends will make sure a lot of people see them."

"Of course," she said.

"Monitor both the east and west entrances of this hangar," I said. Lobo flashed a "coordinates sent" message in my right contact. "The east side will go live in approximately thirty-eight minutes, and the west will heat up about ten minutes later. Your team must either arrive quickly enough for a full stealth setup in advance of the earlier time or come in quietly after they see the ship land on the west and its passengers enter the hangar. I suggest the latter. No one in the building will be able to hear much of anything outside, but they'll almost certainly leave external lookouts. Factor those into your landing approach. Most importantly, make sure everyone on your team knows what my PCAV and I look like and leave it and me alone. If you bother the ship, it will resist."

"Our team is already in route," she said, "and though I've worked with many people who micromanaged, I've never found it particularly effective."

She had a point. I was prone to it, and I needed to stop it. Any team that would be of use to me would have to be able to do its job well.

"We all know what we're doing," she continued. "As for your ship, if we wanted a fight with it, we would have shuttled an appropriate countermeasure to this gate station after your first—" She paused, clearly searching for a term she could tolerate. "—display outside Carne's office."

"I hope so," I said, "but while you're watching feeds of the action, I'll be in the middle of it. My butt's on the line, not yours."

"As it has been from the beginning," she said, "so that's not news. Are we done?"

"Yes," I said.

She cut the link before my mouth had formed the "y."

I stretched again and went inside to wait. The Zyuns followed. We walked the inner perimeter of the building, an unnecessary check but one that burned a little energy and felt good to be doing. The east and west entrance doors stood open. Everything was in place.

We were good to go inside.

Lobo would alert me if anything outside unfolded differently than it should.

Now I had to wait until Dougat arrived, hope nothing went wrong, and find a way to keep everyone alive and safe as this played out.

CHAPTER 36

I PUT OFF the encounter as long as I could, but with three minutes to go until Dougat was due to arrive, I couldn't wait any more.

"Lobo," I said over the comm unit, "tell Maggie to come out." To the Zyuns, I said, "Bring her over."

They nodded as one. The Zyun to my right trotted across the hangar toward the heavy metal door that separated the rear area from the rest of the hangar. The Zyun to my left glided in front of me. Despite the huge amount of muscle they carried and their general blockiness, the Zyuns moved gracefully and quickly.

As the Zyun reached the door, it opened, the Zyun in the hangar acting in perfect sync with the one on the other side of the tall barrier. Maggie stumbled out, pushed from behind. She wore the Followers guard uniform she was wearing the day I carried her onto Lobo after she saved Manu from being shot. Her hair clung dirty and matted to her skull. Her face sagged with exhaustion.

She looked as good to me as anyone had in a very long time.

I shook my head slightly to clear the thought. I had to stay sharp.

The door slammed shut, the metal clanging as its edges hit the permacrete frame.

The Zyun grabbed Maggie's elbow with his black-gloved hand and led her in a slow jog across the floor to me. She didn't look happy.

I hated this part, but it was necessary. Time was short. I had to do it.

"Jon," she said, her eyes searching my face and her tone unsteady. "Why am I out here?"

"Because I need you here," I said. "Stand and—"

She cut me off. "This is not what you told me we'd be doing! The plan was different. You said—"

"Shut up!" I yelled. The look of shock and betrayal on her face hit me like a punch to the heart, but I kept going. "What I said before doesn't matter. What matters is that you stand here, do what I say, and keep your mouth shut."

"What about Manu?" she said. "You promised—"

"I told you to shut up!" I stepped forward until we were practically touching. "We don't have time for this. Dougat is about to arrive. Don't say a word. Understand?"

She nodded slowly, tears running down her cheeks as she moved her head.

"And do as I tell you."

She nodded again.

My heart pounded inside my chest. I wanted to hold her and explain, but I'd thought it all through, and now was not the time for second-guessing. I kept my gaze fixed on her and said only, "Good."

"Your vitals are unusually high given that no hostiles are yet present," Lobo said over the private channel that sounded only in my right ear. "Are you solid to go?"

I nodded to the Zyun who'd escorted Maggie, and he held on to her as I turned and walked away. After a few steps, I subvocalized, "Yes. Dumb reactions on my part. We go."

I closed my eyes and reviewed the plan, inhaled and exhaled slowly and deeply, and my pulse settled to normal. Right here, right now, what I felt was unimportant. Nothing mattered but doing the job, executing the plan, making it work.

"Dougat landing," Lobo said via the comm frequency the

Zyuns and I were sharing. To improve our response time should the situation go nonlinear, I was trusting Lobo to choose which bits of information the Zyuns needed and which should stay private. He switched to the private channel and added, "Last chance to abort."

"No," I subvocalized, not trying to hide my annoyance. "We go."

Back on the shared channel, Lobo continued. "Dougat is over ninety seconds late, but that's within plan tolerances. I detect no support or follow team. Stand ready."

I looked at the two Zyuns.

In unison they signaled ready.

Maggie stared at me, her face showing confusion and hurt. I didn't meet her eyes. We could deal with her feelings if we survived.

In the upper left of my vision Lobo streamed a composite video feed from the ground sensors east of the hangar. Dougat's ship, a dull gray cargo carrier with an AutoHomes Construction logo, landed precisely where we'd directed him. Hatches on the left and right side of its front blinked open and three guards in body armor jumped out of each. The vessel immediately closed.

Fair enough.

"Let them in," I said.

Lobo retracted the east door enough to allow two men to walk abreast through it.

Dougat had upgraded his security team or its members were better at executing scripted scenarios than they were at dealing with unexpected crises. I watched in Lobo's feed as they fanned out on either side of the door but did not enter. One tossed a small ball inside. The metal sphere clanged against the permacrete floor, sprouted four legs and three antennae, and crawled forward.

"Open comm to Dougat," I said.

"Mr. Moore," he said. "I trust you don't mind our precautions."

"Not at all," I said. "As your surveillance spider is telling you, only a few members of my team are currently involved, and your guard is here as a sign of good faith."

"And Manu Chang? We seem to be missing his IR signature. Is he what's behind that large metal door directly in front of our entrance?"

"Yes," I said, "he is, as is another squad of mine. They'll bring out the boy in time, but not until I've seen the weapons and received my cut of the purchase price."

"As I understood you earlier, that last step requires Chaplat."

"It does," I said, "but he won't come until I verify that you've brought everything he specified. So, the sooner you send the weapons inside and let my man verify that everything we ordered is present, the sooner we all get what we want."

"You're making this annoying enough," he said, "that the temptation is growing to send my men to wipe out your small crew and bring Chang to me."

In the upper right of my vision the countdown marched relentlessly toward the moment when Chaplat would arrive. Dougat was such a talker that I'd budgeted some time for him to waste in protesting and threatening, but I couldn't afford for it to go on too long. "Your posturing is a waste of energy. You won't send anyone after us. They'd have to come through that entrance, and we'd destroy them on the way in. What we missed, the team members behind the door and on my PCAV would finish. You said the boy was worth the cost of the weapons—for which you *are* also receiving a rather substantial and quite reasonable fee—so you win by keeping to our deal. Let's get on with it."

"Fine," he said. "Do you want to inspect the cargo in the ship?"

I chuckled. "Hardly. Keep them covered, and bring them inside. My man will check them against the inventory once they're in here."

"We'll start unloading," he said. "Open the door wide enough for the loaders."

"When they're in front of it, we will," I said. "Bring them on."

"Jon, you can't," Maggie whispered. "You promised."

I glared at her over my shoulder and hissed my response. "Do *not* interrupt me."

I looked back at the door. The air in the hangar was still

and cool, but sweat ran down my back and chest until the light armor managed to absorb it. The biolights Jack's team had hung along the ceiling's perimeter glowed a soft red and bathed the off-white permacrete interior in light the color of watered-down blood. I was sure that if I turned around, Maggie would still be staring at me, but I couldn't allow myself to think about that now.

I focused on the upper left contact images of the loaders marching sideways out of Dougat's ship. The soft gray metal bots resembled giants devoid of upper legs, much of their torsos, and heads. Their lower legs and alloy arms emerged directly from the bottom and top of their wide, broad, flat waists. Each pair carried a three-high stack of dull black boxes the size of coffins built for very tall twins. Six loaders with nine total crates emerged; that count seemed about right. They queued up in front of the door and marched forward.

"Open?" Lobo said.

"Yes."

As the lead loader reached the door, the tall metal plate slid further out of the way. The squad of machines thumped into the hangar and formed a rough square with the rear wall as its fourth side, then settled into position. I admired the planning: The weapons were accessible for inspection, but their armored crates also formed a small fort that would shield Dougat. We might have a chance at angle shots, but the stacked containers were high enough that we couldn't see directly into the center of the formation.

I watched in Lobo's feed as Dougat and a four-man team entered the building and went to the protected heart of the group of loaders. Lobo opened a second small display that used the internal corner cameras to show me an aerial view of the man and his guards. His team spread to positions behind loader legs, and one of the guards led him to a safe station as well. He had definitely upgraded his security squad.

Dougat said something I couldn't make out, and the crates shimmered into clarity. The armored and polarized shield glass was a nice touch: strong enough to withstand fire from most common weapons, able to go dark when in public areas, and clear enough to let us do complete inspections without having to unload fully or handle the merchandise.

"As you can see, Mr. Moore," Dougat said, his rich and deep preacher's voice managing to fill our whole section of the huge hangar, "the weapons are ready for your inspector."

Internal projectors could yield the same effects as shield glass, so I said, "He'll perform the bulk of the audit visually from outside the crates, but you also have to let him see inside each one for final verification."

Dougat laughed, a loud, hearty sound that for a change seemed genuine. "My, but you are a paranoid one. Fine, but he has to do it inside this space, because that's where all the easily accessible hatches are."

I didn't point out that he was also paranoid enough to make sure the loaders formed a defensive perimeter with all the crate inspection openings facing inward. Instead, I said only, "Acceptable."

I looked at the Zyun on my right and nodded. I thought for an instant I detected a trace of discomfort in his face, but I couldn't be sure. He neither hesitated nor said anything in response; the Zyuns were worth their premium fees. He jogged over to the rightmost of the stack of crates, climbed up the side of the farther loader as easily and smoothly as most people would walk a gentle ramp, and began carefully checking the contents of the top container.

I shifted my visual focus among the various inputs sharing my attention: the counter until Chaplat was due, its slow downward progress a growing pressure; the external feed showing two guards waiting beside Dougat's ship, not a problem now but a potential one later; the scene around me, all of us waiting, no one happy, everyone tense and everyone except Maggie and possibly Dougat armed; and the relay from the Zyun's microcam, which he carefully but not obviously made sure gave me a clear view of each weapon as he marked it off the list. I didn't let myself check on Maggie.

As the Zyun progressed through the crates, everything

seemed to be in order. Dougat had delivered the goods: pulse and projectile automatic weapons with IR and noise dampening; laser/acid combo next-gen squidlettes far beyond what I'd seen in his warehouse basement on Mund; human-launched surface-to-air missiles that sported enough sensors and computing shielding to let them fly through all but the roughest heat and electronic attacks without losing the locks on their targets; transforming, self-launching missiles that could roll like two-meter-long demon-wheeled cargo boards into position and then sprout launch tubes from their centers; mushroom-headed transmission disruptors that could work on the ground or launch from their thick stems and sustain aerial positions via small rotors that sprouted when they hit the target altitude; and much, much more. No single item was incredibly expensive, but quite a few were pricey enough that many guerrilla groups on poorer frontier planets would pause to lust after them at a weapons mart before having to move on to more affordable alternatives. If Midon's goal truly was to catch Dougat with matériel he could never explain and in the process to put a lot of dangerous gear out of circulation, she'd chosen her weapons well.

"Jon," Maggie said, loud enough that Dougat and his men could hear her.

I turned, glared, and nodded at the Zyun. He clamped his right hand over her mouth.

"And how are you, my dear?" Dougat said, his voice still powerful but now friendly. "How nice that you're on a first-name basis with your captors. I do so look forward to having you back and to hearing all about your time with Mr. Moore and, of course, with the boy. If the child has said anything of interest, I'm confident you'll tell me all about it."

My pulse quickened and my body tensed at the implied threat. I'd hoped he'd find Maggie a small enticement, because she provided a way for him to show his team that he wouldn't let one of their own remain in captivity. Instead, he cared only about extracting from her anything she'd learned about Manu. I glanced again at her. Her eyes were wide and wet with fear.

I hated myself for the thought, but I'd had it earlier as well: Her fear could work for us. I stepped next to her as if I were whispering in her ear but instead quietly said to the Zyun, "In a few seconds, pull your hand away as if she bit you."

I returned to my earlier position, then whipped around when I heard Maggie start to speak. The Zyun was shaking his hand convincingly as she said, "And to think I worked for you, Dougat. You don't care anything about me or the boy! And if you think I'll you do anything to help you harm or take advantage of that poor child, you clearly don't understand me!"

"I'm afraid it's *you* who do not understand *me*," Dougat said. "I care very much about Manu Chang; he may turn out to be the greatest discovery I've ever made. I'm also concerned about you, though I must admit primarily as you relate to Manu. I'm confident we'll be able to persuade you to help us."

"The way you'll 'persuade' him to do whatever you want?" Maggie said. "The way you persuade new Followers to work around the clock without—"

"Enough!" I said. I put my hand on the pistol in the holster on my right hip and looked at the Zyun. "I told you we should have gagged her. Shut her up before I do."

He clamped his hand over her mouth and pulled her next to him before she could speak. Her eyes were wide and her face taut with anger and something else, something worse I didn't want to see.

I turned and spoke to Dougat. "When we're done with the deal, she's your problem, and you two can talk all you want. Until then, I don't care to listen to any more of this."

We stood in silence for a bit as the Zyun near Dougat methodically worked his way from crate to crate. His heads-up display also showed the Chaplat timer, and he adjusted his pace perfectly, so that with ten minutes to go he finished all the checks he could do from the outside of the carriers and entered Dougat's enclosed area for the quick direct visual inspection.

In the feed from the microcam in the ceiling corner behind Dougat I could see that his team had prepped the crates: all the inspection hatches stood open. Two guards trained their rifles on the Zyun's back as he methodically worked his way through the weapons. He showed no reaction to the threat; I once again admired how cool the Zyuns stayed. The Zyun spent almost exactly one minute on each container, checking enough with his eyes and with his hands to make sure the external views had been accurate.

When he finished his inspection, he left the area without speaking, jogged over to me, nodded once, and floated to a front-facing position on my right.

"I trust you're satisfied," Dougat said. "I've brought everything I promised."

"I am," I said.

"Then deliver on your promise," he said. "Bring out the boy."

Even though I wasn't sure Dougat could see me, I shook my head slowly. "No. I told you: not until Chaplat is here and has approved the deal and paid me."

On the comm channel I shared with the Zyuns, Lobo said, "Chaplat's cargo ship has entered the base's airspace. Estimate touchdown in one minute."

"How long will this take?" Dougat said. "You really are forcing me to reconsider this entire arrangement."

"No," I said, "I'm not, because your wait is almost over."

I pointed to the other side of the hangar as Lobo slid the door there slowly open and dust stirred up by the incoming ship swirled inside.

"Chaplat's here."

CHAPTER 37

I WATCHED IN a new small feed from Lobo as the two guards I'd met before hopped out of Chaplat's cargo transport and checked the area for him. They trotted the perimeter of that ship and the rest of that side of the hangar. In the view Lobo was giving me onto Dougat's outside team, that squad returned to positions near their vessel and brought their rifles to ready, but fortunately Chaplat's people stayed away from them.

Everybody was playing by the rules, behaving with sensible and well-organized paranoia, just as they should.

Lobo opened the side entrance in front of Chaplat's ship.

His two guards peeked around the corner of the doorway, then entered the building. After a few seconds, Chaplat and four more guards, all in black and all armed with holstered pistols and rifles, joined the advance team inside. They wheeled mobile shields in front of them, the currently transparent armor slightly distorting their images. Two men formed a second barrier in front of Chaplat. The others spread out along his right flank; the team used the wall to protect his left.

"Mr. Moore," Chaplat said. "I trust you won't waste my time here. I'm quite—"

I didn't want to let him and Dougat start a dominance contest, so I cut him off. "I apologize for interrupting, but

I'm sure we're all eager to leave with what we came for, so I suggest we get to it."

Lobo opened a feed from the ceiling microcam with the best view of Chaplat. My heads-up display glittered with so many images that I had trouble handling them all. I put my hand to my mouth, coughed lightly, and subvocalized, "Fewer feeds."

Lobo closed the images of the exterior teams. Much better. Though I liked having all the information those views provided, I trusted Lobo to show me the outside again if something of note happened. In the meantime, with a smaller number of simultaneous images to manage I could much more easily stay on top of what was happening inside.

I missed a few words from Chaplat in the transition and refocused as he said, ". . . weapon crates, and I have the funds, but I don't see Jack."

"I'd like to verify the payment," I said.

"After we check the weapons."

"My man has already done that," I said, "and we'd be happy to send you the inspection video." I nodded to the Zyun, who thumbed open an unencrypted narrow-range broadcast.

The female guard pulled out a rolled sheet, snapped it taut, and showed the 'cast to Chaplat. He studied it for a minute, then laughed. "Very nice," he said, "and probably accurate, but we will do our own inspection, thank you very much."

Dougat sighed loudly enough that no one in the huge hangar could miss it. He had to be using some amplification I hadn't noticed.

"Must we endure this again?" he said.

Chaplat responded by pointing at two of his men. "Let them do a quick internal physical spot-check of the merchandise, and we'll only delve into the details if that doesn't go well."

"Reasonable enough," Dougat said.

Chaplat's two rear guards jogged to Dougat and entered the area formed by the wall and the crates. I watched in the feed from the camera above that space as one of Dougat's guards took up a position behind each of Chaplat's men and shadowed them as they moved. They opened the hatches and inspected the contents much more quickly than the Zyun, so Chaplat must have been at least somewhat satisfied with the video we'd sent.

We stood in silence for over five minutes as they worked. I checked on Maggie once, and she glared back at me, the Zyun's hand still covering her mouth. I wanted to snap my head back to the front to escape her accusing stare, but I forced myself to keep my eyes on her for a few seconds, as if carefully assessing a prisoner.

Chaplat's guards trotted away from Dougat and back to their leader.

When they'd resumed their former positions behind the barrier and around Chaplat, he said, "Check your wallet, Moore, and you'll be able to see—but not access, of course, not yet—the funds and the pending transfer."

I kept my focus on the two groups of men as I pulled out my wallet and opened it. It immediately displayed the pending transfer.

"The funds are indeed there," Lobo said over the private channel. "I've monitored and double-checked the wallet's query to the bank. Chaplat is playing it straight. It's time."

"I can indeed," I said. "Thank you. Let's do the money and weapons transfer, then I'll get Jack and the boy."

"No," Dougat and Chaplat said in unison, Dougat loudly and Chaplat in a level tone. The timing surprised them for a moment, so neither continued right away.

Chaplat recovered first. "I get Jack," Chaplat said, "and then we do the rest."

"I don't care about him," Dougat said. "The boy is what matters."

Dougat obviously had no real grasp of the type of man Chaplat was, because even if Chaplat hadn't planned to kidnap Manu before, a comment like that guaranteed that he'd go after the boy. I put away my wallet as if by habit.

"I set this up," I said, "so I get paid first." I held up my hand so neither would interrupt, then plunged ahead. Each of them almost certainly believed he had the firepower to overwhelm me. Though each may have thought his team could take the other's, neither could be completely confident on that front, so neither should want to start a war in here. Each was my insurance against the other—at least until they got what they wanted. "But I agree you need to see that I've held up all of my end of the deal. So, how about a compromise?"

"You're pushing it, Moore," Chaplat said. "If you don't have Jack here—"

Dougat cut him off. "What do you propose?"

"I show you Jack and Manu," I said, "and then we do the weapons and money exchange. When we finish that, we'll all have something we want. Then, Chaplat, I'll give you Jack, and Dougat, you'll get the boy."

Maggie screamed against the Zyun's hand, which turned her cry into a squelched roar of pain.

I ignored it and kept talking. "Until we finish all that, Jack and Manu remain with my team. Deal?"

"Acceptable," Dougat said.

"Fine," Chaplat said. "Get on with it."

I nodded and turned to face the Zyun behind me, as if I were going to speak to him. Tears ran down Maggie's face. She leaned forward against the grip of the Zyun, who held her in place with what you might believe was no effort if you looked only at his impassive face. The arm muscles bunched so tightly they strained the flexible armor told another story.

"Send them out?" Lobo said on the private comm channel.

"Yes," I subvocalized. I nodded once at the Zyun, whose head moved ever so slightly in acknowledgment. With one hand he leveled his weapon on the open ground between Chaplat and the rear center door.

I faced front as that huge piece of metal slid slowly open. The Zyun to my right trained his weapon on the space between Dougat and the opening to the corridor.

"We all stay where we are," I said. "My men are aiming only at space, not people. You'll get all the confirmation you need in a moment."

"Here they come," Lobo said.

The third Zyun appeared first, his head rotating from side to side as he slowly checked the perimeter. I knew a feed of the area was playing in his lenses, but like many pros he trusted what he saw in real life more than what any machine could show him.

After he finished his sweep, he stepped back into the corridor and came out with Jack and Manu in front of him. Both man and boy wore blindfolds. Each had his hands tied in front of him. A cable connected their hands, and another cable linked the center of that one with the Zyun who was now behind them. He controlled that main cable with one hand. His other held a small handgun that he trained at the boy's back.

I fought my natural reaction to their plight, a reflex I had trouble suppressing even though I'd caused this situation. If Jack and Manu didn't look like hostages, neither Chaplat nor Dougat would believe anything else I did.

"Satisfied?" I said.

Over the private comm channel, Lobo said, "EC troops on stealth approach from three southern vectors. No sign of awareness on the part of either group here."

"I allowed you to inspect the weapons," Dougat said at about the same time. "I think it's only fair—"

I interrupted him. "No. You put the weapons in crates, so we had no choice but to verify that all the individual items were present. There's only one boy and one man, and you can see for yourself that they're both here. My job was to deliver them safely; it's obvious that I did."

"Good enough for me," Chaplat said. "Jack seems fit."

"You're bound to have scared the boy," Dougat said, "but I suppose it couldn't be helped. Fine; I'm satisfied. Can we get on with it?"

"Definitely," I said. "If you'll ready the payment, Chaplat, we can commence."

When my wallet beeped, I reached for it to visually confirm the completed transfer.

As I did, Maggie burst away from the Zyun, who raised his weapon.

"Park!" I screamed. I held up my hand to signal the Zyun not to shoot.

Over the private channel, Lobo said, "The payment is already on its way to other accounts."

Maggie stopped and turned toward me. "You told me nothing—"

"Shut up and get back here!" I said. "Jack and Manu stay where they are until I'm sure I've been paid." In the feeds in my left contact I caught glimpses of both Dougat's men and Chaplat's holding their weapons at the ready, but I focused on her.

"Money?" she screamed. "This is all about money? I told you I wouldn't let you hurt them, and I won't."

I drew my pistol and aimed it at her. I nodded at the Zyun behind me, who slowly advanced on her. "Stay where you are," I said, "until he reaches you. You can still come out of this alive and rejoin the Followers."

"You wouldn't shoot me," she said.

She turned.

"Stop!" I said.

She took a step toward Jack and Manu, then another, no longer running, just walking slowly, carefully, her head high and determined. I knew how hard it was to stare straight ahead and keep moving when someone was pointing a gun at your back, and I admired her for it.

"Mr. Moore," Dougat said, "surely—"

"She stops, or I shoot her," I said to him, rushing the words so they got ahead of her advance on Jack and Manu. "You want the boy, and so does she. You paid for him. She didn't." My voice rose despite my best attempts to keep it level. "Last chance, Park! Don't make me shoot you."

She faced me, but she continued walking, moving slowly backward toward her goal even as she spoke to me, drawing ever closer to the boy. "You know you're better than that, Jon. You can't give Manu to Dougat. You said—"

I shot her in the chest.

Many things happened at the same time.

The echo of the round I'd fired boomed in the huge space.

Every head I could see in front of me and on the feeds from Lobo snapped toward Maggie and me.

Everyone in the space aimed weapons at us.

The Zyun near the rear corridor led Jack and Manu quickly back to the door, so they were barely in the room.

Jack and Manu tried to scream from beneath their gags.

Maggie crumpled, an expression of disbelief stealing across her face as blood spread on her shirt and her body hit the ground.

CHAPTER 38

"E" VERYONE STAY CALM," I said, tension still evident in my tone. "This does not have to be a problem." I extended my left arm so it was parallel with the ground, then slowly moved it downward. The Zyuns lowered their weapons in time with the motion, and I also lowered mine.

I watched in one of the feeds as Chaplat smiled and nodded his head. His team relaxed and followed suit.

"Not a problem?" Dougat said at the same time. "You killed a woman in front of me. Do you know how much trouble   "

I cut him off again. "Yes, I do," I said, walking over to Maggie's body. "None. This incident won't cause you or anyone else any trouble, because it never happened." I motioned the rear Zyun to join me.

"What do you mean?" Dougat said, reminding me again that he was a man who stayed away from the sharp end and let others do the wet work for him. "I saw it! If anyone were to find out—"

"Will you shut up?" Chaplat said. "You clearly didn't give a damn about her, whoever she was."

"She was one of my Followers," Dougat said, "and I care about every one of them. She was supposed to rejoin us as part of this transaction. And I certainly cannot afford to be implicated in this sort of thing."

"You won't be," I said. "Trust me: My problems are bigger than yours if this gets out, so I won't let that happen. Before we do anything else, my men and I are going to take her body to my PCAV, where it'll keep until we have time to dispose of it properly. If either of you decides to try to use this—" I paused and stared at the body. "—mistake as leverage, there'll be no proof that'll stand up. As for the woman's part in the deal, she obviously had no real value for you, so you haven't lost anything of consequence."

"Leave her," Chaplat said. "It's not like she's going anywhere. Finish the deal, and then you can clean up."

"I don't like her being there," Dougat said. "It's upsetting."

"EC troop lead sent the ready signal on your frequency," Lobo said over the comm unit. "On your sign."

I didn't respond to him. I focused on Dougat. "Yes, and it's dangerous for me," I said. "The sooner this never happened, the better for all of us."

"You stay then," Chaplat said, "and your men take her. I don't like losing sight of any of my colleagues at this point in a deal."

"That leaves me exposed and alone in front of all of you," I said.

"You made that choice when you shot her," Chaplat said, "and now you're wasting my time."

I shook my head and said, "Both of my men take her so we can finish this as quickly as possible. I walk to the door but no further, and my man over there," I motioned toward Jack and Manu, "leads the two of them back behind that door and to the rest of the team until my other two men return from cleaning up the mess. That's as exposed as I'm willing to be."

In the feed from Lobo I watched anger war with control on Chaplat's face, but after a few seconds he said, "Do it, but make it fast." He had to be planning to take Manu away from Dougat; I couldn't imagine what Jack could owe him that could be worth all this stress.

"I agree," Dougat said, his voice regaining its composure.

I nodded. The Zyun with Jack and Manu led them behind the

rear door, which slid slowly shut. The other two Zyuns picked up the body, one lifting under the shoulders and one grabbing the feet, and headed toward the open door behind us. I kept looking forward but walked backward to follow them.

They came to the open doorway and continued moving without slowing. I stopped two meters inside the doorway, glanced behind me to make sure all was well, and saw that they'd picked up speed as they headed to the PCAV. A side hatch in it opened for them. The bright morning light haloed around them so they looked like combat angels carrying off the fallen.

As I turned to face inside again, the world exploded.

Explosive impacts on either side of the door behind me blew chunks from the permacrete. The sound triggered the dampening circuits in my comm units. The dust and stench of spent rounds dominated the air instantly.

"Are you crazy?" I yelled at the two groups in front of me as I dropped to the floor and rolled toward the doorway. "What are you doing? Stop shooting!"

As I screamed, similar explosions at roughly a-third-of-a-meter intervals all along the walls behind both Chaplat and Dougat banged out small chunks of permacrete just above head height. The guard teams didn't know where to turn, so they assumed defensive positions and brought their weapons to ready, some in each group aiming toward the other team and some focusing on me. Two from each group pulled their bosses to the ground, adding to the confusion. All were well trained enough to wait for attack orders, but none of them needed prompting to protect their leaders; they did it instantly and without hesitation.

My roll had taken me to within half a meter of the outside, but I didn't dare move further right now; any action might draw their attention to me.

"Best target here," Lobo said as he enlarged the Dougat feed and focused on a very angry guard near the outer corner.

"Yes," I said.

Lobo swiveled two small automatic weapons Jack's team had

built into the opposite ceiling and fired just above the man. At the same time, the doors behind the two groups snapped shut, showing for the first time the true speed the slabs of metal could attain.

The guard Lobo had targeted screamed, leaned around one of the crates, and ripped a burst at Chaplat's position.

Chaplat's team spotted the motion and returned fire as the first rounds hit the wall behind them.

Dougat's squad scurried to positions facing Chaplat's and returned fire.

I scanned Dougat's group. They were all focused on Chaplat and his men; good.

At first glance, I thought Chaplat's guards were also ignoring me, but then I noticed the woman had turned her weapon on me. If I rolled toward the door I'd expose my back, so I pushed off on my hands and feet and shoved myself forward and to my right, doing what I could to get out of her sights without straying too far from the exit.

Before I hit the ground, a round smacked me in the chest and slammed me backward, my breath leaving as the body armor stopped the shell from penetrating me but couldn't do much about the force of the impact. My chest spasmed and shook with pain. I focused on the shooter in time to see her head vanish in a wet mist and her body drop a second later, Lobo demonstrating flawless accuracy with the ceiling-mounted guns.

The two groups were firing madly on each other, the projectile and beam weapons booming and sizzling in the now acrid air. Neither side was taking much damage; none of these people must have served any serious time in a real military unit.

"Trajectory analysis said her next round would be a head shot," Lobo said.

"Thanks," I gasped. I checked both sides: No one was pointing in my direction. The need to breathe screamed for attention in my head, but there was nothing I could do about it but wait for my chest to recover, so I ignored the summons. I rolled to face the door, scrambled to my feet, and darted out of it and immediately to the right.

The contacts compensated as the bright light hit my eyes. I gulped, and a few shreds of air made it into my lungs. It wouldn't take either side long to realize something was wrong, so I couldn't wait any longer.

"Midon," I croaked.

Shots boomed and rang and echoed inside the building. A few rounds clanged on the door only meters to my left; they'd noted my absence. Men shouted, their words lost in the cacophony. In the display from Lobo I saw that one member of each team was watching the door. The others continued to fire on each other.

"Stage two," I said.

"Starting," Lobo said, and at the same time that he added "and Midon online," explosions ripped the permacrete along the rear wall between the two groups and on either side of the door.

Through the open hatch twenty meters in front of me, one of the Zyuns waved me forward as the other jumped out and crouched to provide covering fire should someone make it through the battle to my position.

I held up my hand as Lobo connected me to Midon.

She and a female voice I didn't recognize spoke at the same time.

"Finally ready, Moore?" she said. "It's about time."

"Ready," the other female said.

"They're firing at each other," I said. "They started arguing, and then it escalated. One of them had wired the place ahead of time, so charges are going off everywhere. They're heavily armed with both weapons and explosives. The whole place could blow. Go with caution."

The other voice's tone didn't change. "We can tell," she said without any trace of irony, "and we're always careful. Exit while you can."

The link went dead.

I sucked in a bit more air and forced myself to run.

At least two dozen soldiers in EC active-fiber urban camo rose from the permacrete in front of me like desert heat waves coalescing into a squad of hell's own warriors. They rushed by me.

I reached the first Zyun. He pushed me forward as the second grabbed my hand and pulled me in beside him. The hatch snapped shut as soon as we were all inside.

"Taking off," Lobo said.

As we rose, Lobo overlaid my vision with feeds from the front and sides of the hangar, battles raging everywhere I looked. I closed my eyes so the Zyuns and the interior in front of me didn't add to the visual overload, but adrenaline surges and residual chest pain impelled me to move even though I was now out of danger. I opened my eyes and subvocalized, "Take it off the lenses and onto displays. Add audio."

The feeds from the battle flashed and screamed to life on the front wall, each image fighting for my attention, the sounds mixing and remixing in rapid audio mutation. I scanned along the different scenes, flitting from one to the next, pacing as I followed the action, seeing what I could in parallel but facing so many viewpoints that I had to process much of it sequentially.

The EC troops at the front of the hangar mirved, squads of eight heading east and west of the building, the remaining group fanning left and right of the door I'd exited less than a minute earlier. Two soldiers from the central assault team rolled a pair of mobile speakers inside the facility. Amplified shouts of "Cease and desist or Expansion Coalition forces will engage you!" soared on high notes above the battle noise as the speakers did their best to evade the shots and pulses filling the air around them.

"Kill the EC warning," I subvocalized.

A second later, pulse and projectile shots hit the speakers and the cease-and-desist notice stopped, the evasive circuits of the agile sound balls no match for Lobo's aim.

More groups of eight EC troops sprinted from hiding places to the left and rear of Chaplat's team on the west side of the building, joining their comrades on the front to surround the gangster's rear guards and trap them against the building.

A similar scene unfolded on the hangar's other side with Dougat's exterior team, but there it turned ugly when one of Dougat's men fired on the EC soldiers approaching them from the rear. The shot had barely left his weapon when the man's body shook as if electrified, then part of his head vanished as the EC troops on all three sides returned fire. The remaining Followers watched the shattered body fall and quickly placed their weapons on the tarmac.

On Chaplat's side, the ship guards did the same, each surrendering all weapons, kneeling, and putting hands on heads.

Smoke and dust and flying debris dominated the inside of the hangar. EC troops fired on both groups from around the sides of the front door. Explosions shook more and more of the rear walls, then spread along the side walls and advanced on the building's front, chunks of permacrete flying into the center area at random heights all over the facility. Sections of the ceiling shattered as noise and dust filled the space, and still more explosions rocked the weakening structure.

"Exits," I subvocalized.

The doors behind Dougat and Chaplat snapped open so quickly that both groups didn't realize for a few seconds that new exit options were available. Their firing slowed as light flooded in from the open doors and the opportunity for retreat became clear. The external EC troops spotted the change a second earlier and focused most of their members and weapons on the dust-filled interior, the remaining troops continuing to control their captives. Chaplat and Dougat wasted no time in leading their teams out of the hangar, only to run straight into their own surrendering ship-side men and the squads of EC soldiers pointing guns at them.

More explosions smashed chunks from the hangar's walls, and holes appeared along the sides even as blasts tore at the front wall.

The EC squad at the front entrance checked the inside, then split, one half running along the outside toward the west and Chaplat's captured team, the other sprinting for their comrades who had taken Dougat.

As Dougat and his soldiers who'd tried to leave the building put down their weapons, four men from the EC squad ran inside and prodded the loaders into action.

The front corner of the building on Chaplat's side collapsed in a heap of rubble, the walls there too weak to support both their own weight and the ceiling's.

"Midon online," Lobo said.

"Connect," I said, "but mute hangar audio."

Silence stilled the air as Midon's voice came over the comm. "What's going on, Moore?"

"What are you talking about?" I said, gasping as I talked even though I could now breathe normally. "How should I know? I brought them to you, and I ran—as we agreed."

"The place is coming apart," she said.

"What? What are they doing? All I know is that I did what I said I would, and those jerks shot me. I'm heading to ground. It's your problem now."

On the displays in front of me another chunk of the front of the building silently fell into heaps of rubble.

"An exploding building wasn't part of the deal," she said. "You didn't warn us about this."

"Because I didn't know about it!" I shouted.

On the displays, the last of the weapons loaders exited the rapidly decaying hangar.

"I warned your team as soon as I saw charges go off." I paused for a few seconds, then continued more slowly. "Dougat said he had a source in the EC; someone on your side must've traced me—thanks a lot—and wired the place. Did you get the weapons?"

"Yes," she said, "and both Chaplat's and Dougat's squads."

"Then what's your problem?" I said. "You caught Dougat with the goods, so you got what you wanted, and you even captured Chaplat in the bargain—as I said you would. Our deal stands. If Dougat wired the place to blow up and destroy the evidence, you have only someone in your own organization to blame."

In the rightmost display, the entire eastern wall of the hangar trembled and then fell inward, small chunks of permacrete flying outward and over the heads of the EC troops and the Followers.

"What about the boy?" she said. "He was part of the deal."

"Getting him there was all I promised," I said, every word flat, "and I delivered. If he's not with Dougat, he's trapped inside. Either way, it's not my problem."

"We're talking about a boy here, Moore."

"Yes," I said, forcing my voice to remain level, "we are: a boy you wanted to capture. A boy Dougat wanted to buy. You'll find him there, or he's dead; I don't see how he's much worse off if he never made it out. Regardless, I delivered, so you owe me."

Midon didn't try to conceal the contempt in her voice as she said, "And we'll pay. I keep forgetting how cold you are."

I watched as the hangar's west wall and central ceiling shattered and fell. "Are we done?" I said. "I have a wound to tend to."

"Yes," she said. "See you in three days."

The link went dead.

"Audio," I subvocalized.

Booms and crashes assaulted our ears as chunks of the rear ceiling of the hangar crashed down, further weakening the last standing parts of the building. The west rear corner trembled, shook, and in a final scream of weakened permacrete collapsed into a mound of rubble.

No more explosions, no more crashes, only permacrete-on-permacrete scraping noises as the last chunks settled and then were still.

The hangar was gone.

I stared in silence at the huge mass of shattered and dust-covered permacrete that marked where the building had stood only minutes before.

"Nooooo!" came a cry from behind me, pain and surprise mixing in the strangled sound.

Maggie was sitting there, her gaze alternating between the displays and me, back and forth, back and forth, her mouth struggling to form words.

"You shot me," she said, the words coming slowly and pain-fully as the drug that had knocked her out released its control on her system.

I nodded, waiting for the rest, my face hot, my eyes wet as the hate in her expression blasted me like a cold, stiff wind.

"I'm alive," she finally said, sounding more sad than pleased.

"Yes," I said.

"And you let them die," she said. "You told me you'd take care of him, you told me to trust you, and I did." She shook her head slowly. "Instead, you were going to sell him, and now he's dead. You could have taken him away, you could have saved him, but you didn't."

She stared at the floor for a few seconds. When she looked up at me again, tears clouded her eyes and streamed down her cheeks.

"It's your fault," she said, "and mine for trusting you. You killed him. An innocent boy."

The tears stopped, and she rose to one knee, snarling as she spoke.

"You killed Manu Chang."

CHAPTER 39

MAGGIE LAUNCHED HERSELF at me faster than I believed she could move, but even fueled by anger she was no match for the Zyuns. One stepped between us even as the other grabbed her shoulder with one hand and stopped her forward progress, the muscles in his forearm straining with the effort.

"And you two!" she said, focusing on them. "How could you help him do this?"

After a pause, as if the third brother had begun the answer, the Zyuns answered, one word coming from each, ". . . our job."

"That's all this is to you people?" Maggie said. "A job? You two were willing to sell an old friend and a boy, and now both of them and your own brother are dead, and your excuse is that it's a job?"

The Zyuns didn't answer, and neither did I. Even if I'd asked them to talk—and I hadn't—they wouldn't have bothered. Nothing we could say right now would convey our feelings, and nothing would do more good than harm.

She stared at the three of us, whipping her head from person to person, and when no one spoke, she sobbed quietly.

After a minute or so, she pushed at the Zyun's hand that was holding her shoulder. He stared impassively ahead but didn't release his grip.

I nodded, a motion so slight Maggie never saw it, and he let her go and stepped forward and to the left, ready to grab her again if need be.

"Drop me anywhere," she said. "I'm sick of the lot of you."

"No," I said. I put my left hand on the shoulder of the Zyun in front of me, and he stepped half a meter to the side, out of her way but still able to protect me easily should it come to that. Maggie and I were little more than a meter apart, with nothing physical separating us, yet I couldn't recall feeling farther from her. "Not yet."

"I'm a prisoner again!" she yelled. She stepped forward and both Zyuns moved to stop her, but I shook them off. She came so close I could smell the fading effects of the drug on her breath, the permacrete dust that had worked its way into her hair when she fell, the tang of adrenaline and fear in her sweat.

"Only for a time," I said. "If I let you go now—"

"What?" she yelled again. "Something bad will happen to me?"

"Yes," I said. "They all think you're dead, and for now we need to keep it that way. The EC couldn't care less about you, but if either the Followers or what's left of Chaplat's gang found out you're still alive, we could all be in trouble."

"So I suppose you did all this for my own good?" she said. "You shot me to save me?"

I considered the question, pondered whether I could explain everything in a way that would make sense and not cause further damage, wondered if I'd made the right choices, and finally decided that the potential cost of any explanation outweighed the possible benefit. "Yes," I finally said.

"Well, you should have let me die," she said.

That was too much. It was all finally too much. I stepped into her space, bridged the last few centimeters between us, and caused her to back up. "That's very noble, very dramatic," I said, clipping each word as I fought for control even as part of me knew that I'd surrendered too much to anger. "But you can say it only because you don't understand what it means. Watch more people die, stare as life leaves them and you realize to your darkest animal core that this is it, this is their last moment alive and then they'll be no more, they'll be gone, lost forever. Then you won't wish for death. When your only options are unending pain for your few remaining hours or days or weeks, then you've earned the right to want to die. Until then, shut up and be damn grateful for the time you have!"

"Maybe you're right," she said, her eyes locked on mine, her words coming slowly and with care and a tinge of fear. "But some of us believe there are things worth dying for, causes more precious than life."

I thought of all the men and women I'd known who'd died in the name of such causes, the bodies ripped apart in jungles and deserts and oceans on half a dozen planets where I'd fought alongside people whose only real sin was being so stupid or so poor or so idealistic that they were willing to join forces like the Saw and fight at the sharp end where the decision makers would never be. Not once had any of them bothered to make a noble speech about causes. They did their jobs, followed orders, and if they were lucky they came home. If they spoke nobly of anything, it was of taking care of each other and of destroying their common enemy. Other people, usually those far from the action, made the speeches; the comrades with whom I'd served lived and died from the consequences of those words.

Lobo interrupted my thoughts on the comm channel we shared with the Zyuns. "One minute from the hangar," he said. "The EC is surely tracking."

"Do as I tell you," I finally said to Maggie, "and soon enough you'll be able to leave, go and find more causes, or do whatever else you want. Try to run before I give the okay, or disobey any instructions, and we'll restrain you." She started to speak, but I held up my hand; we'd make no progress by talking. "None of this is negotiable, and this is not the time for conversation. We're about to move."

I turned away from her and walked to the front of the ship. The Zyuns formed a barrier between us. "I understand," I subvocalized to Lobo. "Take us in, and then we'll go to ground."

➤   ➤   ➤

We hopped out of the hatch and in three steps were at the side door to the low-rent parking hangar. One Zyun stood on point. I followed him, Maggie came behind me, and the other Zyun brought up the rear. I turned toward her and said, "From here until we reach the safe house, you don't say a word. If you scream or try to run or do anything else we don't like, he"—I pointed at the Zyun behind her—"will knock you out, and we'll carry you and explain to anyone who asks that you had a seizure. Got it?"

She nodded.

I faced front again and tapped the lead Zyun on the shoulder.

He opened the door, and we stepped into the heat and noise and bustle of midmorning in Shinaza, Malzton's shiftiest district. Buildings here served function and paid little respect to form, the block in front of us lined by rows of pale gray permacrete two- and three-story structures that either touched or shared walls, as if the genetic material of each had reproduced with only minor mutations to produce the next. The permacrete road glowed a dull, darker gray in the bright light, stained by the passage of people and vehicles. All the windows for as far as I could see were barred, and cold, gray, quick-shut metal shutters flanked all those on the first floors and most of the others. Similar covers stood to the sides of all the doors.

No wonder the EC didn't want to bother governing this place: Every building was a small fortress ready to repel intervention of any sort.

The people walking the street in front of us only reinforced the notion that you did *not* want to pick a fight around here. Men and women alike moved in careful, calculated flow, never touching one another despite the congestion, each one sliding past the others like electrons whose random orbits drew them momentarily too close for safety and would soon enough take them to blessed isolation. Every person in view also carried at least a pistol of some sort and often more than one weapon, the variety lending the street the aspect of an industrial runway show for those with deadly intent: swords, short and long and straight and curved; rifles and shotguns and pulse cannons whose weight made their carriers walk with visible extra effort; knives in sheaths and on loops and tucked into armored clips on pants and shirts; and various extending and otherwise self-configuring clubs, dormant now, only their matte black grips visible, but holding the portent of pain only a flick of the wrist away.

No one paid us any more or less attention than anyone else; everyone here could be friend or foe, alliances as fluid as the traffic.

We walked up two blocks, merged with the human current flowing right, and stopped in front of the fourth house. Another gray permacrete structure, it stood out from its streetmates in two ways: It was the one place that wasn't attached to the buildings adjacent to it, and it was surrounded by scrolling warning signs on the ground on each side and across its front. Text and graphics fled backward from the street on the wired black tarmac in a constantly changing stream of languages and images, all of them delivering the same message: Don't Walk Here.

"Stands out a bit, doesn't it?" I said.

"Harder to blast through," the Zyuns replied, alternating words now that there were only two of them, the cadence having completed the switch from triples to pairs. "Wired and mined and poisoned substrate," they added, pointing in unison to the two-meter-wide black tarmac that ran down the sides of the building. "Double armor, walls, windows, and doors. All exterior surfaces mined. Five buried escape tubes, all armored." Their mouths twitched in the closest gesture to a smile I'd yet seen from them. "Quite expensive. Your money. Most suitable."

The Zyun in front touched a comm inside his sleeve and a thick, gleaming walkway extended from the low front porch to the road in front of us. It cleared the black mini-moat by mere centimeters. Despite my initial doubt, it had no trouble supporting all of us as we crowded side by side onto the two-meter-wide small porch. The walkway withdrew rapidly into the building, and the front door swept aside as a small hatch clanged into place over the now hidden metal plank.

As soon as we were inside, the door slid shut. Sounds of metal in motion followed its closure. I raised an eyebrow in question.

"Armor re-forming," the Zyuns said.

We stood at the edge of a single large room that measured roughly ten meters wide by twenty deep, considerably smaller than the structure's outside. Wood plank floor, yellow verging on gold, ran lengthwise from the front to the rear. Bare walls, also wood but composed of wide pieces whitewashed to a soft purity. Kitchen in the rear left corner opposite a stairway, a counter with a floor-standing oven, a sink, and a refrigerator, plus a garbage chute in the middle of the back wall. More planks and an ancient pull door, no visible lock, covered the area under the stairs. A low-slung table two meters long squatted on the room's left side just in front of the kitchen area, cushions surrounding it, enough room under it for crossed legs. Along the floor to our right were two thin, tightly rolled futons. Identical sets of ten security displays perched on each of the four walls, images in them showing views from security cams monitoring all sides of the exterior and the roof.

Small, furry creatures I didn't recognize, somewhere between cats and rats in size, scampered around as if the place were theirs. At least half a dozen of them remained in view, running indifferently to and fro in the space, occasionally arcing near us and then warping away.

The Zyun in front pointed to the kitchen. "Gas and water tanks inside here," they said, "with no external power. Self-contained. Plenty food."

"And them," I said, kicking at one of the creatures that strayed near my right foot.

"Extra precaution," the Zyuns said. "Meal tasters. React identically to humans."

Maggie spoke for the first time. "You can't be serious!" she said. "You'd kill these innocent creatures?"

"Only if food bad," they said.

"The trash chute?" I said, happy to change the subject.

"To remote buried furnace," the Zyuns said, "with backwash safety valves. Sewer, too."

"Of course," I said. Despite all that had happened, the two of them looked as content as I'd ever seen them, though I couldn't pinpoint the reason for the impression. Perhaps they were simply more relaxed, the building their idea of a happy place. "And the rest of it?"

They led us upstairs and to another single large space. The floors near the stairs and all the steps emitted high-pitched creaks of various pitches as we walked.

"Nightingale boards," the Zyuns said. "Classic. Good."

As we walked up the stairs, I said, "Isn't this whole place more than a little bit of overkill for three days?"

"You wanted safe house," they said, "and gave no budget. Great place."

I hadn't figured them for big spenders, but I should have realized that everyone has weaknesses; security was one of theirs.

The second-floor room was identical to the one below it save for having no kitchen and only a single rolled futon. The glow from similar banks of security displays illuminated the room.

"Your space," the Zyuns said.

"Clothing?" I said.

"In bathroom," they said. "Yukatas. Not here long."

Another flight of differently creaky stairs led us to the third floor, a twin to the second.

"And I suppose this is mine?" Maggie said.

The Zyuns nodded in unison and said, "Thickest armor. No roof access. No escape. Safest."

"As if my safety mattered in all of this?"

The three of us stared at her in wonder, her perspective so very different from our own that I'd forgotten for a moment how this must all appear to her. I knew they wouldn't speak, and I had nothing useful to say, so I shook my head slightly and left, the Zyuns on my heels.

"Wonderful," Maggie said as we headed down the stairs, anger and despair and frustration dripping from the single word. "This just keeps getting better."

Small grunts and thumping sounds from below brought me awake. I launched off the futon on which I'd been taking a nap and raced downstairs, wondering if we were under attack and how anyone had gotten through the house's defenses so quietly.

We weren't. The Zyuns were doing clap-hand push-ups on the floor, moving up and down like machines. They pumped out another dozen while I watched, then stood and stared at me, sweat pouring off their faces and necks.

"When I heard the sounds," I said, "I thought someone had gotten in."

This time, I would have sworn they actually smiled for a second before in the usual alternating speech pattern they said, "With this house's walls, you'll know."

"Of course," I said. "Habit."

They nodded, stretched out on the floor, and started doing crunches. When I didn't leave, they said, "Join us?"

Their tone made it clear the words were less an invitation than a dare, but it wasn't like I had anything else to do, and exercise burned tension, so I nodded and got into position. "Set the pace," I said. "I'll keep up."

We started again on the crunches, and after seventy-five I stopped counting and focused only on keeping my stomach tight and encouraging the nanomachines inside me to clean out the muscle toxins as quickly as they could. I always wonder in situations like this whether taking advantage of that enhancement is cheating, but I also always end up deciding that it doesn't matter. We all use the resources available to us, and from the looks of the Zyuns that included more than a little biochemical assistance.

We moved from crunches to a wall sit and then directly into squats. From there we reversed position and did handstand push-ups, them in the middle of the floor, me against the wall, my balance not up to the job of staying steady without any support. We flowed smoothly from exercise to exercise with no breaks, as they led me through more bodyweight workouts than I'd realized existed. Time vanished, the world narrowed to my little area in this one room, my troubles evaporated in the heat of the repetitions, and all I knew and all I felt was the work, the muscle pain, the effort, and the constant focus on the next rep, just the next one.

It was glorious.

After a particularly long and brutal set of alternate-leg lunges, the Zyuns said, "Enough now."

We stretched out on the floor, spread our arms and legs, and lay there, breathing hard. Even though I wasn't moving, every muscle in my body hurt intensely, my breathing came ragged, and I was exhausted.

I couldn't have felt better. The combination of the rush of the endorphins and the rare freedom of the long period without worry relaxed me even as the exercises tightened me. I was so happy I started laughing, a little at first, and then heartily.

The Zyuns stared at me as if I were insane, but then their mouths twitched, and in a minute they were laughing, too, the first time I'd heard them make any noise that didn't sound completely controlled.

We heard Maggie coming down the steps and stopped laughing as her head came into view.

"What are you idiots finding so funny?" she said, fury warring with incomprehension on her face.

I couldn't help myself: I burst out laughing again, louder this time, and the Zyuns were right with me. After a few seconds and clearly with no understanding of what we were doing, Maggie shook her head, cursed us, and ran upstairs. It wasn't funny, I knew her pain was real, I hated it, and yet I laughed harder, release winning over intellect. The Zyuns did the same, and for a few minutes the sound of laughter filled the room and all was right with the world.

"Why won't you explain it to me?" Maggie said a few hours later, after I'd showered and napped and we'd all eaten. She put her hand on my face, and I expected her to claw at me, or pull me closer and punch or knee me. Instead, she closed her eyes and for a few moments seemed to drift away.

I had no idea what to do; in most of my experience, when someone touches you, it's as part of an attack. I wasn't comfortable, but I also didn't see any harm in it, so I remained completely still.

She opened her eyes, pulled back her hand, and shook her head slowly. "Maybe I completely misread you," she said, "but I would never have figured you for someone who could watch two people die and show so little feeling."

I considered all the reasons I couldn't answer her, and I even wondered if I was wrong for believing them, but in the end all I could say was "I can't."

She continued shaking her head slowly as anger and sadness warred openly on her face. "In the beginning, all I wanted to do was save the boy," she said, "but then I hoped for more. Now, though, now all I want is to leave." She headed upstairs two steps at a time. Though in my mind I was reaching out to her, my hands never left my lap.

I'd told her the truth, and I believed in what I said and the path I'd chosen, but truth and belief are all too often not enough.

The Zyuns and I worked out again early that evening, but this time there was no joy, at least not for me, only anger, rage at what I'd had to do, at myself, at the way my life had unfolded, at the universe. We pushed it longer this time, flowed from exercise to exercise until the Zyuns stopped and sprawled on the floor, and still I kept going. I stopped when in the middle of a set of squats my trembling legs gave out and I fell, my emotions and my body spent.

When I'd recovered, I used the house's secure comm lines to troll the local data streams for news of the fight at the hangar. Dougat's and Chaplat's arrests sent ripples through the infosphere, but they weren't the hot news they would have been on a more government-friendly planet like Mund. There, Midon's smiling face would have been everywhere, transforming the capture of a fanatic arms dealer and a dangerous gang leader into political capital. Here on Gash, the EC came across as just one gang inflicting damage on two others. What stories and threads I viewed focused on the arrests themselves, the disposition of the weapons, the fate of the Followers, and so on. Beyond the obligatory few clips of the trashed hangar, no one paid the setting any special attention, and before the night was out the story was already fading, beach patterns washing away under the incoming news tide.

Lobo and I had agreed the smartest option was to not communicate for the three days, and we were right, but I found I missed him, even his sarcasm.

I stuck to the plan and didn't contact him. I set a countdown timer on my room's displays and watched as a few of the seconds between now and the end of our time in this house vanished in the count. Waiting is never fun, but despite all that I didn't like, passing time here was so much better than many of the situations I'd survived that I shrugged; the hours would come and go soon enough.

The night and the next two days unrolled in a pattern like the first, working out and eating and checking the data streams and resting, but with one exception: Maggie didn't talk to us again. We ate in silence, at the Zyuns' insistence waiting to begin each meal until one of the cat-rodents had swallowed a bit of the food and showed no ill effects. We communicated primarily by pointing, and when we bothered to speak at all, we doled out words as if they were precious gems. The Zyuns seemed at perfect peace with our ritual. Though I knew I should be doing something to improve the situation with Maggie, I couldn't come up with any option that helped more than it hurt, so I did nothing.

Precisely when the countdown timer hit zero, I used the comm line to contact Midon. Her face appeared quickly; midmorning was clearly more to her liking than earlier in the day.

"Prompt when it comes to payment, Mr. Moore," she said. "Of course."

"Is there a problem?" I said.

"None at all. All my news is good."

"From what I can tell, the news barely registers."

"You must have stayed on Gash," she said, feigning surprise even though I was confident she knew exactly where I was. "Back on Mund and on many of the other planets where we released the story of my daring capture of these two criminal organizations, the event is getting major play."

"I'm glad I'm proving to be a good investment," I said, not particularly meaning it but wanting to bring the subject back to money.

"That you are," she said. "How does meeting in an hour at our offices in Malzton sound?" Coordinates streamed across under her image.

"Why not do the transfer now?" I said, though I knew her answer and was counting on it. "I can receive over this channel."

"And leave a money trail over links we don't control? Surely you're not that naïve, Moore."

"If we must meet in person," I said, "I'd prefer the gate station, which should be quite safe for both of us. I'm sure you understand."

"Fine," she said, "but then the meeting can't be until early this evening. I'm jumping out of here then, and no way can I afford to make two trips there today, so you'll have to wait until I'm already at the station."

"Fair enough," I said. "I'll be with a few people," I paused, "and, of course, my PCAV. So—"

She held up her hand and shook her head. "Save your threats. Trust me, if I wanted to do something other than pay you off, even that extraordinarily secure house you're in—" She paused and smirked, making sure I understood all the implications.

"How?" I said, playing the role as she expected.

"Did you think we couldn't track you?" she said. "We know where both you and your PCAV are, and if we wanted you badly enough, neither the PCAV's arms nor that ridiculously fortified building would have protected you. But why would we bother coming after you?" She leaned forward, held up her hand, and ticked off points with her fingers. "First of all, we got what we want. Second, you're not worth the negative public exposure on Gash that any such attack would cause us. Third and most important, you've done good work for us: Between what we'll get for the weapons we confiscated and the value the story is delivering on other planets, this whole affair has yielded massive ROI, both direct and indirect." She leaned back. "Paying you is by far the easiest and cheapest option, so I'll see you tonight at the station." She cut the transmission.

I went downstairs and said to the Zyuns, "Pack up, grab Park, and get ready to move. We're leaving."

CHAPTER 40

WE JOINED THE street-level flow of Shinaza and merged rapidly into it, another cluster in the fast-moving human traffic. As soon as we were out the door, I fell behind the others and opened a link to Lobo.

"All normal here," he said. "Of course."

"We're heading out," I subvocalized, "and with an unexpected bonus: Midon is jumping tonight."

"Excellent. I am—"

I interrupted him. "I know, I know. Gotta move. Out."

We wound our way back to the hangar by the same route we'd taken a few days earlier. Midon was right: At this point, we'd have known if she wanted to hit us, so there was no point in trying an alternate route. Besides, our best defense was to get inside the gate's area of influence; no attack would happen there.

We took off as soon as we were inside.

The screaming red jump gate grew and grew in the front displays until it filled them completely and a single arc of it became all that we could see. None of us spoke, but that wasn't unusual at this point. I wondered, as I did every jump, at the cold beauty of the gates, their power, their mystery, and their origin. I glanced at Maggie, wishing we were again sharing that feeling, but she continued staring away from me. I tried to lose myself once more in the gate, but the mundane world interrupted as we asked the station for permission to dock.

We had a few hours to kill before Midon would arrive, so we all passed through the series of locks and went inside.

Partway through a passable but thoroughly unexceptional dinner of a small-grained starch covered with sauce and chunks of fish, Maggie finally spoke.

"Exactly what am I doing here?"

"Eating dinner," I said. I pointed to her plate and added, "Though not much of it. I know it's not great, but it's better than the insto-food we had at the safe house."

"Don't play with me, Moore," she said, her eyes widening in anger.

So much for my attempt at levity.

"Why did you drag me with you?" she said. "You could have left me on the ship. You don't need me for anything else."

"Insurance," I said, telling the truth, at least all of it that she could handle.

"Exactly how does my presence help you collect your blood money?"

Dumb idea. I should have known that talking was a bad plan. I shook my head, spooned a bit of the fish, and chewed slowly.

Maggie stared at me for a bit, then took a bite of her own food.

I was glad to see her eating. We had a lot more to do today, and when you're on a mission and have the time, grabbing some food is almost always a good idea.

Midon was neither subtle nor over the top when she sent for us. A guard found us in the media lounge at the rear corner table we'd taken from four unhappy bureaucrats.

He walked straight to us, kept his hands away from his weapons, and said, "She told me to tell you to follow me."

We did. I expected to make another trip to Carne's office, but I was wrong. The guard led us to a plain, unlabeled door near the docking area for the larger ships. He stood to the side as it opened and the Zyuns, Maggie, and I filed in. He didn't follow us inside.

Midon sat in a chair in the corner of the otherwise empty room. When she saw Maggie, surprise flickered in her expression before she brought it under control.

Before she could speak, I said, "Why here?"

"No cameras, no sensors, no recordings, nothing," Midon said. "This meeting never happened. Speaking of things that never happened," she nodded in Maggie's direction, "I'd heard you'd shot her dead."

"I might as well have been," Maggie said, "for all the good—"

"Shut up," I said. I faced the Zyun whose black-gloved hand held her elbow and whispered, "If she starts to talk again, gag her."

Both Zyuns nodded.

"I see your talent for making friends knows no bounds, Moore," Midon said. "But as I was saying, I'd heard you'd shot her and she was dead. Why was my information wrong?"

"I shot her," I said, "but as you can see, I didn't kill her. I needed to fake her death." I shrugged. "So I did."

"Why?"

"Both to save her life and as part of my exit plan."

"Too bad you couldn't have done the same for the boy," Midon said, her anger evident.

Out of the corner of my eye I saw Maggie glare at me and open her mouth, but I cut her off by holding up my hand.

"Yes, it was," I said, gritting my teeth and speaking slowly and carefully. "I had hoped to save both him and my previous client."

"But you didn't," Midon said.

"That was not my fault," I said. "I had no way to know Dougat and Chaplat would start firing."

"Really?" Midon said, standing and walking closer to me. "What did you think would happen when you put an arms-dealing religious fanatic and a gang boss in the same room with a shipment of weapons and a boy they both believed was psychic? Or did you even think?"

I stared at her for a long enough time that she took two steps backward before I answered. "I *thought* they would do the deal they'd said they would do. I *thought* they were the businesspeople they claimed to be. And I *thought* your team would arrest them without destroying the whole giant permacrete hangar!"

"My team didn't bring down that building," Midon said. "Those two groups of idiots did it themselves, though no one on either side will admit it—as you'd know if you'd stayed around. But I guess the one life you made sure to save was your own."

I didn't say anything. Nothing would help.

Midon finally filled the silence. "So why are you showing her to me now?"

"So you wouldn't find out later and think I'd hidden anything from you," I said, anger still sharpening my voice. "This way, you know exactly what I did, you encounter no surprises in the future, you pay me, and we're done."

"What about what you didn't do?" Midon said. "You didn't deliver the boy."

"I promised I would get him there," I said, "and I did, but that was also never our main deal. What you most wanted was to catch Dougat in a weapons trade, and I made that happen."

"You did," she said. "And I'll pay." She pulled out a small comm unit.

I thumbed my wallet to receive in a high-quarantine area. No point in taking chances.

"You know," she said, "you have a remarkable talent for alienating people, even those you help." She pointed at Maggie. "Do you really think she's thankful that you saved her? She obviously cared for that boy. She'll hate you forever."

I wanted to look at Maggie, but I didn't. I kept my voice level and said only, "You said you'd pay."

"Of course," she said. "What you'll see is a massive credit for overcharging of jump fees in this sector. The records at all the stations under EC control will reflect various aspects of this error. So, as this transaction and your acceptance of it prove, the EC is only returning money it had previously accidentally charged you."

I studied the incoming flow. The total was right, and the accounting was as she stated. The wallet found nothing wrong with the transfers. I waited as Lobo took the time to grab the data, vet it with the originating bank in Malzton, and then shuffle it through a chain of other banks on Gash to the accounts we'd established. It took well over a minute; transmit times in exchanges with the planet's surface are always slow. When my wallet showed the all-clear signal, I closed it, looked again at Midon, who was waiting with visible impatience, and said, "And, I assume, we never had a deal."

"Why would we ever even have talked?" she said. She brushed past me and stopped at the door. "I'm heading to Mund for some interviews and from there to Drayus and on to Immediata. Visit our worlds for as long as you like. Spend lots of that money on EC planets; our economies love tourists. But," she paused and stared at me, "don't ever call me again."

She left, but the door didn't close behind her.

Maggie stared at me and said, "Will you now finally—" but stopped when she saw the guard come into the room.

"I understand you'll be leaving," he said. "Let me help you find the way out."

CHAPTER 41

THE GUARD WATCHED us through the lock portal until we'd pulled back from our docking position.

As soon as we had, displays popped to life on the front wall, aspects of the gate glowing red in all of them, and Maggie spoke.

"You have your money. Will you drop me off yet?"

I stared at the images as I spoke. "Lobo, I need to see Midon's ship jump to Mund, and I need to know if anyone is tracking us. Give me a view of Malzton as well." I then looked at Maggie. "No. We're not done."

"What do you mean?" she said, making no attempt to hide her frustration or anger. "What else do you need?"

"Not now," I said. "Be quiet and wait."

Several seconds later, one display changed to an image of the aperture to Mund, and a second shifted to a projection map of all the vessels in the area. A third snapped to a highly magnified view of Malzton at night, lights shining throughout the city, the abandoned EC base on its southern edge a solid black mass.

"Only one EC ship," Lobo said, "an executive shuttle, is jumping for Mund. The EC of course doesn't publish its passenger list, but Midon's a safe bet for it. No current signs of

361

pursuit or surveillance, but sitting still makes that all too easy to hide."

"Would you please listen to me?" Maggie said. "All I want is for you to let me go."

I kept my eyes on the display and said, "Lobo, take us Gashward at max speed on an evasive course. Show me anything that might even possibly be following us."

Adrenaline spill, frustration, and anticipation combined to leave me exhausted, but I pushed back the fatigue, buckled into a pilot's couch, and watched for signs of trouble. If our evasion run yielded no pursuers and Midon was indeed through with us, we could finally be done, but we weren't there yet.

I looked again at Maggie. "Soon," I said, "when I'm sure it's safe. Until then, please take a couch, be quiet, and let me work. Sleep if you can. We don't know for certain that no one is after us, so it's not over yet."

As we raced away from the gate, a ship passed through the Mund aperture.

I heard Maggie clear her throat as if to speak, and I said, "Not now."

"The ship most likely to be carrying Midon has jumped," Lobo said. "No signs of pursuit yet, but if there are watchers and they're very good, we might not see them." On the map display, Lobo overlaid a route that resembled the path of a drunken man careening off the walls of a wide hotel aisle in search of his room and bed. "Unless you object," he said.

"I agree about the watchers," I said, "and of course your plan is fine. Run it."

Ninety minutes later, we were flying at treetop level along the southeast edge of Malzton when Lobo said, "To the best of my ability to monitor, there are no pursuers and no active surveillance. This data is, of course, imperfect, but it's all I can provide under the circumstances."

"Good enough," I said. "I didn't think anyone would come after us, but we had to make sure. Take us in."

"Ninety seconds to touchdown," Lobo said.

I stood and faced the rear. The Zyuns and Maggie were sitting in couches. I'd kept my communications with Lobo private, so they had no idea what we were doing. Maggie had obviously been napping, so I waited until her eyes focused on me, then said, "Time to move. We're landing."

"Where are we?" Maggie said. "Are you dropping me in the middle of nowhere?"

"We're back at the hangar," I said, "or, more accurately, at what remains of it, and no, I'm not leaving you here."

Her eyes widened, and her face tightened in anger and horror. "I can't believe you!" she said. "Why—"

She stopped when we settled to the ground, a side hatch opened, and I stepped out. Lobo had brought us to a spot sixty meters from where we'd first entered the rear of the hangar so long ago—a few days ago, I reminded myself. It just felt like a very long time.

"Follow me," I said as I walked a bit closer to the hangar, "but don't go anywhere."

I heard Maggie and the Zyuns approach. Rather than have a long discussion, I decided to show her. "Lobo," I subvocalized, "it's time."

"What are you doing?" Maggie said. "I don't want to be here!"

"Wait for it," I said.

Slight, almost imperceptible tremors, so small you wouldn't notice them if you weren't expecting them, ran through the permacrete.

"Why are you staring—" Maggie said.

I held up my hand and repeated, "Wait for it." In my peripheral vision I saw one of the Zyuns grab her arm.

"Wait for—" she began.

I couldn't hear the rest of her words because chunks of the destroyed hangar screeched and banged as they began moving and grinding against one another. With the light of the star-filled sky and the illumination pouring from the hatch behind us we could just make out the tumbling gray permacrete pieces.

More and more of them shifted, and the screeching grew

louder. The roar of engines added to the noise, and the volume rose.

Another sound, maybe a pounding, clawed at the edges of the din, trying to get in but not yet powerful enough to be more than a feeling. A few seconds later, the pounding clarified into a powerful bass note repeating in a steady rhythm: a drumbeat. I would have sworn the falling pieces were moving in time to the beat, my mind imposing a pattern and order where I knew there could be none.

The ground ahead levitated slowly, as if the bits of the hangar had decided it was time to leave this planet for somewhere better. Shards of light poked out from under the chunks, centimeter-high beams thrusting into the night in random places.

As the sounds of rocks in motion and engines and drums grew louder, the section of permacrete ascended further. Its ascension produced more light, then more, and more still, until a yellow-white glow surrounded and defined a perimeter, as if an invisible giant were uncapping the planet to reveal a secret sun within.

Suddenly, the entire floating permacrete area shot fifteen meters skyward, lifted into the air by the now-visible Lobo, a giant sheet of reinforced metal balanced atop him by struts extending around his exterior. He froze, loose pieces of debris falling off the sheeting on all sides, light streaming from him as the beat intensified and quickened.

What a show-off.

When no more chunks of permacrete had fallen off the sheet for several beats, Lobo floated slowly toward us, moving a fraction of a meter a second, until the hole he had exited was visible behind him, and then he halted.

The drumbeat picked up speed.

The long side of Lobo facing us lifted while the other side held its position, and slowly the remaining permacrete chunks poured off the sheet into the pit where he had spent these last few days. When he had rotated to about sixty degrees and most of the chunks had fallen off the metal sheet, he accelerated abruptly skyward at the same time as he rotated further and triggered the small explosive bolts that disengaged the support struts from his body. The beat reached a frantic pace, the sheet tumbled backward into the hole, and Lobo darted up and away from the metal as it fell with a deafening noise and a cloud of wraithlike dust.

Lobo righted himself and settled to the ground five meters in front of us, the dusty air swirling behind him like clouds around an angel, and then all at once he cut the running lights, his engines, and the drums.

He opened a hatch facing us.

Light streamed from inside him and backlit the man standing in the center of the opening: the third Zyun.

The Zyun reached to his right and pulled forward first Jack and then, a heartbeat later, Manu Chang.

CHAPTER 42

"Welcome back," I subvocalized on the private comm link to Lobo. "Nice entrance. But drums?"

"You have no idea how good it is to be back," he said. "Manu came up with the idea for playing music, and I chose the taiko. He thought it would be a fun touch, and I had to agree. I told you I could do fun."

Before I could respond, Manu yelled, "Maggie!"

The Zyun holding the boy tilted his head slightly. I nodded in response, and he released his grip.

Manu ran straight to Maggie, who grabbed him and held him as tightly as if he were the last good dream she'd ever have. He clung to her just as hard, bouncing up and down in happiness. I hadn't realized they'd bonded so much in the short time they'd spent together. They whispered to each other, his expression animated, hers hidden from me by the fall of her hair.

Jack tried to walk out of Lobo, but the Zyun stopped him.

"Let Jack go," I said.

The Zyun released him and followed him to me.

Jack smiled broadly, spread his arms as if to hug me, and said, "So it all worked out and they paid up?"

I nodded and punched him in the stomach hard enough to cause him to double over.

"You caused all this," I said. "You put a boy at risk, you exposed me, and now all you can talk about is money? How about a little contrition and some gratitude?"

Jack straightened slowly and gasped for air for a few seconds, then slowly brought his breathing under control. Finally, he said, "I appreciate all you've done, but you should consider thanking me as well." He held up his hands as he spoke. I resisted the urge to slap them away and let him continue. "Manu was never in real danger; first I and then you made sure of that. I knew you would; you're good at what you do. We improved this whole sector of space by helping put a gun-running religious fanatic and a dangerous gang boss in jail. We both made a lot of money, and so did Manu. Speaking of which, where's my share of what you made?"

"Expenses," I said. "Like renting that faux PCAV from Li. Like the safe house." I shook my head. "No, you caused this, so most of your share went to paying for it. Besides, I'm confident that you spent far less on the warehouse setup than the value of those gems you snatched from the Followers' Institute; consider them your payment."

"Even if I agreed that was fair," Jack said, "and I most certainly do not, what about Manu's cut? His family is so poor that they agreed to go along with this whole thing just to make some real money. He earned more doing this than he could ever have made pursuing any of the other opportunities available to him—and, trust me, the other moneymaking options were way more dangerous and worse for him than anything that happened with us."

"What do mean his family agreed to go along?" I said. "You told me he needed the money for medical treatments to help him deal with the pain his ability causes him."

Jack backed up a couple of steps. "I admit I said that, but all I was doing was extending the con they were already running with the boy. He really does have ancestors from Pinkelponker, so they knew he'd pass any background check Dougat might conduct. The whole psychic abilities angle was just a way to tempt that old zealot into buying an interview; who knew the guy would turn so crazy about Manu or that other people would get interested in the poor boy?"

"What about the accident he saw?" I said. "He called it before it happened, his reaction seemed genuine enough, and the victim sure was badly hurt, maybe even dead."

"I don't think you ever worked with him," Jack said, "but that 'victim' was Carlos, Carlos Corners, a low-end grifter still grinding it out doing the hit and fall in parking areas and anywhere else vehicles move slowly enough that he can handle the impact. I thought Manu blew his timing and overplayed the reaction a bit, but you're right about the badly hurt part: Carlos did actually get knocked into the air and torn up. I promise you, though, that hurting Carlos was never part of the plan. Some idiot's overly ambitious truck cut off our driver, lost control, and hit Carlos at full speed. It was a freak accident. Fortunately, thanks to the top-notch med units in Eddy, Carlos should be as good as new by now."

"So Manu's not a psychic?" I said, stepping closer, fighting the urge to pound Jack's face into pulp. "And this has all been just another of your cons?"

"Not *just* another con, Jon," he said as he backed up further. "You hurt me. This was, if I may say so, a masterwork, and one that I must remind you has earned all of us, including Manu, quite a lot of money."

Maggie, her left hand holding Manu's right, stepped forward as if to cut between Jack and me but stopped a meter away from either of us. She stared at me and said, "He's wrong, Jon. Manu really is everything he claimed, everything you and I thought."

I forced myself to look away from Jack and at her. "How exactly would you know?" I said, anger coloring my tone.

"Because Manu saw the planned accident go wrong before it did," she said, the words tumbling out like heavy stones rolling off her. "Because he knew Jack would come to his home before Jack ever met his uncle. Because he saw that Jack would let him meet others like him. Because Dougat was right about the children of Pinkelponker—not the name, that's just stupid, but the existence of such a group—and Manu belongs with them."

No one spoke. No one moved. Maggie's eyes widened but never left mine. I couldn't believe what she'd said, maybe because it was so incredible, or perhaps simply because I wanted it so much to be true. If it was, then maybe Jennie might have gotten off Pinkelponker before the accident, maybe I could learn whether she was dead or an incredibly old woman or at least what had happened to her since the time I last saw her.

Finally, I spoke, my voice softer than I intended, almost a whisper. "How do you know all of this?"

"I'm one of them, Jon, one of the descendants of that lost world. I'm not like Manu—I'm not sure anyone alive has as powerful a talent as his—but I am a sensitive. I catch glimpses of what others are thinking."

"You read minds?" Jack said.

She answered him but kept staring intensely at me. "No, nothing as clear as reading. If I touch you—touch your skin, it has to be bare skin—I usually get a jolt of your thoughts, like a wave of impressions washing through me. It's how I knew you, Jack, were running a con on Jon, and it's why I tried to warn him. It's how I know Manu's telling the truth."

"You can do this to anyone?"

She nodded, her eyes still on me. "As long as my skin comes into contact with theirs."

"That's amazing," Jack said, his voice vibrant with excitement. "Do you realize what you could do with that ability, how wonderful it is?"

She shook her head. "No, it's not. I can't touch anyone without them invading my mind for at least a second. I've spent my whole life avoiding even brushing against other people. It's no gift at all. Can you imagine what it's like for every contact with another human to carry that penalty?" She stepped closer to me, leaned forward and tilted her head until I could feel her breath on my ears, and whispered so quietly I had to strain to hear the words, "Except you, Jon. I don't know why, but I could never read you. You, I could touch without worrying what would hit me."

Jennie had always seemed able to tell exactly what I was

thinking, to know my mood and to be able to help me any time I needed it. I wondered if her abilities were limited to healing, if perhaps she, like Maggie, might also have been a reader.

"What are you saying?" Jack said, leaning closer and yanking me back from my reverie. I glanced at him and saw him notice Maggie's hand holding Manu's. "And what about Manu? You're holding his hand, and you seem fine."

"I can't explain it either," she said, "except that it must be part of his talent. The first time we touched, his thoughts smacked into me, but somehow he knew what was happening—"

"And I stopped it," Manu said, his tone as matter-of-fact as if he were discussing breathing. "I can let her in, but I know it hurts her, so I don't, except when we need to talk without you hearing."

Jack laughed and clapped his hands. "This is great! Do you have any idea how much money we could all make? With my skill at working marks, your talents, and Jon and Lobo as backup, we could be rich." He stopped, concern visible in his face. "What about the treatments?" he said to Manu. "I thought your uncle and I made that up to help increase the payday, but is that true, too? Do you really need them?"

"No," Manu said. "That was a lie. I felt bad saying it, but I saw I had to meet Dougat so Maggie would find me. My uncle said we couldn't trust you with the truth." He shrugged and looked unhappy. "I didn't like lying to anyone. I'm sorry."

"It's okay," Jack said. "Of all people, I certainly understand that sometimes you have to skate around the truth. What about the accident, though? Were you really as upset as you seemed?"

"Of course," Manu said, a tinge of sadness creeping into his voice. "Carlos was nice to me, and I didn't want him to be hurt." He was still unhappy as he added, "I wish we could have stopped it."

I focused again on Maggie. "So this is why you were working for Dougat, why you cared so much?"

She nodded. "I had to stop him from getting Manu."

"Why?"

"Because we'd heard about Manu, and he belongs with us. It's the only place he can be safe."

"Where—" I stopped before I could voice the question. The knowledge wouldn't help me, and I knew myself well enough to realize that no matter how much I tried to avoid it, violence followed me. "I don't want to know, because then one day I might tell someone else. Besides, I'm sure you wouldn't want to tell me anyway." I had started to say "couldn't," but I know too well that anyone can and will say anything, no matter how much they don't want to, if you apply pressure on them over a long enough period of time—and if you're willing to hurt them. I'd come close to breaking on several occasions, including during the most recent torture session, which had lasted scarcely more than a day.

She smiled in acknowledgment of my restraint.

"Who are you to decide for all of those people?" Jack said. "Maybe some of them would be interested in a business proposition that could make them rich. Why don't you let me talk to them, and then they can decide for themselves?"

Maggie shook her head and looked at Jack. "No, I can't do that, and I wouldn't even if I could. All I know is where I'm supposed to take Manu. Someone will be watching, and if we're alone, I'll receive instructions for the next stop." She turned back to me. "As you might imagine, the core group moves around constantly, and most of us operate in small cells."

"Let me come with you," Jack said, "and make my case. I don't think you appreciate what we could accomplish with my talent and your abilities."

I hadn't expected any of what Maggie had told me, couldn't have planned for it, but I'd known Jack wouldn't give up Manu easily, wouldn't simply let me take the boy back to his family. That much was as certain as gravity, so I was prepared.

I stepped closer to Jack, shaking my left arm slightly so the tiny needle fell from its perch in my sleeve. I lifted my hand to his shoulder and thumbed free the protective tip, much as I imagined Jack had done when he knocked me out as I was climbing into Lobo after the conflict at Dougat's institute. "Let it go, Jack," I said, clapping my hand on his shoulder in comradely fashion. "Let it go." I raised my hand as if to clap his shoulder again, then turned my palm and brought the needle down hard against his neck. The drug hit him as swiftly as whatever he'd used on me, his eyes only beginning to widen before he drooped and started to fall. I caught him and held him upright. "Would you guys put him in Lobo?" I said to the Zyuns.

One remained behind Maggie and Manu, cutting off any rear escape route, doing his job. The other two took Jack from me and carried him into Lobo.

"Strap him onto the medbed." To Lobo I subvocalized, "Keep him unconscious until I give the word."

"Of course," Lobo said. "My role was obvious."

I ignored him as I realized we'd been standing here longer than I'd planned. We needed to move.

"Is Jack okay?" Manu said.

"Yes," I said. "I gave him something to make him sleep. I'll wake him when you two are safely away."

"Manu," Maggie said, "would you please go wait in Lobo? I need to talk to Jon alone."

The Zyun behind them cocked his head slightly.

I nodded once.

"Okay," Manu said. He headed into Lobo, the Zyun right behind him.

Maggie opened her mouth to speak, but I held up my hand and turned away from her. "Lobo," I subvocalized, "I trust the Zyuns, but if any of them looks like he's going to do something to Manu, put him to sleep."

"Permanently or temporarily?" Lobo said.

"Temporarily, of course. I said 'sleep.'"

"Will do," Lobo said.

I turned around and said to Maggie, "Go ahead. You were about to say something."

She slapped me across the face with her right hand, struck me hard enough that my head whipped partway around.

"What?" was all I could manage, because all my energy went into controlling my natural reaction, into stopping myself from hitting her until she could never hurt me again. Anger flooded me, a bitter taste filled my mouth, and smell vanished as my body focused for combat. I forced myself not to move.

"That's for not telling me what was going on," she said. "You made me live for all that time sure that Manu was dead. How could you be so cruel?"

I didn't answer at first, couldn't do it. I inhaled slowly and deeply through my nose, exhaled even more slowly through my mouth, and repeated the actions twice.

"Don't hit me again," I said. "As to how I could do what I did, the answer is simple: I promised I would protect the boy."

"And making me think he was dead protected him?" she said.

"Yes."

"How did that help? Why couldn't you trust me? I thought you cared about me?"

I ignored the last question, couldn't let myself hear it, couldn't even consider its existence or what that might imply. "Two reasons," I said. "First, I'd learned you betray your emotions under pressure. I couldn't risk you giving away the fact that he was alive. More important, though, was that I knew you were covering up something, so I couldn't risk Manu's safety by trusting you."

"How could you know that?"

"Because you cared too much too quickly," I said. "From the beginning, you were too eager to come along with me, too willing to put up with too much trouble for someone whose only knowledge of the boy was supposedly a single viewing in the Institute."

"So why didn't you get rid of me?"

"Because by keeping you close I made sure you were the one variable in this mess that I completely controlled."

"But what if I'd still been working for Dougat? I could have shot you when you met him in the desert or given him information while I was in the hotel."

"If you'd trained the rifle on me, Lobo would have taken you out," I said. "Except when you were in the SleepSafe, you were never anywhere we couldn't control you and monitor any attempts at communication with anyone else. When you were in the SleepSafe, you still weren't a threat, because I made sure you didn't know anything that could put Manu at further risk. All you could ever tell anyone was that I appeared to be going through with the deals I'd made but might be planning some tricks. That wouldn't have surprised or helped any of these people."

She stood silent for a few seconds, considering everything. "Weren't you still taking a big risk, there at the end? I mean, what if the crashing building had destroyed Lobo?"

I chuckled. "Not much chance of that. He could have withstood the whole thing falling on him if it had come to that, but it didn't: Jack's team had prepared the hole and the metal sheet ahead of time. All Lobo had to do was keep Manu, Jack, and the Zyun alive for a few days, a week at most. For a machine built to house a much larger crew for as long as several months at a stretch, that was no big deal." I looked at her closely. "The hard part was spending those last few days with you and not saying anything, so that when we met with Midon you'd be genuinely furious with me."

She closed her eyes, finally understanding—or, at least, I like to think she understood. "So it wasn't easy for you, was it?"

"Nothing worthwhile ever is," I said.

"You're wrong, Jon," she said. "Some very important things are all too easy." She opened her eyes. "Like caring for people. Like loving them."

I couldn't speak, not without giving away more than I could safely tell anyone. I couldn't explain to her how neither of those statements had ever been true for me, how caring had always led to pain or trouble or violence or all of those, how loving would require a kind of trust and openness I could not afford, how the simple fact that I never appeared to age would all by itself doom any relationship. All I could do was stand there, mute, unable to answer, trapped in my head, pinned down by my life.

"What happened to make you this way?" she said, her hands reaching up and holding my face.

Another question I could never answer.

"And why are you the one person who's closed to me?" she said. "Why can I touch you and receive nothing?"

"I have no idea," I lied, happy to have something to say but knowing the truth had to be related to the way Jennie had healed me all those years ago.

I saw the insight hit her. I suppose it was inevitable. Even as she opened her mouth to ask I began to calm myself for the next untruth.

"Is there any chance you have ancestors from Pinkelponker?"

I chuckled. "No. There are plenty of bad things I could say about my parents, but I can't accuse the bastards of adding that particular strain to my life." I couldn't actually remember much of anything about my mother and father, had only the wispiest memories of them, but the statement would fit with the childhood image I was building for her.

"It's so strange," she said. "Maybe I could talk our people into letting you come with us. You've earned it by protecting Manu, and some of the others might be able to figure out what stops me from being able to read you at all."

And we could spend time together. I saw the thought in her as clearly as if she'd spoken it. I had the same dream myself.

It could never come true.

"I can't," I said. "My life—well, you've seen a sample of what it's like. I've done a lot of things, not all of them good, and sometimes they catch up with me. It wouldn't be safe for any of you." Or for me, I thought but did not add, because the fact that you all share the same heritage and even the same types of talents doesn't mean that I can trust all of you. All it would take is one person to figure out the truth about me and let it slip, and I'd never be able to run far enough. Some corporation or government or rich jerk would catch me, and I'd either have to kill everyone who chased me or end up spending the rest of my life as somebody's specimen. The memory of Aggro, unlike what little I had left of my parents, would never fade. I won't go back to that. "No," I said, "it wouldn't be safe."

"I'm sorry," she said, the hurt obvious. "I don't think you're right, but I obviously can't change your mind."

"I do have one question," I said, knowing that even asking it was taking a risk but unable to walk away from the small chance that her group might be able to help me learn more about Jennie. "Are there any people in your group who are actually from Pinkelponker, not just descendants?"

"No," she said, shaking her head as some obvious sadness hit her. "We had one, a man who was old when the group found me, but he died several years ago. He was the only one."

Even though it had been a long shot, disappointment still washed through me. If Jennie had made it off Pinkelponker and away from the government agency that was keeping her captive, this might have been the kind of group she'd try to find.

I stared at Maggie and wondered if maybe I was wrong, considered whether I should go with her, if there wasn't a chance we could be together.

I was kidding myself. I'd have to be satisfied with the little time I'd spent with her and with thoughts of futures that might have been but never would be.

"I hate to break this up," Lobo said over the machine frequency so only I could hear him, "but we've lingered here way longer than your plan, and I see only risk in increasing our exposure by staying. Couldn't you two finish your little chat inside me?"

"We're done here," I said aloud.

Maggie stared at me oddly for a moment, then nodded. "If you say we need to leave, then I trust you're right."

"We do," I said, "but unfortunately we can't go quite yet." I turned to face Lobo and loudly said, "If you guys have secured Jack, come on out. It's time we finish up."

The Zyuns emerged from Lobo walking three abreast and stopped a couple of steps in front of me.

"You're set to take the faux PCAV back to Keisha Li?" I said.

"Yes we are," they said in their usual speech style. I found the presence of three voices instead of two to be surprisingly pleasant. They certainly seemed happier.

"And you're still comfortable keeping the return of my deposit as the last part of the fee?" I said.

"Yes," they said, "we know her, and we know the ship."

"It was a pleasure working with you," I said. "If I ever need backup in this region again—"

"Then call us," they said.

They turned as one toward the other ship but stopped when Maggie said, "May I ask you one question before you go?"

All three nodded.

"I could read you on the few occasions our skin touched," she said, "but I could never get a glimpse of any thoughts that weren't directly about the situation at hand. Why is that?"

"Now is all," they said. "All is now." They headed into the ship.

I couldn't help but chuckle: Zen backup, a beautiful thing.

"Let's go," I said to Maggie.

I headed into Lobo. She followed.

As soon as we were inside, Lobo closed the hatch. We watched on a forward display as the Zyuns flew away to return the ship.

When they'd vanished from view, Lobo lifted off and said, "The hole is different enough to be noticeable. Is that a problem?"

"Show me," I said.

Lobo popped an aerial view onto the display on which we'd been watching the Zyuns. Chunks of rubble sat in random spots around the perimeter of a pit that was much bigger now than it had been. Sections of the metal sheet protruded here and there from under permacrete boulders.

"Had scavengers come yet?" I asked.

"No," Lobo said.

"Then they'll solve the problem for us," I said, "because they'll want to see if the collapse exposed anything of value. They'll take away the metal for salvage, and their diggers will hide your escape well enough for our purposes." I looked at Maggie. "Where should we take you?" I held up my hand before she could speak. "I'm not asking where you're going; I need to know where to drop you."

"Remember the market on the southeast section of Nickres?" she said. "The one I didn't get to see because you made me wait in the SleepSafe?"

"Of course," I said, flashing back for a moment to the ride in George and hoping that whichever of the two guys ended up with him truly appreciated him. "We'll take you."

"What about the device you put in my arm?" she said. "Will you finally remove it?"

I smiled despite the hurt look on her face. "It was never an explosive," I said. "I'm sorry I had to lie to you. It was a tracker. I don't even know if it's still active; we used one that would decay automatically. Lobo?"

"It's still working, though barely," he said audibly.

I led Maggie to the medbed. She blanched slightly at the sight of Jack unconscious and strapped onto it.

"Don't worry," I said. "He's fine. I'll release him, but not until you and Manu are safely away and we're far from here." I hated being the cause of the lingering fear in her eyes. "I also wanted to say how sorry I am for tying you up there, and for the threat and the tracker. It was all—"

"I understand," she said. "You explained, and you were helping Manu. I just can't stop myself from reacting to this room."

Lobo extended a probe from the wall. Its end glowed dully. "Put your right arm under the light."

Maggie did and held it there.

"That's it," Lobo said. "The device would have stopped transmitting on its own, but now it's incapable of sending or receiving. In about two weeks, it'll break down completely, and your body will absorb or excrete the remnants."

Maggie nodded and said, "Thanks."

We headed back to Lobo's front. "Where in that market do you want me to drop you?" I said.

Manu came over to her and took her hand.

"Anywhere near it," she said. "Where we landed before would be fine."

"Then take us there, Lobo," I said.

Maggie and Manu stared together at the forward-facing display Lobo had opened. I stood beside her, no more than half a meter from her, maybe less, as close as I was ever going to come and still so far away.

Lobo accelerated southward.

For a few seconds I wished he were slower, or that his engines would fail, that we would hover there over the deserted base, just us, alone and safe and together, so that I might have a few more minutes with Maggie, but of course Lobo functioned flawlessly, and we rapidly picked up speed as we hurtled away into the dark, dark night.

CHAPTER 43

LOBO PARKED IN front of a hangar three buildings over from the one where we'd hidden him what seemed like forever ago. The sky was clear, but light pollution from the landing station and the rest of Nickres greatly diminished the number of stars we could see and robbed the evening of its full potential. The air was crisp, but deep breaths revealed the unmistakable trace of fuel. Is this what we humans do? Go to a beautiful, unmarked place, invade it, pollute it, lessen it, and then leave, only to repeat the process over and over, on world after world after world?

I stared openly at Maggie, who was waiting outside Lobo for me, as I realized I was only dragging myself down. Standing on the permacrete, holding Manu's hand, her long red hair glinting here and there from the landing lights, she, they, were proof we also brought joy and could do good things, *did* do good things, maybe not always, but often enough. I pictured her twirling in the blue dress; such beauty.

"What?" she said, smiling a bit, but only a little.

"I—" I struggled for what to say, then gave up trying to be clever or coy. "You're so beautiful that I couldn't help but look, couldn't stop myself from doing everything I could to make sure I'd always remember you." My face felt hot, and I was embarrassed, ashamed, both of burdening her with unwanted affection and of my own lack of control.

She leaned toward me, but I shook my head slightly.

"You have to go," I said.

She nodded, her rear foot raised slightly, her body momentarily frozen.

"I'll walk you to the street where I entered the district last time."

I brushed past her, our shoulders touching for only an instant, all I thought I could handle, and she and Manu fell in behind me. I led them around the hangar, to the right for two hundred meters, and then onto the street I'd walked so recently, so long ago. I gave her quick directions. She listened closely, but too late I realized she must have already known the way. Though morning had not yet risen and we were in the deadest time of night, the magnetic pull of the market's commerce had drawn scores of people and vehicles into the street, all streaming toward the same destination.

"Want me to walk with you to the edge of it?" I said.

She released Manu's hand, glanced down at him, and he looked away from me as he shook his head ever so slightly. "Yes," she said, "I really, really do, but it's not a good idea. We need to be on our own, so it's clear no one is following us."

"Of course," I said, turning to leave. I didn't trust myself to look at her for a second longer. "Goodbye."

I felt her hand on my face, pulling me toward her, and when I turned she was there, right next to me, leaning into me. She kissed me, lightly at first, then hungrily, holding my head with both her hands, and though I wanted to remember always how she looked, I couldn't help but close my eyes. The kiss went on and on, or maybe it lasted only a few seconds; I couldn't tell, didn't want to know.

And then she stopped, pulled back, and whispered, "Oh, Jon. I wish I didn't have to go, but I do."

I kept my eyes shut as her hands left my head. I kept them shut as I heard Maggie and Manu walk away. I kept them shut until I trusted myself to open them, and when I did, I could barely make out Maggie's head blending with the crowd of pedestrians, Manu invisible to me but, I was sure, safely with her. I took a few steps so I could keep her in view, then stopped and stared until the crowd swallowed them and, like a view of a distant happy land fading as a sun set, they were gone.

I touched my lips. "She did care about me," I said aloud, not to anyone, simply so I could hear the words, so maybe I could believe them.

"Of course," Lobo said. "I could have told you that from her vitals many times before."

I wouldn't have thought Lobo capable of speaking those words without sarcasm, but he managed it, somehow made them feel like a welcome affirmation from a friend. How pitiful is this: to get consolation from a deadly machine? I knew I should feel that way, and for a second I did, but then I shook my head and reminded myself that I should always be grateful for the few friends I had, whatever form they took.

"Thanks," I said, "both for saying that now, and for not saying it earlier. Had I known, it would only have made what I had to do even worse."

"Of course," he said again, this time adding nothing, not needing to.

I headed back to him, focusing on bringing down my pulse as I walked.

"Now, let's deal with Jack." I thought about him as I drew closer to Lobo, and about friends, which Jack was, sort of, as much probably as he could be, and an idea blossomed. "Here's what we're going to do."

CHAPTER 44

THE COOL GLOBE of fruit, its surface imparting onto my tongue a taste I'd never experienced, exploded as I bit into it, and a warm, animal-rich broth flooded into my mouth. I closed my eyes to focus on the flavors as they blended and created something entirely new.

"Joaquin is truly a genius," I said. "Amazing."

Jack's eyes were still shut, his mouth closed, enjoying the last vestiges of this *amuse bouche*, the tiny but potent beginning to the very long lunch ahead. "He is that," Jack said. "We haven't even really begun, and already it's better than most meals dare dream of being." He sipped water from the glass etched with images of the four waterfalls that had supplied its contents. "How did you persuade him to put up with"—he waved his arm slowly, taking in our surroundings—"all this?"

"And what's wrong with having a great meal inside me?" Lobo said audibly.

Jack and I laughed and sipped more water.

Lobo was hovering parallel with Falls, high above the canyon and the four waterfalls that inspired the restaurant's name. Displays and open hatches all around us granted amazing views of the stunning setting. Our tableside server stood discreetly outside Lobo on the transparent, padded gangplank that connected the interior where we sat with the pathway that led to the back door to the kitchen. I wished Maggie could have joined me, wondered if fine cuisine was an interest of hers, realized how little I knew about her, missed her nonetheless.

"Nothing," I finally replied to Lobo's question, forcing myself to admit it was true, taking the time to enjoy the views, the light, cool breeze that played inside him, the warmth of the afternoon. "Nothing at all."

Our main server cleared the table. Immediately, two of his colleagues appeared and in perfect unison placed our next dishes in front of us. They vanished as quickly as they had arrived, Joaquin honoring my request not to have anyone provide the customary and rather lengthy explanation of the ingredients and cooking magic that yielded each of the dishes before us. I had no idea what we were eating, and I didn't want to know; I wouldn't be returning to this sector anytime soon, so I wanted the meal to remain mysterious, a magical conclusion to an entirely too real mess.

"And how did you convince Joaquin to open on one of his dark days?" Jack said.

"The answer to both your questions is the same," I said. "I explained that he owed me after one of his staff gave us up to Chaplat. I also warned him that if anything happened while we were dining today, if Lobo detected even a hint of a threat, he'd have fifteen seconds to exit the restaurant before a pair of missiles reduced it to dust. And," I raised my glass to Jack, tilted it momentarily in his direction, and took a sip before continuing, "I promised Choy that you'd pay him an enormous amount of money for this most wonderful meal."

Jack was about to bite a small piece of what appeared to be a sauce- and leaf-covered, whole miniature fish, but he paused, slowly returned the food to his clear glass plate, and said, "How enormous?"

I raised my hand, and Lobo opened a display behind my head.

"Rather," Lobo said, "though given that we know how much we've transferred to your account, it's nothing you can't afford."

Jack sat very still, his face unmoving, an internal argument immobilizing him for many seconds, until at last he smiled broadly and said, "Given that you came through and paid me despite what you said before, I have to agree that I can." He leaned back in his chair. "In the end, Jon, we did it again, and we did it well." He lifted both hands as if to push me away, though I hadn't moved. "Yes, I'm sorry we hurt others, and I never meant to put anyone at risk. But we were every bit as good as in the old days. You have to admit that."

Maybe we were, though it seemed to me we spent more time fighting each other than working together. Still, I saw no point in arguing with him; open a conversational door with Jack, and you can find yourself stuck for a long time on the other side of it.

When I didn't speak, he continued, "If you've got nothing else going, I have quite a few great ideas I'd love to run by you. We'd need to go elsewhere, of course, to implement them, but that's no problem. What I have in mind—"

"No," I said, interrupting him, "I'm not working with you again. I agree that though we messed up a lot, we also did some good—" I paused as I pictured Manu walking away with Maggie. "—and we cleared a sizable chunk of money, but we're done. After we finish this meal and you pay Joaquin—" I paused again to reinforce that he *would* be paying, that I wouldn't take advantage of Lobo's presence to skip out on the bill. "—I'm jumping to Drayus. I'll leave you at the gate station there."

"Where are you heading?" he said. "Perhaps we're going to the same place."

"I don't know yet," I said, telling the truth, "and wherever it is, you can't come along."

"There's no need to be like that, Jon," he said, hurt in his tone and expression.

"We both know there is," I said, chuckling, "and we also both know you should stop trying to con me."

"True grief affects many different human vital signs," Lobo said, "and none of yours are showing its effect."

Jack's face relaxed into a smile. "Fair enough. I'll stop. Let's enjoy the meal and the stupendous day, both of which are better than some people will ever experience, and be thankful that we have them."

I thought of the Zyuns. "Now is all," they'd said, and "all is now." At one level, I couldn't agree with them. The past traveled with us, suffused us, shaped us, and even those people and events that intersected our lives only briefly—I thought of Maggie in the blue dress—had the power to mark us forever, as she had touched me. At another level, though, the Zyuns were right. Each moment was unique, an instant you could appreciate or pass by, an opportunity for joy or horror, beauty or ugliness, good or bad. You had the chance to make the very most of each of those moments; what you did with those chances, one after another after another, was up to you and ultimately defined you.

Nothing would ruin this lunch, I resolved.

I raised my glass again. "Yes," I said. "Yes, indeed."

ACKNOWLEDGMENTS

As with my first novel, David Drake reviewed and offered insightful comments on both my outline and the second draft of this book. All of the problems herein are my fault, of course, but Dave again deserves credit for making the novel better than it would have been without his advice.

Toni Weisskopf, my publisher, has my gratitude for taking a chance on promoting a first novel and buying more in the series before the initial volume had even seen print.

To everyone who purchased *One Jump Ahead*, my great thanks; you've made it possible for me to get to live and write a while longer in the universe I share with Jon and Lobo.

My business partner, Bill Catchings, has both done all he could to encourage and support my writing and also been a great colleague for over two decades.

I've traveled a fair amount while working on this book, and each of the places I've visited has left a mark on me and thus on the work. I want to tip my virtual hat to the people and sites of (in rough order of my visits there during the writing of this book) Portland, Oregon; Santa Clara, California, and other parts of Silicon Valley; Florence, Italy; Baltimore, Maryland; New York City; Holden Beach, North Carolina; Yokohama, Kyoto, and Tokyo, Japan, as well as all the country-side I glimpsed in moments of thought while writing on the wonderful high-speed trains, Philadelphia, Pennsylvania; and, of course, my home in North Carolina.

My gratitude always extends to my children, Sarah and Scott, who continue to be amazing teenagers and wonderful people despite having to live with The Weird Dad and put up with me regularly disappearing into my office for long periods of time; thanks, kids.

Several extraordinary women—my wife, Rana Van Name; Allyn Vogel; Jennie Faries; and Gina Massel-Castater—grace my life with their intelligence and support, for which I'm incredibly grateful.

Thank you, all.